She fainted again. He let her sprawl forward, and her body, whitened by the polish of the night, kept stirring, pricked by little spasms. He moved on her, leisurely now, unhungry, just feasting.

Predawn light started to gray up the narrow spaces between the shutter slats. He finally detached his body from the woman's and stood up. He contemplated her satedly, eyes following her curvatures, as if remembering them for a later, lonelier time.

Then his grotesque-looking hands scooped her off the floor and carried her back to bed. He took a towel and wiped the drops of blood off her neck. Her body was young and strong, her blood coagulated superbly. He stepped into the bathroom, wetted another towel, moved back to her and with an artist's gentleness, washed the face, neck and shoulders of his most recent masterpiece.

IN HOT BLOOD

Petru Popescu

FAWCETT GOLD MEDAL • NEW YORK

A Fawcett Gold Medal Book
Published by Ballantine Books
Copyright © 1988 by Petru Popescu

Library of Congress Catalog Card Number: 88-91299

ISBN 0-449-14554-9

Manufactured in the United States of America

First Edition: January 1989

To Iris

PART ONE

VOICES

1

AT THE airport, going up on an escalator, her body was rigid with fear. Lining up before the check-in counter, with the boarding gate to her right, the plane clearly outlined beyond the terminal's window, she was terrified that Michael might suddenly appear and call, "Laura," in his deep and rather monotonous voice. Voice aware of its power, voice of a man used to taking control as a matter of course, as a natural right. Laura, what are you doing here? With annoyance, but also amused at the absurdity of her action. Let's go back *home*.

She was carrying a small tote—a Vuitton she had bought in anticipation of a honeymoon that never happened. Facing the seating agent, she felt a tremor radiating sideways from her spine to the edges of her ribcage. Her back was totally exposed, totally vulnerable. *Don't let me go,* she begged silently.

" 'Scuse me."

Another body touched hers. She jumped, but her right foot stayed crushed to the floor. Blood hammering hotly inside her temples, she turned to look behind her. A man.

Not Michael.

He removed the bag he had dropped on her foot. One of her brand-new Capezio flats had acquired a dusty smudge.

"Sorry," he growled, without a trace of compassion. Tall, in a business suit. Blue, gooselike round eyes.

She didn't have the strength to feel offended. She moved her toes inside her shoe. They felt mashed.

She took her ticket.

She was terrified. And yet wanted Michael to appear, to materialize absurdly, and stop her.

She was among the first to walk onto the plane. A handful of passengers were already inside, stuffing things into overhead racks. Passing them, she inspected fleetingly and furtively the faces of the men. Back to the old habit. Seeing him practically every day in other men of similar age and build, encountered on the street, in a restaurant, on the BART train. Even in movies, when some subtle director chose to introduce a new character by dollying the camera toward a turned back, till the actor turned again, and faced the lens.

Defeated, she found her window seat, crumpled down. The feeling that Michael was everywhere was familiar to her. Some people live a lifetime with pain in some part of their bodies. She was chained to a memory that had invaded her and taken her over. A year and a half had passed. Now, without much hope, to time she was adding distance.

All right. I won't martyr myself anymore. Let whatever has to happen, happen.

She'd been awake most of the night. After the plane took off, she drifted into sleep. From San Francisco to Los Angeles. From Los Angeles to Dallas, the last stop before New Orleans. With sunlight pouring into the plane from port, from starboard. While waiting on the ground in Dallas, it started to rain hard, and they flew up into a sea of clouds. The seatbelt sign went off, and Laura got up and walked forward to one of the bathrooms. She plugged up the little washbasin, filled it with water, and looked in the mirror before washing her face. For this day of farewell to the past, she wore a denim jacket and a prairie skirt, with a mauve cotton blouse under the jacket. Her hair was brown, slightly shagged, with golden highlights. Her face had a pale leanness from not sleeping, but the eyes were strikingly alive, and the lips were well drawn and carnal. In a quiet, unadvertised way, she was beautiful.

All of a sudden she saw the water in the basin gather up

and rush at her face. It didn't reach her, though, because Laura herself was flung upward, and a freshly unwrapped cake of soap soared past her nose. Somehow, miraculously, Laura's hands clawed at the bathroom walls, and her nape and back didn't hit the ceiling too hard. She cried out, and landed uninjured just as the plane finished its plunge into a pocket of thin air.

A red sign, flashing, like a live heart: RETURN TO YOUR SEAT! The water from the basin had stained her blouse—a sleeveless camisole, crisp and attractive a few minutes ago. What could she do about it? RETURN TO YOUR SEAT! She buttoned her denim jacket over it, flipped the lock open with shaky fingers, and stepped out.

She bumped into a knot of three stewardesses hurrying past drinks spilled off a trolley, to help shocked passengers. A man held his head, a woman with a bruised nose fumbled for a pocket mirror, someone was staggering after a fall. The initial clamor of surprise had been silenced by the captain on the intercom, growling an apology. The storm had worsened in a matter of minutes. They couldn't really avoid it; it hung over most of Texas and Louisiana. Under Laura's feet, the carpet rocked like the deck of a boat in a gale.

She started toward her seat, passing eyes staring straight ahead, darkened with anxiety. The last rebels were putting out their cigarettes, Laura noticed how many people had a look of absent concentration, as if praying silently. She arrived at her row, brushed against two pairs of knees: A black Navy man and a middle-aged Texan smiled at her. She sat and buckled up.

"Look, Daddy, how pretty." From behind, an excited little girl. The scary plunge hadn't been too much for her.

"Yeah, strap up, honey." Daddy sounded tense. Laura looked outside.

The sky, as in a turn-of-the-century seascape, was a maelstrom of clouds, and lightning flared up between layers of clouds, illuminating miles of nebulous space. Suddenly, the plane shook as if hitting some solid obstacle, and Laura saw the wing almost fold. The huge aluminum bird swooped down, groaning with the strain.

God, what if this was one of those airliners fated to lose a piece of tail or rudder, and smash down into a forested hill-side? Years of wear and tear, she recalled reading in an article on aviation disasters, create tiny cracks in the metal which can grow into clefts and fractures under the erratic pressures of a storm. *Michael, if tomorrow I become a paragraph in another air disaster story,* Laura prayed, *I hope we'll be together.* Her imagination raced forward and she saw a smok-ing wreck scattered among burnt-up trees. A year and a half ago, numbed by Michael's death, she would've welcomed a chance of dying, too. With a kind of sick pleasure, she had raced along wet, slick freeways. Climbing to the top offices of high-rises, she had stared down, tempted: How much of a thrust would it take to break this glass-plate and tumble fif-teen stories to the street? And she had told all the men who approached her, quite clearly: She couldn't respond, she hadn't stopped loving Michael. It was her only way of keep-ing him alive.

Six weeks before the wedding. The invitations were being printed. Stubbornly that Saturday morning, she had forced Michael to take her sailing. A storm had caught them, over-turning the boat, drowning him, sparing her. It had been her fault.

Please. I don't want this pain to start again. I've paid enough for what happened that day.

She had learned a trick to apply at such moments: Do something physical, anything. She rubbed the back of her neck. It wasn't too painful; she and the bathroom ceiling hadn't collided that hard. Then she pulled her headset out of the pocket of the seat in front of her and fitted the plastic buttons in her ears. A little symphonic music, to combat the storm. Laura turned the dial. Ah—a harp.

Plucked skillfully, the strings sounded as powerful as a piano. Then came a note, a long resonance, like the fall of a gem into a spiraling depth. And at the bottom of the depth, a flute piped sweetly, irresistibly, wooing the harp note. Pa-ganini's Concerto for Harp and Flute in the middle of the second movement. Laura tried to set the volume at a soft, drowsy level—but the music was alternately loud, then muted, then loud again. As if a full orchestra, following the plane, flew right on its tail for a while, then fell behind.

She closed her eyes.

Then she blinked, aware that the music had stopped before the end of the piece. The headset wasn't dead, though, just unaccountably silent.

"Laura," a voice said.

2

Startled, she shot a glance at her neighbor. The middle-aged Texan was reading papers out of a ponyskin attaché.

"Laura," the voice called again.

It definitely came out of the earphones. A male voice, as far as she could tell—slow, almost a whisper. In the way it pronounced the sound *r*, dragging it, it seemed to have a slight accent.

And then for the third time: "Laura?" Close. Real. As if whoever it was, wherever he was, had located her.

She felt her insides tightening. Her shoes shuffled of their own will on the carpet, and her knees, trapped in the narrow space, shook. She pulled off the set.

Wondering whether she'd imagined the voice, she tapped on the Texan's shoulder. "Excuse me, I'm having trouble with this set. Do you mind trying? I don't seem to get anything."

A pair of gray sight organs leveled on Laura. Yellowed whites, streaked with whiskey veinlets. The man took the headset, stuck the buttons into his cabbagey ears. He pulled them out again.

"I hear some kinda flute."

Paganini. He had heard Paganini.

"Thanks. I guess I was doing it wrong."

"There's a volume control, honey."

"Thanks."

As he handed the headset back to her, the captain's growl echoed in the cave of the plane: They were starting their descent toward New Orleans, and hold on to your hats, folks, this one's gonna be rocky.

She put the headset back on. Not a sound now, not even Paganini. Then:

"Laura," the voice said, sweetly and reproachfully. The roots of her hair prickled. "Only *you* can hear me. I'm talk—" Frantically she switched the dial, killing the voice, but when the dial fell into the next channel's groove, "—king to you," the voice said, with an incredibly sad and sincere ring.

A second passed. "Laura," he called again, louder now, the *r*'s definitely sounding foreign. "I'm talking to you, yes, to *you*, yes. Don't come to New Orleans. Don't come to New Orleans."

Then the same unnatural silence. As though he were watching her reaction.

Her mouth was dry. Even the tip of her tongue felt parched. She wetted it on the roof of her mouth and switched the dial again.

"Trust me," the voice urged. He was on all the channels. "Go back." The sound lingered, "back . . . back . . . back . . . back . . . back . . ." fainter, fainter, until it was gone. Laura listened, waited. Meanwhile, the plane was descending. She ventured her eyes over the back of the seat ahead, fearing irrationally that she might see turned faces, inquisitive looks.

She saw only that the plane was tilting forward at an impossible angle. The central aisle appeared like a steep-grade San Francisco street. The moan of the wind was cyclopean, and the clouds outside the windows churned, dark like ocean-bottom mud.

What had she just heard? What did it mean?

It wasn't Michael's voice, she was sure of that.

From very far, the voice returned. It was singing!

Actually, not quite singing. Rather, lengthening musically its syllables, like in an opera recitative. The voice was declaiming some sort of poem: ". . . from thy daughter, sister, wife," it recited, adding lines to a beginning she had missed.

At that moment, the descent grew steeper, and the copilot

tried to chat with the passengers on the intercom. They were going down real fast and hard, but everything was under control, no worse than a Disneyland ride, and as safe.

> From thy daughter, sister, wife,
> At midnight drain the stream of life . . .
> Wet with thine own best blood shall drip,
> Thy gnashing tooth, and haggard lip.

Torn between the fright from the abrupt descent and the inexplicable message, Laura noticed that the voice exhibited great skill, like the voice of some truly consummate radio actor, shaping and personalizing every phonetic unit. The word *gnashing* came out gritting and clenched, *haggard* with a raspy *h*, *lip* with a pop that sealed it. Then . . .

> Then stalking to thy sullen grave.
> Go—and with the ghouls and afreets rave . . .

By now the voice had begun to sound familiar—she had listened to it long enough.

> Till these in horror shrink away—

At that moment the voice interrupted itself: "Away! I'm warning you! Stay away, Laura!" Emotional, with a moving urgency, as if a catastrophe could be eluded, if only she would have the sense to heed the warning.

Just then the plane banked so hard that people screamed around Laura. It righted itself. The captain ordered all the attendants to take their seats. Both he and the copilot were hunched over the commands, and although the systems read an altitude of a few hundred feet, no landing lights had broken through the storm. The plane rocketed down like an express train headed for derailment.

"Laura! I know you can hear me! For the love of God, stay away, Laura!"

She ripped off the headset, and the other reality, the speed and the seeming imminence of the crash, invaded her. The plane jolted as if shells were exploding around it. Laura glanced at the aisle, to register some last scene in her before-the-crash memory, and saw a stewardess with an Eastern profile crossing herself, Russian-style.

Her entire body contracted, ready for the impact. She tried to think of the man she had loved and lost. Together in heaven, if there was a heaven without such storms. The wheels rumbled out of the fuselage. An instant later, they bumped brutally onto the runway.

Taxiing now. Across the chaos of runways glistening with rain. Fogged-up lights, baggage carriers steered by drivers in yellow slickers and rubber boots.

She mustered the courage to check the headset one last time. It was finishing the Paganini.

Grateful to be alive, she didn't move. The plane, the rain whipping the ports, the Texan beside her, proved that they were real—reassuring pieces of an easy-to-understand reality.

Voices. Who heard such voices—strange, otherworldly, oracular?

Joan of Arc, a far memory from a history book. Also, she remembered a question from the Minnesota multiphasic psychiatric evaluation test that a shrink had asked her to take, two months after Michael's death, when her depression was at its highest point: *Do you ever hear voices?* She had answered no, then. But she had unmistakably heard a voice now. A voice warning her about what? About New Orleans? Why?

In San Francisco, she had managed a successful clothing boutique. She was here to start another boutique, in the heart of New Orleans. Denise, her friend and partner, had traveled down here three times before her, finally deciding to buy from a Mrs. Marion Voguey (''Real estate, commercial/residential'') a former clothing store on Bourbon Street that was easy to remodel with a wider, all-glass front, to rerack and reshelf. Marion Voguey also represented, among other properties, an apartment in the French Quarter, for Laura to lease if she liked it. She was waiting for Laura right this minute in one of the terminals ahead of the plane.

Laura touched her forehead and found it damp. She scavenged in the pocket of the seat ahead, found a crumpled cocktail napkin from a Perrier she'd had after lunch, and

mopped her forehead. All the while she paid attention to her
normal, benign gestures: *See, this is happening. But you have
no proof whatsoever that the other thing really happened.
Maybe you had a hallucination. A very elaborate one.*

Maybe . . . She hated that sort of theory, but it was quite
logical: She *wanted* to hear someone (Michael undoubtedly),
and she made it all up. And the fatigue from the sleepless
night and many other sleepless nights, the tension of the departure, the fear of the storm. Oh yes, the storm. She fastened
on to it, gratefully. Fear alone was enough to trigger a fertile
subconscious.

But why that queer poem? A phrase came back: ". . . stalking to thy sullen grave." To *thy* grave, Laura?

As a kid, she had gobbled horror dime novels and spooky
Saturday matinees as greedily as ice cream and candy. She
had, in fact, met Michael for the first time in a line at the
Opera Plaza, buying tickets to *Quatermass and the Pit*—
aliens hiding under the London "tube," and breeding there
before invading the planet. After moving in together, how
many times had they sat up in bed, tired from making love,
she tickling him into getting up and switching on the TV in
search of a B-movie chiller. They were delicious. The omi-
nously drumming music. The jagged, blood-dripping titles.
Spiked and scaly letters immortalizing forgotten casts. Dis-
solves into haunted long shots. She loved that fear, and Michael thought her charming for it.

She didn't experience that sort of fear at his death. She
experienced the brutal awareness that life can mean loss, instant and unannounced, like a knife stabbing a sleeping innocent. The fear of a few minutes ago, when the plane had
seemed doomed. There was no childlike delight in that.

Besides, she didn't believe in the spooky toys of childhood's attic. The cheaply printed tales, the double bills—life
had showed her what they really were. Pills to relax tired
people. Women in the work force. Women who were lonely.

She recalled the stillness in her San Francisco apartment
after Michael died. The chimes of the microwave announcing
a factory-cooked dinner, warm enough now for her to eat.
She could hear those chimes even from the bathroom, where
she was drying up after a shower—trying to use every minute

profitably even at home after work. She put on a facial mask before looking at the shop's sales report, or whatever other piece of work she brought home. Workaholic. Driven. Key to success. And to forgetfulness.

The sounds of loneliness. When you're alone, every little sound grows in volume. Her own breathing became a tired wind. Loneliness does that.

The plane's engines stopped and the passengers got up. Laura picked up her little Vuitton. Surprising herself, she slipped the headset into the bag, then moved into the aisle.

"We're very sorry." A bulky pilot with gray temples was talking to one of the deplaning travelers. "There was no way we could anticipate a pocket like that."

"It was terrible. I got whiplash," said a woman.

"I'm sorry, but . . . maybe just a little stiffness is all there is. I get it from just sitting there, you know, reading my gauges." He tried to laugh, but it didn't come out—he was too tired.

"I *know* it's whiplash."

Laura passed the captain. The copilot stood beside him, greeting the other passengers. He smiled at Laura. "Have a great stay in New Orleans and thank you for flying Delta." No, his voice didn't sound like the warning from the headset anymore than the captain's did. She stepped onto the covered ramp and heard the rain pelting the roof.

Let's find that realtor, Marion Voguey.

Two immediate impressions struck Laura striding into the terminal under an Excuse The Inconvenience sign. There were many police and airport security officers around, in uniform and armed. Noticing the full holsters slapping their hips, Laura's detail-trained eye saw that the gun grips were of checkered wood, or ebony, or ivory with nicely shiny finger grooves. From the weapons, her eyes moved up to the men who carried them. They swelled their chests and strutted about, mustachioed, imposing. They were big in a meaty, well-fed way, many of them showing paunches. But they didn't seem to care about that. With a sort of ferocious confidence, they prowled the place, telling the world that they were the masters here, trespassers beware. They were *men*,

and they were in control, said every pore of their faces, every
bristle of their mustaches.

Her second impression was from the terminal itself, which
was being refurbished. Whole panels were missing from walls
as if ripped off by bombs, crooked wires writhed out of holes,
heaps of unmixed cement lined the base of one punctured
wall, contrasting with the cops' well-shined boots. *Where am
I,* she wondered, *Beirut?* The prospect of a brusque purse-
search clutched her throat—taking that headset was theft, no
matter how insignificant. No, no, she'd shoved it in by mistake; did she look like she couldn't afford two bucks to rent
a set the next time? Come on, officer . . .

But the cops weren't stopping anyone. They seemed to be
simply patrolling. Her next impression was of the crowd.
Quite a number of them were black—without really looking
black. Some dressed in city clothes, some in overalls and
trucking caps suggesting farms and two-lane roads, these people were every shade from light gold, gold and coffee cream
to terra-cotta and tobacco brown, even a sort of red. An unbelievable mixture—the sins of the lords of the land, the anguish of the young girls bending over cotton blooms, rushed
from behind by rutting overseers. Quadroons, octoroons,
double octoroons. In this melting pot, Marion Voguey seemed
even harder to spot.

Unexpectedly, a beauty of forty-five stopped right by Laura.
She looked like Elizabeth Taylor after her third divorce.

"Hi," Elizabeth Taylor called happily, as if greeting a
sister. "I can always tell an out-of-towner—you're forty minutes late, I was worried. I thought you wouldn't come down
whole from that party in the clouds!"

She gave Laura a big hug and Laura hugged her back before she knew it. The woman's hennaed hair flowed onto her
shoulders. She wore a Chanel suit and white gloves.

"My word, you're so pretty! So much prettier than Denise!
Oh Lord, there I go again—" She slapped her made-up lips
with her white glove but then reaffirmed, boldly, "But you
are prettier than Denise, and that's a fact."

"Wait—Denise . . ." started Laura, ready to defend her
partner. Marion didn't give her a chance.

"She's too serious, my dear, and that's threatening to men.

I might as well tell someone who could tell her. You, you're sweet, it's what this town wants. Oh, by the way . . ." She aimed a gloved finger at Laura's tote; Laura noticed an imprint of lipstick on the finger; served her right. But she fought a smile while Marion prattled on: "That all you're bringing to this den of perdition, where looks come third after dresses and makeup?"

"No, I have a suitcase. And some trunks too, but they won't be here for a week; they're being shipped."

"You're smart. I always travel with a million things, like a camel. Hell," she cried out, "you *must* be smart—you've made your business into a winner without any capital."

"We *did* raise some money," Laura protested.

"Peanuts. Denise told me."

Jesus, what else had Denise told her?

"Are we ready to get going?" asked Marion, pointing to a sign that directed the crowd away to the baggage area. "Or do you want to use the powder room?"

"That would be nice. You know, I've had—" She crushed her lips together. "We had a really rough flight."

"Over there, love. I'll hold your bag."

With a quiver of hesitation, Laura let the tote slip into the gloved hand. Marion was looking at her with unadulterated affection.

"You're a little tired and pale, but you're quite beautiful."

"Thank you, Marion." *I've been alone too long, I'm drinking in all this praise.* "I won't be a second."

Marion smiled. "Take your time."

Laura swiveled around. People flowed back and forth across her path, and by the bathroom door she saw two cops. She had to walk right by them to get in. Her face received their stares, concentrated, heavy.

"What's happening? Did you have a bomb scare or something?" she asked one of them, careful to sound friendly.

"Nah. Just routine." The denial bared his lower teeth, swampy brown. He was chewing tobacco.

She shook her head and entered the sanctuary of disinfectant and weeping porcelain bowls.

When she walked out again, the cops weren't by the bathroom door anymore. All the action had shifted to a spot two

gates down. Passengers and police were trampling in that
direction. Marion, feet tapping impatiently, smiled in relief
upon seeing Laura.

"Come on." She started ahead with the tote, as if eager to
catch the beginning of some entertainment. Laura broke into
a run to keep abreast of her. "Why are we rushing?"

"Laura," said Marion, trotting. "Have you been to New
Orleans before?"

"In a way. Dad took us on a trip around the States when
I was five. All I remember is the French Quarter, and getting
sick from some oysters."

"That's what's left of us," said Marion with an undertone
of rancor. "The Quarter, and the oysters." As they passed a
rain-beaten window, Marion pointed at the shark nose of a
Lear jet maneuvering to a halt. "My dear, this little spectacle
will tell you something about what we *used* to be. See that
plane?" Her voice rose proudly. "You're in luck. The most
talked-about local men just flew in, and you're going to see
them!"

And she zoomed forward. Suspecting she had meant kids
with football logos on windbreakers, Laura lagged behind for
a moment and was surrounded by a group of cops and airport
officials converging toward the same area. She feared losing
Marion and forced herself to run toward the gate along with
an older police officer. The man was fat, with golden rank
stripes, and a .45 with deer-antler grips dangling against his
thigh.

"Hey, Cabot," someone yelled at the fat cop. "Nevah
seen ya heah at this hour, what's happenin'?"

The man puffed on with an irritated expression: "Them
L'coovers's back, that's what's happenin'."

The other grinned and yelled again, in the same lilting
drawl, which Laura found hard to understand. "No kid'n. I
thawt Alain was gone a-hun'n."

"He's back on accoun' his dog caught a cold," said a
third, and all of them guffawed, except the policeman named
Cabot.

"Nah, it wadn't hun'n this tahm. They flew up to Galveston for a shrimp deal," grunted Cabot.

"Now let's see how they face the Mexes," said the second man.

"Yeah, let's see, let's see," others exclaimed excitedly.

"Heard them Mexes got grease guns. Macs and things. What if they start shootin' at 'em?" The second man again, to Cabot. There was some personal challenge there.

"Teyya whut," said Cabot, and just then his eyes went up to Laura. *Who the hell is this dame?* said the brief glitter of anger in his eyes, but he was too far gone to stop talking. "None o' those no-goods can grease a L'coover. They can load their Macs with silver bullits, they still won't grease a L'coover."

That being said with finality, they all spread out ahead of Laura. Laura saw Marion inserted tightly in the crowd, and elbowed her way toward her.

"What's going on?" she asked, catching up with the realtor.

"Look over there!" instructed Marion.

Laura looked toward the opposite end of the terminal. Behind two electronic gates and more police, she saw another crowd, with picket signs and banners. They were waving the signs in tune with shouted slogans, but she couldn't make out what they said. The police had them cordoned off back there, and the crowd Laura was part of drowned out the protests with its own gabble.

"The men you'll see—Emory and Alain Lecouveur," Marion narrated hurriedly, "they own a lot of the river barges, and they're very powerful in the harbor and in the financial district. Now those longshoremen"—she grimaced toward the distant demonstrators—"I don't know what sort of row they've had with the Lecouveurs, but for the last six months they've been harassing them constantly. That's why all these police, isn't it disgusting?"

Television lights suddenly came on. The police parted the crowd in half, forming a path in the middle.

"There they are!" Marion jumped up and down, and searched for Laura's hand. "Here!" She handed her the tote, as if needing the use of her whole body to enjoy the moment.

Over Marion's shoulder, Laura saw a group of Southerners in business suits advancing into the terminal. Just then, someone taller broke through the group from behind, almost elbowing the others aside. Unprepared, Laura saw a man, a giant well into his sixties, eyes shining with arrogance, mouth pouting royally. He took the lead like a star, and Laura felt an unease that tightened her fingers around the handle of the tote.

Stepping quickly into the glare of the television lights, the man looked incredibly pale, like a moving man of wax. He was probably about six four, but appeared interminably tall, being so thin. His double-breasted black suit, though buttoned up, flapped a little around his body, as if hung on a wire mannequin. A crimson cravat embellished his stiff high collar, and a handkerchief of darker red flowed from his breast pocket.

Above this theatrical attire, Laura saw features that once had been gorgeous. The nose, once as straight and resolute as a condottiere's, was now beaked by age. A forehead sculpted into a wrinkled slope was topped by rich hair. Even slicked down on his skull with some sort of spray that didn't let one strand out of place, it was thick, and minerally white. His cheeks, fleshy once, fell in folds, like an old lion's, yet retained a sort of battered majesty. *What a magnificent old rogue!* was the first thought that crossed Laura's mind.

Without slowing down, he shrugged out of a sort of black cape that was draped over his shoulders, folded it over his left arm, and Laura saw his hands. They were large, with muscular palms and knotty long fingers, blue veins outlined sharply against alabaster skin, like an anatomical sketch. She glanced at his collar: The old-fashioned cut and the starch made it look like a piece of frozen cake glaze. The skin above it *shone* . . . Laura had never seen such paleness. Not even political dissidents appearing on TV after years of solitary, their pigmentation mutated by uninterrupted darkness, looked that way. That gave his eyes, narrowed now in the bright lights, a sparkling phosphorescence—as much as she could see of them. His lips—she focused on his lips and stared at them: red, as if glossed with makeup, arched sensuously and sardonically. They curved up and down quickly, in absentminded little smiles thrown at the onlookers, and the glimmer of teeth behind them was perfect. An expensive set of dentures for this eccentric who, Laura guessed, had never hesitated to spend on himself. A young, vital mouth in an old face.

With each step that brought him closer, Laura noticed the details more clearly, somewhat like the clarity of a movie close-up. His lapels were very crinkled—in fact his whole suit was—but there was a note of elegance in that, a sense of antique style braving the present.

"Which one is he?" she whispered in Marion's ear.

Marion, savoring the moment, didn't turn her head: "EMMmory, my dear." She pronounced it like "the Emm-peror of India."

The other onlookers were wowing and giggling with amused incredulousness, like on the passage of a matinee idol. To her right, a man raised a boy on his shoulders, to help him see the apparition. Laura turned and scanned the reactions around her. A single negative: A black security guard watched Emory with deep distrust, cheeks blank like dark slabs.

Just then, the yells of the demonstrators grew louder. Hearing them, Emory Lecouveur turned his profile in that direction, and his lips knotted up defiantly. Then he stared around at his fans. Marion waved at him with a flourish, he returned a much more restrained wave—and his eyes fastened on Laura.

She felt x-rayed by a stare of intense curiosity. Emory's eyes were translucent green, and so direct they seemed incapable of averting themselves, of filtering their intensity in any way. Something dizzyingly male lay in them. Without contact lenses, she thought, the old geezer *had* to stare hypnotically to see anything at all, but Laura felt herself struggling to survive that magnetic glare without being totally possessed by it. She countered with a stare of her own, and put a touch of anger in it, one that said it was an indiscretion, a gaffe for him to eye her that way. He maintained his stare for a second, then looked away; the business suits were trooping along after him, and he pretended to be interested in how close behind they were.

The brief instant, however, felt like a full minute. In fifteen years since puberty, Laura had been examined by a lot of men's eyes. She had started in her business as a model before going on to fashion school and concentrating on design. She was well equipped to meet such stares. What this one had was a depth of mystery, a power that she couldn't instantly identify. Not the cockiness of a well-endowed male. Not the confidence of age and experience many old beaus displayed. Not even hostility for a woman who reminded him, perhaps, of some romantic defeat. Whatever lay behind the green of the stare was stronger, and chilling, because it seemed to assume, with honest selfishness, that what this man saw— became *his*.

She decided to break away from the crowd. She fought her way back, to where the congestion thinned, and breathed deeply. Let this little pageant be over.

Back turned, she bumped into someone, jumped, and dropped the tote. He bent to pick it up at the same time she did, but her hand was faster than his.

"Sorry. Are you all right?"

As if resting from Emory, her eyes took in a young male. Also tall, in a tweed sports jacket and jeans.

"Oh yes. No problem."

Then she started, seeing that he had Emory's features. Was this the other one, Alain? He looked like Emory, but in reverse time-sequence: What was old in the other was young in this one; he looked about thirty. His skin was tanned, and a slight haze of beard surrounded his mouth. His lips smiled relaxedly, none of the sneer the old one couldn't seem to control. The same high forehead gave him a touch of loftiness, but auburn hair, rebelliously tousled, brought him back among humbler humans. His nose was strong, with nostrils that flared at her nearness, as if trying to read her fragrance. Shrinking from another roguish appraisal, Laura tried to avoid studying his face, but her eyes slipped into his, and were held there.

The younger man's eyes were also green, but much softer, much more soulful. He, too, held her eyes, but with sympathetic concern instead of the old man's rapaciousness, and even with a touch of innocence. Ready to be friends, it seemed. He glanced swiftly at the rest of her, and he smiled sunnily. He had liked her. He was letting her know.

Almost simultaneously, however, a dark cast drew his features down, narrowing his face into a stronger resemblance to the old man. He appraised her now as if from a distance, lips straight and determined, eyes darkened by contained passion.

"Excuse me," he murmured.

He put a hand on her arm, easing her out of his way. He strode on, but snapped his face around one last time to imprint her in his memory. Then he cut energetically through the throng until his tall head floated next to Emory's group, and joined it.

She felt back to normal now. The discomfort Emory had stirred in her completely erased, she chuckled silently. *Oh, Laura, your emotions are an inch beneath the surface. Everything you feel seems to multiply and become grandiose and symbolic and impossible to handle.*

The Lecouveur group, pulling most of the onlookers into its orbit, flowed away. Looking right and left, Marion reappeared. "So what did you think?" There was pride in her voice.

Laura shrugged. "That old man, what a theatrical personality."

"Yeah, Emory. Isn't he a mess?" laughed Marion. (As Laura was to learn, mess down here meant eccentric.)

"Why are they having trouble with the unions?" asked Laura. She expected Marion to start walking in the wake of the crowd. But Marion made no move.

"As I said, Emory and Alain own a lot of boats and barges, a fishing fleet." She paused, as if counting in her mind. "Also storages and warehouses—and they need a lot of dockworkers to handle all that. Now the dockworkers' unions, they want the Lecouveurs to hire their people only, but Emory also employs those Cajun bargemen from upriver. So the unions are baring their fangs, forgetting who gave them jobs in the first place . . . can you believe that ruckus?" She shook her head despondently toward the unseen demonstrators.

"Maybe they have legitimate claims," offered Laura. They started down, toward the baggage-claim area.

"Legitimate my backside!" Marion snapped. "First of all, most of them come from across the border. Here, they have it better than they ever did before!'' She noticed Laura's knitted brows: "I'm sorry, I should've warned you, I'm a protector of our old ways. Or as a friend of mine put it—oh, I must remember to introduce Merritt to you—we are the custodians of history. The dust we gather is sacred.''

"You like Emory,'' Laura remarked, conscious that she wanted to mention the younger man.

"He's always been crazy.'' Obviously, Marion relished tattling about him. "D'you know, sometimes he rides across town in broad daylight in a horse-drawn carriage.''

"Indeed!'' Laura felt obliged to say.

"Pretty high-stepping. Always reminding us that they were here when the Choctaws traded a slave for a dog collar, and drinking water was collected in rain cisterns.''

The baggage area was in sight. The serpentine carousel rumbled with suitcases right in front of them.

"I had a fling with him once, thirty years ago. Well, not really a fling—more of a flirtation. Totally platonic on his part.''

Two questions formed in Laura's mind. What did that arrogant old rogue look like thirty years before? And, platonic *on his part*—what could Marion mean by that?

"Did you see Alain?'' Marion threw out suddenly.

"Ah-lain?''

She feigned misunderstanding the French pronunciation. Insincere. Madame de Vincy, her favorite teacher at the fashion school, had insisted that she take French, to be ahead of the competition when dealing with Paris designers.

"The nephew. He's going to inherit the whole pile soon. I don't think Emory's got long, though he's trying to act rugged. Alain almost never comes to town, he stays on the river. That's where their wealth is.''

Hmm. For a wealthy young heir, Alain dressed very unassumingly. She pictured him in a silk-blend jacket; with pleated gabardine pants, a crocodile belt, high-cut loafers . . . Muted French blues would go great with his tanned face. *Hmmm.* Under Alain's clothes, she could tell from a few seconds of proximity, was a body all muscle and health, taut and agile like a panther's.

"They've got class,'' Marion concluded her little lecture.

"I mean New Orleans class, my dear, not repainted water-fronts with carriage lamps. We were a *city*, once."

"So," commented Marion when her Cutlass was on the free-way, "Denise said you work and work and reward yourself with more work. She called you the Iron Lady. Oh my *God*!" A pickup truck missed them by inches; it swung ahead of them, and both cars honked. "Maniac!" choked Marion. Laura caught a glimpse of men packed in the back of the truck, under soaked blankets and collapsed cowboy hats. Latins. Some held the picket signs she had seen at the airport, limp with rain. "They can't even drive like we do, but they harass us," huffed Marion.

"We've got a lot of Latins, too. They're okay," countered Laura. Quickly, because she didn't want to be dragged into an argument, she asked. "Where are we?"

The elevated freeway ran through a suburb with trees filling every space between clapboard houses. Reluctant streetlights illuminated porches with battered screen doors, and all the parked cars looked defunct. In contrast, a bright diadem of light lay ahead, and above it towered an agglomeration of glittering high-rises.

"What you see on your left and right is a section known as Metairie. It used to be Bayou Metairie, you know, one of those sluggish outlets of the Mississippi, with sunken trees?"

"I only see houses."

"The bayou is no more, it was drained." Marion pulled at one glove, then at the other. Well-kept hands speckled with liver spots grabbed the wheel again. "In fact, most of New Orleans is built on reclaimed land."

"I didn't know that." Laura was intensely aware of the humidity. Even the air coming out of the car's vents was humid. She was used to rainy days in the Bay Area, but this sort of dampness was like a second skin, wrapping itself like a lukewarm liquid around anything uncovered by clothes.

"Oh yes. We're a swamp, dear. You'll see here a lot of houses with cracked walls and slanted window sills—that's because their foundations aren't solid. They're sinking a little every day—like us."

Marion's tone, no longer exuberant now, sounded thoughtful and real, and Laura felt like forgiving her her prejudiced remarks. After all, she was a nice lady, who had ventured into the rain to pick her up, had put on her best appearance of enthusiasm and flattery, and was now winding down to her usual self. "A terribly clever date of mine once told me we have more drainage pumps in New Orleans than in the rest of the world. We're draining tens of thousands of . . . what is it . . . not square feet . . ."

"Cubic feet," answered Laura.

"That's right—cubic feet. Tens of thousands of cubic feet of water, *per second*. It's incredible that we're here at all. You know, people have all these romantic notions about the tropics. Lush greenery, juices flowing, all that. My ancestors died of typhus in cabins covered with cypress bark. Someone in my family got lost upriver in 1724 or '25. The story goes that he was taking up a barge loaded with raw hides that he hadn't sold—so he was going to barter them back to the Indians he had bought them from in the first place . . . Are you interested, dear?"

"Of course." Downtown's high-rises were growing rapidly in front of the speeding Cutlass.

"At that time, barges made it upstream under power of teams of convicts or slaves, usually twenty men chained together. The Indians ambushed my great-great-great-uncle, killed the slaves, and tied him to the barge by his waist with what remained of the chain. The barge sank, and settled on a sandbar. He found himself chained to the railing, half of his body under water."

Laura imagined the ordeal. Marion gave her a swift look.

"Guess what saved him? The raw hides."

"How so?"

"Flies gathered to feed on the hides, and some banana spiders sewed their webs all over the side of the barge, to catch the flies. Sewed them right over my uncle. You know how big banana spiders are?" She balled up her liver-spotted hand in a fist.

"So my uncle was protected from the flies and mosquitoes by the cobwebs, and he lapped rainwater to quench his thirst. But he was dying of hunger. Well, the sixth or seventh day, as he lay in a stupor with his mouth open, a bug ventured into his mouth, and a spider followed it. So he found out, quite by accident, how tasty the spiders were. Fortunately, his hands weren't tied. He started to wait for the biggest spiders to gorge themselves on those bugs, then he caught them and ate them. He survived six weeks on that diet, but when the search party found him he was a living skeleton.''

She stopped and watched Laura with interest. Wondering whether this had been some subtle battle of wills, Marion trying to repulse her, she not letting herself be repulsed, Laura asked, ''What's the purpose of telling me this story?''

Marion smiled. A light flying fast above the car threw a quick feral shine on her made-up lips, then disappeared.

''There are many stories like that behind the charming carefree ways of New Orleans. I just thought I'd tell you one of them. There's blood and suffering behind our cast-iron balconies and beignet breakfasts. Oops! Nearly missed it.''

A ramp. The Cutlass changed course and spattered through a huge puddle. A sign flashed past, its letters disintegrating from the speed, but Laura's eye caught the pieces and put them back together: Esplanade.

She had read about it. It was one of the mythical streets of New Orleans.

''Now, if you want to admire the Quarter's architecture, keep your eyes up,'' advised Marion. ''The second floor, that's the true soul of the Quarter.''

To acquaint Laura with the famous birthplace of the city, she insisted on driving back and forth from one street to another. Wrought and cast-iron balustrades, mansard roofs, grilled and latticed windows, arched *portes cochères* for carriages of yore, outer stairways, rusticated walls paraded past the car, colored pink, ochre, Paris green, Venetian red, or simply weather-beaten gray. It was like a cramped history of styles: The pioneer upstarts had erected in French colonial, Spanish, and even Greek revival and Victorian, a monument to their triumph over the swamp.

What held it all together was an uninterrupted patina, a sort of stagey effect, incredibly fake and yet real. Fascinated, Laura saw people of today walking out of *portes cochères*, parking their cars halfway on the historic sidewalks (''banquettes," Marion called them), entering bars darkened by candle smoke. The other unifier was the smell. Food scents, reeks of fish from restaurant garbage dumps, coffee brew, strong at this late hour, mixing with a muddy flavor from soaked little patios. Wet wood from rain-beaten porches, old sewers; and flowers, a profusion of unseen flowers. Laura inhaled the breath of the city, exhaled, drew in another chestful; more water-saturated earth, mixed with oleander and jasmine, and crushed leaves, and decomposing mud. The totality was inebriating. Leave anything alone in this climate, ignore it for a few hours, and it'll germinate, bloom, rot, and fertilize the next blooming. Through all of this walked the locals, white and not-so-white, golden faces, mixed blood turned into handsome tans. Lilting along, "where y'at, where y'at," Laura heard them, shuffling into gangways echoing with Forties' jazz, chipper, happy, without a care. She remembered how New Orleans was known by visitors, and by its own children—The Big Easy, they called it.

"Here we are," Marion brought her back to the moment.

A two-and-a-half-story building on Ursulines Street. Louisiana Spanish, cast-iron balcony hanging above an enclosing brick wall. A pink magnolia tree rose by the balcony, looking suffocated between wall and building.

Marion parked the car. Laura got out, grabbed tote and suitcase. Marion walked through wrought-iron gates under an arched opening, and Laura followed, noticing how silently the gates swung open. They must've been recently oiled.

"D'you mind waiting here just one second?"

"Not at all," said Laura, not knowing what to expect.

Marion headed toward an outer stairway. Clicking a set of keys, she climbed to the middle landing and vanished inside a door. *So that's my place. On the second floor, with that lovely grilled balcony.* The magnolia tree sent branches, thick dark veins, all across the front of the house, screening off half of her balcony with foliage and flowers. To the left the patio was a mass of azaleas. As for the first-floor apartment, it was dark and silent at this hour.

The grilled balcony door made a loud dislocated noise; a quivering light appeared behind it, illuminating Marion's face. "Come on up," she said.

With bag and tote, Laura climbed the stairway, and Marion met her at the door. She held a lit candle in a ceramic holder.

"I hope you'll like it," she giggled, as if unwrapping a gift.

She led the way, her candle pushing shadows on the walls. Intrigued, Laura stepped in and stopped, like a traveler shocked at the size of her cabin before a long cruise. The place was small, perhaps a third of the size of her San Francisco apartment.

But it was all paneled in rosewood, even the ceiling. Marion had lit candles everywhere, and the gentleness of the old wood, streaked by irregular darker threads, was like a decoration in itself. From a little hallway, Laura stepped into a dining room, with a carved table and six carved chairs. The dark top of the uncovered table, shiny with age and skillful finishing, looked like a peaceful pond.

Two adjoining openings followed after the dining room— on the right, elevated by a step, the deep niche of the bedroom. A canopied bed waited there, with drawn-up curtains wrapped around the posts. On the left, a long kitchen, lit by common electricity. It gleamed cleanly with empty shelves.

"Boy. This is a museum."

Was that what made her uncomfortable? From the hallway, a contraction in her chest, a sensation of enforcement, held her back, though what she saw was stylish and lovely. She touched a chair's back. Tapestried with French pastoral scenes. Then she saw a sideboard to the right of the table. Its marble top carried a sixteenth-century timepiece of gold, with a round porcelain face supported by gilt mounds. The back of the clock, chiseled and coffered, was visible in a wide oval mirror.

"D'you like it?"

"Yes. It's . . . fabulous."

It was fabulous. Why did she have to force the words?

"Oh, I forgot!" Marion fluttered away into the kitchen. "Come on in, you have to see the appliances."

Laura followed. Counters, stove, butcher block. On the other side of the sink, a microwave—now, that was a valuable feature. Marion was pulling something out of a layer of ice in the sink.

"Get the glasses, they're above the microwave," she commanded, struggling with a bottle of champagne. Laura saw the brand: a five-dollar celebration, but it was a sweet thought. She grabbed the glasses and held them out. "To men!" Marion foamed out the champagne.

"To men," agreed Laura.

"They're the most important thing," sighed Marion. "Crying shame, isn't it?" Glasses in hand, the two women walked back into the historic section of the apartment, and Laura remarked that there was no living room.

"The dining room was a sort of day room, that's the way they were built in those times," explained Marion. "Let's see the bedroom."

The bedroom was almost all bed, except for a secretary table and chair. The secretary could double as a dresser. It was inlaid with miniature scenes on porcelain plaques, and carried a TV set and a phone—two time travelers, among the other pieces.

"I don't know what to say—this place is so . . . unusual." Laura dropped her body on the bed. It gave her the vigorous welcome of a new mattress.

"You can draw these curtains to separate the bedroom from the rest of the house," Marion encouraged her.

"I will—I've never had a bedroom that any visitor could peer into."

"But that'd be such a pity," said Marion. "This bedroom's so unique, why not let people see it—after you make your bed, of course. Or . . . look at that mirror." Laura looked. The mirror in the dining room was close enough to capture her clearly, seated on the bed. "Imagine yourself with a beau," Marion grinned, "here on your bed, after the . . . preliminaries? Your body and his, reflected in that mirror. And the shadows, if the candles are lit, the shadows of the two of you . . ."

The same feral touch glowed in her eyes, as when recounting the spider-eater's misadventures. Laura rose with a look of disturbed privacy she didn't try to disguise any more. What was this game Marion was playing—this prying, sprinkled with morbid little stories, in between sweet gestures like the airport welcome and the champagne?

Marion instantly sensed it. "Forgive me. That was utterly tactless." She took Laura's hand and seated them both back on the bed.

I won't give her a hard time. "Look," Laura said, "it's no big deal really, we're both women. But we're not friends yet or anything . . ."

"Forgive me, please." Deeper tone, truly genuine feeling. "I'm . . . Maybe I should've explained." She squeezed Laura's hand and Laura noted the power of her fingers. "I'm a widow, and not a very merry one." She tried to laugh. "Despite the appearances. My last gentleman friend just gave me the boot."

"Oh. I'm sorry about that."

"I saw you arrive, so fresh, so pretty. Young and yet so successful, so ready to conquer us . . . I . . . I felt jealous."

She took a deep breath.

"The furniture's not really matched," she announced suddenly, and for some reason it sounded comical—both women started chuckling at the same time. "But most of the pieces have been here for longer than I've been alive. Not the bed, though." That sounded comical, too, and Laura laughed more, and the feeling of unease dissolved in laughter.

She asked how much the place would be.

"Twelve a month is what everyone would pay. You can have it for a thousand. Remember, you're in the *heart* of the Quarter!"

Chimes—*dling, dling*—suddenly started to count the hours. *Dling.* A caroling so minute and delicate it hurt the ear. Laura pulled her wrist up to look—ten already?

"Is that a church nearby?" she asked.

The corners of Marion's mouth crinkled. "That's no church. That's your own clock there on the sideboard. It's an authentic Boulle, my dear, and you'll see how wonderfully it keeps time!"

Dling—the old spring added the last hour. As though prompted by the sound, Laura decided to finish the negotiation. "Nine hundred?" she asked.

"Nine hundred," approved Marion. She rose, descended into the living room, and found her purse. "I'll drop by the shop tomorrow to bring you the lease, all right?"

"Sure. Thanks for picking me up, and spending so much time with me."

"Oh, time's my cheapest commodity, now that I'm rid of my last *soupirant*. In a way I'm glad, he was always in such a hurry with me." She stopped, hand on the doorknob. "Have you ever met a man who took his time with a woman, I mean, really took his time?"

"As a matter of fact, I have," confessed Laura imprudently.

Marion had opened the door, letting in a misty magnolia smell. She instantly reclosed it. "Is that true? And why are you not married to him and blessed with his offspring?"

Lord. Will I have to go into that with Marion Voguey?

"It wasn't meant to be," she whispered evasively.

"Well, if he's still around you'll have to tell me. I'll take a shot at him myself. Good night now."

"Good night. And thanks."

"Oh, I forgot—important. Read the *Times-Picayune* tomorrow morning."

Same look, surprise-surprise, as when she had led Laura into the flat, carrying the lit candle.

"I will. Thanks again."

"We'll be friends. Good night."

"Good night."

Marion smiled, became Liz Taylor again. Liz Taylor trotted over the threshold and down the stairs. Laura closed her door.

As soon as Emory and his nephew Alain had spent ten minutes inside the Moisant Airport, Cabot's instinct told him that the police might have a riot on its hands.

Cabot patted his holstered gun. In strained situations, many cops reassured themselves by instinctively touching their weapons, but with Cabot particularly, after years on the force, the gesture had grown as habitual as a Muslim's fingering his beads, and as obscurely mystical—he *was* the gun, and the gun was him. Stroking the antlered grip, he climbed to the concourse above, trying to think of a way for the Lecouveurs' party to avoid a confrontation. Yet he found them here, too. The demonstrators.

They were kept back from the concourse proper by a thick floor-to-ceiling partition of glass. They were shouting in Spanish, and Cabot spotted some organizers he knew. A massive docker whose first name he remembered as Braulio, from Guatemala or some other shithole, hammered a ram's head of a fist on the glass, punctuating the crowd's slogans. Not far from him was a wiry little monkey with glasses, Arata: a troublemaker who made speeches. Big fist and l'il fist. Under his cheap windbreaker, each man could've easily concealed a MAC-10. (Eleven hundred rounds per minute, Cabot knew their hot feeling in his palms from firing them at the police range.) Seeing the uniformed police lieutenant, they chanted louder, with a belief in their right to be there and raise hell that made Cabot part his legs and face them daringly, like a tree in the way of fire. Just to show 'em, he stood there two full minutes, his hate staring at their hate.

Then he turned and walked to the duty-free shop, where he knew he'd meet the man in charge, Captain Knowles. He found him, and Knowles asked what brought Homicide here. Careful of what showed in his blue eyes and puckered red face, Cabot said he thought there was a link between his investigation and the dockers: All the murders had occurred in the waterfront/dockside area. Is this the way he was sniffing around, fully bedecked in uniform? asked Knowles. Might as well carry a big sign with THE LAW on it. Cabot swallowed, mumbled about a rookie class he'd just finished teaching that evening, no time to change, while swearing internally: *I'll have your job in two years, you son of a bitch, if I have to buy a death spell on you from some hoodoo in Tammany Parish.*

Also wordlessly, Knowles gave himself a few months to kick this sack of grits off the force, Cabot being the last unconquered bastion of an older regime that Knowles had vowed to demolish for the sake of principle alone. Then Cabot came to the point, told the captain that they had to find another way out of the airport for the rich barge-owners. Otherwise "that crowd out there, suh, they're ready ta skin 'em lahv."

"You're such a sweet mama to those Lecouveurs," said Knowles, studying him with interest, and Cabot protested,

"No, suh, I ain't no sweet mama to nobe'dy. It just so happened I started on the force when Clair Lecouveur was mayor. You know, Alain's daddy."

"But there's no other way out of this place, is there?"

"There might be one." He led the captain to the railing. They peered over it, saw that one of the walls under reconstruction down there gaped with missing panels. They could take the party out through the wall and to their cars without using any of the regular exits. Then remove a couple of roadblocks, let the motorcade gun off onto an access road, from there to the River Road (as Highway 44, serving the old plantations, was called), and good-bye. If those hotheads wanna crack skulls, let 'em get drunk over missing the chance and do it 'mong theirselves.

Knowles was nervous about presenting Emory with the idea of such an inglorious passage. Might buck the old rooster into walking out the main gate on purpose. But Emory was still doing his popish march through the crowd, so Knowles went looking for Alain, and found that Alain was looking for him.

Alain was alarmed by the idea of confronting the dockers. Knowles outlined the alternative. Alain turned his muscular torso toward the demonstrators' racket, and then toward his uncle.

"We'll do it," he approved cold-headedly. "Get the cars ready on the other side."

He hurried after his uncle—his mind still filled with images of the young woman he had just bumped into.

The protracted negotiations with the union in Galveston had resulted in a fiasco. At home, Alain knew he would have to deal with Emory's ego, furious at the disaster he himself had precipitated with his high-handedness. Sometime in the next few days Alain would have to come down here again, approach the unions, and put out this fire once and for all. Pressure, pressure, pressure. In Alain's mind, the body of the woman with the pale face and the pure eyes fought the weed of pressure, like a supple flower.

He found the lawyers who had accompanied them to Texas clustered around Emory. "What is it, *mon brave*?" Emory asked Alain.

Mon brave, a condescendingly French way to address younger acquaintances, or servants. Alain explained the situation. The lawyers, most of them tight on the bourbon and champagne served on the plane, frowned and tensed up. They stared back at the old man, whose airs and tempers they knew well, ready to hear a tirade—"A Lecouveur will never . . ." etc. etc.

And the tirade came, infallibly. Emory's lips curled, delighted at the affront. "Me, run away from this rabble? A Lecouveur . . ."

He saw Alain cross his arms over his chest, and felt like an actor who knew his lines brilliantly, yet either the feeling wasn't there, or a new audience was filling tonight's house, not willing to clap, not ready to worship. As he kept talking, he noticed Knowles, one step back but obviously not missing a beat, and the lawyers' expressions: paling beneath the sweaty flush of the drinks.

The main omen was Alain, and his nephew's attitude was clear: *If the old fool insists on taking a stand here, I'm going to grab him bodily and hurl him through the wall.*

"But of course, I was joking!" With surprising agility, Emory arranged his face into amused compassion for his poor companions; they had been so easy to trick.

"I always travel through walls in an emergency," he quipped in his creaking, French-accented voice. The voice he used for small talk. When he wanted to assume his full eminence, Emory used a bronzelike tone, vast and grandiloquent like a master's in the resonance of his baronial hall. Alain also had it. As if the genes of a clan with roots buried in legend never spared the vocal cords.

The lawyers laughed, and Alain turned and nodded to Knowles.

Immediately, a team of cops walked into the breach in the wall, tearing off any loose ends obstructing the passage. In minutes, the whole party was on the other side.

There they waited for the cars to be driven over. A limo pulled up first, and the lawyers climbed in it. Alain was about to get in after them, glad to relax in the limo, and have his first drink of the day.

"Alain," Emory called after him. From spoiled, his tone had turned now to meek, almost obsequious.

Alain knew this pose too. *The hypocritical old reprobate gets us all into trouble, then cries for loyalty and protection.*

"Ride with me, please. How would I look, returning all alone?"

While Alain hesitated, Emory closed the car door, and the limo pulled away from the torn-up curb.

A second car pulled up. A vintage Hispano-Suiza. Hand-made in 1924, it had required eight months of careful construction, from the chassis made of an alloy including silver to the walnut interior paneling and the gray cushions of *cuir de Russie*. Emory's own beloved vehicle was driven by Malcolm, an ebony butler/chauffeur born in the Caribbean. He had been in the family as long as Alain could remember.

Malcolm held the door, and Alain stepped in first. Emory sat next to him, and Malcolm took off.

Emory—his name was really Amaury, but the merciless Americanization of these parts had touched even him—kept shooting reconciling glances at his nephew. Then he exhaled a resigned sign, and tapped his fingers on the windowpane. His overgrown nails produced a sound like bone on the glass.

"After work, revelry," he whispered, talking to the outside darkness.

On Alain's side, an adumbrated little lamp mounted in the car's upholstery illuminated a vial of water nursing an orchid. But the water was thick and yellowish, almost puslike, and the orchid's drooping tissues exuded a sad obscenity. Malcolm was letting things slide. No, not Malcolm, Emory. The labor conflicts, the deals killed by pretense and ego, were part of the sliding.

"I'm turning in early," said Alain. "I've got a bitch of a day tomorrow."

"You'll turn in when everyone else does—pray remember, we have guests." Emory put the right amount of vibrancy in his tone. "It's in the best interest of business . . ."

"It's in the best interest of business to do business differently," Alain pounced, surprised he could muster passion after all that had happened tonight. Emory, shocked by the direct attack, turned and contemplated his nephew, who stared back. For an instant, the car sped away with two enemies in the back seat, profile angled aggressively against profile. Emory's forehead was tall, slanting upward with the dusty smoothness of old marble. Alain knew that the old man powdered himself occasionally. Emory's nose, though aquiline, had full manly nostrils, and the high battlements of his cheekbones made him look haughty no matter what mood he was in. But the eyes, and the moving red lips, broke the mask. He was alive, not a statue.

Alain had the same features, but smoothness of expression and the fresh carnality of his skin changed them completely. His cheekbones weren't as high. His eyes were large, and let no inner feeling go unbetrayed. The nose and the mouth carried a stamp of contained passion, like a signature. *He's mine,* exulted Emory proudly, watching in Alain's face this seal of uniqueness. *Even though I wasn't his father.* A sort of selfish adoration seeped up in him, for the young savage who understood figures and spent body-racking hours on the river with the pilots maneuvering loaded vessels pregnant with precious Lecouveur goods, in lawyers' back offices fumigated with cigar smoke, in vulgar city hall lobbies and sweat-smelling union negotiation rooms.

He's made for love, he thought. But for Alain, he knew, life wasn't a romantic exercise. Right this second, Alain was thinking that they'd have to reduce their overhead. Finish this useless war with the unions. Project a new image.

"Alain," Emory said, mildly.

A flicker of distrust across the handsome forehead. Then, "Yes, sir."

"You're overworked. You miss the company of women. I've noticed at the airport your eyes darting into the crowd."

"Your eyes were darting, not mine. That's called projection."

Along the road, pines and oaks hugged each other. Rare lights on tar-coated posts sent shivers of reflection into overflowing ditches. Water, water everywhere, reminding the humans that the bayou was all pervasive and ready to creep back.

"Did you like that girl?"

"That . . . ?" Alain trailed off, taken by surprise.

"She was with Marion Voguey. Interesting young female."

He missed nothing. Alain took a deep breath.

She had looked pale and tired, and yet wide open, absorbing a new world. Her mouth, the way she carried her head, an ineffable breath of perfume as both had bent to pick up her bag. Little gems of memory, they had dropped inside him, sunk to the bottom, and now they clinked down there.

In the silence that followed, the Hispano-Suiza's beams swept around a turn in the road, and hit the limo's taillights. The old car had caught up with the new one.

"Alain, Alain," chanted Emory. "We're so different and so alike."

He was right. That was his triumph. That was the family's triumph over Alain.

Both cars turned into River Road, as the moon, one quarter full, showed a shard through ruptured clouds.

Entrances, driveways to famous plantations sped past. Destrehan, Saint Just, the Cedars. Places to bring wives and children on Sundays, and then eat late picnic lunches on the grass.

Not far beyond, Belle Hellène sprawled on acres and acres between the highway and the Mississippi River: the Lecouveur plantation, still owned by its founders, in the midst of this tumultuous century. The road toward it went over a succession of little bridges. The water gleamed pitch-black under the bridge supports. Stagnant bayou water, myriads of plants and microorganisms releasing their foul nitrogen in it, liquid poison all the way to the captive lakes, Maurepas and Pontchartrain. As a little boy, Alain had often mirrored his face in it, expecting hands to come up suddenly and pull him in, toward a submerged face. The black cooks and maids told stories of the mudman who hid in the swamp and fed on children. Of deathly beauties, girls who had lusted and loved before their wedding vows, and had buried their shame in the bayou. They lived at the bottom now, yearning for lovers.

The past had been different then. Like a sad but wonderful book, for Alain the child.

"Are you going to take care of that nuisance?" Emory meant the longshoremen.

"Friday I have to be in town. I'll meet with our man and see what can be done."

For a few minutes there had been not one light on the road. An after-rain mist festooned the trees. Then a wall appeared and ran along the road—peeled in many places, showing the inner brickwork. Spiky corroded iron bristled along its top.

Emory sat up, and his eyes sparkled. The little sconce in the upholstery couldn't have done that. The old man's eyes caught some unseen reflection, perhaps the luminescence of the mist, perhaps the moon. It was the look Emory always had when he returned home. The power of the past revived him, gave strength to his arrogance.

Alain clenched his fists. The muscles on his arms awoke—ready from palms to shoulders to flex and obey any command from his brain. Awareness of his strength reassured Alain any time he returned to Belle Hellène.

The gates loomed up ahead of them.

What had been once a huge *porte d'entrée des equipages*, enabling two carriages to arrive and depart simultaneously, was now blocked by vast and ugly panes of iron surmounted by arabesques of iron. A medieval square of sliding iron looked like a patched eye in the right wing. The gates were sinister, like a gothic concentration camp's.

Malcolm swung the Hispano-Suiza ahead of the limo. He stopped before the gates, and honked.

The eye patch rattled sideways. A rocky head leaned out to look: Steve, the groundskeeper, had been crippled in a forest fire. His face had been sewn back together.

"Welcome," he mouthed, grinning hideously. Emory saluted him with a wave, and the cars hurtled in.

The pines and oaks continued for a mile, then gave way to a wide French garden. For years it had been shaped by trimming scissors, making the trees and bushes look like fastidious poodles, but the family's recent cash-flow problems had caused them to discontinue many time-honored customs. Emory had let the garden go wild. Weeds killed the flowers. The whole looked like a giant funeral wreath, sumptuous but wilted.

Lack of money had brought other changes. Old servants had been let go, and temporary help insured from the ranks of local Cajuns. The family Dobermans, however, were still fed and cared for. Right now, their growly masses rolled over each other beside the barn-sized kennel by the mansion, gutturally welcoming the masters.

At the end of the garden, gravel once raked in fantasy patterns preserved now the dents of car tires. Behind the gravel, two Greek temple structures side by side communicated through a glass-enclosed gallery. The left-hand temple, repainted, bore a complicated television mast on its roof. The rooms Alain used were right underneath it. Emory lived in the other temple.

The cars stopped. Lights started to flick on in the house. As usual, the windows were open on a hot humid night. While Malcolm rushed to hold Emory's door, Alain jumped out unaided and gave the windows a look. The gauze of the curtains flapped a little, sucked out by the night breeze.

Like a sleepy face, eyelids blinking, trying to wake up the sleeper, thought Alain.

Yet the sleeper was too deep in his sleep. Didn't feel the impending danger. It was only imagined, it was a wisp of a dream.

As the drunken bunch tumbled out of the limo, Alain turned his face east, toward the unseen city, toward that woman.

3

So, if I dreame I have you, I have you,
For all our joyes are but fantasticall.

JOHN DONNE

AFTER A bath, Laura put on a nightshirt and finished unpacking. She threw the headset in the dresser's bottom drawer, and covered it with a stack of T-shirts. Exhausted and wired at the same time, she checked the front and back door and the windows, decided to sleep with the door to the balcony open a crack, then changed her mind and closed it. Finally she remembered that she had brought a book.

There was a lamp on the bedside table: a dancer lifting a little bauble of glass with a blazing curl of wire trapped inside it, and an on/off button on the side. Laura left it on. The button was polished and caught a glint of light.

It was hot, and the apartment had no air conditioning. That had to be put in, Marion had said, hopefully with care not to ruin the decor. Laura undid the bed's curtains, and they fell off the posts, filtering the light and making the couch inside nicely dusky. She could even read, straining her eyes a little, and she counted on the strain to put her to sleep.

She read for a minute but the room seemed hotter, so she sat up to strip off the nightie, sprawled again, read again. Her eyes were weighted with the day, the semidarkness, the heat.

She knew what would happen if she closed her eyes: Michael.

Michael came back to her every night, behind her closed eyelids.

It always started with one of the day's last thoughts hooking into a slumberous memory of them together. An intimate moment, a talk, some place they had visited, one of the many hours of lying next to each other, naked. She rewarded herself that way after a workday of responsibilities and conflicts, a process that sleep finally completed.

Michael, who took his time, as she'd told Marion. He also took over, giving her pleasure, most often leaving her nothing to do, making her feel spoiled and protected.

This time she didn't give him a chance. She was ripe for sleep, lying on top of the covers. Her fingers unclenched and dropped the book. She debated unclearly about the bedside lamp, but couldn't find the energy to stretch her arm, and flick it off through the parted curtains.

"Where did you get these hands?" Denise asked Marion.

They were in Denise and Laura's boutique in San Francisco. The clothes racks had been pushed against the walls, chairs had been brought in, and despite the storm that raged outside, she and Denise were having a party. Everyone was here, the salesgirls, Madame de Vincy and the other instructors from the fashion school, Mom knitting, Dad in his work outfit, and Marion sitting next to Denise, drinks on a little table between them. Laura was circulating with a tray of hors d'oeuvres brought by Dad from his own store.

"At the mission on Geary Boulevard," answered Marion. "Share Thy Limb, you know the place? It was started by missionaries who worked in Vietnam, with children burned by napalm, and in Central America."

She clasped her right hand around her left wrist.

"You wouldn't believe how light they are, and practical."

With a rotating gesture, she unscrewed the left hand and offered it to Denise. Laura's heart jumped straight into her mouth: *My God, the spurting blood will flow onto the carpet, which is rented!* But the hand dripped nothing, no blood at all, although Laura saw at the unscrewed end the white of the severed bone, the bright red of sectioned tissue and the purple of cut-off veins. Mom and Dad and other people stepped closer, someone took the hand and examined it, and then it was passed around with *aahh*'s and *mmm*'s of appreciation.

"They do it out of love. My hands belonged to a young missionary who gave them away during his training," Marion explained placidly, as the hand went the rounds.

Someone opened the front door, a man whose face Laura couldn't see. "Is this the love seminar?" he asked a little too loud, and several voices hushed him. Yes, he was in the right place, it had just started.

"That's what I call love," someone said with conviction, returning the hand.

"You've got to be careful, though," said Laura's mother. "I mean, today people think they're in love and say the words all the time—what'll happen to the world if we all start carrying our hearts on our sleeves?"

"Helen's right,"_ agreed Dad. He was wearing a red apron with his store's name embroidered on it. "Me and her, we never even told each other mushy stuff for the first twenty years of our marriage. Only now, that the girls are grown : . ."

"I think that love is a currency," said Denise. "Everything's currency anyway. We trade in love, like in everything else."

Where the hell was Michael? Laura also wanted to talk, wanted to impart to everyone her own opinions about love, but she had to find Michael first. She spotted him behind an improvised bar—the counter with the cash register had a lot of bottles and glasses on it. He smiled at her. She made her way to the bar: "How you doing, honey?"

"Stretching my arm, crooking my elbow—nothing to it." He smiled again, lips sensuous and shiny and Laura quickly brushed the tip of one finger on them. They were his own. They weren't from Share Thy Limb, thank God.

"Can I leave this tray here?" she asked. "They don't seem to want to eat."

His lips made her horny.

"Sure, sweets."

"Can we slip to the back together?" she asked. "As soon

as they start really talking to each other, and we don't have to wait on them?'' She had put a bed in the boutique's back room, she remembered.

"Sure. I'd go anywhere with you.''

"Oh, Michael . . .'' Her chest filled with such gratitude, she felt she could tear off her hands, her arms, her legs, even her heart, and screw them onto any body part Michael might ever miss.

"Let's go,'' she pleaded, "let's go and make love, *now*!''

"They'll want to hear you talk first,'' he said reasonably.

"Let's listen to what Laura has to say. Laura! Laura!'' Voices were ringing in the shop. Dad was grinning like when she read poems at graduation and Mom was squinting near-sightedly. She arrived in the middle of the room, drew a breath, opened her mouth:

"Love . . .''

No other word followed. Her mind voided completely. She had forgotten what love even meant. How could she have forgotten?

She stood there, pitiful, surrounded by all those warm gazes. Mom nodded encouragingly, and seeing her daughter stuck, rounded the air with her lips: love . . . But that didn't help. She just didn't know what the word meant, she had absolutely no notion. A sense of emptiness, so powerful, so searing, tore her insides like the talons of a bird of prey, lacerated her entrails. One couldn't live without knowing the meaning of love. She had experienced love, and it had been heavenly, that she remembered. Now she carried in its place a low, cold desperation, like lead in her womb. And a rend-ing, blighting shame. She couldn't stand that shame in front of everyone, she simply couldn't.

She turned to run away, trying to escape toward the bar and Michael, but lightning flashed suddenly outside, bathing the street in an appalling aqua light. Blinded, she bumped into the man whose face she had not seen . . .

and *screamed* in her dream. He had no features, absolutely no features: a lean oval visage, like a mannequin's. What could be more hideous? She stumbled over a table with drinks. Denise rose to catch her. Marion rose, too: Jesus, the poor woman had rescrewed her hands wrong, left onto right, right onto left! She screamed again, her own voice shattering her temples, but it didn't shatter the dream.

"Hold on," Michael said calmly, in control. "Steady, girl." She was shaking so wildly that he crashed a slap on her cheek, sending her head into another orbit. Oh, Michael, that wasn't necessary, that wasn't nice! But all of a sudden she got her memory back. How sweet that was, Michael, thanks. She was inundated by the knowledge: Love is love. Love is love is love is giving yourself completely. She could dance with joy, she remembered what it meant.

"Young lady," Dad said, "come back here and get hold of yourself."

She minced her little steps after him, a little girl now, a good little girl. Ready to do anything to please Dad—didn't she love him? And Mom. And oh, Michael. But now she was eleven—she hadn't even met Michael yet.

She followed her father into the back of the grocery store. The store he had in Carmel, before they moved to San Francisco. Male voices gibed and scoffed outside—the truck driver, his help, a shop assistant unloading boxes of coconuts.

She was naked under her dress. A coconut fell out of a box and rolled on the floor. They usually came fibrous and hairy, but this one was huskless, polished.

She stole it, while the jeering voices mingled, buzzed behind her, like a swarm of giant gnats. She took it to a cliffside, where she could sit down on it, and rock back and forth, letting the polished roundness warm up her thighs.

Roll back, roll forward. Press flesh against shell. Free the thighs a little, crush them together again. Skin starting to dampen. She liked the smell.

Thighs red from rubbing, shell getting slippery. Under the shell, the meat one eats. Inside the meat, the milky sweetness. She saw Michael at the bottom of the cliffside. Down she rolled, down the cliffside, *wheeeeeeee*! Riding the coconut, thighs burning, toward Michael, who grew taller by the instant, arms opening . . .

She felt a long spasm, from her throat down her back, along her calves, into her heels. A dream. Just a dream. Michael.

In a suspended state, she lay there, unconscious yet aware that the dream was over. The lamp was still on—the liquid space behind her eyelids wasn't dark, it was twilight. She thought she heard pages flipping. Her book was on the bed. The night was breathing into the balcony door, moving the pages. Feeling the back of her thighs warm as if the dream ride had really happened, Laura wanted to smile, but her face was fixed, all muscles asleep.

As much as she could concentrate without breaking the floating state, she wanted the dream to continue, to ramify, to grow into Michael's presence. She tried to get hold of the yearning inside her body, to make it remember and create fantasies. The yearning was like the milk in the coconut, under her flesh.

She sensed that something was going to happen. A second before it occurred, she thought of a touch, and then something lighter than fingers touched her.

On her naked shoulder.

She shivered from head to toe. The touch repeated itself in the same spot.

Nice. What a considerate, patient, unrushing fantasy.

The touch landed again, and stayed.

Then fingers lighter than fingers slipped down, over the curvature of her shoulder, along her forearm. Laura held her eyes closed, as if trying not to scare a very rare beast. She inhaled, recognized a man's smell. Strong. Lust with some crushed spice in it. His body, as if gaining courage, pulled closer, and she heard a spring in the mattress, distending under the double weight. She didn't really feel his body, only its warmth, fitting the flexuous line of her back, padding her from shoulder blades to buttocks.

Like a bow string, the virtuoso finger played on her side, moving from waist to thigh. She heard her heart pound more strongly, feared waking up. No. Her heart stabilized at a responsive rate—she was all right. Her eyelids were glued shut. The body behind her, its warmth, were welcome now. Through the balcony door crawled a humid coolness, and the curtain folds swayed, caressing her right hand.

The man reached for the inside of her thigh. A very slow throb began to build up in her, and sleep assailed her from

all sides. Dark slumber tide, it always drowned her before
the end of her fantasies. Resigned, she let her cheek sink
deeper into the pillow. An arm burrowed under her waist,
and clutched her middle. The arm of sleep, no doubt, girdling
her waist like a parachute strap. Into the stormy sky the parachute bloomed, and then umbrellaed her down onto Geary
Boulevard, San Francisco.

Michael and she had a date on Geary. A date in front of that
mission, Share Thy Limb.

Geary was deserted. Not a car, not a soul. Streetlights
clicking, pools of rainwater.

One man.

One man on a street corner, with his back turned to her.

Snapping herself out of the parachute straps, Laura realized
that the throb inside her had increased. How could she feel
pleasure when she was so frightened?

She advanced toward the man on the corner, begging God
not to let her glimpse the displays in the store windows she
was passing—peasants' heads, nuns' breasts, in ample supply
from the mutilations in Central America. Fingers, hands, arms
from the shoplifters in the Sudan and Libya who had offended
Allah and his Prophet. Michael, Michael, why did you choose
this place?

The man without a face sprung up in her mind. What if it
was *him*, standing at that corner?

Dang! A bell tolled, yanking her off her feet, propelling
her up into the air like a string puppet. J-Just a church bell,
she stammered to herself. One A.M.

It had to be the man with no face. That was the mission
shop, and he . . . she knew now why he had no expression.
His face . . . his face was made up of bits of all those other
faces. So many features resulted in no feature at all. No. No.
She wasn't going to the corner.

He started to pivot around. No ears clung to the sides of
his face.

I can't look at him. He turned further. Glabrous cheeks,
no detail to them, a ghastly nothingness. She was positive
that she couldn't take it when he'd finally turn to face her
fully.

He did.

She screamed and whirled around, crashing into Michael.

"Come here," Michael said. His breath was heavy and repulsive, but his arms were comforting. He pointed at a store front. Behind the glass, a canopied bed, with a lit bedside lamp, in a French-period interior. Her ears were pierced by high crackling trills, groans, monstrous hiccups from around the corner.

"They're coming for us!" she cried. Panic, reproach at how unruffled he looked, he was always so damn self-possessed and impassive, made her pound his chest with both fists.

"We can hide in here." He led her into the store.

They lay on the canopied bed, while the groans and whistles and meows and rattles and grrrs grew deafening. "Easy, sweetie," she begged him. "I'm a little raw from all that lack of practice." He didn't even hear her. He lay behind her, his hand between her thighs. She aimed her face away from the street, toward the bedside lamp. In hot little puffs, he blew his breath at her shoulders, while the hand between her thighs kept moving. She wanted to be afraid, she wanted to be horrified, to be able to rip her eyelids open, scream, wake up. She experienced the most excruciating tug inside her: She craved the end of what had been started, yet wanted to wake up and save herself from it.

Dling, went the little Boulle clock.

If I count, I'll wake up. If I count, I'm awake.

What he did to her wouldn't let her. His breath and hers were in sync, quickening, galloping together. She heard the clock stop. He had brought her to the edge of the bed, and the brilliance of the bedside lamp blazed through the curtains. It burned her closed eyes. He was weighing painfully on her neck, panting more furiously, holding two kindled breasts in one hand. Michael had big hands. She was so close, the bastard light was going to spoil it.

"Michael," she moaned.

He responded with an angry snort.

So close, and yet the light. She did the only thing she could do—stretched out her arm and tried to reach the lamp's off button.

She couldn't. He was holding her, his chin cutting painfully into the back of her neck. Like a rooster on a hen. The contortion inside her was torturous. A spring that should uncoil, or break. Her middle finger swabbed at the button, missed it.

Outside, a throng of witches was gathering on the sidewalk. They were watching. They whistled, commented obscenely. She trembled, wished she had taken a sleeping pill, had never dreamed any of this.

Her finger tried again. Landed on the polished little tit. Killed it. She closed her eyes so tight that purple glitches danced before her irises. The spring inside her gave way, exquisitely. She rippled, melted, felt his weight lift off her back. *I'm waking up,* her mind whispered.

Crusted by sleep, her eyelids popped open to total darkness. The ripples kept curling her body, but otherwise she was deliciously loose and liquid. Then she felt the pain in the back of her neck, where dream-conjured Michael had mortified her flesh. *I slept crooked,* she told herself.

God, how sweet it all would've been, without those ghoulish apparitions. She very rarely had nightmares. Thank Marion, with her bizarre tales, for this one.

But she had been with Michael.

A sadly languid sensation stirred in her. Loneliness. What a friend loneliness could become, what convincing sensations it could give birth to. Remaining, though, what it was: aloneness, seclusion within herself, bittersweet familiarity with having less, with living less.

Night sat on her face now, balmy, asking for nothing. And then . . . *Wait a second, I didn't turn off this lamp. That was in the dream.*

Frowning, she sat up, trying to remember.

A creaky noise, very light but real. A floor plank right there in the bedroom, crying under a weight, then stopping. Another plank, buckling under a weight, creaking. A footfall.

She felt her mouth go dry. Another footstep, this one in the living room. Two, three, four more, as the intruder, a little less cautious, strode further away from her bed.

She squatted on the bed. With a sense of vulnerability she had never experienced, she groped, found the nightie crushed in a bundle. Its silk on her fingertips cracked electrically as Laura pulled it over her head, blessing the brand-new mattress for not betraying her movements.

She put foot to floor, heart pattering, expecting . . . No. Just the floor. She advanced to the bedroom threshold. She saw a silhouette in the living room, and stopped dead.

It looked hellish, a dark demonic body with a Medusa head; snakes shooting out of wild hair.

Somehow her mind, sorting and retransmitting millions of scraps of reality per second, squashed the cry in her throat, held down the dread, flashed instead: The demon was *her*, in the mirror.

The footfalls had ended, but would she have heard them had they continued? Her heart *dang*ed like the church bell in the dream.

She whipped her head around: By the balcony door, a creature stood straight like an angel of vengeance, arms folded on his chest, narrow waistline betraying an athletic body, a body that could leap and run faster than her, faster than anyone.

Her mind circuited backward, to all the scares of childhood, the bogeyman, the devil, the hirsute bum who flashed her once in a park. Then forward—burglar, rapist, maniac. The balcony door was right by the apartment's front door. Even if she made a beeline for it, he'd catch her.

The balcony door. The balcony door behind him looked closed. *Was* closed.

How the hell had he gotten in? The kitchen . . . Oh Jesus . . . The back door, at the far end of the kitchen.

"Stay where you are," she managed to articulate. Her tongue was sandpaper. She scraped it against her lips. "What do you want, money?" She had money in her purse—two hundred in cash.

He made no movement, no sound. *Good Lord, look down with clemency upon this, your servant, Laura.* "What do you want from me?" She had to do *something*. She took a step. "Look, I'll get the money out," she promised. "I've just got to turn the light on, for just a second, to find my purse."

She didn't even know where the switch was. Her palm

touched the wall, started crawling, searching. A hard square edge, an excrescence of plastic . . .

The light came on.

Her eyes goggled from her head and she felt about to swoon. The balcony door was flanked by curtains, just like the bed. A fold of curtain stood where she had imagined an intruder. Erect and martial, it was tied together halfway from the ground by a cincture with tassels, and *that*, in the dark, had turned into the broad-chested, slim-waisted silhouette she had hallucinated in her panic. A blasted curtain, a hanging column of lifeless folds—there he was, her haunting demon!

She pulled out one of the carved chairs, sat giggling madly, jumped up and ran to touch the thing—yes, that's what it was and nothing else! She felt like rushing out into the street to grab a passerby, to bring in a witness, and had to restrain herself. Then she shoved back the chair, ready to race to the phone and call someone, Denise in San Francisco, her mother in Carmel (she'd moved back there after her father's stroke). She found the strength to just pace, still tittering like an idiot, until the laugh wetted with tears, and she walked to the bed to get her handkerchief from under the pillow, dab at her eyes, blow her nose.

"Laura, Laura," she mumbled, "this just can't go on."

She staggered into the kitchen, looking for a drop left in the cheap champagne bottle. Two fingers of it laced the bottom with expiring bubbles. She poured it into a glass, threw it back too fast, and felt the acid nettle her nostrils.

She was still shaky. She felt like dragging the bed into the kitchen. In the whole place, only this little room looked friendly, mediocre, and normal.

By the stove, she saw a cupboard door, starting at the floor, some three feet tall. She wondered how she had missed it.

Glass in hand, she stooped to clutch a wooden knob, pulled, and opened. A cool darkness brushed her ankles. Bending, she saw darkness, except for a sort of wooden platform at floor level, a fairly wide one. Maybe two by two.

It was square, like the dark shaft above and below it. It didn't rest on something; it hung from four lanyards that passed through little holes in each of its square ends.

Stunned, Laura knelt and laid her palm on it. The slight

pressure instantly tautened the lanyards, sending the platform down a few inches, and Laura almost tilted into the shaft.

She withdrew her palm and her weight. The platform had stopped a few inches below the sill of the cupboard door. Laura looked up to see where the lanyards led. In the dim light, she saw that they continued up past her floor and the one above.

At the top, the square shaft became a square opening. She strained her eyes. The clouds hadn't dispersed, but she made out a patch of sky, and a sort of grating, closing the shaft. Under the grating, the lanyards contrapted into a knot that slid on what look like some ancient pulley. And then the rest of the ropes, braided into one rope, redescended. The end of the braid hung just above the top of Laura's cupboard door.

An elevator, she decided. Ancient like the house and the furniture.

What a funny place to put it, though. And why the low door, as if designed for the body of a dwarf?

She looked up. The lanyards vibrated subtly. The night seeped in through the grating.

She strained her ear. Whispers?

Of course. What an ideal acoustic conduit. A great rumor shaft.

Just then, a woman's wail sounded from the depths of the house. A long, resigned lament, as if after pain. Hearing it, she put her head back in the shaft, careful not to lean on the platform, trying to determine whether it came from above or below. She couldn't. It was too weak, too tremulous, and it didn't last long enough.

Laura got up and closed the cupboard door. She picked up the empty champagne glass, put it to her lips, sucked hopefully and absorbed another atom of sparkle.

She wondered who her neighbors were, above and below. She would ask Marion tomorrow.

What if the footfalls had vanished into the kitchen?
Someone could have . . . Oh, come on!

And it was the grating closing the shaft that finally reassured her. No one could squeeze through the grating, up or down, even if anyone—chimney sweep or goblin—would seek such an entrance to pursue the money or maidhood of

Laura R. (for Renée) Walker, and one scare per night, she decided, was enough.

Thank God for exhaustion. It helped her common sense.

The Boulle timepiece read three in the morning.

She checked the balcony door to make sure it was closed, got back in bed with the book, confident that sleep, good sleep, would soon follow.

The phone rang at nine in the morning. Its distorted echo plunged to the bottom of the lake of sleep, and found Laura there. She stuck her arm out of bed, knocked the phone down, fished it off the floor by its cord.

"Hay-lo," sang a girl's voice. "Is that Laura Walker?"

"Mm-hm," she said, sitting up, feeling a heaviness in her temples like the unconsumed effect of a sleeping pill. The back of her neck creaked, and warm pain spread from it into her shoulder blades. She gritted her teeth, massaged the spot with her free hand. "Who is this?"

"Oh, hi, boss-lady," the girl sang on. "This is Charlotte."

Oh. Yes, yes. The assistant Denise had hired for her. Laura looked down at her naked legs and found them lying in a battlescape of ravaged sheets.

"I'm sorry about this, first day'n all. But I'll be a little late for work, I hope you won't get too mad. I've had an emergency."

"Oh. What happened?"

The girl hesitated just a second, then: "Sort of an adventure, know what ah *main*? Started the night in one place, ended up in another. But I shouldn't bother you with the details—som'un'll drop me there in about an hour."

"Wait a second." Laura heard her own voice; the grogginess of sleep was gone, the tone was sharp and unambiguous: "Are you a heavy sleeper, or did you forget to wind up your alarm?"

The strong, no-nonsense tone of professionalism. If we work together, I've got to know that I can rely on you. If I pay, you deliver. It had been a problem for her to develop that tone. But there was no survival without it, no success in business for a single woman. She had learned the hard way.

Denise had helped, and so had Laura's own mistakes. Mostly her own mistakes.

"Oh no," protested Charlotte, sounding for the first time just a little fazed, "no, this isn't a habit or anything. I won't make trouble for you, don't worry." And hastily: "I'll see you there, okay?"

"Okay. See you at the store, Charlotte."

"Bye," said Charlotte, and hung up. As soon as Laura touched down the receiver the phone rang again, with the impatience of a living being.

"Hi, Cinderella," said Denise across 2,000 miles of wires.

She forgot about the pain. "Denise, darling! What a sweet thought to call me, but I wish you didn't have to get up at the crack of dawn to do it."

"I didn't really sleep that well last night, but I guess I rested," Denise said in that detached way she had about herself. Marion had said it, she *was* a little too serious. Maybe, it dawned on Laura, she attracted even-keeled people like Denise and Michael, because she needed them to find her own balance. Meanwhile Denise continued, "It's so strange not having you around. I suppose it's as big a change for me as it is for you."

"I didn't sleep either. Well, I didn't sleep great; I had a nightmare, and you were in it. Oh, by the way, the girl you hired just called to say she'd be late for work. On her first day."

"Charlotte? Did she give you a reason?" inquired Denise, her tone an octave higher. When it came to work, she was rigorously dependable. She was wondering, Laura knew, whether she had hired the wrong person.

"Sounded like she had a prolonged date. Promised not to make a habit out of it."

"Oh, well," Denise, said and laughed. "She may not make a habit of coming late, but prepare yourself. Charlotte goes out just about every night."

"Is she that attractive?" God, it was enjoyable to talk to a good friend, especially after last night.

"She is, but I don't think it's the looks, I think it's her attitude. Anyway, a date a night. Not like us winners," Denise chuckled sarcastically, and added, "She's a quadroon."

Aha. One of those gorgeous golden skins.

"What was I doing in your dream?" asked Denise.

"You were saying . . ." She remembered. It seemed funny now. She laughed, rolled on her stomach, and threw her feet in the air. The movement hurt her neck, but not too bad. "You were saying that love is a currency."

"Sounds like me," agreed Denise, who read books like *How to Win Through Negotiation*. "So, d'you feel like a new human being down there?"

"In a way, I do. Everyone here's so different. I don't feel really like myself."

"They're quite trippy," laughed Denise. "I think it's that quirky city. Meet any men?"

"Already? I saw a guy at the airport."

"And?"

"He almost knocked me down running past me. Marion told me his name. From a prominent family, supposedly."

"Call me when he makes a move."

"What move? We haven't even been introduced."

"Would you like to meet him again?"

"I don't know."

"What do you mean, you don't know?"

"Exactly that." Loyalty, loyalty. Loyalty to Michael? Is that why I left San Francisco? "Well, I guess I wouldn't mind running into him again. Denise, don't you want to talk about the business at all?"

Denise said sure, and asked what Laura's immediate plans were. Laura said she was planning a fashion shoot, and the store needed a glossy brochure. She was also toying with another idea—a lingerie fashion show. Denise thought that very radical. Laura agreed, but it could be done by invitation only, with a strictly female audience. That would be a great way to start, particularly since the decor of the store would be tastefully Victorian, and the name, Whispers, was so romantic. Denise advised Laura to use Marion Voguey extensively. The woman moved in the most exclusive social circles of New Orleans, she was a pillar of several uptown clubs like the Ice Breakers, she'd raised money for jazz festivals, she had a finger in everything. Now, the local banks Denise had contacted were . . .

"Listen," Denise concluded around 9:45, "even though I already miss you, I'm glad you moved down there. Only the best can come of it, I'm sure."

"I'm sure, too," answered Laura, and she *was* sure at that moment. They exchanged I love yous, and said good-bye.

Laura jumped out of bed and put her watch forward two hours. Checking the time on the Boulle, she noticed that one of the clock's lateral mounts was missing. It made the bulging golden shell look like a big crab with a broken claw.

The bathroom was the apartment's narrowest accommodation. Open all the way, the shower door hit the toilet seat. Oh well, the hot water was abundant. Laura soaped her shoulders, and her fingers slipped over a craggy little swelling right under the roots of her hair. She started, thinking it alive. Her nails scraped, a speck came off, and she held her fingers up in the penumbra of the shower stall. A dark stain instantly dissolved under the hot water.

She stepped out, hit her shin against the toilet bowl, turned her back to the shaving mirror, and twisted her neck as much as the pain would let her.

A copious bruise stretched from under the ends of her hair, more than two inches down her neck. A half-inch scab, ripped off, was dripping minuscule liquid rubies.

It must have happened on the plane.

The cut stung from the soap and water. It had stung even in her dream.

She had no rubbing alcohol or Band-Aids. She'd have to shop today for a million little things. She finished showering, dabbed Yves St. Laurent over the laceration, and found a smaller one right next to it. Puffed up a little, with a tiny gem of blood marbled under the skin. If she left it alone, it would reabsorb itself.

She put on pumps, a white skirt, and a blouse with a high collar—no need for a scarf to hide away the bruise. Eager to go to work, she flurried back and forth, stuffing money, sunglasses, lipstick, and appointment book into a canvas shoulder bag. With each spin of her body, her clothes brushed and rustled against the crampedness of the apartment. A crash pad, that's what it was, a nicely decorated crash pad. Good for youngsters like Charlotte. Well, it'd have to do for a while.

She checked the door in the kitchen, and, on her way back to the front, shot a glance at the mysterious cupboard by the stove; it was shut, lifeless.

Whirling down the outer stairwell, she heard the bells of St. Louis Cathedral tolling in the old Place d'Armes, saw the chocolate, ochre, and mustard housetops shining in the morning sun, the gray and pocked brown of pigeons flapping from one roof crest to another. A burly man's silhouette was just entering the patio. Laura saw him from above, fragmented as he passed under a crown of magnolia leaves, then stopping at the door of the ground floor apartment. He stooped, picked up something off the doormat. *Neat, a neighbor.* Laura bounced off the last step: "Good morn—"

The rest of the greeting wheezed out of her as the man returned her glance. A black beard crawled up his whole face, almost into his globular, fatigue-ravaged eyes, and more black hair ate down into his eyebrows and even sneaked out of his ears. An odor of tobacco reeked from his old army sweater, olive shirt, wrung-out tie, and faded corduroy trousers. Why was he dressed so heavily? He had in his hands a folded-up *Times-Picayune.* Past the paper, Laura glimpsed his feet: sockless, in leather sandals, more shrubs of hair on each toe.

"Oh. Ah yes, aha. Good. Marion told me. You're the new one, huh? Good morning."

The voice sounded mechanical, like a robot's. His eyes were black like Greek olives, and he looked not quite all there.

"Yes, I'm the new one. You live down here?"

"Everywhere," he said. "And down here. I'm the Egyptian. What's your name?"

"Laura Walker."

"You're in the paper."

"I am?" She raised her voice, surprised.

"Yeah. Marion wrote something. You have a store. For women." He started to laugh oafishly.

"For women," he repeated, as if that was the joke. Then his face darkened. Laura felt like looking away from the thin slit of his mouth, which showed almost obscenely in his curly beard. "Incomplete aura," he grumbled, studying her with such concentration that Laura felt split into little segments. "Strong, but incomplete," he repeated, then stuck the paper under his bearded chin, jerked up the doorknob to lift the door with both hands from its comfortable bed of long usage, and vanished.

Three, Laura counted, walking into the street. Marion, Emory, now this guy. Any more characters? This last one took the cake.

The Quarter was alive, house doors open to visions of breakfast, bedsheets flying out of windows to hang and regain their freshness, garbage collectors lifting round iron lids in the sidewalks and extracting obesely stuffed bags of refuse. *So that's what those iron lids are for,* Laura smiled, enlightened. The men and women of the Quarter hopped in and out of buildings, hailed each other from balconies, nonchalantly ignoring the tourists. This is Venice, this is the Left Bank, their attitude said. These natives, too, had grown used to living, loving, trading, and visiting in the very heart of history, under the stare of big-spending strangers. From birth till death, they lived on this floodlit stage, like circus artists in their conspicuous caravans, never escaping the scrutiny of ordinary folk. She, too, was going to live on this stage, thought Laura excitedly. She was going to be part of it.

She found herself unexpectedly staring at her store, its brand-new glass front filled with OPENING SOON banners. She looked at it from across the street, with heartbeats of pride and belonging.

This was her store. This will be Whispers.

They had opened the first Whispers in San Francisco three years before. It had done well enough for bigger chains to offer to buy them out. Denise and Laura had resisted any takeover, and here she was now, looking at the toil of years, months, days, and hours, materialized, ready to break free from her chrysalis.

She noticed the stores flanking hers. On the right, a bed and bath shop, and next to it a contemporary sportswear boutique. That was good. On the left, Le Beignet, a fancy little place with marble-topped tables invading the sidewalk, European style. Advertising the strong *café brûlot* of old Dixie reputation. All this meant good walk-in business for Whispers.

She fumbled in her purse for the keys to the two locks—one right above the sidewalk. She ventured inside with a nice thrill of curiosity, even though she had codesigned the decoration and Denise had shown her Polaroids of the almost completed work.

The front of the store was done like a Victorian seamstress shop, with antique sewing machines, a settee for waiting customers, pulled-out drawers and mirrors, and mannequins and racks for turn-of-the-century pantaloons and whalebone corsets mingling with the panties, bras and stockings of today. The rest of the store's interior was for the sales counter and the wares proper, from slips and underpants to nightgowns and bedroom slippers. In her mind, Laura saw the women of New Orleans coming in, chatting, asking her and the other salesgirls questions, then trying on things, with that particular female attention, almost scientific, that women give to choosing new attire, checking in fantasy the responses of men they know, anticipating the reaction of men they dream of meeting. They were serious at such times, Laura's fellow women, as if their lives depended on their choices of clothes. God, she loved women. In a sisterly way, not with the passion one gives to a man, not as she'd loved Michael. But she loved them. She had had a good mentor in that sort of feeling—old Madame de Vincy, with her fashion school on top of Nob Hill.

Madame de Vincy had taught her some great basics. That a woman could turn off men and lose them not because nature hadn't endowed her with enough, but because it had endowed her with too much. That less is more. "Breasts, for example," the Frenchwoman cautioned, "should be indications, not statements." Men feel more rewarded by a little at a time than by getting everything immediately. Love's secret was a process of distillation and gradual tasting. Exactly what Michael's love had been for her—distillation, slow uncovering, delight in waiting. "Ma chère," quoted Madame de Vincy in her gargling Parisian, "toutes femmes sont nées jolies, tous hommes sont nés aveugles." All women are born pretty, all men are born blind.

Laura stopped in front of the back dressing rooms, still awaiting their light fixtures, and pushed a rotating stack of shelves. It supported pimpernel bath crystals, Victorian frames for wedding portraits, lotus shampoos, crushed rose petals in sachets. Mirrors lined the back of every shelf, to double the perspective and the number of items. Pushed, the shelves swirled around, setting the view behind Laura in motion. In the shimmering reflections, she saw a vaulted chest, a grinning face. *A pair of reaching hands!*

She froze. She felt even the scabs of her scratches contracting. Panting not to scream, she let go of the swiveling racks. The mirrors moved back, the man behind her disappeared.

She waited, neither alive nor dead, feeling him inches behind her, hoping she'd faint before he touched her.

She heard a rap on the front window of the store. She turned her head infinitesimally. She took a breath, turned further, preparing to call for help.

Standing on the sidewalk outside, three people were peering in: two women, one man.

She found her courage, pivoted around, and saw . . . "Oh, God," she whispered. "Oh, Jesus."

A tailor's dummy was what she had seen. A tailor's dummy without a head, without raised hands. Her imagination had added the head and the hands to the innocent object she'd seen all by chance in the mirror.

It must've belonged to the old store. Denise didn't have a chance to get rid of it.

I must slow down. Slow Down.

She combed her fingers through her hair and hurried to open the door. "Hello, I'm Doug." "Hi, I'm Cheryl, Doug's wife . . ." "I'm Fran," the three instantly chattered. "You must be Laura. How nice to have you next door to us. Marion wrote such a sweet piece about you." Doug was holding a copy of the *Times-Picayune*. He and Cheryl ran the bed and bath place. Fran owned the coffee house. Should she have some coffee brought over? wondered Fran. "No, but thanks. You're too kind," answered Laura, grateful for small talk. In the middle of it, a Rabbit convertible, top down, braked spectacularly in front of the store. Behind the wheel, a boy who looked eighteen, hair cropped ruthlessly to a yellow brush-cut over scalp and temples, and beside him a woman in her twenties in a cocktail dress, smacked their lips together and lolled their heads about in kiss, till they had to part for air. Then another kiss, even longer. The woman's hair looked straightened, her naked brown arms wrapped like creepers around the driver.

"Isn't this your girl?" asked Fran. "I've seen her when your partner was around redecorating."

A third kiss for good measure. Then the woman jumped out of the car and flounced into the store while the Volkswagen vroomed away. "Hi," she announced, "you all know my boss already? I'm Charlotte. I made it," she added to Laura, as though deserving congratulations.

Great. Great entrance, Charlotte. Great aplomb. Great everything.

The coffee house and bed-and-bath excused themselves— "See you later, Laura, take care"—leaving Laura and Charlotte alone. Charlotte said she kept a change of clothes in the back, and rushed to slip into it. Laura heard her flush the toilet. Charlotte resurfaced in a cotton dress and barefoot.

"Listen." Laura had been thinking of the tone to adopt, decided that direct but fair was best. "I don't care what you do with your personal life, Charlotte. But I do care that you arrive here punctually, and if a boyfriend drops you off, please enjoy that last kiss two blocks before you arrive. I don't want customers or even the people next door to gape at my saleswoman, because we're trying to create a certain image here, and I want the other girls we'll be hiring to learn from you."

It stopped Charlotte in her tracks, and Laura had the time to acknowledge how attractive she was. Five eight, maybe, with sumptuous breasts, limber all over, looking older than she was because she was big. Her lips were full, vaguely African, her eyes lazy and long-lashed. Yet more than in her features, there was something in her skin, in her carnality: a will to absorb and relish life that Laura had sensed even on the phone, and definitely witnessed in the kiss she had given the driver. The disarming élan of a ripe twenty-year-old. *I like her,* Laura decided, curious for Charlotte's reaction.

Charlotte stared back at Laura, digesting her calmly stated

words. Then she smiled, not entirely good-naturedly but not phonily either. "Okay, boss-lady."

Laura asked to be called Laura.

"All right, Laura."

"I hope your boyfriend wasn't too late for work," said Laura, to smooth the moment over.

"Oh, Rush? Made no difference to him, he was going to church."

Laura gawked, then took it the way she was starting to take everything in this remarkable place. In the mornings, Charlotte told her, Rush ran a service for the elderly at a Redemptorist convent. He was a seminarian.

Work avalanched over both of them right away, and the little rub was forgotten. They looked up photographers for the fashion shoot, talked to the mannequin artist who promised to be at the store around two with the models, called employment agencies and explained what sort of young ladies Whispers needed as saleswomen, moved racks and shelves around, measured space. At lunch, Charlotte suggested muffulettas—ham/salami/provolone/mozzarella sandwiches on Italian seeded bread, and reminded Laura to read the paper. Laura had barely had the time to scan the gossip column: "New Gal in Quarter Loves N.O." Marion described Laura as a California celebrity, gave her quotes she hadn't said, urged all women to march to Whispers, and signed herself M.V. Over her half-eaten sandwich, Laura turned a page back, to a block of metro news. Suddenly solid bars of print, with flat ends like railroad nails, pegged her attention to the bylined story:

DOUBLE SLASHING OFF FRENCH MARKET PLACE

At loss over confusing leads, Lt. Cabot ready to consult psychics.

It was business as usual at 2 A.M. last night for Dale Cabot of the city police—with a morbid twist. As a woman collapsed on the sidewalk fronting the French Market Place,

her jugular vein severed, sailors walking out of a bar hap-
pened to see her writhing on the ground, unable to cry for
help. While several picked her up and lay her on one of the
empty market stalls, one of them ran to call the police. Dale
Cabot was there in minutes, with squad cars and paramedics.
No name was released, but a source close to Cabot revealed
that she was a prostitute.

Though the area was sealed off, the killer or killers were
still hiding in it, holding prisoner a young man—perhaps the
woman's companion—who was later found literally floating
in a pool of his own blood atop a two-story apartment build-
ing on Decatur Street, which commands a view of the French
Market. His throat was cut similarly and, according to the
coroner, perhaps no more than an hour after the first victim
was killed.

This raises the number of waterfront killings to fifteen and
sixteen, respectively.

Laura fought her curiosity and looked up. Starved after her
antics with the seminarian, Charlotte had inhaled her muffuletta.

"Did you read this?"

"Yeah. Gross city." Charlotte smacked her lips.

Laura tried to turn the page, but her eyes returned of their
own to the story.

The second body was found as Lieutenant Cabot deployed
a substantial force to scavenge nearby alleys, cul-de-sacs,
building lobbies and stairways, in the hope that the killer or
killers had not yet fled. Meanwhile, helicopters were scouring
rooftops from the air—and within minutes a searchlight shone
on victim number sixteen. With good reason to hope for a
capture, Cabot's people gave chase to shadows while the
helicopters kept up their prowl. They regrouped, however,
empty-handed.

"As little as we know about this latter-day Jack the Ripper,
his pattern suggests a perverse enjoyment of his own acts,
notably the possibility that he may have finished off his sec-
ond victim while . . .

Charlotte reached over the round little table for the rest of Laura's muffuletta:

"Going to eat this?"

"Please, I'm not hungry. Take it."

. . . while peering from the rooftop at the very market stalls where paramedics were trying to revive his first victim. Perhaps he forced his second victim to watch, too, to see salvation almost within reach, yet impotent . . .

God, what a gleeful hack this reporter was! How satisfied with his own penny-paltry prose, tapped out before dawn on the office computer!

"What d'you think about these murders?" Laura asked, angling the paper so that Charlotte could see the article. Charlotte shrugged, pushed the last of the sandwich in her mouth. "It's the Big Easy. We do bad stuff like any other town, just kinkier." She paused, her peevish expression disappeared, a fleeting twitch of anxiety deformed her sexy mouth, and she resolutely chased it away, "Listen, the way I look at it is, he's into hookers, so I've got nothing to worry about."

"Are the streets safe here?"

"For single women? In the Quarter, yes, almost any place before midnight. Just stay close to the crowds." Her eyes became animated. "D'you want to come with me tonight? Rush has a friend who plays jazz at Tipitina's, and then we can go to a party."

"Ah, no thanks. I have so much to do in that new apartment."

After lunch they took an hour off from the store, and Charlotte helped Laura shop for her most immediate needs. They walked out of a mom-and-pop store like Laura's father's in Carmel, pushing an overflowing cart. They left the cart in the patio and trampled up and down three times to get everything into the apartment. Charlotte offered to push the cart back to the store, Laura said thanks, and would she hurry to the store right after that, the mannequin models were due. She'd follow Charlotte back there as soon as she put the stuff away.

"Wait," she called, bringing Charlotte back from the door. "Do you by any chance know what this is?"

Brow furrowed, Charlotte joined Laura in the kitchen and looked where she was pointing: the low little door into the queer inner shaft. Charlotte got down on her hands and knees and opened it.

The platform was right there, where Laura had last seen it. Swinging gently from its lanyards.

"Well, blow me down and roll me over," Charlotte cursed softly, as half of her disappeared into the shaft, and her voice totally changed resonance. The vertical dungeon made it low and cavernous. "No, never seen such a thing before."

"Is it a chimney?"

"Without a fireplace?" marveled Charlotte. "Looks like it's for ventilation or something. Though I don't see what it could ventilate down there. And this little platter . . ."

"Is it a domestic appliance of some kind?"

"Could be, though I don't see who'd use it or for what. It's a spooky old thing." Charlotte whistled inside the shaft, and the shaft responded sonorously. Then she pulled herself out, hair tousled. "Laura, it's two o'clock, I better hightail it out of here."

"All right. Go, and tell the mannequin guy to wait."

The front door closed. Laura waited a few seconds, then crouched and looked inside the shaft again.

It was perfectly square, walls blackened by smoke or time, she couldn't tell which. The grated opening on top, aimed at azure sky, caught inside its rim half a scoop of sunlight.

"Ooooooooo-hooooooooo," she called childishly.

A couple of seconds. Then she felt a slight shiver, hearing, "Aaaaaahhhh." The same long plaintive sigh. Female. Born in the depths of the house, it grew, matured to a wail, then trailed off, giving way to a humming silence.

Very, very faintly, yet real, not imagined, she could hear the Boulle clock on the dining room sideboard, scoring away the seconds.

Then she heard the wail again. Coming from afar, yet from close-by. It started, built up, became strong . . . and personal, as if a woman was really crying in one of the three apartments stacked up under the common roof. The intonation was indescribably sad—exhausted suffering, hopeless.

Laura listened, trying to control an upswell of fear. With

the cry came a sort of cool underground breeze. Was it just the air, flowing up and down, translating its own crawling inside the mysterious shaft into the semblance of a human voice?

It sounded like the soul of the house itself. Captive, crying. Giving the place a sort of direful poetry.

She was afraid. She realized it as she extended her arm and put her hand out to touch the still platform. A blood rush in the tips of her fingers, a heightened awareness of her capillaries, of her skin.

Yet, more than afraid she was intrigued. Was it really a human voice? Wailing like that from the first time she'd heard it, in the dead of night, till now, more than twelve hours later? But why hadn't Charlotte heard it?

She slipped her fingers between the shaft wall and the wooden platform, pushed the platform away, and brought one eye as close as she could to the narrow crack.

Hollow darkness.

No question. The explanation was the air. The shaft might descend to some basement far below, some vaulted catacomb of the old city. Or . . . a remembrance jumped to the fore: the pumps. The pumps Marion had mentioned. Draining so many cubic feet of brackish water per second. Maybe *they* were wailing.

I'm crazy, crouching here, trying to remember my physics. Back to reality, Laura, back to work. Now.

The mannequin maker had brought three samples of his work, and Laura was disappointed by them. One was of twisted wire, following the general shape of a body, and ramified at the shoulders and hips to hold clothing. It looked like a Martian skeleton, and for lingerie it was the worst. The next was of plaster—dull gray, impersonal, body shapes unnecessarily streamlined. Laura told the man how tired she was of unnaturally long legs and tight, unfertile hips—did any women look like that in real life? Of the third, the artist was most proud: He unwrapped an anatomically correct woman of translucent plastic, fitted inside with a lighting system. It gave the plastic breasts and pelvis a shine of bionic skin. Laura thought it was an eye-grabber, but cheap-looking.

While this went on, Marion dropped in with a male friend. Laura thanked her for the article, and everyone conferred about the bionic mannequin. Marion's friend was a man in his forties, with gold-rimmed glasses and blond hair combed forward to block off a progressing baldness. He took one look at Laura and made efforts to indicate that he wasn't Marion's date. His name was Merritt. Merritt Bonheur.

Laura asked him what he did for a living.

"I studied to be a doctor," he said, "but it wasn't for me. I love history. I'm a curator now at the Louisiana State Museum."

"Then you're the man to ask." She mentioned the shaft in the wall. He listened, remembered no such architectural innovation in the city's development, offered to check or drop in and take a look. Marion said she had never opened that funny little door; though she'd rented and re-rented the place several times, she'd always surmised it was a closet.

Merritt's keen eye, meanwhile, noticed between Laura's hair and collar her bruised neck, and he was ready to offer remedies. Reminded, Laura realized that it didn't hurt anymore. Merritt had graceful long bones, an elongated head, and hadn't shaved: The manly shade of his stubble didn't go with his face.

"By the way," he announced unimportantly, "I'm having friends for dinner in a week—would you and Marion care to come?"

Marion said yes. Laura promised she would try if her schedule didn't get too crazy.

Merritt said good-bye; he was due back at the museum. After he left, Laura ordered the artist to make a simple impression of a young woman's body in plastic with realistic colors, then Marion gave her a ride to a car dealership nearby. On the way, Laura found it surprising that even someone like Merritt had no idea what the shaft in her kitchen might be.

"Honey, would you like me to find you another apartment?" asked Marion.

From her mire of indecision, Laura groped around and found nothing solid to cling to. "I don't know. It feels sort of silly to put you to work again because of something that may have the simplest explanation."

She really hadn't meant the shaft. She had meant the wailing voice.

"I'll do it gladly," said Marion patiently. "Except that you might have some other fears right now, and that thing in the wall is just some back way you're taking to get to your fears faster." Driving, she gave her a sideways glance, and seemed impatient to hear a confirmation. Laura didn't speak. "Some people get spooked by motel rooms, cause they're so white and shadowless. Besides, what's wrong with your fears? I'm sure you love them."

Cheeks hot, Laura looked away, like an apprehended truant schoolgirl. "Why do you think that?"

"It makes sense," answered Marion. "We're all habituated to our preferred emotion. Anger, love, fear, whatever it is. We like to have it back again and again, and when we don't, we miss it and feel like we're not quite ourselves without it."

Laura blew air out of her mouth to cool off her upper lip. She looked at the street; some obscure meaning seemed to beckon to her, blended invisibly into the street's pettiest details, yet unarguably there.

"Otherwise, you'd stop it," concluded Marion. "If you didn't *like* your fear, you'd drop it one-two-three."

Laura was silent, and the apartment issue was dropped. At the dealership, Laura leased a Jeep Wagoneer—the ideal type of vehicle to haul merchandise around.

Parting from Marion, she drove the jeep to the store. In her absence, Charlotte had taken a call from the airport: A shipment of bras, garter belts, slips, knickers, from Laura's wholesaler in Rome, was waiting in customs. Laura made an appointment to pick up the shipment, then offered Charlotte a ride back home, and they locked up the shop.

Not two minutes later, at Bourbon and Bienville, they were blocked in traffic. "Take that," Charlotte pointed to a squalid little alley.

"It has a No Entry sign."

"This is the Quarter. We all do it."

It looked too narrow for the Wagoneer. Fearing the loss of a door handle, Laura hurtled the fat wheels over the mounds of offal behind a famous restaurant, brushed a tree with the jeep's top and, sensing Iberville open ahead, eagerly stepped on the gas . . . then braked as suddenly as she had accelerated.

"Wow," she uttered.

Inches from her front bumper was a closed carriage, an authentic turn-of-the-century phaeton or brougham, drawn by a single black horse, driving up Iberville Street. Motor cars piled up behind it honked deafeningly. Unperturbed, the horse, caparisoned richly in black leather, clippety-clopped along, and the driver perched on the front boot's tall bench flourished a shiny whip, and bit on a lit cigar as thick as the whip's handle.

"Look who's here," laughed Charlotte. "He climbed out of his coffin."

On the driving bench, Malcolm pulled luxuriously on his cigar, steering the horse right down the center of two lanes, so no cars could overtake Emory's phaeton. A folded triptych of steps finished the carriage door, and on the door Laura read an emblazoned monogram: *L.*

Inside the carriage, Emory had turned half-profile, reviewing the sight of the street. Because of the darkness of the interior, his skin looked even whiter than usual. In fact, it had the pallid look of a wax effigy. Yet the stubborn contraction of his jaw muscles was real, and so was the defiant mien he presented to these contemporaries in summer clothes, swarming about caught in their vulgar interests. To Emory, it was these people on the outside who were outdated, not him. He was dressed in a sharply tailored gray jacket, and his chin was nursed by a yellow silk ascot with red-and-black dots. He made a point of keeping his glance as impassively static as possible. So his eyes, like marble balls, slipped over Laura and pretended not to notice her.

The high axle of the jeep brought Laura's face exactly level with Emory's. The fixedness of those eyes was too much to take. She tried to avert her eyes from his, but they seemed to attract what light there was in the carriage, leaving the rest—the man's face, the oval viewing port behind him—in a sort of theatrical penumbra.

She took the whole weight of the immobile pupils. Their sharpness was daggerlike, making her feel drawn out of the

jeep, even out of this moment in time, and sucked magnetically into the rectangle of past slowly sliding before her and
Charlotte.

Seeing the waxlike face, fear moved inside her. Beloved
fear, according to Marion.

Steel springs berthed the phaeton gently as it passed. The
spokes rolled inside the iron hoops of the wheels. A buttoned-
up leather trunk at the back of the phaeton floated by as a last
impression—the sword case, in its time. It contained no
swords now, yet Malcolm dusted its inside and shined its
outside religiously. Malcolm loved taking as much care of
the phaeton as of the Hispano-Suiza, because they were what
the city saw. Hopefully soon, more money would be available to take the house and the garden out of their morass.

Emory passed, taking history with him. Laura drove down
Iberville, honked her way across to St. Charles, and remarked
to Charlotte that these local old boys were so *heavy*, she just
couldn't deal with them.

"You'll get used to them. We all did," said Charlotte.

Laura asked a couple of questions about the illustrious Lecouveurs. A bunch of loose screws with money, Charlotte
diagnosed them. Yet she liked them around; they gave New
Orleans something, helped her feel special because they made
the place special. What about Alain? Charlotte had never met
him, but she'd heard stories that he was terrible with women.
Nobody seemed to measure up to his lofty standards. Laura
put a stop to her inquiry, drove Charlotte to her place on
Magazine Street, off Audubon Park.

They agreed to jog together in the park, day after tomorrow, Saturday. If they survived tomorrow: The new counter
was coming in, two Victorian chandeliers, and the fixtures
for the dressing rooms.

"By the way," said Laura, stopping in front of a clapboard
house, "you can pick your underwear from our supply from
now on."

Charlotte smiled. "Can't afford it."

"It's free. I'll give it to you."

"What?" A look of distrust spread on the big girl's face,
then turned quickly into one of embarrassed delight. "Oh
boss-lady, that's . . . that's . . ." She was so thrilled, she

couldn't find the words. Laura sensed behind Charlotte's cool and cockiness another Charlotte. A kid, not used to niceties, not lavished with gifts.

"It's okay," she said, to stop Charlotte's awkward search for the appropriate thanks.

"Oh, my gawd." She sounded more Southern when she got emotional. "I'll never be able to keep my ankles crossed. Rush'll *dee*-vour me. Hey!" She leaned out of the jeep toward a male figure seated philosophically on a step before her door, "When'd you get into town? Why'n't you call?"

Laura looked. It wasn't Rush. It was a boy with a saxophone case. Clear-eyed, getting up to greet her with open arms.

Oh, Charlotte, Charlotte. Oh, New Orleans.

Let's see what sort of sleep I get tonight, she wondered driving back, the smile that Charlotte had put on her lips still there. And she became aware of how different, how separated she'd felt in the last few hours from the Laura who had left San Francisco yesterday morning, terrified of looking back, terrified of looking forward, terrified of looking in any direction at all. Maybe she was beginning to handle her fears differently? Maybe she was already beginning to love them?

Just then a pinch of anxiety gripped her chest, and she almost squirmed in her car seat as she entered Ursulines. The two and a half stories of her building towered before the car, as if rising to greet her.

4

"I'VE NEVER seen anything like this. Never in my born days," said the woman.

She stood her ground upright in the basement lab of the morgue on La Salle Street, her five feet ten topped by a foot-tall beehive hairdo. From her barrel-shaped body, from her rope-thick arms, even from her flaming-red beehive, energy exuded and rippled around her. Then the energy rose and seemed to push up the low ceiling with light bulbs inside inverted domes of wire. From there, her energy refracted toward the windows buried under the ceiling's west side, then dropped along the tiled wall, and flowed back: to the faucets spitting into enameled sinks, to the surgery tools waiting to be reused, to the infrared spectrophotometers and stereoscopes, to the dead.

Dr. Jackie Webster.

Unique in Dixie law enforcement, she was the head of the forensic division of the New Orleans Police Department. A curiosity that went practically unnoticed. The Big Easy, the department, kept her hidden down here, occupied from dawn till after pink of evening. So she had her meals brought in, and routinely warmed them up in the crime lab's fume chamber. Cabot sniffed the air: something was boiling in there right now. Smelled like pizza.

The windows were open. This Friday morning, the temperature was barely 60, cold for May. It had gone down overnight, like an aftereffect of the storm and rain of two days before, but Cabot, a local boy, knew why. It took that long for a weather change to affect the lakes, the great repositories of water northwest of the city, which neither warmed up nor cooled off easily. From their silent expanses came cool or warm breezes, like wrath or thanks from closed-in, unreadable people. Unspontaneously, after the fact. A frosty front was floating south now, misting up the Mississippi, shrinking the open flowers, unifying the morning colors under a coppery hue. Even the sun wore a frigid coil around its glare.

"The blood, Jerry," said Jackie. "What in the dickens happened to the blood?"

The three of them were posted in a loose triangle around the trays with the two bodies. Jackie by the dead man's midriff, Cabot and Jerry Mayberry, the senior crime analyst, over by the dead woman's feet. Cabot reached to touch his gun, felt the empty holster, and remembered he had signed off his piece at the security desk. A new regulation from Knowles. A patrolman had chosen to off himself in the morgue john last Christmas, using his own gun. Since then, in his wisdom, Knowles had decided that the morgue could affect cops' psyches unpredictably. If there was one unstable psyche in the department, Cabot knew, that was Knowles.

Extra lights had been positioned around the two trays, illuminating them from every conceivable angle. Beyond the tag lassoed to the woman's big toe, Cabot's eyes crawled up the columns of her legs. Their doughy whiteness made her freckles look like clusters of dead red lice. Where the lab people had handled her, her flesh had conserved the dents of rubber-gloved fingers. Her pendulous breasts had sagged sideways, as if wanting to leak off her body. Too much light wrapped fuzzily around her pubes, around the sandy fur on her legs and arms, and the rigid down in her nostrils.

"The cutting object," said Jerry Mayberry, "ripped the external jugular vein, which in this case I gauge at twice the size of all the other veins, the posterior external, the anterior jugular, the internal. It was double in size possibly because the victim had a heart condition—unless the enlargement was temporary, due to the use of cocaine, of which traces were found in the urine. The attacker stood behind her and to her right, raised the death tool, and slashed, severing first the big vein. I think the spasms of the victim helped the blade penetrate further, in the process sectioning pretty much all the stuff around, superficialis colli nerve, auricularis magnus, et cetera, and then—"

"Hold your Latin," said Cabot. Jerry stopped, pleased to be not fully understood. "You say her own twitching helped the killer cut the other veins and whatever. Or was he of such mighty strength it woulda happened anyway?"

Jerry shuffled in place. "Well, I don't have really a theory. She was possibly leaning on him close, in some sort of embrace. Some other action might've been going on between them."

"You mean he was giving it to her?"

"We couldn't determine that. She'd already had a busy night."

Fifteen-dollar girl, thought Cabot. "But the blood, Jerry," he urged, his voice inflected with raspy disquiet, a rare thing in this jaded cop, "where's the blood?"

"I don't know. He slashed from behind, inward and forward. A lot should've spurted out on the spot, even though we're talking veins not arteries."

"But she's big enough to've had ten pints in her. Now, the killer wasn't standing there with a can to catch it, was he?"

"I don't know. From the male victim, I took samples of marrow."

The three shifted around the trays, closer to the dead man. He was the woman's pimp. They had established the nature of their relationship from the duplicate keys they carried. They fitted the same crummy door in an impoverished, crime-rife area, in the suburb of Algiers. There the couple slept in the daytime, shunned by neighbors, on the brink of eviction.

"I just had this funny idea." Mayberry quickly blew his nose. "You know, bone marrow's fire-red in infants, but a lot of it becomes inactive in adults, and gets kinda yellow. It's yellow in the arms and legs, for instance."

"Jackie, your breakfast," Cabot reminded her.

"I don't think I'll have it," said Jackie, and moved to turn off the fume chamber.

This had spooked her appetite, reckoned Cabot. Not the cruel, gruesome death. She lived with that. The *un-usual*.

"I cut from the spine," continued Jerry, "and from the ribs, the flat bones of the skull, the hip bone . . ."

"Jerry got carried away," confirmed Jackie.

". . . and guess what?"

"What?" asked Cabot impatiently.

"All his marrow is discolored. As if he'd lost not just his blood. As if he'd lost . . ." He hesitated, searching for an appropriate description. "The memory, yeah, even the memory that his bone marrow ever got involved in any sort of blood formation."

He waved his arm despondently toward the second victim.

The pimp lay next to his woman, hearing nothing, seeing nothing. His eyes were open, fixed glassily on the ceiling. A few shiny swiggles of his hair, black, ancestrally African, poked out of the bandages hiding his open skull.

"Wait a second—whoa!" Cabot's face turned massively towards Mayberry, like a battleship maneuvering in straits. "Discolored bone marrow? What the hell you talking about?"

Mayberry was observing him coolly. *I knew he'd blow his top sooner or later,* the crime analyst thought. Old model cop. He doesn't use technology, or deductive logic, to apprehend killers; he tracks them by the seat of his pants. Look at how he's been calling the killer *he,* with no evidence that it was a man. He figures a lot of men hate women, and most of the victims are women. Now, who would kill *American* women around the waterfront and the docks? Foreign workers of course, wetback dockers. Cabot has already fitted the crime to the handiest set of suspects, and heaven forbid that new evidence might challenge his preconceptions. Yet new evidence would, and so would Jerry Mayberry.

"Bone marrow is what produces human blood, red bone marrow. This victim exhibits *no* red marrow. As if it's been sucked out of him, or he's never had it."

Cabot looked like he wanted to stuff Mayberry's smart grin down his throat.

"There's more, actually," Mayberry punished him. "You

know, don't you, that the human spleen is built like a sponge, and it stores up blood for emergencies.''

''I know,'' Cabot snapped back.

Mayberry's face curled into a question mark: *Do you really?* and he talked on: ''When a human hemorrhages, a command from the brain squeezes the spleen, and pours all that reserve blood into the system, to restore the balance. Now this guy's spleen, I tried to sample some blood out of it— *nada*. It's like made of old rubber.''

''Whazzat? The killer cut his spleen open, too?''

''Oh no. The victim presents no incision anywhere close to the spleen. Yet when I opened the spleen, I found no blood in it.''

''Is all this . . . physiologically possible?'' Cabot always took a breath before using highfalutin terms.

''I don't know. I can ring someone who knows more than you or me.''

The implication of *you or me* was brightly clear, but the lieutenant just shook his head and stared down with fascination at the woman.

Her neck had been so shattered that on the way to the morgue an assistant had had to clamp it back to the head to keep the victim in one piece. The red fluid of life, the precious essence of her being, was already gone. It had escaped through the gash, making her the cold, juiceless feast that she was now. Too little blood had been found on the sidewalk, or on the market stalls. Almost none of the man's had been found up on the roof. Where was that precious blood, marveled Cabot, singing in its complicated pipes and conduits minutes before the attack? Every cell of it, so lively when alive that it took each drop less than sixty seconds to circle joyously away from the heart and back again, couldn't just have evaporated. What beast or beasts had gorged on it, and where? Right on the spot of the kill? Somewhere else? Who was he? Who were they?

In Cabot's mind, trained like that of a paleontologist's to reconstruct from a few petrified fossil joints the image of a whole dinosaur, a killing was usually told and retold, blueprinted again and again around its own scraps of evidence until it emerged like a detailed scenario: The victim was here, performing this action; the killer came from here, snuck behind her, pulled out such and such weapon, and did the deed. In the shattered-throat cases, however, Cabot's mind wrote scenarios that made no sense. How could that killer have followed the prostitute so closely through the streets filled with sailors and other drunks in search of cheap fun, stood behind her right there in the street, finished her with one blow, and somehow piped out her blood too—all without being seen or heard?

She had no money in her purse—the collections from the previous customers had been found on her partner, apparently untouched. Working girls always asked for the money beforehand, but this time no money had changed hands yet. Were they still talking a deal when the killer slit her? Was he—again and again, the same torturing question—was he alone? What athletic skills, what unnatural calm, what intimate knowledge of the human body did this culprit possess, to dispatch her so perfectly and so quietly? A deranged premed student? But young intellectuals whom Mama had dressed in girl's clothes, screwing them up for life, were—though occasionally brutal—usually messy in their methods and not great at erasing traces. They talked in their sleep, or to their shrinks, or spilled the beans at confession. Cabot's informers at the hospitals and medical schools, his choir-boy recruits, the psychiatrists who asked him about police trivia to write in their first detective novels, none had come up with anything, not a hint, not a token of a lead. Above all, the killer himself left no marks of any sort, not fingerprints, not footprints; as yet, not even hairs.

"Dale." Jackie's voice pierced his reverie, soft, surprising for her three hundred pounds. "D'you think maybe I should open the freezer, pull the old ones out, and let you go over 'em again?"

"No, I'm done with those." He shook his head, trying to appear casual, but he felt in his back, unhampered by his padding of fat, the below zero chill of the crypts. Fourteen other victims lay in there—three men, eleven women. He felt how out of their blood-depleted carcasses, stopped in midrotting by the arctic of the freezer, wafted a mute accusation of inefficiency, of slipping in his old age. *Maybe Knowles is right.* He felt his shoulders slump under the whole weight of the building, which was erected in granite and shaped like a giant urn for ashes.

Fourteen unsolved cases. Not all slashed—some ripped at the neck by sharp tools that couldn't be identified. One bitten all over the body—hundreds of nips and nibbles, ripe as flea-bites.

"Mornin', ma'am. Hey, fellas." Six eyes went to the door and found there a diminutive cop with one large organ: his nose. Les Vitrolly stood in the doorway, beaming good spirits. A recent addition to Homicide, Les had been with the narcs for three years. The time spent digging up scag and playing father confessor to snitches with fried-up brains made him as thrilled as a puppy dog about solving murders. Murder work was slow, methodical, dignified. Murder, the ultimate crime, the end of a man's humanity, gave Les a greatly improved sense of himself.

"You look like something the cat drug in," remarked Jackie about Les, who was a boozer and unmarried.

"You look terminal," added Mayberry in a jolly voice.

"You look like you need some Jamaica ginger to rub the rye outen your eyes," said Cabot, kinder.

"I'm right peart!" The little man, as hard as kindling, swelled his chest. "Where's the new gal? Hope she's pretty, th' last one was plainer'n homemade soap." He sauntered over to the trays and his cheeriness died. "Mother of Jesus," he whispered, entangling his eyes in cold hair, gaping gashes, greening nose tips.

"You heard anything?" rocked Cabot's voice.

"Nope, but the whole street's working!" declared Les, trying to fight the feeling of the room. "I had an idea," he confided to Cabot more than to the others. "I'll get Horsey, my main snitch, outta the jail. With him, the street'll be buzzing news to us like a radey-ho."

"Yeah. Crap in one hand and wish in another, and see which fills up first—beg yo' pardon, Jackie." Cabot turned to prowl purposelessly, and heard Les say, "Dale, why d'you let the papers run off at the mouth like that about these cases? The *Times* said yesterday you found a body sogging in its own blood on that roof."

"So what shall I do, print a denial?" Cabot's boots crashed onto the floor as he spun around. "He wadn't sogging. No, suh, he had no juice left in 'im at all. He was cleaner of blood'n an unborn leech!" He exploded, not able to keep his arms at his sides any more, his fists battering the air like a ram at a rock-house. "I gave orders that no one talk to the press! I called the paper and tol' 'em that if I met the ink-pisser who wrote that story, I'd wring his neck personal! You know the feeling I got? They din' *care*! They didn't, cause Knowles himself is behind it! He wants my hide, so it's just as well that the papers are blowing it outta all proportion. Never mind the tourist trade, let all the comers and goers know that we got an ogre here, and Cabot, after thirty years of practice, can't find a shred of evidence to take across the street to the D.A.'s office!"

Drained, he leaned back against a tray. The coldness of the metal cut into his kidneys. It felt good, cooling him off a little.

"That carpetbagger from Ohio's been trying to clean me off the force for quite a while. He'll nail me to the barn door over this, and I don't mean maybe."

In the silence that landed over people and objects, a fresh voice was heard. "Yeh, yeh. Cap'n Knowles don't suffer 'tenant Cabot, he brung that out into the open right at the beginning."

Cabot knew who it was without looking: Cahill, a black lab technician. Hard-working, knew his place, Cabot liked him. But oh, how he hated these cases, and hated, loathed, abhorred the sympathy of friends, the compassion of subordinates. He was used to *their* sorrows. Now they were nodding gravely, thoughtfully, to his.

Les expressed the common feeling: "What shall we do?" he asked.

The one who secretly enjoyed himself was Mayberry. "Let's go sit someplace and talk about it," he suggested. He sensed a chance to inject some intellect into the discussion. No easy feat, with these hicks. The temptation was simply tantalizing.

They went and sat in Mayberry's office, because Jackie's was being repainted. Mayberry had put his stamp on the place in the form of primitive artifacts and blown-up photos of tribal ceremonials: Kenyan tribal circumcisions, *kurdaitscha* men from Australia pointing the bone, famous anthropologists in the bush surrounded by natives. They contrasted with several embossed plaques of maplewood he hadn't been able to remove without tearing holes in the walls. "Never be afraid, for I have redeemed you"—Isaiah, 43:15. "The branches are holy if the root is holy"—Romans, 11:13. His predecessor had fought the daily tides of death and madness by becoming born again.

"Dale," Mayberry began somewhat officiously, "have you heard of Gilles de Rais, or Henri Blot? Or Sergeant Bertrand?"

"No, who are they?" Cabot rumbled gruffly. Likely, some fancy cops from Baton Rouge or Houston, as the sergeant rank seemed to indicate.

"Gilles de Rais was a baron and marshal of France, in the mid-1400s. He lived a life of such splendor that he had his own clergy of no less than thirty priests, owned half a dozen of France's richest estates, and wasted fortunes on alchemists trying to turn sand into gold. But his claim to fame is the killing by refined torture of a few hundred boys and girls, whom he sexually violated, and while doing that opened their necks, shoulders or stomachs with small bores of the bistouri, to drink their blood. It was said that his castle had a dungeon with three hundred drainholes in a floor of marble, one for each lovely young soul he sported with. The blood was gathered underneath in a tub of youth where he bathed, convinced that would prevent his looks from fading. Pleasure was his only religion, and he was an artist at others' suffering. He even had scribes take down the feverish pleas for mercy of the victims, and composed poems from them. He kept an accurate list . . ."

"I hate to interrupt one of your lectures, Jerry," Jackie Webster cut in. "But what does all this have to do with our cases?"

"It has to do with *understanding*, that's what," said Jerry irately. "Gilles de Rais was rightly called a vampire in his time. Henri Blot, four hundred years later, was a necrophiliac who broke graves open to satisfy his base lusts with the corpses. It is related that he was caught *in flagrante delicto*, making love to a dowager who had died of a cerebral fever, and had been interred only a month. At the trial, d'you know what he had the nerve to tell the judges? *'Chacun a son gout,'* which translates sort of like 'To each his own hobby.' "

He paused, waiting for a reaction.

"And the other'un, the sergeant?" asked Cahill. Of Jerry's audience of four, he seemed the most interested.

Jerry rushed back in enthusiastically. "He was the most famous. He was a true military man, and used the battlefield to make dates—so to speak. I mean, he carried comrades in arms, dead or dying, away from the trenches, and on the way to the morgue or the infirmary he molested and mutilated them. He was actually renowned for bravery, because he often rushed ahead under enemy fire, to save those casualties he'd had an eye on. Now, I tell you, Dale—and all of you," he posited, "we're dealing here with someone who could be worse than all of them."

He had wished the four to pull their heads back and grow round eyes, as if he'd unleashed an incubus into the room. Instead, Dale Cabot clenched his jaws, hostile. Jackie knitted her brows. Les chewed at something he didn't quite get. Only Cahill let out a whistle of amazement.

"Thass crazy stuff. But it ain't like in the movies; I mean, the guys you're talkin' about don't go 'round suckin' on gals till they gets pale an' look like the stuffin's falling outta them."

"What's the difference really?" bristled Jerry defensively. "Except that most movies are about fantasy and legend. And there have been a few films about people who *think* that they're vampires—therefore, they vampirize."

"Jer, listen." Jackie sounded like she was trying hard to keep from losing her temper. "Let's not get all blooey here. What you said about those Frenchmen is one thing. They were perverts, and we're dealing with one too, perhaps with several. But what does it have to—"

"Not perverts," said Jerry ardently. "Not perverts—vampires."

"You mean bats?" asked Les.

"No, I mean people. People who drink blood."

"Come on, Jerry," sneered Cabot. "There are no such people. Killers, yes. Maniacs, sure, a gracious plenty of them. But bloodsuckers?"

"You're missing the point!" Jerry agonized. God, these backward cruds. "These are not simple serial killers, not normal psychopaths"—normal wasn't quite the word, but no one else seemed to notice. "These people kill to suck blood, and it makes no difference whether you believe it or not. *They* believe it. They are persuaded that they are vampires, so they act like vampires. Like real ones."

"Real ones?" Les looked completely lost.

"Yes, real. Because, looking at reality . . ."

"Jer," said Jackie, still patiently, but with soft authority. "Jerry."

Jerry swallowed his crescendo like a radio performer hit by a power cut. "Yes, ma'am."

"You're just being curly-minded. What difference does it make whether people think that they're something and act it, or they just act it without thinking? I want to know who's at work in this city, who's out there maybe right this instant, snuffing out another life?"

Jerry felt an inner tremor. "So do I."

"Is the killer hitting on dead ones too, like those old crazies you were talking about?" asked Les.

"I don't think that makes a difference," Jerry persisted.

"Oh? Sho'nuff?" roared Cabot. "What would I care if we found that some morticians diddled their dolls while painting up their cheeks? We've got sixteen citizens in here who were very much alive before they got it. And more lives may go down the drain just like those sixteen."

Cabot suddenly marched on Mayberry. Mayberry shrunk back, smelling the sour aroma coming from Cabot's mouth. Whiskey. Late at night, knocking them back on a porch with swings of old tires. The cars that had driven on those tires were long gone, the kids had moved to other cities and better prospects. His own best years were gone, too. The stars twinkling over his porch were showing the path of luck and achievement to other humans.

"I'll ask you something else, boy." Cabot's blue stare had

steeled up; his face was red and threatening. "And watch how you answer."

Mayberry shrugged. The intelligent debate was over. Once again, he'd lost. "Ask," he dared.

"Are there any vampires that you could call . . . *real*?" A nasty twitch shook Cabot's shoulders, and he fought it angrily.

"See, you call them real, too." Mayberry couldn't contain himself.

"Real, goddamnit! I mean sleep the day off in caskets, come out at night, dry up in sunlight, live till kingdom come? Now answer me—are there?"

He looked like a puffing bull, head hanging forward, eyes frenzied.

But inside he was afraid.

The God of his Baptist childhood had never spoken to him. The unexplained, the darkness that wouldn't open to one without initiation, those were for the newer brand of men. In his life, he'd met not just with death, but with witchcraft and hoodoo, with cruelty and craziness, and he'd knocked them all out of his way with a swing of the billy club, a punch of the fist, or, if they lingered in his mind, with a swig of whiskey. But now he felt something different. A sediment at the bottom of himself, like dregs from all these years. A core of anxiety that wouldn't melt or crack. And it wasn't because of Knowles. What if, right now, right here ahead of him, lay a crossing that would lead him into what muscle and bullets couldn't deflect, and he'd be left, just rounding 53, at the mercy of that angel unfolding its dark wings, his own immortal soul?

Mayberry took a deep breath, and stood on tiptoe, as if trying to measure up to the question: Are they real? The tie in the opening of his lab gown throbbed as his Adam's apple slipped down, up, down. And then he deflated like a bagpipe. "I don't know," he squeaked.

"Should we call Tulane, speak to someone smarter than you or me?" snickered Cabot.

He hadn't missed the earlier jab, noticed Mayberry. He wasn't that far gone, the bastard.

Jackie Webster moved impatiently in her seat. "Jer honey,

my throat's parched. Go make us some coffee.'' The crime analyst rose and headed for the door, but Jackie stopped him over the threshold. ''I guess we all deserve a fresh brew. Why don't you step out and buy a pound down at that new deli?''

''What's wrong with the coffee that's left in the can?'' mumbled Mayberry.

''It's deader than the dead,'' answered Jackie Webster.

''Why d'you send him away?'' asked Cabot as soon as Mayberry's footfalls were lost in the outside lobby.

''Because he's a bigmouth. Now, us here, we've got to deal with the facts. Knowles is out to put Dale to pasture, isn't that so?'' asked Jackie, all female softness vanished from her tone, sounding in fact rather teacherish.

''That's so,'' acknowledged the men. Cabot didn't. He knew all too well that was so.

''We've built our lives in this department around Dale and our friendship with 'im, and we've had it sweet together, isn't that so?''

''That's so,'' chorused the class.

''You, Dale, and you, Cahill, you have wives and families. Les here needs whatever it takes to play young stud round the community. I mahself . . .'' The men waited suspensefully, but Jackie didn't disclose the nature of her own private predilections. ''We want our paychecks undented, our chairs warm from our own behinds, our privileges whole. And if Dale goes, all that goes—isn't that so?''

''That's so.'' Cahill had rested his chin in his open palm with a melancholy expression. He had pearly Jamaican eyes, and the frizz on his temples was beginning to turn gray.

''We're Dale's friends. And Knowles is a pretty thorough fellow.''

No one made a noise any more. At the far end of the lobby, an elevator whooshed open for the coffee-bound Mayberry.

''Jerry gave me an idea. And I don't want any of you to laugh or make faces when you hear it.''

Faintly, doors shutting. The elevator starting up. The office, like the lab, was in the basement.

"Now this is what I thought to myself while Jerry was smart-pattering. Why is this heat on Dale and on us? Because there's a maniac out there, and he's just a run-of-the-mill ol' maniac. But Dale hasn't been able to catch him yet. So all the shame and blame goes to Dale. Now if we had some new element involved here"—her voice thickened tentatively—"if we had a monster on the loose, one that was, well, supernatural, like an undead from a coffin, like a real vampire."

"Whatcha mean, if we *had* one?" The chin in the palm mangled Cahill's question.

"I mean, what if it was established that something inhuman, some zombielike, can't-put-shackles-on-it kinda beast, is wreaking all this havoc?"

The sediment of disquiet kicked in Cabot's stomach. "Jackie, what are you saying?"

"I'm saying we need something so big that Homicide alone can't handle it. Something that would shift the attention away from you to Knowles, to the police commissioner, to the mayor. I'm saying we need a monster." She inspected her class again, then finished, forcefully and definitively; "And if we can't find one, we've got to invent one."

"Jackie, for Christ's sake . . ." Cabot jumped up, while rapid images from his police life machine-gunned his mind: his office, the neighborhoods tirelessly cruised by black-and-whites, the phones ringing daily, nightly, the hundreds of cases he'd worked on, the hundreds of suspects he'd turned into jail inmates. "I've made it this late in life to come to *this*?"

"Hear me out, goddamn it!" She shook with a passion that quaked her entire hairdo. "Dale, guys, just imagine. Dale, you take the waterfront and harbor—spook the hell out of the wetbacks and the dockers. Les, you leak it to the junkies. Cahill, you talk to your people . . . Cahill?" She said suddenly, with apprehension, "Are you in with us on this one?"

Cahill's eyelids beat; he was astonished. "Me? With y'all, ma'am, for sure with y'all."

"Then you take the rumor to your bunch. Spread the word that we've got . . ." she enunciated emphatically, "*a real big one* here. The Immortal Bloodsucker from ages past, alive

and well and suckin' in New Orleans. No ordinary police can
catch him. No regular bullet can stop him. No protection at
all works against him. You'll see how the town starts be-
havin' when they live under latch and key and can't even
screw up the guts to walk to their outhouses.''

For a moment, the men stared into abstract points, envisioning the collective lunacy.

"It's a far-out idea," said Les. "I like it. But how d'you
reckon it helps us?''

"It's a big crisis," answered Jackie. "Big and without a
fast answer. Who can catch a killer that can sift through a
keyhole? That's what we need to put out there. So that everyone's tongue starts wagging. Why is this happening to us?
Have we sinned and here's our comeuppance? What says science? The shrinks? Is it a sign of the times, is it the decay
of the schools, the TV?'' The phantasms of all these possi-
bilities glossed her eyes while she enumerated them. "You'll
see how the town rises up in arms and marches over to City
Hall to demand action, and Knowles and Commissioner Har-
ris and Mayor Dutoit start pissin' in their pants. And then,
just then, in desperation, Knowles has to call on *you* to save
his ass . . . Dale, *I'm talking to you!*''

Dale felt his brain popping at the prospect of such a plot.
"Yes, Jackie?''

"And you bring in the killer!''

Exhausted, she sat down on a stool, spilling over the sides.

Les looked ready to cry with hope. Cahill hissed a snake-
like sound of admiration. "Ma'am, you's so brilliant!'' Cabot
alternately choked and gasped for breath.

She started again. "You bring him in, and you'll be back
in favor. Hell, you'll be a goddamn hero! And you'll see
who everyone turns against: Knowles, the mayor, all the
biggies. For allowin' such a brainless panic to start in the
first place!''

Now that *was* brilliant, thought Cabot, as he resumed
breathing normally. Women. Damn creatures had such an
innate sense of politics, even when they weighed a ton and
lived buried in this meat sorter. Jackie, Jackie, how did God
ever think of baking up one of your kind?

Jackie didn't have to ask for approval. She knew she had

struck the right chord. Cabot clutched and unclutched his fists rhythmically. Les no longer looked about to cry; instead, he grinned like he wanted to bite his own nose. Cahill was still hissing.

"Can we do it?" asked Jackie.

For a second the three men scrutinized more than just their skills. "We'd be starting something pretty big," pondered Les, "but I don't see us having no other choice."

"Be fun," Cahill summed it up.

"To work, then," Jackie dismissed them.

"What about the coffee?" asked Les.

"I'll tell Jerry you were called out."

Cahill and Les got up and headed for the exit. Cabot stayed behind for a moment. "Jackie, you don't think that in starting this ruckus about a monster, we might . . ." he fidgeted with his empty holster, "we just might rouse a . . . a real one?"

"*What*? Don't be ridiculous, Dale. What are you, a child?"

"Awright then, dawlin'. Bye." Chastised but not comforted, Cabot hurried after the others. He caught up with them by the elevators. They were laughing like men laugh when talking about women. Cahill was asking who smoothed Les's creases last night. An *ac*tress, was Les's proud response.

Cahill accompanied them in the elevator and over to the security desk, where the cops checked out their guns. Then he said take care, he had to plunge back into the pit and do some piss-readings. The cops said take care, too, and hit the streets to create a monster.

Saturday morning, Laura and Charlotte jogged in Audubon Park.

The weather was warmer, and an iridescence of steam rose from the grass, making the trees into compact masses of green. Laura had driven over in white shorts and a sweatshirt and woolen socks, the all-white of her outfit accentuated by a yellow sweatband she wore close to her eyebrows. She parked the car outside the Magazine Street gate, walked into the park, and found Charlotte reclining on the grass, in wild red shorts and a T-shirt with an alligator and a joke printed inside its open jaws. Charlotte rose and held up two Walk-mans: What was her preference, Peter Gabriel or the latest Madonna?

"I guess Peter Gabriel," Laura opted without enthusiasm, remembering the headset. She had meant to drop it off at Delta's downtown office, but the opportunity hadn't pre-sented itself. She looked at the park: A few people were scat-tered on the grass, but the jogging paths were as busy as rush-hour downtown sidewalks. "We're gonna get run over in that traffic."

"Don't worry, I have my own jogging track," Charlotte said and smiled.

Laura had slept well, the insteps of her feet enjoyed the snugness of her Reeboks, and she felt strong and physical. Seen close, Charlotte's body was more muscular than she had realized. Laura watched the sinewy architecture of her arms and legs, building and rebuilding itself, as the quadroon fit her Walkman onto her waistband, and trod away on the grass. "Did you ever lift weights?" asked Laura.

"I did, but Rush stopped me. He doesn't like that, says it reminds him of a guy's body."

Crushed selfishly by the women, the blades of grass broke and collapsed in damp little patches behind them. "Let's go!" commanded Charlotte. She bent under the white explosion of a flowering dogwood and rocketed off, throwing back dirt and ripped-up grass. Taken by surprise, Laura bent too late: a quick bite of twigs and flowers from Charlotte's takeoff burned her eyes and forehead. She hadn't jogged in a while, and when she burst out into the open from under the dog-wood, Charlotte had already vanished in a breach between two thickets.

By instinct, she followed, her heart starting to pick up the rhythm, calves and thighs responding, elbows beginning to pump back regularly, breathing accelerating to short, hot gasps. She saw Charlotte flashing straight at a stand of mixed cottonwoods and oaks, and then disappearing into them. Laura doubled her speed, pounded the ground, bent to duck the branches, but still had to close her eyes against twigs and leaves. The row of cottonwoods and oaks passed, and another appeared. Charlotte was still ahead. Knowing her own strength, Laura smiled. *If that's the way you want to play, let's play your way, Charlotte, honey.* She wasn't even hearing Peter Gabriel and a full rock orchestra, playing surrounded by trees and grass and baby leaves whose pale green bellies made them look like schools of little fishes, swayed by the breeze as if by an underwater current.

She gave her heart a precise order, leaned forward a little more, and her body became a flash of white skin amidst the hues of summer. She saw a narrow crack between bushes and a willow swaying behind like a green parachute. She zoomed through and knew she was ahead. She looked, and to the right of the willow, *boom* came Charlotte out of the green, breasts buffeting like wayward sailboats. They saw each other and grinned, and Laura kept the lead, her heart and body in sync now, wishing she could run like this forever, with shadow and sunlight streaming over her face. They left the willows behind and broke into grass, and Charlotte pointed at the jogging track.

It wasn't as crowded here. Better runners, mostly men. As if energized by the sight of the men, Charlotte hopped onto the track. The men made room for her, eyes turning to see this female moving so abundantly among them, their chests exhaling an extra puff. Laura ran on the grass to be able to see Charlotte, majestically full and young as she charged through. The men were running faster, to keep up with her. Laura cut in front of someone, joined the path herself, and the men noticed instantly the more fragile second woman. The body made of toned, lighter flesh, the ankles narrow but vibrant, the smaller breasts fighting tightly inside the sweatshirt, the pelvis more delicately carved, more mysterious. For her they made way. She kept up with Charlotte, who maintained the pace for a few minutes, eyelids lowered to tease male stares searching for contact; then she led Laura back onto the grass. Getting her second wind, Laura ran unchained, faster than Charlotte, toward a paper birch rising solitarily in this unusual climate—and suddenly she became aware that Peter Gabriel had faded on the Walkman.

"Laura," whispered someone through her headphones.

Laura's eyes bulged from her sockets.

"So you're here," he continued—with sadness and resignation.

For some reason she didn't think of taking off the Walkman right away. She kept running, in a sort of moving inertia, though she couldn't feel the beat of her heart anymore, and her mouth filled with a sour, oxidated taste—the taste of fear.

"You're here and they've found you," said the voice—the same one that had spoken to her on the plane.

"But you can still leave. Leave, Laura, please leave New Orleans," the voice begged, in the intense tone of sincerity and concern she remembered from the plane. "Please, leave New Orleans. I don't want to lose you . . ."

"Leave me alone!" she shouted.

"I don't want to lose you forever, Laura! I don't want to lose you to them!"

"Leave me alone!" she shouted again, at the park and at the rapidly approaching birch. No, she wasn't dreaming. She wasn't dreaming any of this, it was really happening.

She felt the knotted roots she was landing on battering her insteps—hard, real. She felt the fatigue. She felt the inebriation from moving so fast. All of it real, unfantasized, *here*.

"Laura, it may not be too late . . ."

"*Shut up!*" she countered furiously, running straight toward the birch.

"I want you to listen to me . . ."

"I don't want to listen to you!" she screamed as loud as her running rhythm allowed. "Give me peace! Leave me be!" Just before she reached the birch tree, she suddenly felt a snap inside her right ankle, and tumbled onto the grass. The Walkman popped out of her ears, and she called desperately, "Charlotte! Charlotte! Help!"

A few minutes later they were seated on a bench. "I don't want to talk about it!" was the way Laura had started, followed quickly by "I'm sick of this, sick of keeping it in."

"Then let it out!" had been Charlotte's answer.

Now, in halting sentences intercut with darting looks around, she was pouring her heart out. It didn't really matter that Charlotte was, after all, only an employee who might

walk out of her life tomorrow; she spilled the whole essence
of the last three years, told her all about the voice on the
plane and the one that had interrupted Peter Gabriel. Then
she and Charlotte experimented with the Walkman: Charlotte
put it on and heard nothing; the tape was rewinding. Then
Laura tried it and heard the band and the lead singer, and
nothing else.

"Seems to me that you gave all of yourself to that guy,
and you felt really betrayed when he died on you, and got
mighty angry," said Charlotte at the end of the confession,
and Laura almost jumped off the bench: Was there no place
for guilt in Charlotte's explanation? But it was *she* who had
insisted they go sailing that day, said Laura. So why did he
give in to her fuss and take the boat out in a gale? asked
Charlotte. And sure, it made sense not to go out with other
men for a while, but now it was high time she did, and neither
love nor loyalty should hold her back, insisted Charlotte.

"You've been locked up so long, you're afraid of going
out on the open market again."

As Charlotte said it, two of the men who had run behind
their cantering womanhood on the jogging track approached
the bench. They had watched Laura's fall and asked if they
could be of help. When Laura snapped at them, they drawled
apologies and left.

Charlotte gave her a perceptive smile. "See what I mean?"
she asked. Wondering why she felt irritation instead of relief,
Laura asked, "what about the voices?"

"But they didn't mean what they said," shrugged Charlotte. "They're like dreams, you know? One thing means just
the opposite, like wedding—death, butterflies—worries."

"So you wouldn't be afraid?"

"Of what?"

Laura got up ready to shower her with a waterfall of data:
neuroses, the subconscious, split personality, the paranormal.
Lazy eyes staring upward, Charlotte waited, and Laura chose
not to do it.

Charlotte offered her shoulder to lean on, but Laura staggered a little and said it was fine; the movement would do
her twisted joint good. As they started back toward the jeep,
Charlotte embroidered a little on her theory by saying that

anything unnatural, like not dating men, or feeling guilt for something that had happened totally out of one's control, put a strain on the mind, and the mind talked back with voices. She was just superb, thought Laura. She had a perfectly protective thinking mechanism. "Hey, Charlotte," she said, "you could make money with this kind of philosophy."

"I know it," replied Charlotte energetically. "Rush's been trying to get me onto one o' those Christian radio talk shows. He thinks I'd be terrific."

"I think you would be, too. Listen, I haven't told you the whole story." Briefly, Laura recounted her first night scare, with the dream, the fantasy and the footfalls she'd heard hurrying back into the kitchen.

"Aw my Gawd," Charlotte moaned. "Aw Jeez," with an inflection Laura couldn't quite read. But she looked in the quadroon's eyes. The taint of jealousy polluted their luster.

"What's the matter?" she asked.

"You've got the greatest fantasies. If you need a lover, you make him up! I could handle any man if I had your fantasies; I could play hard-to-get forever! Come on, give me a ride home, you lucky tart," she said with a familiarity that Laura felt unable to resent.

They climbed into the jeep, and Laura put it in gear. "But didn't you say that fantasy was unnatural and strained the mind?"

"Sure, but not your sort! Who needs men if they can get your kind of Prince Charmings—they're great, they take their time, they're dirty, and they don't knock you up!"

Despite herself, despite the Walkman that lay between them in the front seat next to its twin, Laura started to laugh. "Charlotte, Charlotte. You're just impossible."

"That's the way we grow 'em down here," Charlotte said, and laughed, too. Laura laughed even harder, and so did Charlotte, till they were both in a fit of laughter. And Laura laughed until two swells of tears started to glue her lashes together. Sweat from the running was still hanging heavy on her forehead, so she wiped away tears and sweat with one sweep of her bare arm, and it felt good.

"Hey, Charlotte, are you going to a party tonight?"

"No, I've got a date. Listen, can I take him to the store?"

"Rush? You mean, this evening?"

"Not Rush. Someone I meet now and then—he's from out of town. You know, my place isn't grand, and this guy stays at the Hilton. If he sees the store, he'll be impressed."

Laura wrinkled her forehead. She could hear Denise's voice: You can't allow her to do that—that's utterly unprofessional.

An hour ago, she would've had the same reaction.

She stared at Charlotte, feeling how a solid principle was being shattered right this instant, and couldn't find anything to say to the pretty eyes and candid smile.

"You *gave* me the keys," chided Charlotte, and Laura said okay, *if* they weren't drunk, and stayed just ten minutes, and locked up again properly. Any mess she might find after them, even a loose hair, she'd take out of Charlotte's pay.

She got home in a state of mind she didn't really understand, except that she was ready to laugh at the slightest provocation. Exhaustion, emotional exhaustion. She ate a sandwich, then turned the TV on. Instead of watching it, she started to write to Denise, then stretched out on the bed and dozed off to the TV sounds.

A moment later—or was it an hour?—she bolted up, thinking she'd heard someone.

It was still broad daylight. The TV babbled on reassuringly.

She turned on one side and shut her eyes, as though inviting the fantasy to return; it could only creep up on her from behind—it feared her eyes.

She dozed off again. A slight movement of air touched her back, and then a pair of lips brushed ever so delicately against her still bruised neck.

How wonderful. The fantasy lover hadn't abandoned her. Her protectiveness, her protests hadn't put him off. How right Charlotte was: she was so lucky.

Sweet and soothing, the lips kissed her bruise. Sweet and soothing, a tongue licked the spot. It'd be completely cured by tomorrow.

He didn't feel like Michael, and she didn't care.

"The violent labor unrest witnessed at the airport the other night has been followed by sporadic vandalism to Lecouveur property . . ." boomed the TV set.

She sat up: The screen sparkled brightly in the dusk of the apartment. The six o'clock news rushed at her, with those men at the airport waving fists and banners. "At issue in the conflict," the commentator said, "is the vast barge fleet owned by the Lecouveur family. Traditionally, those barges have ensured the traffic of goods up and down the river"—a map flashed on, with the crescent-shaped city tweezed between the Mississippi and the lakes; a red arrow shot along the blue contortions of the river, marking the movement of the barges—"And faithful to tradition, Emory Lecouveur persists in hiring local nonunion Cajuns to pilot, load, and unload his barges, in violation of his labor contract . . ."

Laura got out of bed. It was 6:20. She had slept like a child back from a hiking trip. *I'll go out,* she decided. *Preservation Hall or something like that. I've no reason to stay here.*

"With posturing on both sides, the conflict is getting worse," the news droned on. "Running for councilman, young Alain Lecouveur is likely to lose votes and credibility . . ." Laura fumbled in the closet, flipping the hangers back and forth. What should she wear? Ah—a black linen dress. Ralph Lauren, halter style. Usually worn with high heels, but her ankle . . . wait. Black-and-gold sandals. Charles Jourdan, this season's.

"Concerning the waterfront murders, uneasiness is beginning to spread in Algiers and other depressed areas, where the population sees itself as a prime target. The lack of information and police progress is giving rise to superstitious rumors . . ."

Looking in the mirror, Laura missed the last words. Her skin seemed blindingly fair against the black. Nice. Striking combination. The fine veins in her temples were amethyst blue. A golden necklace. No earrings, her watch.

When she walked out, the sun was just slipping below the skyline, like a red-hot wound. The branches of the magnolia, crudely black, tore against the sun.

Teeming with pedestrians, the streets instantly convinced her that she was safe. She walked to Jackson Square and

entered the church, sat quietly for a minute in one of the
pews, then came out just as a local band dressed like min-
strels started a concert of old instruments, *fistulatori et tub-
ulatori*, on the steps. She smiled at their temerity—trying to
compete with all the jazz. She walked to the wooden bridge
at the square's waterfront end, leading to the Algiers ferry
landing, and looked down at the river. Beneath her were fifteen, perhaps twenty couples kissing while standing up against
the waterfront's stony embankment. Kissing like there was
no tomorrow.

At 7:30 she was inching past the doorstep into Preservation
Hall. They were playing inside already—Dixieland. One of
the players had a great Ornette Coleman kind of sound. She
felt a thrill of alarm, packed like this between strangers, and
this time it seemed like the appropriate emotion. The yearn
for the unknown. Life, her own, moving forward. She was
standing in the middle of a drunken bunch of men. They were
passing between them beer bottles and plastic cups filled with
cocktails. "Hey, sister!" She was accosted by the one standing right behind her. "You look short tonight, what happened?"

"I'm standing in a hole," she quipped back smartly.

"But you're missing the show. Don't you want to see those
great old-timers?" She felt a hand touching her waist, and
was so dumbfounded by his audacity that she almost dropped
her purse. "You've got some nerve," she told the man, pushing his hand away.

"I'm known for my bravery," he replied with a belch. He
had a short haircut and a fastidiously trimmed mustache. In
San Francisco, someone looking like him would've been gay,
and no nuisance to a single woman. "I just thought I'd lift
you up, feather-light that you are, and help you see the band."

"No, thanks," she said, and tried to smile. The four or
five other grins surrounding her came from his friends; she
couldn't expect much assistance. "I'm fine just listening."

"You have dynamite skin," he persisted. "Make other
women look like calico next to silk, like they say." Suddenly
the hand was on her waist again, lower. Instinctively, she
slapped at it, felt a puffy moist roundness, like an unbaked
pie. "Hey," he said, "you're not nice."

"Could you keep your hands to yourself?" She heard her voice tremble.

"Don's just bein' friendly," said one of his acolytes.

"Can't keep my hands to myself—cause you ain't keeping yerself to yerself," her torturer said, finding his own words so clever that he howled with laughter. Several voices protested, they were there to listen to the music, what was the matter with that drunk? She started to ask for help, and someone beyond her immediate circle ordered her to shut up, too. Don winked at her with complicity. "See, if you'd let me lift you up, I'd be quiet and we'd all be happy here." Again, the hand on her body. She felt like she was losing control. People were literally stacked up behind her. How was she going to get out? "Would anyone please . . ." she called out loudly to that indifferent multitude, ". . . please tell this gentleman to stop annoying people?" Don's friends found that funny. Inside, the band was playing on. *Jesus, I could get raped standing here!* "Let me out of here *now*!" she yelled, and the man who liked her so much said she was so uptight she could use a drink.

And then a little commotion happened at the back of the crowd. She saw a head of chestnut brown hair bobbing above the rows behind her, like a swimmer's cutting across waves. "Excuse me," a voice said determinedly. A ripple went through the crowd, and Laura felt it unpleasantly as the man behind her was shoved tighter against her. An athletic body pushed two of the drunks apart, and stepped right next to her aggressor.

She saw the chestnut hair invading his forehead, and his eyes glittering underneath, like a fire under a bush. His face looked even more tanned than at the airport.

"Would you leave my friend alone?" he asked. He was closely shaven now, not stubbly, and under the tan his skin had a dark ivory polish.

"She's making friends fast enough to—" the drunk began.

"That's none of your business," said Alain Lecouveur. His tone was light, almost amused. He made eye contact with her as if he'd been away for just a few minutes. "D'you want to stay?" he asked.

"Sure, she loves the music," slobbered the man with the trimmed little mustache.

"I want to go," she whispered tensely, finding Alain totally different from the way he had looked at the airport. Then she realized that she had simply forgotten what he looked like. All that she remembered—and recognized instantly—was her own tingle at being so close to him.

"Come on," the man named Don said to her. "You want to stay." And to Alain, "We just had a lovers' quarrel."

"Step aside and let her pass," he said amicably. In response, the man with the trimmed mustache stretched an arm between Alain and Laura, and propped his fist against the wall of the passageway.

Laura saw Alain grab Don's arm slightly above the wrist. He neither twisted it nor pulled at it. His jaws contracted as he squeezed Don's arm. Don's color, already pink, turned to purple. He made a crying sound, and his knees buckled. Alain let go of his arm. Don's friends caught him under the armpits to hold him up.

Everyone around was watching. After Don's cry, the only sound was the band playing on.

"Let's go," urged Alain. The crowd parted. She followed his back. He wore a suede jacket and needed a haircut—his hair overflowed the jacket's collar.

They stopped on the sidewalk. "How d'you like New Orleans?" he asked, amused, almost mockingly.

She didn't answer. She stared up at him: Without heels her eyes were level with his chin.

"I was just passing by, and I heard you. I was on my way to dinner."

She must've called out for help quite loud. She felt two simultaneous and conflicting fears: that he would spend five or ten minutes with her, and never want to see her again; or that he would hurry off to dinner right away. *Dinner by candlelight, with a woman?*

"Where are you having dinner?" she asked. He wasn't dressed up, though—he wore a simple white shirt, and the suede jacket, she noticed, wasn't new. It draped around him with the natural grace of clothes that have learned every sinuousness of a body.

"Nowhere in particular. My date stood me up."

The uneven lighting of the street made his eyes dark, but she could still see the sunny glow they'd had under the neon glare of the airport. Oh yes, that she remembered well. Suddenly there was a change in his stare. The tinge of mockery vanished. For just an instant he took in her face with a sort of voracious attention, as if breaking it into its component parts, to understand each one of them: her skin, her bone architecture, her makeup.

Dizzily drawn into the depth of his eyes, she tried to exercise some inner detachment and couldn't. His eyes were like spiraling tunnels. *I'll let myself go. I'll enjoy it just one second.* She tumbled in vertiginously. The tunnels closed as fast as they had opened. The facetiousness, the slight biting edge were back: "Would you like to go to dinner with me?"

Don't agree instantly. Good. Now, like a good sport. "Well, I haven't eaten yet, so why not? Her loss is my gain."

He started to laugh. "You think it was a woman?"

Shrug. "Yes, I was assuming . . ."

"That woman could have our kneecaps smashed, or worse, have us dangle from cypresses in the bayou with dead pigeons in our mouths. Welcome to the real New Orleans," he said, seeing her flinch. "Sorry. I was supposed to meet a labor organizer, to try and straighten out the family mess. No need to save appearances before strangers—it's all over the news."

His lips crested down dejectedly. *He has a great mouth.* "So—dinner?"

"Why do you want to have dinner with me?"

"I'll tell you a secret." He lowered his voice suspensefully. "I'm tired and confused and my pride is hurt. I need a good night on the town and someone to impress. Here's my car."

He pointed: a white Chrysler Le Baron convertible, parked right at the curb in a red zone.

A thought dawned on her: "Did you stop for me?"

"I was crawling behind someone else, and heard the commotion," said Alain. "Now, we have to pick up some wine first, because the dive I'm taking you to has only rot-gut.''

He arched his arm away from his body, and she understood that he was offering it.

She took it.

PART TWO

CRYSTAL OF FEAR

5

Come live with me and by my Love,
And we will some new Pleasures Prove.
JOHN DONNE

SHE SPIED on him on their way out of the Quarter. His forehead was higher than his hair revealed, his nose was straight and determined, and when he came across the obstacle of a slow car in his way, his eyes hardened, his nostrils flared, and a fleshy pout stuck out his lower lip. Taking chances at passing cars in the narrow streets, he gripped the Chrysler's wheel like a racer. His forehead lowered, he gunned forward, and the contained passion she had noticed at the airport was all over his features. Once he was ahead again, his cheeks relaxed, the mouth softened into a pleased, almost feminine carnality, his eyes reliquefied, and he gazed proprietarily at the street. *So male*, thought Laura, almost touched: Men were such innocent prisoners of their own expectations of themselves.

Alain drove into Marais Street, where a wine cellar's yellow lights seeped out from cobwebbed windows, and an aproned vendor came to take his order outside. Alain asked for *"mon regulier,"* also named another wine, and as they waited he told her that he came to town only on business. When he wasn't traveling, he slept at Belle Hellène, the family estate, and spent his days at a loading spot upriver, to which and from which the Lecouveur barges chugged full or empty, continuously. And what about her? *Oh, great*, Laura thought, *terrific opportunity to invent a new personal history*. But she told him about Mom and Dad and Denise and the store and implied she had dated some other men. The wine man came out with a white Cabernet, and two sturdy unmarked bottles of red: from Alain's personal stock. The Lecouveurs had tried to start vineyards here. Emory's father had even shipped over soil from France. Fruitlessly. Louisiana was too hot and humid.

"Hold the bottles," he told her, gunning the car eastward on Marais. Watching his profile again, she was jolted to a stop in front of a ramshackle two-story clapboard house. A crippled neon sign advertised Cafe Paris.

"Is this it?" she asked incredulously. He nodded, opened his door, and asked a teenage valet about "the boss." "He in th' kitchen," said the boy, and Alain tossed him the keys. She stepped out on dirt ground battened unevenly into hardness. Blues music rolled out of the house, over a bunch of dusty acacias and over parked cars.

"Come on," he said, "and you'll eat better than in your sweetest fantasy."

A black busboy was rushing down a flight of cracked steps toward them. He greeted Alain deferentially and raced straight to the Chrysler to bring out the bottles. Alain took her elbow and whisked her into a bar where the stooled patrons she saw were wearing hats and caps. Savoy Brown surrounded her from all sides, together with vapors of food, cigarette and cigar smoke. The food smell was fortunately stronger, an aroma of fried okra and sausages and red beans—earthy, greasy, and yet somehow doing the right thing to her stomach. She looked away from the bar and saw tables around a dance floor lit only by narrow blue and red floodlights. Only the faces of men and women and the bare arms and backs of women were visible in the shadows of the floor: suspended masks and disjointed limbs dancing exuberantly. She started to laugh the way she had with Charlotte. "Where have you taken me?"

She turned, not finding him by her side. Several men had gotten up to greet him and he was caught in a knot of bodies dressed in almost comical Sunday finery. "What a doll! *Ow!*" one man squealed in her direction. She reached out her hand; it disappeared into hands that the lack of light made invisible, and Alain slapped backs and had his slapped, and then the noisy friends went back to wives and dates, and Alain pulled out a folded handkerchief to mop his forehead. "So this is Paris?" she laughed.

"No, ma'am. *Ah's* Paris." A small round black man with white hair grabbed her hand and rested it from the previous shakings. "Paris Johnson. Ah has jes' the spot fo' you."

"Come on," said Alain, and smiled at her smile. "Careful going up." Her sandals felt uneven boards as they climbed to a second level with booths. The booths had curtains of chenille, some of them drawn shut.

"Raht heah," said Paris Johnson, opening a booth. "Ah'll get you a tebble cloth an' can'les an' yo' wine." He hurried away.

"I could've taken you somewhere stodgy, like Antoine's, but I'm tired of those places. Sit down," said Alain. "You won't catch anything." She laughed and sat, and as soon as she was down, a delicious dread spread in her whole body. From her temples, down her spine, around her buttocks, down thighs and calves. She was alone, alone with him.

"Open those," he said, pointing at curtains on the other side of the booth. She pulled them open just a crack. A balustrade came up to her elbow, and over it she saw the dance floor below. The fascinating pantomime of faces and arms and legs swinging with *joie de vivre*.

She let the curtains fall. A waiter had brought one of the unmarked bottles, and the Cabernet, both open. Another waiter started to light candles. The unmarked wine dribbled slowly into Alain's glass, its consistency tinting it seemingly to pitch black. Alain sniffed it, tasted it, and closed his eyes for a second. The waiter started to fill her glass with Cabernet.

"Wait a second—why aren't we having the same wine?" she inquired.

"I don't think you'll like mine," he answered, and sipped with satisfaction. "It's sort of an aquired taste."

"I want to try it." She tapped with her glass on the table.

"All right." He pushed his own glass across, still pretty full.

She filled her mouth, finding it cooler than she had expected, then swallowed a thickness of velvet—so thick that it overrode the taste. Trying to get to the taste, she took a gulp. It went down, she tilted the glass for more, and suddenly her temples were pounding and her pulse rate seemed to double. She lowered the glass, and he promptly took it away.

"You drank almost a whole glass." He sounded surprised.

She looked down, studied the wood of the table. A busboy slid a checkered tablecloth under her eyes, and she studied its pattern. She hadn't eaten anything since that sandwich.

Her pulse slowed, and on the roof of her mouth she finally found the taste. Almost sweet, but there really wasn't a word for that sort of sweetness. It felt more like a depth. Yes, that was the word. *Deep.*

"I think it's a great wine, but it's too heavy for me," she said.

"You drank it as if you've had it before."

"I'm sure I haven't had it. It's incredibly potent."

"Cabernet for the lady," he commanded to the waiter. "Something to wash away my wine, and quench your thirst."

He had his glass filled with the heavy one, and explained that it had been imported years before, from a vineyard the Lecouveurs used to own in the South of France. Now it was aging in the bottles cellared away on Marais Street, because— something she didn't know—a wine's life is never really over. It continues to ferment even in the bottle. Every spring and fall it "moves," until someone drinks it.

She didn't listen to any of this. She was looking at his face.

The fleshiness of his lips curled down into a heart pattern, and where the heart curves met, right under his nose, a tiny spot of shaven skin shone so deliciously naive and younger than the rest of his face that she felt like reaching over and touching it.

"Alain," she interrupted him.

"Ma'am?" he responded automatically, a Southern boy for that short span of reflex action.

"Did you mean what you said about being hanged from cypresses?"

He thought. "What I meant is that my family has a serious showdown with the unions coming. And so far, it hasn't been defused."

She felt like laughing, and caught herself. This was serious. No reason to laugh. She rinsed her mouth with more Cabernet and looked at his mouth. Incredibly attractive. Didn't want it on a cypress tree.

"Anyway, I want to relax here," said Alain. "Relax, and impress you."

"Impress me," she acquiesced. When had they ordered? Paris arrived with a team of waiters with baked okra, beans and rice and sausages sprawled lasciviously on the rice, and steaming fresh cornbread. She felt so hungry that she stuffed a huge piece of cornbread into her mouth, and Paris patted her paternally on the back. "Eat, it's good for you."

"Let's eat like pirates," said Alain. "Paris, you have any special desserts tonight?" Paris had pie and pound cake with whipped cream, homemade, and would bring them with the coffee. He grinned and said he'd knock with a broom on the ceiling right under them before bringing the desserts up, and closed the curtains. Alain started eating ravenously. Her first pangs of hunger past, Laura asked him how French his family was.

"Originally not French at all. They moved to Marseilles around 1760. There, they became totally Frenchified. My uncle, though he sailed over to New Orleans as a young man, is still as French as I'm American."

"Where were they coming from originally?"

"From the lower Danube. From Romania."

She was plunging a forkful of okra in her mouth. She burst out laughing, and it went down unchewed. "Romania?" He seemed almost as entertained as she was. He explained that two centuries before, Romania was a cluster of principalities—Wallachia, Moldavia, Transylvania—and that the clan of Calovaru, grand *boyar* and landowner, had a quarrel with the reigning prince. Consequently, the clan was forced to leave Bucharest, the see of princely power, though not without their money chests. Lecouveur was a loose anagram of Calovaru, and his uncle Emory was a walking chronicle of all those deeds and ancestors. For Alain, it was all buried in legend.

"But it *is* legend, isn't it? You don't really come from there?"

"I never knew what to believe of Emory's stories. I think Emory made it up, quite frankly, because that part of the world is so obscure and mysterious, and that's Emory's act." Laura laughed and agreed, remembering the brougham driving across the Quarter. Finally she veered her eyes from Alain's mouth to his hands. As a rule, men's hands weren't that pretty. She liked his a lot.

"D'you know anything about Romania?" she asked, feeling tenderness, even compassion, because if Alain's family was originally from there, then he had lost not one but two homelands. The second glass of wine was working, she told herself.

"I know what Emory tells about it when he's in the mood." Alain was laughing now almost as much as she was, and his bottle of wine was empty. "You care to listen?" He gave her the portrait of an unspoiled, primitive culture. Villages nesting in the Carpathian mountains, villagers living in their own time capsules because the roadways were so poor. People who endured a kind of tragic solitude, among the mountaintop stars and the sheep they raised. A sense of honor upheld with the knife and the pistol. If a brother was killed, the survivors lived to avenge him. A cruel sort of innocence.

"D'you think it's really like that?"

"How would I know? I've never seen it. Emory tried to go back there in 1947, when the Russians were closing in. He took the Wiener Waltzer express train from Vienna, bound for Bucharest . . ." *That must be a gorgeous trip*, thought Laura dreamily. ". . . but he was stopped at the border. The Russians didn't want any Americans poking around."

"Can you speak the language?"

He opened the curtains and called. The waiter brought his second bottle of wine, filled his glass, and obligingly closed the curtains.

Alain took a healthy sip, and his breath reached her over the table with whiffs of wine and wet cork. "If anyone had told me that I'd be talking to a California career-woman about this . . . No, I can't. In fact, the only Romanian words I know are the beginning of a folk song that Emory taught me." He put his glass down, raised his head, and said with a different intonation—white, toneless, suspended in the air: "I like you a lot."

She counted a few seconds, then said, "What's that song?"

"I can't sing it. I can only say the words."

He recited:

> Varcolac, moroi, strigoi,
> Vino noaptea pe la noi,
> Stai de pinda la culcare,
> Sa bei stropi de fata mare . . .

It had a roughness she hadn't expected. The words hammered, seemed to break in the middle, then clanged shut. The v's and c's had an animal brutality. People who had learned to talk fighting each other, avenging, mumbling alone with their sheep.

"What does it mean?" She giggled for no reason.

"It means . . . I'm going to embarrass you . . ."

"No, no, I promise you." She giggled more.

"It's sort of coarse . . . It's a peasant song."

"What d'you think I am, a prude?"

For just a split second, he looked like a little boy who'd lost his nerve in the middle of an adult joke. "It means— vampire, ghost, undead/ come and visit us at nightfall/ lie in ambush by our bedside/ and lap drops of maidenhood."

She stared him straight in the eyes, and said nothing.

"It's a song spinsters sing, supposedly." He advanced his hand and took hers. She started at the contact. Then, for just a second, she felt absurdly that all her unseen nudity had been drawn together in her hand.

"That's weird," she said, without withdrawing her hand. "Why would spinsters sing invitations to vampires?"

"Because those mountains are so untraveled, and the men are always away where the grazing sheep take them. So the villages are full of unmarried girls."

"I see." Laura caught on. "Having a vampire lover is better than having no lover."

He smiled and she stopped giggling, aware that he was watching her magnetically, heavily male. His stare had body. A tickle played with the naked skin of her arms. She felt the need to roll her shoulders, brushing them against the linen of her dress. The linen felt rough, stiffened without reason.

"You okay?" he asked out of the blue.

She was shocked. "Yeah, yeah, I'm fine," she mumbled.

He let go of her hand. "I don't think any of the stories are true," he said, as if with regret. "The old buzzard always had a head full of quaint notions. He used to collect gothic novels, the dime-store type . . ." He leaned forward, the laughter dancing in his eyes again," . . . and he read them aloud to the housekeeper and cook to terrify them—look!" He caught her hand again, and with his other hand he pointed at something in the air.

Laura started. Convinced by the realism of the gesture, she looked up: only the dark ceiling, with naked, ugly pipes streaking it. "There, there circled the monster, the *Ungehauer*!" cried Alain in an accented falsetto, and she quickly focused back on him, not to miss the recital. "Folding his wings, he dropped onto the steps, and cast no shadow!" Laura started to laugh hysterically, her hand shaking in his. With his other hand he made a tempering gesture—could she control herself, there was better and juicier to come.

"Careful to fold his wings so that they wouldn't burden his passage through the narrow crypts, Gorgaunt climbed and climbed. With each step his breath grew ranker and his visage acquired another detestable wrinkle of perversity."

Laura realized that she had kicked off her sandals under the table. Her feet were playing unguiltily on the dusty wooden floor. *I'm drunk. I'm really drunk.*

"His clawed feet finally brought him at the door parting the rest of the labyrinthian castle, each room and stairway a witness of iniquities, from the modest but limpidly clean room where, unsuspecting, the fair and God-devoted virgin . . . Aprilia . . ."

"Wait!" yelled Laura. "Alain! Are you *remembering* this?"

"Pretty much," he said, "but it's not from one book, it's snatches from God knows how many evenings. I was a kid who wouldn't go to sleep. Now you got me out of my mood . . ." He made an effort, but seemed to have forgotten. "I can't recapture it," he declared.

"Oh," she cried with disappointment, and the soles of her feet rubbed the floor. "Are you sure?"

He took another sip of wine, hung his face close to the table. "Oh shit," he said, like a frustrated actor. Waiting, Laura felt now a tingle, coming from her feet this time, mounting up along her legs, toward her middle . . .

"*Aha!*" he cried suddenly with a mad flame in his eyes; it took her by surprise and she squirmed on the cracked vinyl of the booth. "Yes! Yes!" He pretended to suck his teeth and chafe together monstrous paws, raspy like parchment. "Yes, Aprilia, yes. Gorgaunt's purpose. The aim of his debased urgencies. Aprilia was just taking off the crucifix that nestled daily between the treasures of her breasts, protecting her against the castle's miasmatic calls to evil. Preparing for bed, the girl stepped out of her humble servant skirt, and sinlessly showed the flower of her maidhood to the polished brass of the chamber pot . . . and . . . Can you take over?" he asked Laura, but not in a normal tone of voice; in the same falsetto—fake, yet lewdly effective.

"Me?" she asked, amazed. "Oh, I see . . . and then she, she . . . She flung aside the bedcovers and stretched on the hard bed . . ."

"Very good . . . palpitating . . . palpitating at . . . Go on!"

"The thought . . ." Beside herself with laughter, she fought for dear life to lower her voice, and tried to stare back at Alain with the same lubric hypnoticism. ". . . at the thought of peaceful hours of blessed rest? No. At the elevation of her soul toward angelic heaven, high above the dreaded castle's spires?"

"A little namby-pamby, but not bad. You got her in bed too quickly. Gorgaunt is terribly disconcerted."

"Then let's take her back to the pot!" roared Laura.

"I think we must. Back there she was, satisfying nature. Ha! Did she ignore the danger peering at her through the door's peephole? As she straightened herself, Gorgaunt's incontinence almost dribbled on the doorstep. With matchless brute force, he pressed himself against the ancient padlock.''

"Stop! I got it!" shouted Laura. "The door flew open in splinters, and Gorgaunt used his wings for just one flap that landed him atop the horrorstruck child." Pleased at her inventiveness, she kept her eyes locked into Alain's, who instantly picked up:

"Unyielding though she was, Gorgaunt's toil in subjugating her was brief. Knowing that screaming was no use, that Gorgaunt was sure to get his reward, Aprilia used all the soul left in her . . .''

". . . to invoke the Virgin and the forty martyr saints in prayer."

"Terrific! She prayed, he tried. She cried, he pried. He tortured her faultless limbs, while she begged for a miracle. But heaven's occult design was that she would be excruciated. In minutes, by using abject blows and language even worse, Gorgaunt became the tamer of her chastity. As he possessed her, he opened his wings and down they soared together, into the pit."

"On her bed the next morning were found . . ." Laura groped for a nostalgic ending.

"Still moist," he interrupted, "the vestiges of her virtue."

She howled with laughter again. "Alain, you're so gross!" And then both took a deep breath. Laura's jaw ached from laughter.

"This was a hoot," he said.

"I haven't laughed so hard in years." She shook her head, stunned from the last ten minutes, then stared at Alain. Attentively and warmly. She saw him avert his eyes.

That was a surprise. He unblushingly played such games, but when she gave him a truly direct look—he was shy? She watched him, decided that she was right: behind his randy facade there was a core of shyness.

She liked that even more than the game they had played. He finally looked at her, eyes clear of laughter, and not totally sure of her reaction.

"Would you like more wine?"

"No, thanks. I've had more than enough."

She found her sandals under her table and pushed her feet into them. "Listen, d'you think I can go powder my nose without meeting Gorgaunt?"

"Give forth a shriek of distress; I'll instantly to your succor," he promised. "Meanwhile, the dessert will make it to the table."

When she came back, pecan pie, pound cake, and date loaf were on the table, with a pot of coffee and a bottle of *fine de champagne*. A big unlit *puro* clenched between his teeth, Alain rotated a cognac glass in his hand, to spread the aroma around the inside. He asked if he could smoke and she said she didn't mind, the place was smoky anyway. She had pie and coffee, he took a few pulls of his cigar, poured her a glass of *fine*. She said she had drunk too much already.

"Try just a taste. It's the only decent liquor this place has."

She took the glass, looked at the dance floor below through it. Doubly distorted, legs and arms and buttocks were still frantically at it, while the music plowed on, from Savoy Brown to Big Mama Thornton. Happiness. In this smoky, smelly place, to the tune of forgotten hits. It was the best place. Better than Antoine's, or any other fancy restaurant with its haute cuisine and its fastidious service.

"Wouldn't it be nice to be children again?" she whispered.

"Or at least teenagers?" he echoed.

"Were you in love as a teenager?"

"Don't you find it extraordinary that we met at the airport, and then again tonight?" He had changed the subject so abruptly that her mind went along with the change, without protesting.

"I wouldn't say that we really *met* at the airport." After eating, his mouth looked rich and red, like a satiated carnation.

"I feel like we did. And yesterday Emory mentioned your name, after a phone call from Marion. Marion periodically calls him with a full report about what's happening in town."

"So you've been around since Wednesday night?"

"Yes, but later tonight I've got to hit the road and be back at my loading station before dawn. So drink that *fine*, or don't drink it—I want to show you a view of the city." He pulled out his wallet and looked inside it. Laura spotted his wine glass: A dark mouthful of wine lay sleepily at its bottom. Temptation shot her hand forward. She grabbed it, threw the wine back before Alain could pull a roll of bills out of his wallet.

She swallowed the wine too fast. It burned her throat and lit a smoldering fire in the food in her stomach.

This time it had plenty of taste. The same deep taste, even deeper. So unusual that she licked her lips trying to define it. Food helped it. With practice, she could like it.

"Let's go, the night is young!" Alain smiled. He crushed out his cigar, and threw some cash on the table.

The place was shaking and jumping, the old clapboards rattled in tune with the music and the dancers, and legions of parked cars surrounded the packed Paris Cafe. A breeze was up, and their hair flapped as Alain ripped away from the parking lot. The stars seemed big like blooming magnolia flowers, and they rained across the car's windshield.

Alain took Highway 10 and circled downtown, then switched to 90, toward the bridge, and Laura was getting tipsier and tipsier without being sick—just so high that everything was possible and in reach, like this man she liked so much, and was riding with, and could touch if only she put out her hand and stretched her fingers. The car shot across the bridge, its huge steely accordions heaving inside Laura. He looked at her while the big steel transversal beams hummed above the fast-moving car, and she looked back at him. The city, a mass of burning jewels, glittered in his eyes. They zoomed to the other end of the bridge, and then again toward downtown New Orleans, just to enjoy again swinging under the colossal ropes of twined steel cables, and finally left the highway at Annunciation Street. Laura's eyes were drunk with stars as they sailed back to Rampart and reentered the Quarter. They found it wrapped in a fog of tired jazz. In front of the cathedral, a bridegroom in tails was throwing confetti at his bride. Each tree trunk seemed tripled by a pair of lovers leaning against it. He asked her for directions, and turned a corner toward Ursulines.

"Look at the moon!" she called, astonished. She thought she had never seen it like this: a shard of silver, floating somehow in the night sky, without tipping over and sinking.

"The varcolacs ate it," said Alain with a smile.

"What do you call them? Vrrr . . ."

"Var-colacs. Means vampires in Romanian."

Even the word felt perfectly descriptive. Vrrr—winglike, batlike. *Colac.* Like a squeak from a thirsty, dried-up throat.

"You're going to make me believe in all this. Do they have anything to do with the moon?"

"Oh yes, and that's another legend." He slowed down behind a police car. "According to the Romanians, the varcolacs are born in the moon, which is full to begin with. Being lustful little monsters, they multiply too fast and grow so hungry that they start to munch on the moon—till they wear it down to a sliver: that's why the moon decreases. As the moon shrinks, the vampires fight for space, and more and more of them fall onto the earth, till none are left. By now of course, the moon is thin like a maiden's brow."

"What an ingenious explanation of the phases of the moon," she whispered.

"Isn't it? But there's enough room on the new moon for the eggs the vampires laid before falling off to earth. As the new moon starts growing again, the vampire eggs approach maturity. By the time it's full, the vampire eggs hatch. A new generation is born. It starts munching at the moon again, and the cycle goes on, repeating itself forever."

"So the moon is like a vampires' paradise, before their downfall?" asked Laura.

"If you want to make this folk tale into a genesis kind of myth, yes. The moon is paradise before the fall, and the vampire's original sin is hunger. All myths about a beginning are the same. There's a cosmic state of felicity, which primal man—or primal vampire—invariably shatters."

I'm so clever, thought Laura. She looked up at the moon shard. It seemed to wink at her, familiar, friendly.

All right now. When we get to my place, what do I do? Do I ask him in?

Alain brought her to Ursulines, and she invited him in. They went up the outer staircase together, and as she tried her keys, his silhouette blotted out half the sky and the city lights, and she felt like grabbing that big hunk of man and pulling him over herself. They walked into stuffy air and he remarked, "You afraid someone might come in and hide in your wardrobe?" She opened the door to the balcony. He was standing in the middle of the main room, hands in his pockets, with deep eyes, with chestnut-auburn strands of hair streaking his forehead.

She felt so certain that just by passing she'd invite a kiss that she furtively wetted her lips as she started toward him. She walked past and he didn't move. *Missed.* She walked into the kitchen, not knowing what to do, then turned on a tap and drew herself a glass of water.

"I actually am afraid of something. Well, not really afraid. Curious."

He ambled into the kitchen. She sipped from the glass, put it on the counter, and looked up at him. The bright overlight streamed down his face. *If I look at his eyes, he'll get it.* She let her eyes slip into his, and the depth made her dizzy. They were deep, but not all that warm. *I'm moving too fast, and he can tell. Easy, Laura, you only saw him once before.*

"What is it?" Alain asked.

With the tip of her sandal, she pointed at the little closet door. "This. It opens into some sort of . . . well in the wall."

He looked at it, narrowed his eyes and furrowed his face, and crouched by the closet door. Swinging it open, he looked in. He lay his open palm on the platform, stared up to where the sustaining lanyards vanished into the dark. "Aha," he said finally, and Laura throbbed slightly, like a patient awaiting a doctor's verdict: "It's a *sommelier volant,*" he said. She hadn't the faintest idea what that meant.

"A flying wine steward. Like a dumbwaiter, but this type was used exclusively for lifting wines from cellars."

"By whom?" she asked, resigned to waiting for that first kiss, and fearing that her mood would change.

"By whoever had the house before it was remodeled into apartments. The flying steward was originally a French device and it was imported into the Quarter, oh, I think in the 1800s. Usually the cook or a servant stepped on this platform and lowered themselves to the wine cellar." He touched the lanyards. "They took what they needed, then pulled themselves up again." He pulled at them, and observed that they were in very good condition.

"They went down this way rather than take the stairs?"

"It was a lot more convenient than traipsing up fifty steps, carrying big flagons or cases. Taking a chance of missing a step and breaking fine bottles of imported wine."

"D'you think someone could still use this to pull themselves up and down between the floors?" she asked, looking at him, striving to put nothing but earnest interest in her stare.

He stood on one foot, took off one shoe, then the other. "Let's see." He grabbed the braided rope and stepped on the platform. He straightened up inside the shaft. "Laura," he called, his voice muffled by the acoustics of the shaft.

She squatted to peer in. She saw his dark silhouette towering over her, and a very faint gleam in his eyes, from the shaft's top opening.

"There's a block up there, with a pulley," he said. "And this thing's solid enough to hold both of us."

She nodded, watching the lanyards. They were taut like violin strings.

"Want to come in and see what this is all about?" Alain asked.

She pondered. *Why not? Forget about the kiss, let's solve this puzzle.* She felt the defiance of alcohol, and courage in the company of this strong male. She unstrapped her sandals.

He made room for her by flattening himself against the wall. She crawled in, he took her hands and pulled her up, and they stood face to face inside, like in an elevator.

The lanyards throbbed, but held. "Look at these cords," she said, amazed at their strength, but that didn't surprise Alain. *Sommeliers volants* were designed to support big demijohns of wine totaling a few hundred pounds. He started to chuckle.

"What the hell are we doing in here? Being children again?" She felt his breath, heavy with food and cigar, a little too heavy. But the closeness of his body made her heart pump fast. He suddenly clutched her hand: "Ssshhh!"

They listened. Silence.

They listened more. A ripple of voices. Coming from below.

He grinned suddenly, and the paleness of the night glistened on his teeth. For a second, she felt he was unknown, and scary.

"Shall we go exploring?"

She shrugged, not ready to say yes. She felt claustrophobic, dizzy with drink, suddenly uneasy about leaning on him for support.

He tested the leather braid by pulling on it, then tugged. The platform shook, clattered against the shaft, and mounted a few inches. The light from Laura's kitchen almost disappeared below them.

"What are you doing?" she asked, insecure all of a sudden. Who was this man? What was he up to? What if this contraption suddenly snapped and they took a neck-breaking tumble into the dark?

"Ssshhh," he said imperatively. He was learning how to operate the flying steward. He stopped it, then let the braid creep out of his hands, and the platform descended. The open closet door flew up toward them, and Laura saw his face almost in full light: normal, nothing to be afraid of, just interested in this extra bit of fun.

He lowered the platform more. Far above them, the block and pulley creaked. She tried to make no noise, and heard the voices again. And then just one voice.

A woman's voice. Crying.

Alain kept maneuvering the platform. The braid slipped through his fingers for a second, the platform shook, and they were thrown against each other. He rebalanced the platform. Looking down, Laura saw a dagger of light slitting the wall horizontally. The crying was perfectly audible. *Aprilia*, wondered Laura, *weeping her shame after Gorgaunt had his way with her*? The sense of security from Alain's strong hands helming the precarious vehicle excited her, however. What might they find? Creatures of the night, catacomb dwellers, perhaps a different race tending those pumps? She stood on tiptoe, touched the rim of Alain's ear with her lips.

"Aren't you scared?"

"Of what?" he whispered, steering.

Wonderful answer. Her hero.

"Where is he now?" snapped a female voice, seemingly inches under them. The daggerlike cleft in the wall ascended, throwing a stripe of light on Laura's dress, on Alain's shirt. Careful like a balloonist, Alain slowed the flying steward to a crawl.

He brought the cleft in the wall exactly level with Laura's eyes, then silently and efficiently wrapped the braid of leather around a forearm. Her eyes adjusted to the light: a rectangular opening, just like the one in her kitchen, had been bricked up. A thin vein of mortar between two layers of bricks had crumbled. Like a child, she put one eye to the cleft, and her cheek touched Alain's. The touch made her skin tingle. Not just on her face. On her arms, her back, her legs.

"I don't know," answered a basso voice.

Peeping in, she saw the Egyptian's face, dead ahead of her. His eyes were at half-mast. He seemed to be pressing his fingers against his temples.

"I don't know where he is," repeated the Egyptian. "He exited this state."

"Bring him back, bring him back," the woman demanded, hysterically, like an addict needing a fix. "Can you bring him back?"

"Take your position. I'll try."

A silhouette cut across Laura's view, hiding the Egyptian. Probably the woman's. It dropped below the edge of the cleft, and made a sound as if collapsing in a heap on the floor. As though obeying a signal, the woman started to cry again, softly but with complete conviction.

Alain touched her shoulder. "Laura."

"What?" she whispered back.

"This is a séance. In progress."

They waited another few moments, listening to the sobbing. The beam of light carved Alain's face. "Let's go back," he whispered.

She nodded. He unwrapped the leather braid and started hoisting the platform up.

"So now we know," said Alain, pulling himself on all fours out of the shaft and into the kitchen. He helped her out. "Your downstairs neighbor is a medium of sorts."

"I guess." She shuddered slightly, and realized he had

noticed. "I can cut those lanyards if you want," said Alain. "Put the flying steward out of commission."

"It's not worth the trouble." *Don't let him think you're neurotic.*

"You could also nail that closet door shut. It obviously serves no purpose." He sounded like he was ready to say good night.

"You're right. Maybe I will."

Disappointed, she stepped back into the living room, turned to look at the Boulle clock, and he surprised her by wrapping his arms around her. She raised her face, he printed his lips on hers, and the warmth of the kiss spread through her body like a drink. "Alain!" she murmured. He kissed her again, and while kissing her he forced her body down.

With delicate strength, he guided her body to the floor, and she let herself stretch out on the polished wooden planks. She saw the bottom of the chairs and the edge of the table over them as they kissed a third time. This time she opened her lips completely, put both hands over his temples and pressed, eased the pressure, pressed again thirstily, breathed through her nose, kept his mouth, kept it till she left not a square inch around her lips dry. He pulled away for air.

"Some first date," he said. He dried his lips on her cheek. His weight made her feel the hardness of the floor. She put both palms on his chest and pushed him away, just for the pleasure of feeling a statuesque set of pectorals (the chest of a statue, a pharaoh statue, flashed through her mind, and she killed the vision).

"I'm sorry," he whispered.

"For what?" she asked, a little hoarsely.

"For pulling you to the floor like this.'

"You're acting like you haven't dated anyone in a while," she said with hope.

"I haven't," he confirmed. He got up, and with the same delicate strength he brought her to her feet. "We can sit on your bed," he suggested.

"Why not?" She turned to lead the way, and wiped off the wetness of the kisses with the back of her palm, *like a regular type schoolgirl.*

They sat on the bed, kissing for perhaps a minute, then

started tilting over like one body, and she fought his arms. "Wait." With useless concern for her dress, she straightened it, brought her legs up, and lay on her back. He immediately rolled on top of her, kissing her lips, her neck, her face, her lips again and again, endlessly. *Good. Take over. I don't want to have to make any decisions.*

He finally stopped. Lying on top of her, his weight felt like a resplendent, muscular mass. Under her dress, Laura's knees had parted, and her cheeks were ablaze from the warmth of their clothes and of his body. She felt a subtle film of sweat where her forehead met her hair.

His powerful hands lay under her back, arching it upward. "Close your eyes," she whispered.

He smiled a spoiled little smile, as if guessing what would follow, and his eyelids dropped. Holding his head, she began to kiss him. He tried to respond and she ordered him to be still. She moved her lips slowly from one corner of his mouth to the other.

She did it once, stopped for breath, heard his heart thumping.

She started again the other way. His lips were salty now. Lying on her back, she felt tipsy all over again. Thank God kissing didn't need that much coordination.

She finished, started again. She heard his breath growing shorter. He was aroused to a peak, but made no attempt to seize her determinedly. He just held her, not even trying to slip his hand toward her breasts, or her waist. Smart guy. Enjoyed the same sort of game she did. Laura stopped by one mouth corner and morseled it, and suddenly paused.

Somewhere inside her, an obscure rumble was about to start. A shiver was beginning to gather, ready to inform her limbs and agitate them, and she anxiously started to kiss him again, not wanting Alain to become aware of what might happen. Trying to bring together the sensations of the kissing and the inner rumble, her shoulders shook. He was still taking her kissing like a good boy, though starting to respond as much as she would let him. The rumble grew louder and closer; it was unmistakably there. She tried to control her throbbing shoulders, her tingling throat. *Just one more second, one more.* The rumble was filling her. She pressed his lips too hard and her teeth clicked against his, but that didn't inhibit her. She experienced a pleasure that stopped her heartbeat for one instant, and sighed, "Oh, Michael."

She was so instantly aware of the mistake that she tried to muffle the word by crushing her lips against his again. But Alain had heard her. He slipped one arm from under her and rose on one elbow.

"Who's Michael?" he asked.

She averted her eyes, painfully uncomfortable. "I'm sorry."

"Who is he?"

She looked and found him above her. Red in the face from arousal, but his stare dark and hostile.

"Someone . . . someone from the past. Does it matter? I'm here with you."

He moved off her body. "*Now* you are. Who were you with a minute ago?" His green eyes were almost red with anger. She closed her lips, feeling his taste on them, and was silent.

He stood. "All right," he said. "It's well past midnight."

She stood, too. He was in the main room already, pulling on his suede jacket. "I'll see you," he said indirectly, sounding calm now.

She clung to his farewell. "When?"

"I'll call you."

"You don't have my number." Right this instant she found him incredibly handsome, and the whole misunderstanding ludicrous. She hurried after him. "Alain, wait just one second." She tried to say that Michael wasn't in her life anymore, that he . . . and came up with, "I had a wonderful time," uttered defeatedly, and with anxiety.

"My pleasure." He punched his way into the jacket's other sleeve.

"Is there a number where I can call you?"

"I'll call you," he insisted. "At the store."

She stood on tiptoe, hoping for a kiss to tell her that everything was all right. It didn't come. He opened the door, showed her a piece of sky and the vampire-nibbled moon, closed it behind him.

She hurried to the balcony, peered out across the mass of

the tree, to catch a last glimpse. In a gangway across the street, something moved quickly, like a person stepping back out of sight, and then she heard the well-oiled gates to the garden being banged shut by Alain. Then she heard the Chrysler's engine come alive.

Ten minutes later, she had somehow put it all in perspective. No use kicking herself. She would see him again, or maybe she wouldn't. She knew nothing about him. He didn't owe her anything.

Anger began to surface as she peeled off her dress, then her underwear, and let it all fall in a useless pile on the floor. She slipped on her nightgown. It was even stuffier in the apartment than when they had arrived. She opened the balcony door wider. A vague coolness touched her skin. She paced into the kitchen and back. Could something that had started so smoothly, and felt so right, be turned off, just like that, by a silly little mistake? Except that the mistake had to do with calling a man by another man's name. God knows what Alain had made out of that.

Why had he left so abruptly? Was he truly jealous?

Maybe, if he was jealous, that meant something.

Finally, she put out the lights and plopped into bed. She crushed her face into the pillow, hoping for the kindness of sleep.

The apartment was oppressively dark. The Boulle clock ticked away the seconds.

It seemed only minutes before she opened her eyes again. She had had a brief dream. About Alain.

Her tongue felt like a piece of bark, her stomach was wallowing in nausea, and her lips . . . her lips stung and pricked. Was it that spicy meal at Cafe Paris? She sat up higher against the headboard, and . . . something popped in the kitchen. Like a cover opening. Like a lid coming off a box.

I'm dreaming.

A floor plank creaked.

One, two, three, four seconds chinked inside the clock, swept away by its tiniest hand.

Another creak.

She put the three sounds together, shot out of bed like a

fury, knocked down the lamp on the bedtable, pulled it up, flicked the switch.

Darkness. She had broken the bulb.

She breathed in the moist air of the night. *It's nothing, I can make up a whole horror movie, I know it.* In her fluttering nightie, she rushed madly to the dining-room switch. Her fingers gripped. The light came on.

The flat seemed empty. The kitchen was plunged in a dim haze coming from the little square of glass in the back door; its lifeless contours looked harmless: counters, stove, refrigerator. She made another dash, flicked the kitchen light on, stood reeling, ready to be sick.

The little door by the stove was open.

Had they left it that way? Had Alain closed it? Could it have opened by itself?

She thought of the grating at the top of the shaft. Could it be removed? Could someone lower himself from the roof into her apartment with the same ease with which she and Alain had traveled one floor down to spy on the Egyptian?

Suddenly she remembered. Nails and hammer. They were in the bottom drawer of the last counter. She stumbled to the drawer, pulled out the hammer and a square package with a cellophane window. American Tack & Hardware—made in Taiwan. Nails, all sizes, household assortment. They were rolling inside, fighting for space like Alain's varcolacs on the moon. She squeezed the package and a trickle of them jingled onto the kitchen floor.

She thought of the neighbors. The apartment above was unoccupied. The Egyptian? She shut the cupboard door, chose the spot, secured a nail between thumb and pointer, struck and missed, struck and hit it, grinding her teeth at the pain in her temples—it flared every time she crashed the hammer down. A second nail. She landed the hammer on her finger, sucked her finger, went back to work. Eight nails. The hardest job she'd ever done. It took longer than forever.

She breathed, dropped nails and hammer back in the drawer, turned off the light. She walked back into the dining room, turned off the light, stumbled into the bedroom. She spun around, streaked to the balcony door and latched it. And backtracked again through the darkness.

Her naked knee found the bed. She was ready to roll in like a big clumsy ball, ready to see before her the spread of the open bed. Two pillows were heaped right in the middle of it. She reached to push them away, and they became . . . *a human body*: a man whose face whitened the night around it, the ashen complexion smoothing his features into no features, like the man in her nightmare.

Bells rang in her head, as if disintegrating her brain. His eyes *electrocuted her*, two blooms of yellow-green in the dark. Blinded, she batted her eyelids together. When she looked again, his beaked fingers were by her neck. She sighed and passed out straight into his arms.

A second of silence reigned in the apartment.

The creature of the night bent over her. Touched by his lips, the woman responded with a stir, but remained unconscious. She didn't feel his nostrils burn her skin. His lips kissed the scar on the nape of her neck. Then they chose a fresh spot, and his teeth cut through her skin and into her jugular vein.

Another moment passed. Then the creature freed her neck, and contemplated her in the dark. His breath was loud, his hands convulsed around Laura's wrists, and, buried in the shadows, he seemed to struggle for a decision. He stroked the unresisting woman through her sheer nightgown, and gathered the strength to rise. His dark clothes made no impression on the night in the apartment. Only his white face seemed to float toward the door, and float out through it.

At 2:30 A.M., Cabot's wife was awakened by the phone. As usual, she made sure it was a call worth disturbing the lieutenant for, then punched Cabot's back, and stuck the receiver to his ear.

"How many this time?" Cabot's tongue clucked through the routine words before his brain even caught up with their meaning.

"Two more," growled Les, who sounded barely awake himself.

"Where?"

"In the Quarter."

* * *

I want Alain, thought Laura, coming to.

Her brain, with its incredible capacity for survival, got her up, stopped her before the mirror, and helped her not scream. It made her march into the kitchen, where she armed herself with the hammer. Then she called the operator, and asked for the emergency number of the police, all the while spying right and left in the apartment for an undetected presence. The number rang and rang, and while she was waiting, she stretched the cord over to the wardrobe, pulled out some clothes, and started boxing and kicking her way into them, phone glued to her ear, hammer right at hand. *It was that maniac on the loose. I'm not staying here.* For a second she wondered whether Alain had made it safely out of her killer-haunted street. "N'awleans Police Department—please ho-old . . ."

She held, and the connection went dead, and just then she heard something in the apartment. She didn't wait to see what it was. She flashed out the back door, brandishing the hammer. *I'll go to the store and call the police till someone answers.* Holding the hammer sheathed in the flaps of a skirt that didn't match her top, she made it to the carport behind the house. She locked the jeep's doors before starting the engine.

From Ursulines into Dauphine, from Dauphine to Bienville, from Bienville to Bourbon. *Killer, killer, mad killer. But something stopped him from killing me. There* is *a God up there!* Her store was two doors from the corner. She nosed the Jeep around, braked. A police car was parked halfway onto the sidewalk, domes turning. She grabbed the hammer, dropped it on the floor, jumped out of the Jeep. The door to her store was standing open; two stretchers were lying on the sidewalk, covered with blankets. She spun around: A black man with graying temples was spraying the front doorknob with a fingerprint atomizer. She galloped inside right by him, and someone shouted, "Hey, don't step on that!" A hand clasped her wrist.

"What . . . what the hell's going on?" she hollered to a red, puckered face.

"Who the hell are you?" answered Cabot. Behind him,

the racks and displays that she and Charlotte had put up were lying scattered and trampled on the floor. "I've been assaulted!" she cried, looking like a crazy woman, her eyes wild, her hair a fright. "This is my store! What are you doing here?"

"What are *you* doing in your store at four in the morning?"

Someone with an unlit pipe between his teeth appeared from behind. "Take it easy, Dale, this lady's in shock!"

They sat her down and someone said, "Let's get her some water," but she sprang up again. Who was lying on the stretchers in front of her store, Charlotte? Charlotte and her date who was staying at the Hilton?

"Lady," rumbled Cabot, gruff but gentle; "I'm sorry to say there's been a double murder in your place." The water glass knocked against her teeth, but she got up and was ready to look. The blankets were peeled off the faces. Unknown faces—boy, girl. Both maybe twenty. The girl had a café-crème complexion not unlike Charlotte's. The boy's face was blue from death. One of the eight or nine police technicians at work in her store was just taking Polaroids of a pair of work gloves lying on the floor, of tools spilled from a box— it looked like a burglar's kit.

"These kids were in your store when someone surprised them inside and attacked them," said Cabot with a can-you-take-this? sort of expression. "Now, why were you coming to the store at this hour?"

"I've been attacked, I told you. In my apartment."

"Where is your apartment?"

She gave her address on Ursulines Street.

"I'm a physician," said the man with the unlit pipe whom Cabot had introduced as the coroner. "Let's see where you're hurt."

The dressing rooms in the back had escaped the havoc. He made an examining room out of one of them, palpated her neck, touched the dried-up little scars on it, and said that she'd been lanced, sort of, with something sharp, maybe a dagger. He took her blood pressure, found it a little high. Natural, considering. He asked if she'd mind having a little blood taken, for tests; he could run them at the police lab. She agreed and Cabot came over with the graying black man who had been spraying the door, her cash register, and other areas of her store.

"I'm afraid your rug'll stay stained, ma'am," he said. His eyes were slippery and gray like Jamaican pearls. "And I had to tear a few samples of fiber."

"Can you do me a favor?" she heard herself ask Cahill. "Can you rip up the rug in the whole front area? I was going to have a new one put in anyway."

"I guess we could. L'tenant?"

Cabot nodded, his attention elsewhere. The coroner slipped the rubber hose off her arm and raised the full phial: Her blood seemed so very dark in it, so very rich in body.

"Let's cart off this batch to the morgue, Cahill," ordered Cabot. "And then let's take this lady back to her place and see what we find there."

The bodies were sent off to the morgue in an ambulance, and Laura, Cabot, Cahill, Les, and another officer drove over to her place. On the way, Cabot asked her what she had done with herself during the last twenty-four hours. She told him her schedule in broad strokes, finishing with dinner. He insisted to know who had taken her to dinner—he called it "supper." She was under no obligation to tell, but it could be useful for the investigation.

She hesitated, then mentioned Alain. Cabot's face widened in a smile. He knew the boy from way back, when Alain's daddy was mayor. How long had she known Alain Lecouveur? She scrambled a little explaining that a common acquaintance had introduced them Wednesday night. At the airport.

"I was at the airport that night, too," said Cabot. "I think I remember seein' you in the crowd. All three of us was there—what an interestin' coe-incidence." The police car stopped on Ursulines. "So you met 'im Wednesday, and planned supper for Saturday night?"

"We didn't plan it. We met by chance last night, at Preservation Hall."

He dragged his belly out of the car and she stepped out after him. The sun was rising from somewhere behind the planet, making her street pink. "And you kinda natural decided to eat supper t'gether?"

"Yeah," she said annoyed by the details he was piecing out of her answers. "Kinda natural."

"What time would you put that at? Supper?"

"Dinner? Around seven-thirty." They all walked through her gates and onto her patio.

"And after supper Mr. Lecouveur took you back to your place?"

"Yes."

"And when would you say he left your place, Miss Walker?"

"It was . . . after midnight." Maybe she was mad at the cop's questions, but now she also felt a rush of anger at Alain. If that . . . that . . . idiot hadn't left in a huff, maybe she wouldn't've been attacked. A flash—the memory of his lips.

"You've got a visitor, Miss Walker," announced Cabot, casually. Rolled up before her door, like a hibernating bear, sat her neighbor, the Egyptian.

Cabot told her to wait down in the patio, and trampled up the stairs. He rousted the Egyptian, questioned him briefly, then sent him down to join Laura, while he and two other cops used Laura's keys to enter the apartment—just to make sure that no one was lying in ambush there, waiting for her.

While she craned her neck to follow these movements, the Egyptian seized the chance to whisper, "I've had astral communications about you all night."

She looked away from the top of the stairs, at the hairy man.

"As you know, I'm a channeler," he said importantly.

"I didn't know," answered Laura. He explained that a channeler was a medium for a spirit who spoke through him.

Laura cut him off; the lieutenant was waving her inside. The Egyptian shuffled up behind her, and Cabot tolerated him inside, but said, "no one touch nothin'." Les and Cahill instantly produced sprays, fiberglass brushes, tiny blades to rake off dust and paint from touched surfaces, "searchie" hinge-lifters to seal in the smudges of fingerprints. Cabot stopped before the nailed cupboard door, and Laura had to go through the whole story about the flying wine steward. That brought all the cops around her. "So you tried to see how the thing worked?" queried an astonished Cabot. "You and Mr. Lecouveur?"

"Yes. Mr. Lecouveur suggested it."

"And in the middle of the night you got spooked and nailed the thing shut? Why?"

"I . . . I thought someone could let themselves in that way."

"And someone did?"

"I don't know. I don't know which way he came in." She would have thought herself quite paranoid, she realized, answering the way she did. Cabot kicked the door lightly with his boot and a couple of the nails, superficially imbedded, popped out. Cabot pulled the door open and he and the other cops peered in. Then Cabot sent the fourth officer to get some other men, climb up on the roof, and check that grating.

While he was gone, the phone rang. Les answered and passed it to Laura. It was the coroner. He'd thought about her lacerations, talked with a colleague, and arranged for him to examine her at noon at St. Vincent's Hospital, and give her a tetanus shot.

By now, the neighbors from the adjoining buildings had woken up to the police activity, and were staring out of windows, conjecturing. The end of the show for them, however, came soon. The fourth officer climbed down from the roof and came in to report his findings.

"Well, he didn't come in the up way," ruled Cabot, hearing that the grating, though old, was well secured and hadn't been moved. "I'm gonna call Mr. Lecouveur," he announced. He went to her phone, called his office, got the number of Alain's upriver piloting station, which was equipped with a radio phone. In the meantime the Egyptian had shuffled around every room of the apartment, forgotten. He finally ambled back to Laura.

"I have an astral meeting in half an hour, but I'll be at my place. Drop by when you get free."

"Okay," she answered, to get rid of him.

The business of getting through to the station took a few minutes. Cahill, hands full of detective paraphernalia, approached Laura and said, softly enough for only the two of them to hear, that he was sorry her acquaintance with New

Orleans had debuted so disturbingly. As for the killer, "He's a bad one," he whispered. "It's a mir'cle you got away."

"Psychopath, huh?" she asked.

"No, ma'am," he lowered his voice more. "This one's not in our books. He's a vampire."

Vrrr. The *vrrr* of *varcolac* throbbed in her ears. Cahill turned to make sure that no one else heard him. "Ma'am, go bah some wolfsbane or sompin' like that. He'll be back heah—what them ghouls taste, they remembers well."

"Hello," said Cabot into the phone, and her heart leaped from where she stood straight into the phone's mouthpiece.

"What's wolfsbane?" she asked, her attention mostly on Cabot, who was asking for Alain.

"Issa sorta buttercup, pu'ple mos'ly—a flower."

"It's still ringin'. D'you wanna talk to Mr. Lecouveur?" Cabot held out the phone.

"It's okay, I can talk to him later," she said, and instantly regretted it.

"Hello?" roared Cabot into the phone, as if loudness could conquer distance.

Cahill waited for Cabot to turn, then stroked Laura with his anxious Jamaican-pearl eyes. "I know a store what sells it, dried up, but I forget its name. On Canal Street. I can find the name for you."

"*Hello?*" roared on Cabot. He waited, then slammed the phone down disgustedly. "They're dead out there. I'll call him from the office." Cahill gave Laura a little gesture of complicity, and excused himself as Cabot—portly, purposeful—came to post himself before her. "Miss Walker, of all the coincidences, and you seem to run into a goodly number of'em, d'you realize that your attacker, and the man who killed those punks in your store, could be the same person?"

I'll have to sit down, she thought. "You mean that killer's really after *me*?" As if reading her thought, he pulled one of the dining room chairs for her, then sat down himself.

"Miss Walker, those kids that robbed your store were professionals. They didn't even break the glass of your door, they picked the lock and opened it. Now, maybe they fought among themselves inside, which means that they were three or four to start with, not just two, but that's a really weak maybe, 'cause the victims are ripped at the throat just like the sixteen before them. No, no." He shook his head with conviction. "There were just two of them inside, pullin' the job. By the way, that alarm you got, it's some invention. It started to ring and brought us in there, but just before us, it brought in the killer. He was passing by. He heard the rings, went in after the kids, and nicked their necks." Cabot said it with such ease, and he looked so incongruous in her dining room, his uniform clashing with the chair's antique tapestry, that Laura looked down at her arm. *Maybe if I pinch myself next to this little Band-Aid, I'll wake up.*

"We steamed over," continued Cabot, "but he was done with them already, and boy, did they fight like bobcats. Anyway, the alarm tells us that the time of the killing was three-thirty at the earliest." He had recited this staring expressionlessly at her; finally he blinked once. "Miss Walker, you were also struck on the neck. Not killed, but hit in the same area nevertheless. What time would you say you were attacked?"

She was feeling chills all the way down to the soles of her feet. She was wearing the Capezio flats she'd had on arriving in New Orleans.

"I don't know. I'd say maybe an hour after Mr. Lecouveur left."

"Not more than one hour? The doc said the cuts on your neck were really fresh."

"What are you telling me? You think the killer, instead of finishing me, hopped over to my store, found those burglars, and . . . and killed them, minutes after he left here?"

She felt like a dangerous game of the mind was opening. *Look how much this guy makes out of everything. Watch out, Laura.*

"For one thing, I really can't grind the fact that this guy didn't finish you," he said brutally. "He hasn't given a break to anyone else so far. According to you, he was with you, alone. He had you, yet he spared you and scooted out there to find someone else? Miss Walker"—he looked a little offended—"I'll believe anything, but not a killer who stops killing right in the middle of it and then takes it out on someone else."

He looked at her. She looked back at him, fixedly. Cahill and Les had quietly pulled chairs on her right and left, and now she was surrounded by cops.

"So what *do* you mean?" she rasped.

"Maybe there was no killer here at all."

"I see." *He's trying to throw me. This is a sparring match.* "So who cut me?"

He chuckled. "You don't really want me to say, Miss Walker."

"Look," she said, pounding the words, "that uniform you're wearing gives you no right to patronize me."

"You," he said peacefully. "*You* cut you, Miss Walker." He took her breath away. "After you cut up those kids. Then you put those holes in your neck, ran out to your car, drove it around the block till we got there, and came back running, looking all deranged and frazzled. Isn't that the way it all happened, Miss Walker?"

Even her new friend Cahill hissed in admiration of this scenario. As for Les, he looked reverent.

Feeling partially paralyzed, Laura managed to articulate, "I wouldn't kill anyone."

"That's what juries hear every day," said Cabot.

"I didn't kill them. I didn't kill anyone, ever. You're crazy. You have sixteen other murders to account for," she suddenly remembered, and clarioned triumphantly, "Did I commit those? I wasn't even in town."

"You weren't in town for only fourteen of them. Two were committed Wednesday, several hours after you and I—don't you recall?—crossed paths at the airport. And that's no proof of your innocence either—you could've been here all along and left town for just a few days . . . And there's your partner, Denise Pratt—she was here looking at property when we had a slew of neck slashings," he said with a smile of brilliant association.

She pushed her chair back. With a dull clatter, it fell over on the floor. "Please, leave. Come back when you make sense, or with a warrant."

He curled his nose. "You wanna throw the law out, li'l lady?"

She didn't miss a beat. She padded over to the phone, bedraggled and pale though she looked, yanked it up, and cracked at the operator, "Who's the head of the New Orleans police? Uh-huh. Uh-*huh*. I want the number of the police commissioner's office."

The operator started dictating a number, but she stopped paying attention: The cops pulled to their feet; she honestly expected them to slap handcuffs on her—instead, they paraded out of the apartment. *Fools. Dolts. Nitwits. Saps. That sap, Alain, too.* She included him in an outburst of wrath engulfing everything that had happened since she arrived, everything since her ill-fated takeoff from San Francisco. She put the phone down, seething, but mentally took Alain off the list. Was he alive up there on the river? Why had he left her last night? Why wasn't he calling, the unintuitive blockhead?

Cabot put his head back in the door. "May I?" he asked almost courteously.

"Come in," she said, spent and reasonable.

He walked in alone, leaving the door open. "You win the round on points, Miss Walker. My apologies."

"Almost sincere, I'm sure," she joked colorlessly.

He settled heavily back at the table. "Miss Walker, let's discuss business. You survived last night, but you may not survive tonight, unless I give you police protection."

"Which you'll give me on condition . . . ?"

"No conditions. I'll have you watched, Miss Walker. Your store, your house, your person. All I ask you to do is help me find the killer."

She righted her overturned chair and slumped in it. "What makes you think I can, Lieutenant?"

He let a few beats pass. "*He* didn't take the trouble to come here at random. He's seen you before. He *chose* you. And he put you aside to come back to you later. You're a gutsy young woman. I can tell you're a good American. Let's catch him together."

Ugghhh. That featureless face, as if polished by water. That mouth opening in it.

"Otherwise how are you going to know who he is?" She didn't reply. He took a new tack. "Mr. Lecouveur likes you a lot."

"He does?" asked Laura, cheeks coloring up a little.

"He met you at the airport—and showed up three days later, just like that, to ask you to supper. He rode that basket in the wall up and down with you, just to please you. He left well past midnight . . . I could tell you really wanted to speak to him earlier. How d'you know it ain't him who did it? To you . . . and to the kids."

"Because I know. You're being outrageous, and if you don't stop I'll throw you out again," she shrieked, surprising herself.

"My gawd. No need to get mad as a wet hen. You know, your cooperation could help, him, too." She asked why. Alain was the last person to see her before she was attacked, he answered. That made him virtually a suspect. "Why meet him again on your guard, your li'l heart goin' pit-a-pat, instead of knowing who it is you're . . . you know?"

"I see! You want me to be your bait—is that it?"

He studied her. "Not quite. Jes' let me know who you're with and where you go. That'll give me enough lead."

Laura swallowed. She thought of this unknown town. Of herself in it, of the people she had met here. She said she'd think about it. She got up, and he read it in her face: time for him to go. He handed her a card with a police shield above his name. "Be a good idea to follow up on those tests. I'm sure you're clean as a pin, but just in case . . ."

"Lieutenant," she said when he reached the door.

He turned swiftly, with a show of consideration. "Ma'am?"

"I heard someone say . . ." she didn't want to get Cahill into trouble, "that this wasn't the work of an ordinary psychopath. That the killer's actually a *vampire*."

"Who knows? I've lived enough," he said, "to marvel at nothing. But we need to find out for sure, don't we, before we start a slush fund for holy water."

"Les," said Cabot down in the car, one minute later, "you get two more men, and stick to this lady around the clock, like stamps on an envelope."

6

SHE WOULD forever remember this Sunday.

Alone after the police left, Laura felt a surge of panic. She called Charlotte, but her line was busy. She called Marion Voguey, who answered, and told her about the burglary and the double murder, and how she herself had survived a bizarre attack. Marion hailed God for watching over the innocent, swore that she'd have security installed in Laura's apartment as of tomorrow, said she'd come over to help her get over the shock. Laura asked her to come to the store instead. Even though the store had been the scene of the murder, she felt less frightened there than at the apartment.

When she arrived at the store, Laura found that the police had stripped the rug as she had asked them. On the store phone, she finally reached Charlotte, who promised that she'd hurry over, too. Then Fran from the coffee house dropped in, and brought coffee this time. In less than half an hour, a comfortable little cluster of friends had assembled to assuage Laura—but they started by taking the bandages off her neck, to examine the wounds. Fran shuddered, and Marion almost pierced her skin with her inquisitive stare. Charlotte had heard it said that a human's bite healed slower than any other. "What did he do to you?" all three wanted to know.

Laura resisted remembering, because almost by the hour the memory sprouted up richer in her mind, with more and more details. The dreadfully brief moment of seeing *him* on her bed, before he touched her, had grown to an interminable horror, during which every segment of her body played a role. Even her womb had responded to the sight of him. As if an ancestral scare, from a past life when she was a naked Neanderthal with pawed hands for burrowing in the dirt for edible roots, and hair on her back and in every crevice of her body, had rung inside her, buried under civilized strata, but not forgotten. The mouth, wet and red, had grown a chin, and the nose she hadn't seen had wide-open nostrils. She was terrified now that a full portrait would resemble . . . could resemble . . . Alain! No, no, it couldn't! It wasn't him, she was as certain of that as she was of the fear in her womb.

Her rational faculties told her that she must have some *reason* for likening last night's aggressor to Alain. When she realized what it was, her naked neck froze as the three women were examining it: she feared another encounter, and from that fear came the hope that if it was going to happen any- way—despite Cabot's guarantees of protection—then she wanted to dupe herself into the belief that it *was* Alain (even though it couldn't be), so that she could close her eyes and breathe without fear of smelling some putrid hulk, and let her trembling body embrace whatever it was and think it was Alain, sweet sweet Alain, taking her, opening her, possessing her.

Jesus, what's going on with me? I spent a few hours with a man I like. I'm certainly not in love with him.

I'm going bats.

The involuntary pun made her titter silently. Marion asked if she was all right. Yes, yes, yes! She needed a shower; there was a shower in the back. Could they all wait till she took a shower?

Alone in the bathroom, she took off her clothes, and looked at herself. Her old scratches were healed, but these two new ones, almost perfectly round and small, not two inches apart, bore dark scabs, and the bruised skin around them was raised into tiny craters. They hurt just a little. Otherwise her neck was pale to almost lilac from exhaustion and lack of sleep, her breasts hung haggard, her belly looked as gaunt as her cheeks. *I'll put some food in me—maybe a hamburger, a juicy rare hamburger.*

Charlotte came into the bathroom while she was drying herself off after the shower. From Charlotte's ghetto blaster out in the main room one could hear John Fogerty yowling out "Rock 'n Roll Girls."

"I would've turned green and peed all over myself," the quadroon said. "I would've *died*, Laura . . ." The poor girl couldn't help it. "Laura, what did it really *feel* like?"

"For Chrissakes, Charlotte, what do you think it was, an orgasm? Why the hell did you come in?"

"A guy just dropped by with this note."

"What guy?"

Scrawled on a lined half-sheet from an official blotter of some kind: *Wolfsbane. At the Butterfly Box—corner Canal and Villere.*

"He looked like a cop."

"He *was* a cop. One of those dunces advised me to buy this . . . this wolfsbane nonsense and sprinkle it in the apartment. Against vampires."

"St. Vincent's nearby. I'll drive you to the doctor's, and we can buy it on the way back."

"Are you crazy?" she yelled, drowning out John Fogerty. "I'm not putting any mumbo-jumbo in my apartment."

"No, *you're* crazy," retorted Charlotte, and Laura glared at her so badly that she blinked in intimidation. "Boss-lady, make sense. You hear voices. Not once but *twice*. You rent places with spooky shafts in the wall. You get attacked, and bitten on the neck. And then you try to act like nothing's happened? I'd drag a whole tree of that plant into my bedroom, if I were you."

She almost threw her comb at Charlotte, who cowered and ran out. Alone, Laura looked at her lips. Closed, they lay on top of each other like two bodies fitting together perfectly, like Alain's body on hers last night. The idiot. They could've done it last night. She had been wholly and utterly and unashamedly horny. Now it would never happen, not with this suspicion.

Now she had to come out and talk to her new friends, who were beginning to treat her solicitously, like a heroine, like a star! Marion, who wanted details not about the vampire, but about dinner with Alain, of course! And Fran—oh God,

Fran. How could she have been so careless to speak so freely in front of her? Now her coffee house would be rattling with tales. No, she had to forbid her. She flashed out of the bathroom in jeans and a sweater, feeling constantly cold, and was met by a rewound John Fogerty tape:

> *Oooooh, let's go-oh*, he wailed,
> *To the end of the wo-orld,*
> *Rock 'n Roll girls,*
> *Rock 'n Roll gi-irls . . .*

She made Fran swear not to say a word to anyone about what had happened, then hurried her good-byes, and left with Charlotte for the hospital—stopping off on the way for hamburgers. Laura's was delicious, though a little too well done.

At St. Vincent's, Dr. Gattery said that her blood tests indicated nothing outside the limits of the normal. He joked about the fact that she was type O—universal blood donor. As for the bites, if bites they were, the pervert must have made himself a set of dentures with two protruding canines; an ordinary human would've produced a little horseshoe of tearings and puncturings, because human teeth were rather dull, blunted by millenia of complex diet, much in the same way as a mammal's from feeding on raw flesh. Her punctures were deep; at least one of them had perforated her jugular vein, and blood had oozed into the neighboring layers of tissue. He looked at the scabs on the back of her neck, right under the roots of her hair. Those could've been scratched in a similar way, but on both occasions the loss of blood wasn't alarming; the stolen plasma and cells had already been replaced by her body, a vigilant and healthy young organism. Listening intently, Laura asked whether someone could live on a diet of blood.

"Blood," sighed Gattery. The butt of a cigarette hung wetly from his lower lip; his left eye had been reduced to a permanent crack by the ever-rising smoke. "Blood has multiple mystical connotations. The ancient Egyptians used to dip convalescents into blood baths to make them heal faster, and even thought that a dead man, mouth-fed instantly with

blood from sacrificed slaves, might be resuscitated that way.
The Romans drank the blood of dying gladiators, the Aztecs
ate still-beating hearts, and so forth. But blood has very little
value as a nutrient—first off, ninety percent of it is water.
And you're asking about drinking it, not having it transfused."

"When did people first start getting transfusions?" she
asked with an interest she never knew she had.

"Here, let's give you this tetanus shot . . . Oh, in the six-
teenth century. Prosper Denis, in France, transfused lamb
blood to an anemic. The poor fool died, because the blood
of one species cannot flow in the veins of another without a
fatal reaction, and the physician was sued . . ." Dr. Gattery
was ogling her with the staid resignation of older males, she
noticed. "So, you see, not even an animal—a bat or whatever—could really use your blood as normal daily suste-
nance . . ."

At the Butterfly Box she lost her temper. Wolfsbane, she
learned, was an extract of a plant called monkshood, and
came in leaves crushed to dust, or in a liquid tincture. Both
were sold in bottles blessed by "Brother Harry"—a black
rural minister who smiled from a picture xeroxed on the hand-
applied labels of the bottles. The place, which smelled like
an unaired pet store, offered a stock of other exotic panaceas:
radix pedis diaboli (devil's foot root); dried-up Jamaica pep-
pers; powder of bones "from frog to heh, heh" said the
kerchiefed saleswoman with a laugh, meaning probably human; not to mention lotions and potions for regrowth of hair,
for virility, fertility, and so on. Laura got senselessly irritated
by the casualness of the saleswoman, who filled orders for
bring-him-back-to-me powder and raise-it-again ointment,
and drown 'im, make 'im-spew, break-his-legs and lay-'im-
in-bed-with-sores stuff. She didn't even want to touch the
bottle of powdered wolfsbane, and the woman finally handed
it to Charlotte. If Charlotte wanted to go back to Laura's
apartment and sprinkle it on her bed, she was entirely welcome. Laura was going to the airport to get the latest shipment out of customs.

By five, she was at the airport stacking up parcels of bras

and knickers in her Jeep. By six she was back at the store putting them away. She had no more robberies to fear now, though the shattered glass of the door was still unfixed. A man with white socks and brown shoes who had been standing outside the store all morning had just been replaced by another one wearing white socks and black shoes, and still others would keep watch during the night. A little before sunset—a somber bleeding light was filling the store—Alain walked in.

She cried out and let the panties in her hand fall and float to the floor. A tentacle of fear distended in her, wriggled in panic, then lay still.

He walked up to her slowly, scenically. He wore a camouflage jacket over a T-shirt and jeans, and army shoes. *He's been up on the river.*

"Show me the palms of your hands," Laura said. Watching her magnetically, he held up his palms. She smelled the river on him, a muddy, musky rottenness, and the dried-up spice of a man's sweat. No hair grew on his palms. And the sun hadn't set yet.

"I'm sorry I filled your head with my ridiculous stories . . ." he said.

That voice, that splendid cracked-bronze timbre.

" . . . Especially before what happened."

News travels fast down here, she thought, looking at Alain's mouth.

"If I had stayed, nothing would've happened. I behaved like a stupid, jealous schoolboy."

That mouth.

His eyes were worriedly, guiltily examining her neck bandages.

"Who told you?" she asked.

"I found a funny man prowling your patio five minutes ago, waiting for you, apparently. He told me."

The Egyptian. "Alain," she asked, her eyes tumbling into his again. "What's happening to me?"

Something in his eyes blocked hers, keeping them midway, not letting them reach all the way in. "I don't know. What I do know is . . . I'm not going to let it happen again."

Oh, he's so sweet. She melted and felt like saying that they should make love right there, right then, and remembered she had said that to Michael in her dream. *No, no more blunders like that today.*

He took her by the hand, and pulled her very gently behind the revolving mirrored racks. She put her lips on his, and she sipped him like wine. Her body, electrified, felt every inch of clothing on it, as if wanting to shake it off, to strip bare. She tightened her arms around his neck, kept the kiss faintingly long, then whispered, "I care for you. Very much." And scared by what she had just admitted, pulled away and said. "Alain—you *smell*."

"One of our barges ran aground. I was wading in water up to my hips all morning."

"It doesn't matter," she reassured him. Even taller than usual in his army boots, he was practically breaking her neck kissing her, and he finally noticed it. So he leaned against the wall, his legs at an angle, and pulled her to him. She pushed her pelvis against his hard thigh and rode it, kissing him, her breasts grinding against his camouflage jacket. "Can you take me home?" she whispered. He couldn't. His famous labor meeting was due to begin, and he was hurrying over to the financial district, but couldn't resist stopping off to see her.

"Can you stay a little longer?" He could. Five minutes.

"Let's make a date for later," she urged, tossing overboard the book of rules.

"Okay." A kiss.

"Tomorrow. Come to my place, at seven."

"It's a deal."

"I'll cook for you."

She kissed him again, knew that if he gave her just a little time she could feel that magnificent rumble again; in fact, it was already beginning to clutch almost painfully at her insides. But he cut the kiss short to ask if she had seen a doctor. She said yes, he seemed reassured, and offered to drop her home on his way to the meeting.

During the short drive, she asked him if he liked tempura. He said yes. She could make it for him if she found a decent deep-frying pan. They got to her place—he sweaty in his rumpled jacket, she disheveled and pale and ringed around the eyes—*I must look like a cat in heat*—and instantly a man's shadow pulled back into an alleyway, so fast that it seemed to Laura like a piece of her retina had just fragmented and fallen off. Cabot's refined tailing techniques.

"Walk me to my door." *Do anything to get more kisses.*

"I'm late." He followed her, though, and put his palm on her back, pushing her up the stairs. She wriggled her ass in his face as she climbed. *I'm gonna do this to your face, tomorrow night, sweetie, and I'm gonna kiss you till I get that river out of your pores. And then I'm gonna put you inside me and hold you like in a tight fist, and see what you're gonna say THEN.* As she stepped onto the landing, he sneezed violently behind her. Hand in her bag for keys, she turned and saw him cover his face with his open palms. He dropped his hands, but another sneeze brought them back up instantly. She watched him, key in hand, while he sneezed a third time. She descended a step toward him.

"Did you catch a cold on that river?"

"I'm probably just tuckered out." He lowered his palms again. He had paled under his tan, and his eyelids looked reddish. "I'm sorry; I'm bone tired and this meeting is all I need."

"Come in a minute? I'll look for some aspirin."

"No, no, I can't!" he exclaimed. "The meeting."

"I don't want you to get sick, I want to see you tomorrow."

"I'll be here. Gotta go." He looked at his watch with anxiety, gave her a peck on the cheek, and ran down the stairs.

As soon as Alain's car turned the corner, Les spouted out of the alleyway. Sideways, crablike, he ran two hundred yards and clinked a dime into a pay phone.

"Where is she?" asked Cabot.

"In her crib. The Lecouveur boy just left."

"Have his ride followed?"

"No need. He's meeting with the Mexes over by Lee Circle."

"Did he make a date with her?"

"I didn't hear, but I'd assume so, the way she swung her hips at him."

"Back to work. Later."

"Later," mumbled Les. He hung up and rushed back.

As the alleyway came into view, it seemed to him that someone else peered out of it for just a fraction of a second. With the same crablike movement, Les swept the wall, fingers crooking to grab whoever it might be.

The alleyway looked deserted. Then he heard a big iron lid rattle faintly by the far side, where the alleyway tunneled into a parallel street. Someone hiding in there?

He pondered, gave his stakeout priority, and resumed watching.

A half block west of the statue of General Lee—whiling away immortality and pigeons atop his Greek column—the union hall, located in a converted old movie house, shook with the boisterousness of some thirty beer-swilling men. Twenty-three of them were Latins; the rest were rednecks who had come as observers, to determine whether the Anglo locals should throw in on this one with the tamale pies. The Anglos looked huge among the short, chunky Latins. They sipped from their cans, smiled tensely, sucked the ends of their straw-yellow mustaches. In a corner, Arata and Braulio parleyed anxiously. If Alain brought a proposal that would douse the fire of revolt, the two of them would lose their respective positions, Arata felt. Careful to sound like an ideologue, Arata mentioned the endangered revolutionary spirit. Both he and Braulio knew that warfare maintained leaders.

"We do dis," Arata proposed. "If de masses say *si* to what de *maricon* says, we go widda masses. Den we get a bunch of tough boys, not dese *descojonados* here, and we go hit one of deir barges *Miercoles* night. We find out once and for all what dey carry. Dey give us a piece, or we sink deir barges."

Braulio approved, starting to line up in his head some gutsy characters, just three or four, who could follow a barge upriver, board it, and expose the Lecouveur scam, whatever it was. Arata thought of all the *tetas* (tits) the union job had brought his way. He dropped in on unprotected wives during working hours, found them wet from his latest fiery speech.

Oh, what *tetas*. *Bazumbas*. *Carrangas*. *Buscos*. Like everything in consumer America, the *carrangas* were bigger, the *buscos* juicer. If he went back to punching the clock, he could kiss the *buscos* good-bye.

Twenty minutes later, Alain walked in, bravely alone, and put on the table—as Braulio and Arata had feared—an unrefusable package. Fifteen-percent salary increase over the next three years, a six-percent increase in the pension fund. And as a gesture of good will, the Lecouveurs would rebuild the union hall.

When Laura stepped into her apartment, she found a crumpled note inside the door.

"Had critical astral meeting about you." The Egyptian's handwriting reeled wildly in all directions. "Made next astral appointment at nine-thirty tonight. Can you come? The spirits want you present."

We'll see about that, she thought, right now envisioning a microwave dinner and a glass of wine. Her apartment, this assemblage of creaking floors and shadowed corners, was actually starting to feel like home—just a little.

Then she bolted at what she saw crawling along the doorsill. An army of ants. Another one lined the bottom of the balcony door. Intrigued by their stillness, she bent down and looked closer.

They weren't ants. They were microscopic fragments of wolfsbane—Charlotte had been here. Laura found them around every window, every door, the entrance to the wall shaft, and, as an extra precaution, along the step leading into her bedroom. The pungent odor, like horseradish, pricked at the insides of her nostrils. *I've got to sweep this away*. But she was too beat now. Tomorrow, first thing.

At eight-thirty, Belle Hellène, the Lecouveur plantation, had lost the last glow of sunset on the twin facades of its Greek temples. From gray the columns turned blue and, as always at this magical hour, they suddenly seemed to elongate upward, giving the house an appearance of gothic svelteness it did not have during the day. The trees instantly grew in shadow, their crowns broadened into rich nests of darkness.

From the walls of Belle Hellène, a profusion of cornices, moldings and entablatures leaned out spikily, like so many beaks and hooks. The garden looked up, oxygenated by the gathering night, and the sound of magnolia petals, falling down, withered, took on the feltlike muffledness of footsteps as they landed on the broad lawn. Across this landscape of death reborn, Malcolm drove into the property in a pickup truck and parked it by the brougham. A man's torso showed in the carriage's window, leaning pensively forward. Malcolm smiled, although he knew that his smile would get no reply, and went in to find Emory in the Carpathian room.

He found him, illuminated by candles, under the *grandiflora*—a huge stained-glass window—below which hung the Lecouveur arms. A shovel was the coat's main symbol, stuck in upturned ground, under an incomplete moon, with the motto "Mors Elude"—Flee from Death. Emory had eluded death so far, but as he sat at his hermit's table—an authentic Jesuit monk's from the Middle Ages—between an astrolabe and a reliquary with a pale bone in it, he looked like death itself.

Malcolm compared for a second how perfectly Emory resembled his twin, the man who sat outside in the carriage. Emory's table wasn't quite beneath the grandiflora, whose predominant color was red. Dead below the stained glass rested a ducal chair as white as ivory—in memory of the Calovaru family who had been *bani*, or dukes, of the lower Danube.

Emory's hands were busy playing a monumentally tedious game of solitaire, the one named Napoleon. The race into the future of a dozen clocks could be heard, for Emory collected timepieces. Three pendula in their upright coffins and nine table clocks were dispersed through the Carpathian room, along walls decorated traditionally with furs and hunting weapons, and household objects of bare wood and iron, from a time without grace, when only honor counted.

"He went to see her again this afternoon," the manservant said. "At the store. And then he took her home."

"Did he stay?" rasped Emory. Malcolm could smell his breath: chill and rank, the breath of a tomb.

"No, sir. He went on to his meeting. And her house is under police observation."

Crashing noises, barking voices reached in through the red glass of the grandiflora. The domestics, the groundskeepers, always appeared at this hour, putting life back into the place.

Emory's eyes studied a card, tried to read the anonymous backs of three others. "We shall invite her to my party," he said, using the royal "we."

Malcolm nodded at the master's decision, then started to leave the room, a huge chamber, past panoplies with cudgels and spears and swords. He saw a weapon hanging askew, and automatically righted it. It was one of those *cannes a sabre*: a stick that contained a long thin swordblade, very popular a century earlier, after the Yankees had banned duels. It looked like an innocent walking stick. Yet one turn of the pommel pulled out the blade, making a duel instantly possible. Its hairbreadth sharpness could separate a limb from a body with one strike.

At nine-fifteen Laura was nodding off over a plate of lasagna. She jumped out of her skin when the phone rang, and before answering glanced out the window and across the street. In the alleyway Cabot's devoted sentinel was standing erect, and though she couldn't distinguish the face, she imagined seeing two sharp eyes in it: his alert attention, all concentrated on her survival.

"Hello?"

"It's me, Laura. Alain."

"Oh, *Alain*." She sat on the bed, heart beating in her cheeks, in her temples. In the background behind him she could hear excited shouts, hoots, laughter, all male, like at a Filipino cockfight. "Where are you?"

"At my meeting with the union. Listen, I can't make it tomorrow night."

"Alain!" Crestfallen, she lied, "I had already started to cook."

"I'm sorry. They want to go with my proposal." He sounded excited. "They'll leave our barges alone. But some details have to be worked out, so they want me here again tomorrow night."

"Oh, well. If they'll leave your barges alone . . ." *Those damn barges. Before this week, she hadn't heard the word "barges" three times in her life.*

"Can we move it to Tuesday?"

All right, damn your barges and your unions, you know already that we can.

"I think that can be arranged," she said composedly. She was upset, but resigned to the delay. *I'll be even readier by Tuesday night, and you will be too, big shot councilman barge owner, important family heir.*

"I was worried you might have something else on for then."

"No, my whole week's unplanned." *I'm going to fill you with food and wine like you did me last time . . .*

"Oh, great. Maybe I'll see you several times." He didn't sound that sure, but he was standing in a crowded hall, she could tell.

. . . and then I'm gonna lay you down on my bed, put all the lights out so you don't see me blushing . . .

"What were you doing when I called?"

. . . and undress you. For every button I'll undo, I'll kiss that spot. "Just finishing dinner." *And I'll be wearing a dress, a loose light big one, with nothing underneath.*

"Laura," he said seriously, "I want you to make double sure you close all your doors and windows tonight. . . ."

"I already have." *And when I have you all naked, I'm going to arouse you so savagely that you can barely breathe, and then, holding your hands captive in mine . . .*

"I was so happy seeing you this afternoon, even for a few minutes."

"I was, too." Her other hand clasped her right thigh, and her fingers buried into the flesh . . . *I'll hold your hands tight. We'll need no help from your hands or mine, anyway. Then I'm going to . . .*

"Can you hang on just one second?"

"Sure." The rowdy sounds grew louder. Was he in a bawdy-house rather than at his meeting? No, no. He wasn't the type . . . *I'm going to straddle you, and put the seam of my body against you, I'll be so ready-ready, my opening will find you all by itself. Still holding your hands. I'll lower my-*

*self around you, ever so carefully, like a very vulnerable little
girl, like a first-timer . . . and then sit on you . . . sit on you
. . . like a bird on her eggs.*

"Laura? I'm here."

"What's going on?" . . . *And I'll hold you still in me,
absolutely still, for at least a minute. So I can watch your
eyes in the dark.*

"They want me back. But we're okay for Tuesday."

"Okay. Say something nice for making me cook twice."
A pang of guilt for the lie. "Actually, I haven't started to
cook yet."

"I'm crazy about you. Lock up." She hung up and sat
with the phone in her lap, her sleep evaporated. Then she
looked at the clock. She wouldn't be seeing him for another,
oh, at least forty-five hours.

The bottle with two inches of leftover wolfsbane stared
directly at her from the other room, from the top of the sideboard. Charlotte had propped up a Halloween card against it,
and wished her "Good luck with the ghoulies!" on the back.
Laura got up to get the bottle out of her sight. She stared
through the tree and didn't see the cop in the alleyway. She
pulled out Cabot's card, rushed back to the phone and called
his office, was given his private number, dialed again. A
grumpy middle-aged woman answered, put him through.

"I don't see your man out there," she said instead of good
evening.

"Good. If you can see him at all times, someone else
would, too. Take a pill and go to bed."

"I don't have any pills. I'm afraid of going out to get some,
and . . ." Crazily, she imagined him behind a deli counter,
selling Brie cheese and cured ham and homemade potato
salad, like her dad in Carmel. "You left that cupboard door
unnailed. Shall I nail it back again?"

He thought, and she moved the bottle in her hand. The
stuff in it sifted around dryly, like bits of ground roaches.

"I'll ask Les to get up there and do it for you. When he
knocks, don't blow his head off." She said she had nothing
to do that with anyway, and he said thank God for small
favors.

Five minutes later, Les knocked on her door, came in,

and strode vigorously to the little cupboard. He detached the
lanyards, took out the platform, and pulled the whole contraption off its block. As he was finishing, another cop
knocked on the door and brought in a cache of Sominex.
Meanwhile, the phone rang, and Marion told her a security
man was coming in before noon tomorrow to install a system.
The cops left while she and Laura were still talking, Les
grinning and making reassuring gestures, not to worry, he
was right outside.

"I asked Merritt. He said that vampires have been sighted
occasionally on Bayou La Fourche ever since the late twenties," said Marion conversationally. "Well, *reported* sighted,
to be precise. I think it's just poppycock." Laura didn't want
to ask what sort of vampires—did they look human, were they
bats?—she just gritted her teeth and said please let's save this
for another day. Marion told her she was a brave girl, and
they said goodnight.

She left several lights on, and slept fitfully.

Knocks on her door pulled her out of sleep. She jumped on
the floor into a pool of morning light. "Yes, Les, I'm coming." Or was it Alain? Her heart beat cheerfully; perhaps
he'd found a way to drop by again between his river-to-down-
town wanderings. She rattled the chain off, flipped the lock
open. A dark human form blotted out the sun.

"Can you come down now?" insisted the Egyptian. "I've
got them coming back in fifteen minutes."

"Who?"

"The spirits. I guess you didn't get my note."

"Oh." Auras, cosmic beams, astral projections for breakfast. She was too numb and tired to think of an excuse.
"Okay, I'll come down. D'you have coffee?"

"And muffins," he promised repellently.

"See you," said Laura, and banged the door in his face
and felt like screaming for her bed in San Francisco, and for
the old store, and for Denise. She staggered to the bathroom
to throw water in her eyes, and saw herself lily pale, but with
a sort of languorous inertia in her mouth and features. The
bandage on her neck hung loose, undone by sleep. The scabs

were dry, shrunken; there were no new cuts, and despite the paleness she decided that she looked better.

In fifteen minutes the Egyptian let her into an apartment so stuffed with furniture, mostly chipped and gimcrack, that she had to follow a zigzagging path into the kitchen to serve herself coffee, which was on the stove. The stove was coated in dried-up lava from meals that had overboiled, but the plate with the muffins looked clean, and the muffins were fresh: baked by a lady, who was an apprentice in mediumship, explained the Egyptian. With coffee and two muffins, she found a corner on a sofa heaped with books, while he slumped in a sort of lacquered pharaonic throne, closed his eyes, and put his left hand and a legal pad on his knees. He lowered his eyelids, and his left hand started skittering back and forth on the paper, writing.

Waiting, she inspected the place. It looked like the sky had opened to rain books into it, anything from leather-bound old folios to finger-stained paperbacks, and her eye absorbed at random words like projection, etheric, atlantean, cosmoconscious. A poster showed a younger and trimmer Egyptian, announcing some kind of conference on ESP. She started at the date: It was for this Thursday, at the Saenger Performing Arts Center.

Push Farther the Frontiers of the Outer Plane!

commanded the poster, specifying that:

We Were Born before Birth!
We Are Here And Now,
and Everywhere Else in Place and Time!
Your Personal Aura is Your Space Passport!
Follow the Egyptian
On A Voyage into The Sixth Dimension
All Navigators Invited to Talk,
to Share, to Learn, and to Helm the Ship.

More discreetly, the poster announced that the Egyptian would sign copies of his book, *The Personal Aura as a Space Passport*, and that there was a contribution entrance fee of twelve dollars. The poster was thumbtacked to the bottom of an easel with an unfinished oil portrait on it. It showed a man in a pharaoh headdress, cobra and hawk twining above his brow. He was captured walking in a moonlit desert, in the classic pose, left foot forward. Laura blinked: Although the features weren't alike, there was a striking resemblance between the man in the portrait and her scribbling neighbor. Perhaps because they both had the same engimatic, half-mast eyes.

"I listened to them and transcribed them," said the Egyptian, reentering Laura's reality. She swallowed the last of her muffin. "They are of rather inferior quality, astrally speaking."

"What? Who?"

"These spirits who've been talking to me about you."

"Thanks," she said, and he didn't notice the sarcasm. "Why is that?"

"Something's torn their aura. It's stretched around them in tatters, sort of, instead of being oval or circular. And they're using a term. I can't read it well, *wmpyr, upir*, something like that. They're trying to use it as a substitute passport, but it's rejected."

The word *vampire* instantly killed whatever fun she'd been having till this minute. *He's making it up. He was at my place yesterday, when the cops were there, and now he's making up this spiel.* "Look, before we go any further—are you charging me for this?"

Her back ached. She straightened it.

"Of course not! I'm a professional."

"If those voices are so inferior and their aura is so tattered, why bother to listen to them at all?"

"Because of what's happened to you," he said. This morning he didn't sound oafish; this morning he adopted a dramatic baritone, echoing as if the outer plane was really there, somewhere between his uvula and vocal cords. "And because they're so insistent. They're having a regular argument about you." Now was the time to get up and leave. Now, thanking him for the coffee and the muffins from his apprentice.

"What are they saying?"

"They're sort of evenly divided into two groups. One group seems to have tried to warn you about not coming here. I don't mean to this dimension, I mean to New Orleans. The other group is trying to prevent the first from warning you, and insists that you should join them."

"Wait a second." She rubbed her palm over her forehead. "Who do they want me to join? You said there were two?"

"Well, that's not very clear. They're all traveling together. But some want you with them, and some don't."

"I see. Can I have more coffee?"

"Sure."

She made it back to the pot on the stove, wondering why she was staying. Was she beginning to go for this, to enjoy the daily mix of fear and pleasure, of threat and temptation that New Orleans had straitjacketed her into from the very beginning?

She noticed the spot where the Egyptian's own shaft door should have been, by his stove. The wooden door had been torn off, and the space was bricked up.

"So what else can you tell me about these . . . these vampires? They're calling themselves that, right?"

"That's the word, yes. There's conflict even among them, where you're concerned. Some of them want you to join them, but one of them doesn't, and this spirit seems distressed, and sort of ashamed. The others are colder and more cynical."

"Do any of these spirits have individual names?"

"Possibly. But I can't read them."

"Do I have any say in the matter?"

"I can't tell."

"Why not?"

"Your own aura appears incomplete, though strong." She remembered his mentioning that on her first morning in town.

Incomplete aura. Curiouser and curiouser, cried Alice—but she wasn't Alice.

"What does that mean, incomplete aura?" she asked, feeling the same fatigue, despondency, and aggravation she'd felt yesterday, buying wolfsbane at the Butterfly Box. "What in the hell does that mean?"

He looked at her, and she felt that the pharaoh in the unfinished portrait was looking at her, too.

"You've been taking a trip for a while," he said cautiously. "I think it's a trip you didn't really want to take."

"A trip to New Orleans?"

"An astral trip," he said, disappointed at her lack of quickness.

She looked back at the pharaoh portrait. Its eyes, placed without any sense of perspective over a poorly sketched nose, had a flatness of cheap canvas. She was all the more surprised that a feeling of some kind emanated from the portrait and its obvious lifelessness, like from the eyes of statues she had seen in museums: empty eyes, irisless, colorless. Of stone, never indicating emotion, or interest. And yet something lay behind that opaqueness. A mute, ghastly knowledge.

And she finally plunged into the chasm she'd been standing next to for the last day: "What *are* vampires, anyway?"

"Let's consult an authority," he said. She expected him to pull out a book, or pick up a phone. Instead, he slumped back on his gaudy throne, eyes half closed, and talked to someone on the outer plane.

When he came back, fifteen minutes later, he read from notes that vampires were present in all cultures from China to North Africa. In very few places were they thought to be born that way, addicted from the womb to the blood of innocent people or animals. In the Balkans, harelipped infants or ones born with teeth were quickly strangled and had their hearts taken out and burned. Sin, vile sin, made a dying human a vampire, particularly if he died without repenting. Killers became vampires. Madmen could become vampires. Other abominations, unconfessed and unabsolved, made the culprit open his eyes in his coffin after the burial, undead and thirsty. Witches and murdered people who weren't avenged by their kin became vampires. So did a corpse over whose coffin jumped a dog, or even a chicken. If a horse never brought to stud stamped its feet by a grave and refused to jump it, there lay a vampire.

To counteract the transformation of likely candidates inside the coffin, Romanians covered their corpse's eyes with silver coins, so the vampires couldn't see their victims, placed pieces of silver in the dead hands, sprinkled wolfsbane and garlic in the coffins. The sure cure against the revenant was to decapitate it, or pierce its heart with a stake, or bury it at a crossroads: the sign of the cross and the confusion of the intersection kept that vampire forever inactive.

They were pleasure seekers. They had sought pleasure in their damnable lives, and kept seeking it thereafter. Pleasure was their goal: relish, delight, reveling, all at others' expense, anywhere, selfishly and relentlessly, to the end of time. They tore, sucked, bit, shredded with craftsmanlike skill, artists in their nefarious labor.

They were lovers. And they were tormentors—tormentors of all people, no matter how strong or healthy. But out of the eternal unrest of their quest for pleasure came understanding. Vampires had been poets, statesmen, scientists, lawyers. The world was theirs to lead and teach a lesson, if only they found the vein in time. And so many more of them had existed, and kept existing, than public awareness openly accepted.

While the Egyptian read his notes, Laura's mind raced back the whole sinuous length of her past, trying to link what was happening to anything else, to anything at all in her life foretelling, prophesying the present. Destined to live a normal existence until now, perhaps at last consoled after her great loss, why did she suddenly find herself on this mystical threshold, under the whirl of monstrous batlike wings? Where was Alain in all this? What was the role he'd been cast into? Why was she so attracted to him—so obsessed, that was the word—that even the movement of her lips sipping coffee reminded her of Alain's kisses, and her body touching its own clothes anticipated touching him, belonging to him? Was she in love? Could she be, so fast, in love with Alain Lecouveur?

What was she to do? Should she run away? But from what? What if the killer was arrested tomorrow? Should she stay and try to untie this knot of mystery?

"Who did you consult?" she asked the Egyptian. He said Dom Augustin Calumet, a theologian who wrote a treatise on vampires in 1746.

"And what's your own opinion?"

"Before the vampire spirit revealed himself through me,"

the Egyptian murmured thoughtfully, "I would've said this was your own repressed sexuality, acting out eroto-violent dreams and fantasies."

"Thanks," she said touchily. "Put it on *me*. *My* repressions. *My* fantasies." She got up from the sofa in a sour mood. The Egyptian invited her to his Thursday-night lecture. He'd let her in free.

"I don't know if I can make it."

"Try. It'll help you."

"I'll see."

Walking out, she gave the pharaoh in the portrait a final glance. Yes, there was something behind those petrified eyes. Knowledge. The knowledge of something lifeless, yet outliving time.

All right, I'll give it another couple of days. I've got the wolfsbane against the vampires, and the police to save me from the killer.

She stormed into work-like a fiend.

Monday passed. Laura was counting the hours.

Monday night she slept almost well.

Tuesday morning came with models sent by an agency, who arrived at the store, stripped, put on Laura's enticing lingerie, and stretched legs and flexed knees, thrust breasts and pulled in stomachs for two photographers. Charlotte wanted to model some underwear, too. She wasn't terrific, but one of the photographers asked for her number.

Laura was getting good responses from people interested in her lingerie fashion show. How to handle it tastefully was the issue.

She took some mail off to the mailbox while the photographers started to wrap up their stuff, and when she came back Charlotte looked like there was something she didn't dare tell her. But she told her anyway.

Someone had called with the message that Mr. Lecouveur had to leave town unexpectedly and couldn't make the dinner appointment. A business trip. Mr. Lecouveur would call as soon as he returned.

Her fridge was stuffed with nice things ready to be cooked!

* * *

What happened? What did I do wrong? What's going on?
Cancel once, then cancel again? Is he really away on business?

I should've moved much slower. Should've been poised. Ladylike. Interested, but not anxious.

Monday, after a double murder in my store, I told him I was nuts about him, I practically panted in his arms. All after calling him by another man's name.

He thought I was easy. California girl.

Is he with someone else? Where in the hell is he?

The port of New Orleans took in eight vessels a day on the average. On Monday afternoon the *Khayati* had crawled in, buzzing from tired turbines. She was matriculated in Panama, but in reality was Lebanese, and her name in Arabic meant sweetheart.

An old cargo boat who dragged herself many times a year across the waves from the Black Sea to Gibraltar and from Gibraltar to Louisiana, the *Khayati* saluted the forty miles of harbor on both sides of the river with a phlegmy siren. Her drainholes spewed water. The skipper was on the bridge, the scanty crew at their posts, chugging the ship along the wharves and cotton warehouses, grain silos and steel sheds and other ships. Eighty steamship lines connected The Big Easy with the confused, fragmented outer world. A big foreign-trade zone, among the top five in America.

One of the *Khayati*'s seamen had met his death on the trip. An American. By law he had to be returned to the nearest piece of American soil. The body lay in a section of the ship's refrigerator, one level above the cargo.

This was going to be a tough one for Captain Baroodi. Seeing the three elegant spires of the St. Louis Cathedral float past, he longed for a minaret and a muezzin's call.

Arata learned about the *Khayati*'s cargo the next morning. It was to be unloaded and turned over to Lecouveur's people, who would put it on barges and whip it up the industrial canal, which linked the river to Lake Pontchartrain. He remembered instantly his earlier plan to board a barge.

He owned a Smith & Wesson "Highway Patrolman."

Braulio had a Mac-10 automatic, easily concealable under his jacket, hanging from his right shoulder. It could be swung forward, trigger pressed, in no time. They had an Anglo docker friend, Candy, who could bring along a couple of buddies.

And they had to find a nice little boat, not too noisy, able to follow a barge without being instantly spotted.

Anyone else but me would've said, gee, poor guy's busting his buns working. What a demanding family business. What a tightly knit family. Their interests come before anything else.

Now, now. They've got a lot of pressure, remember what he said about the longshoremen? They could hang the Lecouveurs from cypresses in the bayou. (Please, not Alain.) It's a real emergency, and you want him to drop everything and call in person a girl he's met exactly twice?

I'm sure he had to leave in a hurry. In the family jet. Are such planes safe?

But there's got to be such a thing as a phone wherever he went off to.

He never gave me a number where I could call him.

Wait a second. Jesus. He doesn't have my number at home. Must make sure I'm listed.

Les and his people kept their watch vigilantly.

Wednesday passed.
Thursday passed.

He's just an insecure guy like so many others. Judging women by appearances. Wanting them to be manipulative, hypocritical kittens. Someone stronger than that scares the pants off them.

I wish.

She felt worse than horny. Cheap horny. Thinking of going to bars alone. She blamed Alain for it.

Thursday night she woke up around three, sneezing. She smelled the wolfsbane. It should've lost its pungence by now.

As the moon sailed above the magnolia in the garden, she got out of bed and sat on the floor by the locked balcony door. The curtains were drawn aside, and she saw the moon. Deformed, yellow, it looked like a pregnant dwarf. She heard a long cry somewhere outside, and it chilled her blood. She popped up to see if the cop was there.

There was no one in the alleyway. *Already slipping.*

The cry repeated itself, distant, but so sad, so desperate in its longing, as if some unfortunate being was lost out there, kept mercilessly away from some warm home, from some loved partner. She wondered if it was a dog's howl. Maybe a *varcolac* was howling in fear, falling off the moon, parachuting to earth. Whatever it was, she was touched by its loneliness and loss of hope, and felt the same way: She was lonely, too, and though not falling from one planet to another, she was definitely in a state of strange transition. Was she still the person she had been in San Francisco?

The cry came closer, closer, closer still. But its sadness somehow kept her from being frightened. The creature was vulnerable and pitiful, not to be feared.

The wolfsbane by the balcony door looked like a rash of tiny corpses.

She kept going to the store—what else was there for her to do? And the store kept her busy, with all sorts of little things that were beginning to push Alain out of her mind. Well, not *really*—but the missed date began to feel more and more like something that had never had a real chance of happening. A man had seen her at the airport on the night of her arrival. Three days later, he had taken her out, self-servingly, he had said so himself—he was down in the dumps and needed company. Her misfortune that night had brought him back again the next evening, with a show of concern and care that might've been simply pity. But he had kissed her. But maybe he kissed all girls he felt pity for, and that was his way of showing it. Then he canceled—he'd gone as far as he wanted to go with this casual flirtation.

She talked to Denise. Laura heard herself describe the burglary and the double murders and the episode with Alain. Shrinking them, cutting them down to the size of ordinary, forgettable events. Denise was upset about the burglary and the murders, couldn't understand the slowness of the local police, wanted above all to know if Laura was all right. Yeah, she was all right. Of the canceled date with Alain, Denise thought it was great that Laura's little muddle with that guy had kept her mind off the shock of the assault and burglary and the murders. He wasn't in any way really important to her, was he? No, he was just sort of cute and that night after dinner he had kissed her well. It might still turn into something, or not turn into anything at all. It didn't matter. *It didn't matter.*

The little things continued. The first customers wandered into the store and bought bras and panties. There was a push-button security panel next to her apartment door now, doubled by another one inside, right by her bed. Even groggy from sleep, jolted out of a dream, she would just need to zap it with the edge of her palm to start a bell that could wake the dead, and make a strobe light flash outside to alert the police. She and Marion were becoming friends. She and Charlotte were becoming friends. As quickly and as violently as it had flared up, her attraction for Alain might shrivel and fall out of her life. The weekend drew near, came, Charlotte and Laura went to see a sweaty Sylvester Stallone picture. Work started again on Monday.

Cabot called her Monday afternoon, asked her how she was, had she noticed anything even slightly out of line, had she seen Alain again? She felt she had lost the momentum to ask him for the Lecouveurs's number (she could get it from Marion, but she didn't want Marion to know how important Alain had become to her). They chatted. The killer hadn't claimed any new victims in a week. The hospital had finished all her tests and given her a clean bill of health. Cabot said he might lift her protection if nothing happened for another week, and that didn't make her too nervous—she had the alarm system now, panel glowing in the dark by her bed.

After she hung up, she wanted to call him right back for the Lecouveurs's number. Wait a second, what was she going to say to Alain if she got the number? "Hi," coquettishly, "so you've been back almost a week? How could you live without calling me? . . ." Or, "Hi," with cheerful camaraderie. "I just took this dress to the cleaners and found your number in my pocket." Nonsense, he'd never given her the number. How about simply: "Hi, let's get together." But what if he didn't want to? By now, he didn't seem to be worth risking a rejection.

It was all going away. Going away!

She knew, however, that the few days when she had felt absolutely *filled* with him and his presence had been a sort of summit—a time in her existence when either her senses, heightened by the lengthy celibacy, or her openness to novelty and life in general, had been at an unequaled peak. Perhaps she wasn't longing for the man any more, she was just longing for that special sensation.

Merritt stopped off at the store and asked her to join him for a drink, and she had a salty dog with him at The Royal Orleans. His face seemed more elongated, his bones even thinner than the first time she'd met him. His neck was narrow, as if strained by the weight of his head. She compared it to Alain's neck—*that trunk thick with muscle, that gorgeous stack! No. No, Merritt, I'm sorry.* "I'll be so busy for a while," she said when he asked for a date, "I don't think we can really plan anything yet." Better go back to her familiar but still rewarding fantasies. She hadn't had one for nights.

She tried that night, but it didn't go anywhere.

The next morning she woke up and almost retched on her way to the bathroom. Then she took a broom and gathered up the wolfsbane, which had lost all odor, and threw it in the toilet. She felt terrible, as if the blood inside her was crying for something, if she only knew what it was. Her scars were almost gone, but she looked and felt like death warmed over. Had she been eating right? She couldn't even remember.

She thought of Michael. For a moment she considered visiting the Egyptian, asking him whether Michael wasn't calling her because he was angry at her. Angry about her coming to New Orleans in the first place, angrier still about her fling with another man. She looked at her calendar. By her memories and calculations, the Egyptian's ship bound for the outer plane was due to sail off the day after tomorrow.

She dragged herself to work. A lot of women came and bought lingerie that day. The cash register was ringing until six o'clock. Charlotte had brought in another girl, and they were training her.

As she was opening her door that night, she heard an envelope crumpling underneath it. The Egyptian, no doubt, reminding her of his public séance.

It wasn't from the Egyptian. It was a plain envelope, gray-lilac, of rather stiff paper. It rasped in her hands as she tore it open.

Dear Laura,

Sorry for running out on you last week. It really couldn't be helped.
Dinner Friday night?
I want to see you.
I'll pick you up at seven.

A.

"*Huh?*" she exploded into an amazed whinny that hit her rosewood walls, and then bounced back to slap the furniture. "*Oh, brother, do you have a healthy ego! How many women have ever said no to you, big boy? Not many? One blind girl? I thought so!*"

What a spoiled brat! *He* wanted! *He* would pick her up! Tomorrow at seven. If and when it suited him.

So clever, so used to this game, so sure of how much she wanted to see him, that again he gave no phone number. Leaving her no alternative. No way to say no. No way to play back, to use a bit of bargaining power of her own before accepting—which of course she would.

Wait. What's today?

Panic. Flames of panic from everywhere, to burn her at the stake of her insecurities. When was this delivered. How?

It was hand-delivered. *Relax, Laura. Today is Wednesday, tomorrow is Thursday, Friday is Friday.*

I'm going to sleep tonight even if I have to take two pills. I want to look good.

She reread the letter.

All right, Mr. Lecouveur. We'll see what manner of beast you really are. And this time we'll do it right. Slowly. I won't give you any breaks, I won't make any advances, I'll let you work for it.

The only thing that bothered her was the letter. Why not a

call? What was this mystery? Like his comings and goings, his terribly important barges and meetings and vanishings up the river. Like he wasn't quite real.

She took Marion to dinner, and casually mentioned her new date with Alain. Marion was spellbound by the idea of such an unlikely couple. "I don't mean it's wrong, honey. You're so very different, you could really make a great match. Now isn't that all love really needs?"

"Oh, come on— *love*?"

She was soaking in the palmated tub when the phone rang. She let it ring twice, then got out wet to answer it.

"Laura?" asked Alain anxiously.

"Alain?" No answer. "Good evening, how are you," she said confidently.

"Did you get my note?"

He sounded hollow, like he was talking from a submarine.

"Did you put me on a squawk-box?" she asked.

"Yeah," he answered. "I'm talking from my office at the station." Anxious. "I sent you a note. Can we have dinner Friday?"

"Sorry, I ate all that food I prepared for you."

"I hope you didn't eat it alone." She squeezed the receiver between her fingers, and as if sensing it, he hurried to say he was joking—and terribly sorry that he had flaked out on her like that, not once but twice.

"How are your barges?" she asked matter-of-factly. *God isn't this delicious?* She felt the delight in her navel, in her lower belly.

"They're fine. Listen, can you make it Friday?"

She counted to five, slowly. "Okay. What time?"

"Seven?"

"All right. See you then."

"Great. Thank you. Good night."

"Good night, Alain." The phone clicked, but a hum stayed on the line, a cavernous murmur, like the flowing of the Mississippi on a silvery moonlit night.

The water was beginning to dry up on her body. She plunged back into the tub.

She was ecstatic.

I'm going to put myself to sleep with you tonight. I'm going to have the greatest fantasy about you. Tonight, and tomorrow night. And then I won't be in a rush to kiss you Friday, I won't be so needy, no, not for a second. I'll be cool and calm and perfect.

7

At SUNDOWN on Thursday, as the sun nuzzled the hairiness of the bayou, the piloting station was buzzing with activity. In the operations room, the dispatchers followed on computer screens the positions of the barges and other Lecouveur vessels. A telex clacked out sheets with the stock's movements, from New Orleans, Houston, New York, and the station's radios transmitted all the relevant information about weather, water levels, river traffic. In the camp behind the station, Alain stepped into his shower, too preoccupied to close the plastic curtain—or to remove the lit cigar in his mouth.

On the walls of Alain's quarters, the river canals were shown on detailed maps. A Walther PPK blowback pistol and a customized Winchester with Redfield scopes hung from a clothes rack right next to the shower. The hot water stung Alain's skin, but massaged his tired muscles. It rained on the cigar, but the size of it kept it lit.

The station, the guns, the cigar, the river. Alain's river. Alain's world, which Emory hadn't invaded yet. He had gotten a message to hurry to Belle Hellène for a conference with his uncle. Driving, he could be there in an hour.

The vehicle he used on the river was a truck, a 1987 Dodge Power Ram, fitted with swamp tires, and bull bars front and back. Alain threw in the cab the morning paper, which had reached the station in the afternoon, and which he had barely skimmed. An editorial about the labor tensions. A local columnist's speculation about the slash-kills, and the superstitious rumors they were starting to give birth to.

Driving with impassive control, though the tires' sidebiters ripped cyclones of mud, Alain recognized every turn in the shrub and the tangled trees, and knew what lay beyond them, on the riverbank and in the river. Poachers' huts, abandoned moonshine stills, and hulks of barges and boats run aground during the last fifty years, some earlier.

The river that flowed in his veins. How could anyone ask a woman to live here?

He knew by heart what he had to tell his uncle: The old ways weren't working anymore. Alain would describe his own vision of a modern empire, based on quick communications and efficient PR, replacing the faded glamor and the old-boy cronyism. He would ridicule Emory's rides in the brougham. Who wanted to do business with a wax-museum family? He would attack Emory's insistence on absolute obedience and loyalty. "We need major changes," he would conclude. "Otherwise we'll keep making enemies, and no new friends. Look at the unions. Before I talked to them, they were ready to blow up our ships and smash our offices and roast us in our mansions. We need to let in new *blood*!" He would bugle out the closing line, knowing what the tall ceiling of the Carpathian room would do to his voice.

He drove through mixed bayou and forest. The shadows were starting to stretch into the frightening silhouettes of his childhood. The mudmen, the zombies. The voodoo witches.

He left the truck by the estate's river gates. Steve, the groundskeeper, wasn't in sight, but the other hired help hobbled between the garden and the twin Greek temple structure: all stooped or limping, or deformed in some other way. In his camouflage jacket and boots, Alain walked to the mansion, defiant *homo novus*, exactly as that unrepeatable twilight hour struck, and the mansion seemed to soar in height from Dixie belle to gothic witch.

He pushed the tall panes of beveled glass in the baronial front door. Here was the moment. The moment when the healthy resolve of outside had to face the stab of chill hallways, the creepiness of sagging stairways, the glacial inquiry and accusation of family portraits.

There were no lights on in the house. Alain stopped by a multiple switch. He tried all the buttons. None worked. But he knew the house blindfolded. He veered left, and strode through the darkness, reassuring himself with the sound of his steps.

He walked into Emory's study, and shivered: Pale and glabrous faces looked up from every chair and sofa, better than a dozen, ghostly from the candles. Cocktail glasses shook in knobby hands, catching feverishly the candlelight. "Hi there, when did y'all drive over?" Alain asked, like a true Southern boy, ripe with hospitable enthusiasm. Coming in from the river side, he hadn't seen their cars.

"Good evening," said Emory, and stepped from the shadows behind his mahogany desk. His eyes were vitreously green, his handshake congealed. He proceeded to explain how a dumb Cajun repairman had crashed a pickup truck into the generator not an hour ago, provoking a power outage. Alain meanwhile slowed his breathing, adapting for the thousandth time to this bone-deep coolness that came not from the air but from these people. To their stares, which were intense, indecent almost in the way they pierced clothes and souls. To the voraciousness of their contact: They all acted urgent, querulous, seeking. And they shook like addicts.

He wants strength in numbers to reject my ideas out of hand, guessed the young man.

"Shall we start without lights?" asked Emory, knowing that in this eerie flicker Alain's words would lose power and credibility.

Alain nodded, shook his cousins' hands: the sepulchral Lignacs from Baton Rouge, Ernest and Jack and "Duff" Lecouveur from Florida. Plus Clark Chadwick, dean of the family's attorneys. And Aunt Flora, who lived in Houston, and had brought her daughter, Rose Janice. Plus a few others. Emory seemed frighteningly cold, though he wore a double-lined dressing gown, of cashmere wool. Afraid. *I've never seen him look nervous before*, thought Alain.

Rose Janice dampened Alain's cheek with a clammy kiss, blew ancient fumes of patchouli on him, lolled her head in laughter: She'd not seen him in eons, was he hah-ding? She was dark, skinny, her wrist joints cracked audibly. The family's expectation was that they'd be married.

"What a nice surprise," he twanged at the bunch, silently damning them all to hell. They all owned pieces of the empire, of the barges, of the stock. Rose Janice alone held three barges in her skinny arms.

Very well, since you're all here, I'll give it to all of you with the bark on.

The barge was pushing slowly up the river. Green light to starboard, red light to port. *Groll-groll-groll-groll-groll* went the engines. The boat that followed her was far behind. Almost invisible, hopefully, to the men on the barge.

Arata was armed with his Smith & Wesson. Braulio had the Mac-10 under his jacket. He also had a Survivor knife in his belt, in its rigid metal sheath with its sharpening stone: the knife was sharp, all right.

Candy had a shotgun. He'd brought two buddies he knew from the street, who sat silently by the boat's rail, eyes focused on the vessel ahead.

Braulio increased the speed of the boat just as the barge started decreasing hers. They all stood up, weapons at the ready, Arata holding a rope with a metal hoop that tied into a rope ladder.

No one had noticed them. The fat *groll-groll-groll* of the barge engines drowned the rumble of the boat as it caught up with the larger vessel. Avoiding the wake of the barge, the boat came up alongside and the hoop sizzled through the air, clamping the gunnels of the barge.

Now the boat was being tugged, and Braulio cut off the motor. Like dream creatures, one after the other, the five climbed to the rails, and hopped onto deck.

They glanced quickly in all directions. Shiny from the river mist that wetted the decks, the barge looked deserted. Ahead, the vast metal covers of the closed loading hatches stretched seemingly forever, as if the vessel were ten times longer than it had looked from the dockers' dinghy. The mist made it look that way, decided Braulio. But that uncanny illusion of length made him grate his teeth and control a rapid little shiver.

Port and starboard, wooden walkways ran along the hatches all the way to the prow. They looked striated, assuring the men that their boots wouldn't slip on the narrow treads.

Astern, only the pilot's cabin showed, like a humpback's silhouette. Braulio saw no bargemen there either, standing by the rail, chatting or turning their cigarettes toward the dark rolling roadway of the Mississippi. The barge seemed to sail and keep course all by herself.

Candy gripped Braulio's sleeve. "You an' me, le's go aft," he whispered.

With mute nods of approval, the others started ahead on the narrow walkway. Candy and Braulio moved back toward the pilot's cabin, closer and closer to the jaundiced light that dripped out of its dirty window.

Clearly, the barge was slowing. Braulio noticed the gap in the succession of knots of cypresses lining the left riverbank; a side canal was opening up unexpectedly and the barge began to veer smoothly toward it. He whipped his head toward the prow, and his eyes slipped along the familiar length of the main industrial canal. Wrapped in the unclearness of distance, a piloting station showed its lights ahead. That, he knew, was the nerve center of the Lecouveur river operation. But the barge was turning left, rather than heading toward the station.

"Where the hell are we going?" he muttered.

And Candy whispered simultaneously, "What the hell kinda trade are the Lecouveurs into, anyway?"

They stopped by the pilot cabin at the same time. Candy, who was short, peered in from behind Braulio and his Survivor knife. They both strained their eyes. The light from inside was thick like beer foam, and Braulio had trouble spotting two human silhouettes. They weren't moving.

He drew closer, Mac in firing position. He gasped so frightfully that he almost let loose a volley of bullets.

The pilot was leaning back against the cabin wall . . . staring straight at Braulio. A knife pinned his neck to the wall, impaling him straight through his Adam's apple. The knife's handle jutted out of the throat; with a sick sense of humor, someone had hung his cap from it.

The side of the dead neck, Braulio saw clearly, was striped

by a long, deep gash. Dripping blood had coagulated into several dark icicles extending down to the dead pilot's shoulder.

Only then did Braulio realize that the other man in the cabin—the one helming the barge—wasn't dead. Just at that moment, apparently sensing Braulio and Candy's presence, the man turned toward them, and showed to the eyes goggling outside the cabin a lustrous yellow face and a wide, snaggle-toothed smile.

He wore strange clothes: brown, woven from some sort of peasant flax, or maybe it was wool—Braulio had never seen such attire. His low forehead was half covered by a round little hat of black lambskin.

Braulio and Candy, eyes bulging from their sockets, stared at the little creature, who seemed malnourished and not terribly athletic. But a monstrous threat came from the beady eyes: They rippled with a sort of childlike glee. *I killed!* they seemed to shout. *I'll kill again!* He couldn't leave the helm, but he beamed broadly at Braulio and Candy, friendly-like: *Be patient*, said his beady eyes. *In a little while we'll all have fun together.*

Braulio felt a power stronger than God push him bodily back from the cabin's window. Both men staggered backward, boots feeling the walkway blindly, until they found themselves midship.

No one burst from the pilot's cabin to pursue them.

"Where are the guys?" rasped Candy.

Braulio couldn't speak—he just gestured, *I don't know.* Someplace ahead, but Braulio was going no place. Candy had reached the hoop lassoing the little boat to the gunnel. The barge was now chugging along into the side canal.

"Let's split," whispered Candy, trying to pull up the rope ladder.

Braulio found his voice. "What about the others?" Candy made a listless gesture—did it matter, did anything else matter to him, apart from getting out of here with his life?

Braulio tried to think of what to do next—anything that might save them. He couldn't. Fear had stolen his *cojones.* Even worse, it had stolen his mind as well.

* * *

The canal widened. Before the nose of the barge, a complete set of wharves started to appear through the screen of creepers, kudzu, Spanish moss. Some were rotting, collapsed in the water. Others showed signs of recent repair. Lopsided storage sheds rose behind the wharves, and the rusting beaks of winches and pulleys dangled cables out of them.

An abandoned loading site.

By the prow, Arata walked past a stack of shapeless masses wrapped in coarse brown blankets. He stumbled over one, and it stirred. Who are these *gitanos*, he wondered, seeing a pale face with long hair and staring eyes, then another, then another. Stepping back from them, he didn't see the open trap door behind him. His foot stepped on air, and with a muffled yell he tumbled into the belly of the barge. He drew his eyelids tightly closed. *That's it, I'll break my spine. Paralysis, impotence, adios tetas.*

But he fell on something soft. His body churned up humid clods that splattered him in the face. While his arms and legs wallowed, his scrambling hands scooped palmfuls of the stuff.

"*Suelo!* Dirt!" he whispered, in total astonishment.

He struggled up, buried to his knees in dark soil. It smelled moist, faintly rotten, and filled the barge completely. Far aft, there were some wooden boxes stacked up on top of it, long and rectangular, like coffins. But otherwise, the whole damn cargo was nothing but *soil*.

With the shrewdness of an *astuto politico*, his mind raced to his next harangue before the crowded union hall. So *that* explained the secrecy, the insistence on working only with their own people. They were smuggling something in. What? Radioactive soil? Didn't the *masses* have a right to know?

Above him, the sounds of a brief scuffle: Candy's men had reached the prow, had stumbled over the slumbering gypsies. A yell ripped the night, interrupted abruptly as if someone had flicked off a soundtrack button.

He grabbed his gun, pulled the hammer back. He saw the stairs and trampled up noisily, gathering courage from his own racket. A lid blocked his progress. He let the hammer down again, stuck the gun in his belt. He pushed the lid with both hands, rattling it loose, and burst up upon the deck.

The pile of brown blankets lay a few yards ahead, and

didn't look like a pile anymore: Six creatures had hatched out
of the blankets, and they were standing by the opening, staring at him with curiosity. His eyes fastened on the closest
face: it yawned, and the moon glinted on a pair of fanglike
teeth, and Arata heard the gurgle of a hungry stomach.

That second, he realized that Candy's men wouldn't,
couldn't come to his help.

The six moved closer, slowly surrounding him. The first
brought his face inches close to Arata, examining him myopically, sniffing at his clothes.

Far behind, Arata heard something plopping in the water.
He didn't even turn to see what it was. Eyes anchored into
the creature's eyes, his brain an empty box of vapor, he waited
for his fate.

Lights, moving lanterns were appearing on the shore.

While Arata was surrounded, Braulio managed to throw
himself off the portside, into the little boat. He almost cap-
sized it. Candy jumped, too, but missed, and landed in the
water.

Flailing his hands for help, he sank, resurfaced bubbling
water from his mouth, tried to call, and went down again.
Poor swimmer or just paralyzed by fear, Braulio would never
know. An interminable minute later, Candy floated inertly to
the surface, blood bubbling from his open mouth, then sank
again. Braulio watched, without reacting.

Somehow, he unsheathed the Survivor knife and cut the
cord. Losing the power that pulled it forward, the little boat
slowed down, while the barge's big dark hips squirmed away,
plowing a deep furrow in the water, toward the approaching
wharves.

Waves shook the boat and Braulio gripped its sides
thoughtlessly. Then the water smoothed itself into a dark
shifting mirror, and Braulio found his mind, and the boat's
emergency oars. Teeth clicking, he started to row back toward a bend in the canal. Once beyond it, he could start the
motor.

8

"I CALLED to remind you about my lecture," said the Egyptian from the other end of the phone line. By the store register, Laura held the receiver negligently, studying her brand-new hairstyle in the mirror. "It's tonight."

"Oh. Yes, yes, yes. Listen, I won't be able to make it. I have a dinner engagement."

"Have dinner, then bring your date with you."

"What time is the lecture?"

"Eight."

"I'd like to catch it, but we're going out at seven. We won't be seated and served before a quarter to eight, so it's really iffy."

"All right, then." He sounded hurt.

Laura wished him good luck and went back to looking at her hair.

It was going to happen tonight. She had a feeling.

She was dressed at six-thirty in a floral wraparound dress, lavender and gauzy. Dyed snakeskin shoes, her highest heels, matching purse. Smiling all by herself, imagining the noise of his approaching car every other second, as plenty of other cars passed beneath her balcony.

Five minutes before seven she had a horrible thought: *He won't come, he'll flake out on me again.* But she still had the feeling that it would happen between them, tonight. Seven struck in her Boulle clock and in the cathedral's belfries, and she took a deep breath.

She gave him five minutes, wondered whether to welcome him with the TV on or off. Finally she turned it on, then sat down to watch, careful not to crease her dress. She watched the screen with unseeing eyes, rubbernecking to check the Boulle clock and compare its crawling progress with her own watch. 7:07. She gave him ten more minutes, then went out to the balcony and looked down at the street. The evening was gorgeously balmy. *I'd like him to take me somewhere by the river after dinner. I'd even sit on the grass with him.* She saw the Egyptian come out of his apartment, bedecked in a collegiate herringbone jacket with battered elbow patches, headed for his conference, and checked her watch. 7:18. That upset her a little, and she gave Alain exactly two more minutes to be at her door.

Minutes after St. Louis Cathedral had clanged 6:30, the Chrysler Le Baron rolled off Highway 10 at Canal Street and slowed in the maze of contiguous little streets, looking for a parking space.

Alain drove it with the same precision he put into executing anything, though his jaw felt like cement under his tanned skin, and his eyes showed their inner turbulence, darting glances back and forth between the road and the rearview mirror. He had had a drink before getting in the car.

Emory's words echoed in his ear. "Alain, you know that I want to retire and let you take over." Said as both of them strolled in the moon-polished garden, its decay looking now like the porcelain embellishments of a giant French miniature. After dinner, after the relatives and attorneys had left. To Alain's protest that Emory might as well remain in charge if he wanted nothing changed after he stepped down, Emory had replied that five hundred years of tradition couldn't be torn up with one change of chairmanship. Those centuries were their taproot.

Alain parked the car right outside the Quarter. Eyes staring inward, he walked toward the river, trying not to think of the woman who had prepared herself for him in the apartment on Ursulines Street.

Why was she so important, Emory had asked. She was a stranger, not even French, not one of *them*. What about his intended, Rose Janice? Alain's face had contracted. That praying mantis, letting a nightgown drop to the floor in a bridal suite, to seize him in her spidery arms? Her organs of generation, webbed like a big dark moth in the fork of her legs, ready for *him*? "Never," he had answered irrevocably, and Emory had signified his wrath with a stony silence.

He walked into the Quarter, gingerly, like a convalescent, a gait that didn't fit his powerful body.

"This desire for change, the way you plead for renovation, is it coming from *her*?" Emory had asked. Without answering, Alain had gazed somberly at the moon. Emory had continued: Was this outsider worth violating a whole tradition? Did Alain actually believe that they were *destined* for each other?

Six and three quarters clanged in the belfries. He was still early. Alain entered Jackson Square, looked left toward Laura's place, then ahead again, toward the waterfront.

He started to walk faster, as if hoping for an answer from his body, from its quickening pace. He looked whole and determined, he knew it: dashing young man dressed for dinner with a beautiful companion. *Were* they destined for each other?

He saw the ferry from Algiers: It was just docking, its broadside bumping clumsily against the landing's clusters of car tires. On the deck, a constellation of eyes already searched the Quarter, ready for a spree.

Seven clangs from the cathedral. Laura was ready for him. Alain's heart felt caught between two pressure drums.

"If you're not sure, don't take the risk. For *her* sake, as well as yours."

The old man was lying. His own sake was what he held most dear, not Alain's, and certainly not Laura's. Under the opiate moon, Alain had stopped and told him that squarely, feeling all the while in his body, like a dangerous radiation, the energy released by the old man. From those ridiculous clothes, just like from those selfish eyes, emanated that desire to possess and control, to bond and fit unnaturally to his purpose and liking. It had been the same ever since Alain was a little boy. He had always been wary of his uncle's cracked laughter, of his crooked hands, of the way he wanted to play with little Alain—exactly the way little Alain played with his mongrel pups, with a child's cruelty. *Dad, Mom, where are you? Save me.* Dad had lost himself in the world. Deserting Mom—or was it the family? Mom was twenty. She had moved out of state, and remarried. The old man's hands had clutched the kid. Now those hands had less than half the power of then. Under his eyes, porously flabby formations of skin betrayed the decay of vital functions. And he was so pale— salt-white, death-white. The grandeur, the absurd pomp remained. It was enough. Everyone responded to it. *Don't take a risk—for her sake.*

A body. A young fleshy body, to feast his eyes on. To wash himself clean of that spectre of decay.

Alain noticed a girl walking off the ferry. A dyed blonde, rolling her hips under a red dress. Her eyes passively scanned the waterfront, saw Alain. The stagnant liquid in them broke its crust and started to flow. "Hi there, sweetmeat," she drawled, her mouth filled with the words.

He looked at her, wondering whether the rolling majesty of her movement came from shoes one size too big. "Hey, honey lips," he answered.

And suddenly he wished the cheap appearance to be an answer. If he just heeded this inferior sign, maybe his searing dilemma would be solved.

"Going any place in particular?" asked the dyed blonde, stopping and posting herself in front of him.

Behind them, the cathedral chimed 7:15.

At a quarter to eight, it became clear to Laura that Alain wasn't coming. She was numb, she felt that her life had been drawn out of her, she felt doomed never to have the luck of other women—just to meet someone, like him and be liked by him, become lovers and go from there.

Now he was a whole hour late . . . Now he was seventy-five minutes late. No, he wasn't late. He wasn't coming. It wasn't meant to be.

Then her phone rang, and she bolted to answer it—landing

on her high heels and nearly spraining the ankle she had twisted two weeks before. Heart in her mouth, she expected a message from the police, from a hospital. *He took that off-ramp too fast . . .*

"I can't make it tonight," said Alain hurriedly, in an unpleasantly grating voice. Over gas-station noises: honks, rumbles of machinery.

She couldn't speak, then stuttered, asking what happened. He couldn't really talk now.

"I love you, Laura," he whispered suddenly. So meekly and emotionally that she crushed the receiver over her ear, to catch every other sound, to collect every other detail that could explain his behavior. Was he drunk? Was he crazy?

"I love you," he blurted, as if the declaration had ripped his chest.

"Alain, wait—Alain, what's happening to you? Please, can I help?" Somewhere in the middle of this imploring speech, he hung up. She was left, receiver in hand, a dead line buzzing in her ear.

Alain.

Oh, dear God, what's going on? Where is he? Why did he hang up so abruptly? Is someone standing over him, training a gun at his head?

Some of the life sucked out of her came back. Enough to formulate questions: Was he in trouble? Did he really mean what he said? That he loved her? Why couldn't he see her—another business emergency? No, no, he wouldn't have announced that so dramatically, in a strangulated tone, in such emotional agony. And she hadn't dreamed it, that was no imagined voice. That was Alain, *her* Alain.

The man she loved. And he had just answered her own unuttered declaration. He loved her. *God, is it really possible?*

But then, what was the meaning of all this? What held him back from their appointment? What held him back from her?

Something was wrong. Was something wrong—with her?

The ugly thought, always the same. The feeling, like a nameless disease under her skin, forgotten until five minutes ago. But now back in full power, wanting to grab back every second since the second she first laid eyes on him, to see what she had done wrong. What explained, infallibly, scientifically, this new impasse, this fresh disaster?

The insecurity, like a sister. Sometimes forgotten. Never lost.

She felt like weeping.

Calm down, said another part of her. *You're just very disappointed. He'll call you soon, tonight maybe.* And the glimmer of hope in the tunnel: *He said he loved you.*

Don't stay here, all dressed up, to psychoanalyze what you can't understand, she ordered herself. She grabbed herself by her hair, winched herself out of a bog of near tears, brutalized a body that just wanted to lie down and sob. Go out. *Go out.*

She could still catch the Egyptian's lecture. It might even provide some insight. More glimmers of hope. Marion or Charlotte might want to go with her.

She decided to call Charlotte. Too bad she had to admit that she had been stood up.

She couldn't find her. Then she remembered that Charlotte had mentioned her friend from out of town, the one who stayed at the Hilton. With diminishing confidence, she called the Hilton, and had Charlotte paged in the bar, then in the restaurant.

They found her in the restaurant.

Charlotte sounded flustered, almost angry; then she softened. "Yeah, okay, why don't we go to that séance? Bond and I were just trying to figure out what to do with the evening. And there's a party later, a friend of mine's sold her house, and she's throwing a farewell bash."

Bond, her man, must've been standing right there: Charlotte lowered the receiver, and Laura heard her outline the plan to someone, in short, curt sentences.

"We'll come pick you up in a cab," said Charlotte.

At a quarter of nine, the cop, Les, was sitting in his car watching Laura's place: A cab stopped in front of Laura's and waited. There were two people in it. The kook in the downstairs apartment was out, so they had to be waiting for Laura.

Les fired the engine, used a dome light to get to the corner of Ursulines, where he turned it off and inched carefully into

Laura's street. Her slender body was just slipping into the back of the cab.

"How nice to finally meet you," Bond said. Fortyish, a little pudgy round the middle, wafting her way a breeze of martinis. Pretty eyes, though. "You're the one who got her into these wild undies—don't mean to be graphic, but, boy, does she get a response out of me with them on!" He was dressed to the nines in a white blazer, wore a gold watch on one wrist, a gold bracelet on the other.

"Glad I'm getting a response out of you *somehow*," said Charlotte with a really nasty edge, and Laura stared at both. There was a guilty, martini-infused smile on Bond's face, a hurt, jealous intensity in Charlotte's pinched features.

Les followed them to the Saenger Performing Arts Center, whose front was wallpapered with ads about the Egyptian's "Voyage Into the Sixth Dimension."

There were still a few seats left in the orchestra, and Laura, Charlotte, and Bond stumbled over rigid sets of knees to get to them, while Les wisely chose the balcony. From there he had an unrestricted view. Two converging spotlights lit a gaudy wooden throne, center stage, on which sat the guru himself behind a microphone, in his herringbone jacket. Overweight, bearded, he looked in no way different from a small town C.P.A.

Clad in white gowns looking like ordination albs, six women stood to his far right, modulating a one-note song: *Aaaaaaaaahhhh*, six voices melting into one unending wail, to create an aural-astral field that would ease the master's navigation to and from the outer plane (Les had missed that explanation on the printed program). Portraits of more bearded men—Paracelsus, Agrippa, Albertus Magnus, Darwin, Freud—flapped gently on white, yellow, and green banners hanging from the ceiling. Les examined the rest of the trees of knowledge and badges of magic craft, written up in olden fonts he couldn't read. The navigators lined up along the central aisle, and the Egyptian turned the "ship" over to each in turn. Les remarked to himself how many of the navigators were women. This guy's gotta be scoring like a rabbit. 'Magine what his phone calls sound like? Help me, swami, get me over this or that, swami, come on over and straighten me out.

I love you, Laura. I love you.

She sat between Bond and Charlotte. What was the matter with those two, had they quarreled? But she couldn't be bothered. She was with Alain, listening to his three words of magic, registering only abstractly what else went on around her.

The Egyptian advised a navigator whose third eye hurt badly that she was going to receive a visitation from "the outer." They all talked about the outer and the inner, but so far Laura hadn't figured out which was which.

The Egyptian finally descended from the stage and strode into the darkness of the filled rows. "Kindred aura," he said, addressing Laura over five hundred turned heads. "I feel that you're with us for the first time."

She started in surprise. *I've got to do it the right way—they're so into this.* "Yes, kindred aura," she replied.

"What is your passport, kindred aura?"

Passport? Everyone was looking at her, but she didn't discern one giggle of curiosity or sarcasm. The navigators appeared religious in their concentration on her and on the medium. "I am applying for a passport right now," she said, getting to her feet.

"To go in or out?"

Everyone else had been going *out*. "In," she announced as if it was a confession.

The Egyptian frowned, and the six vestal virgins seized the occasion: they droned a long *Aaaaaaahhh*. It sounded like the voice inside Laura's wall: That dirge, that mournful sacrificial wail, that had scared her and moved her. Maybe the Egyptian had it recorded, and played it back to himself for inspiration. Unless he had all six of his chorus girls spending hours in his cluttered fleabag apartment, singing that same interminable note while he was tripping.

"Come to the stage, aura," he said. He turned, forcing her to follow him. This obvious favoritism didn't seem to disturb the crowd. She mounted onto the stage, the Egyptian pulled another mike over, and she remembered being a poem-reciting little girl, helped by an encouraging glance from Mama over a verse that eluded her.

"What is the problem?" asked the Egyptian. She felt how the packed theater was staring at her with myriad astral scrutinies. Uncomfortable, she tried looking at the Egyptian's eyes, and received a sort of antishock: They were very hypnotic.

"I love someone," she declared.

"Of course you do," said the Egyptian, as if that was elementary.

"I love him. I'm sure of it. He says he loves me, too. Yet there seem to be some forces opposing our . . . our union. I wonder if I'm creating those forces myself."

He kept watching her, hypnotically. She felt she could fall asleep standing like this in front of him.

"I'm scared," she blurted without thinking. "I've been afraid most of my life, I realize that now. I think I've been afraid of love. I wonder if my fear of love is creating these obstacles between myself, and . . . and him."

She fought the slumber. A minute, perhaps more, perhaps less, passed. The floodlights from above had flattened the scene into only two dimensions, but had somehow opened a third, or perhaps a fourth, inside her, one that was visible not just to her but to everyone else present. She felt that the Hebrew and Arabic characters under the portraits of Paracelsus and Philo and Averroës were penciled directly on her retinas.

"D'you *hate* your fear, kindred aura?" psalmodized the Egyptian.

"Not always. Sometimes I love it," she said, and this time she heard a few outbursts of laughter.

"Wait," said the Egyptian, "if you wouldn't feel fear, what *would* you feel?"

For all his astral powers, he wasn't smart enough to get this one?

"Happiness, of course," she protested.

"Have you ever felt happiness?"

"I . . ." That was interesting. "I guess not right when it happened. I mean, I've always realized that I was happy *after*

I was happy. I know some of you would agree with me."
She turned defensively toward the audience.

"I would, too," said the Egyptian. "Happiness cannot be
instantly recognized, because it happens on a different plane.
A different inner plane. So, can you remember what else you
were conscious of feeling, when you were happy?"

She felt a little less hypnotized. She tried to think back, to
ignore the distraction of the floodlights and of the audience.
She came up with a feeling like seawater cupped in her hands:
It was transparent and colorless in her hands, but thrown back
in the sea it instantly turned green again.

"Same thing—I was scared," she said, "when I was
happy."

She squinted at the audience, and read a sort of sympathetic
twinness on the faces close enough to emerge from the dark.
They had felt the same, at their happy times.

"Because fear is a passport," said the Egyptian. "Without
fear, no newness is available, without fear no different plane
can be recognized. Fear"—he turned his hairy face to Laura,
fastened his hairy glance onto her—"is the passport of the
born navigator. And you are one, kindred aura."

That sounded right, sort of. He flicked off a button on his
mike and shocked her with a sotto voce question: "What are
you doing later on?"

"I think we're going to—" When her answer rang out on
her mike, she quickly located the button and turned it off,
too. "To a party."

"Take me with you," ordered the Egyptian. "You've only
started to move. In a few hours, you'll be cooking."

A little jab of alarm in her heart. Aha. This was as good
an opportunity as any to become intrepid and dauntless. She
pulled back her shoulders. The wraparound dress rustled with
a challenging forward boost from her breasts. "I don't care
if you come—it's not my party."

Courage. Because Alain loved her. Audacity and nerve.
What a blessed feeling.

"You're right on the money, trying to get rid of your fears,"
said the Egyptian as the four of them stepped out of the the-

ater. "But let's not be foolhardy: Your voices mentioned danger."

"Oh, let's be foolhardy," Laura said. "For a change."

The bloodshot eyes gleamed, as if challenged, but his beard stayed shut, hiding his lips. It had rained during the lecture. A cab was just passing, and Bond hopped across puddles to flag it down. He negotiated with the driver, and turned back saying that the driver wouldn't take them. *"What?"* asked Charlotte and Laura in one voice.

"I don't know why, he acted sort of dismayed by the address," muttered Bond. "He asked me for it again. I said up River Road, by the Destrehan plantation, and he said he wouldn't take no one to that ghostly spot, not at night."

"Jesus, Bond, do I have to do everything for you?" said Charlotte.

"Honey, please," said Bond.

"If you can't talk to a driver," croaked Charlotte, "it's no wonder you can't talk to—" A second cab zoomed across puddles past the theater, and the Egyptian ran after it, and stopped it. They got in.

"You wanna go up River Road?" asked the driver. He was wearing fatigues, and there were plaques and stickers all over the car saying "Vietnam Vet." "That's where that troll got his lair."

"What troll?" asked the Egyptian.

"That goblin what kills whores to suck 'em dry," said the Vet, and the very thought of it repulsed him so much he hawked and swallowed his spit. "He's hidin out in one of 'em rundown mansions. I talked to a coupla friends, maybe we'll take our guns and drive over this weekend, find the ruin an' smoke 'im out."

"Gee, I should come down here more often. I'm missing all the entertainment." Bond seemed ready to salivate with interest.

"You come plenty often as it is; don't overdo it," said Charlotte.

The Egyptian asked the driver how come he wasn't scared. "Me? I got a piece right unner mah seat, wanna see it? Any of 'em come close, I'll fry 'em just like we did at Day-Nang.

One point I'd like to see cleared, though: He rapes first, doesn't he?''

"This town sure knows how to fan a rumor!" uttered Bond admiringly.

"Oh, we're the greatest when it comes to that," agreed the cab driver. "This town'll change the meaning o' th' word *sucker*."

Bond turned to the Egyptian with a more complex inquiry: Those vampires, were they ghosts or flesh? If they drank blood, then they were flesh themselves, but how come they could slither in through keyholes or filter through walls?

"That's an interesting confusion," said the Egyptian, "between ghost, which is ethereal, and corpse, which is material. What do you think, Laura?"

"I think we should wait for the police to catch that maniac, and then we'll know he's real," she said. She turned away, toward the steamed window. She could see her mouth in it, floating across the streaming shapes of streets. Her lips looked a little swollen, hungry. She hadn't had dinner, and felt a little lightheaded. *I hope they've got food at that party.* She'd been packing it in for the last few days, but seemed to gain no weight. Must be the emotional overexertion. *Hope they don't serve fish tonight. Too light, not filling. Steak, barbecued hamburgers, ribs. Ribs.*

She looked at her mouth in the car window. *This mouth was made for . . .* She wanted to think *kisses*, but her mind shot forward a different word instead—*eating. This mouth was made for eating. Biting, sucking, gobbling, swallowing. No, no, no. Kissing.* She rounded her lips in a kiss aimed at the window, and . . .

Alain slid right past the kiss. In his Chrysler, with the top up, overtaking the cab.

Alain!

It was really him. She saw his profile cutting through the night with determination, his strong hands mastering the wheel. The same air of contained passion she had responded to on the way to the Paris Cafe—she saw it now in the way he fought the foggy street and the slippery roadway.

Her heart dropped to her stomach. Then to her heels. There

was a female next to him. A big smudge of blond hair above the top of a red dress.

Laura put her hand on the window to wipe off the steam, and one fingernail screeched on the glass. The blond head and shoulders rolled in the seat, covering Alain, and Laura felt like screaming at her to get away from the man who had said he loved her. He must have said something funny to the woman just then: The blond shoulders shook up and down. Laura couldn't see her face; she was turned toward the handsome driver. In her mind's eye, Laura saw a vulgar mass of mascara, overprotruding cheekbones, a forehead blocked by dense bangs, a suggestive grin. A whore.

Alain! Alain, I'm here—where are you going?

Alain sped past the cab, with his passenger laughing her heart out.

Alain, I'm yours! Why do you need her?

The Chrysler's back fanned water over the cab's windshield. The vet cabdriver switched the speed of the wipers, and they swept deliriously—but the Chrysler had disappeared.

Laura couldn't catch her breath. This was the sensation one had, she was sure, when a spike was driven into one's body.

This time she could make no excuses for him. (An acquaintance. A relative. A secretary whose car had stalled in the rain.) It didn't work.

She was hurt, hurt, raw with pain. The humiliation of being deceived. The rage at herself. For believing in him so much, for caring, for worrying about his presumed troubles.

"I sense something." The Egyptian's hand crept over hers. She tore it away indignantly. "I sense that an astral blockage just occurred."

"Uh-huh," she said, without intonation, boiling inside.

"This man who loves you—does he have some gender confusion? It might explain what's blurring your own aura."

She felt like shrieking. Then like laughing insanely. Then the storm in her chest roared away, moved to another part of her. She heard it now in her temples only, like a shutter the storm had unfastened. It rapped in threes, as if by rote: I-love-you, I-love-you, I-love-you.

* * *

There were barbecued pork ribs at the party. She buried her face in them.

"You run Whispers? I bought these there," said Jeanette, the woman who was selling the house. She pulled her dress up, and Laura saw a transparent set of underpants, recognized the brand name. "I'm glad the word's getting around," she said, still mawing the ribs. Jeanette had a punk haircut with beams of hair standing erect all around her scalp. She had to lean on the table not to lose her balance.

"I need a drink," declared Jeanette. "How about you?" Without waiting for an answer, she reeled across the dance floor—a living room and den emptied of furniture—and came back with two nearly full big glasses of bourbon. "That's what we call a drink down here," she said. "Spigot water's on the table if you want it." Laura swallowed half her drink.

"The blockage is still there," said the Egyptian, standing next to her.

"Fine. Check me again in ten minutes." She dug back into her ribs.

"If I could find a room to hypnotize you in . . ." sighed the Egyptian.

She guffawed, with ribs in her mouth, "Boy, are you obvious."

"I'm what?" He hadn't understood her around all that chomping.

"Nothing." *I'm eating and getting out of here. What do I have to do with all these twerps?* She gave an involuntary start and didn't know what had impacted so sharply on her senses, and then knew: silence. The rock and roll blaring in the next room had just stopped. "Strip Ball! Strip Ball!" voices yelled enthusiastically behind the partition.

"We're too old for this crowd," said the Egyptian.

She ignored him, and looked around: Good, there were the paper napkins. She was ready to wipe her hands on the tablecloth if necessary.

With the exception of Jeanette, who looked about forty, the people who'd been sweating on the dance floor were all in their early twenties. A couple of meaty boys with red hands had asked her to dance and she had said no. She felt stupid being here; she felt stupid, *period*. As for anger, she felt like a sack stuffed with five clawing cats.

It just wasn't meant to be.

"Let's look for a quiet room upstairs," insisted the Egyptian, trying to take her arm.

She slipped it free. "Will you give me a break? Why don't we just join the party?"

She moved toward the next room, and he shuffled behind her, heavy like a tusker. The light in the next room came from a few dim bulbs in the wall sconces. Here, where they'd been eating, it came from two bare bulbs hanging right over the buffet table. All the other fixtures had been stripped from the place, and some doors were missing their knobs. Maybe Jeanette would unscrew the water taps before leaving in the morning. Laura stepped into the relative dimness of a corner, and Charlotte suddenly collapsed in her arms, with dissolved makeup streaming down her cheeks.

"What's the matter?" Laura said, swaying under the quadroon's weight. Behind her, Bond was smiling uneasily. "You don't want *me* to play Strip Ball, but it's all right for *you* to play around, you selfish jerk!" sobbed Charlotte over her shoulder.

"Honey, you're drunk," tried Bond.

"And if I am? Ask these people." She indicated Laura and the Egyptian. "Ask them how *they* would feel. Listen to this one, guys," she noisily inhaled her tears, "I was there, in the same room, in *bed* with him if you must know, and he had the nerve to call up his *wife* to wish her happy birthday."

"Honey, it was just a gesture," said Bond. "You know I don't love her."

"A gesture! You were naked, too, naked as a jaybird! You were lyin' there all naked from being with me, and you told her—"

"Hey folks, cut that out!" yelled Jeanette. The hostess and practically everyone else were seated on the floor, some women missing their tops, a few of the boys in jocks; pants and other clothing lay the way they had landed by the walls. Just then, a soft plastic ball zoomed elastically above the craning necks, and hit Jeanette in the knee.

"Now he doesn't want me to play Strip Ball," Charlotte

went on, oblivious. "Why don't you *leave* her if you don't love her? You ain't got no kids with her."

Jeanette started to walk over toward where the problem was, and some of the players yelled that she abide by the game's rules, so she stopped to unzip her skirt and slide out of it. "Charlotte," she called, approaching the four, "you hush now and don't ruin my party!"

"I don't want to ruin nothin'. I just want him to lea' me 'lone!"

Jeanette stood in front of Bond, navel showing under her cotton top, an adumbration of pubes peeping out of her underpants. "Let 'er play, mister, she's free and over sixteen."

She threw her hands up toward Laura, as if taking her for a witness, and Laura used the opportunity: "I'm going to have to leave, unfortunately. Can I use your phone to get a taxi?"

"I'm sorry, the phone's been disconnected," said Jeanette, reeling a little. "You—play or leave," she notified the whole bunch.

"I'm leaving," said Laura. "Charlotte, come on, we'll find a ride along the road."

"I don't wanna leave, I wanna stay and have fun!" whined Charlotte. Bond had turned: He was following with interest the progress of the game, and who was taking what piece of clothing off. Laura pulled Charlotte aside. "Honey, come on, this guy's not worth crying over . . ."

"What do you know?" exploded Charlotte with unexpected anger. "What the hell do you know about me? I've been seeing him for four years; he's been promising for four years to divorce that porcupine!"

"What about Rush?" asked Laura, and was sorry.

"Rush? He's a *plug*, that's all he is!" Charlotte erupted.

Laura squeezed her arm. "Charlotte. You're a little loaded. Better come home—"

"I wanna stay! *You* go home and be a spinster!" she bellowed, and warm spit from her breath sprayed Laura's face.

Sickened, Jeanette stepped back into the game and a ball hit her in the shoulder instantly. *"Ow!"* she cried; starting to pull at her cotton top, she yelled at the seated guys: couldn't they get off their asses, come over here and drag these killjoys into the game?

Laura looked for Bond. He was taking his shoes off in preparation.

"Charlotte," Laura tried one more time.

Charlotte stared at her with hostility, and smirked. Laura wiped the spit off her face with her hand. The guys in jocks were getting up, so she threw a "Good-bye, all" over her shoulder, and hurried to the entrance.

Opening the door, she stepped onto the front porch and saw bushes wrapped in misty darkness: bristling, sharp, like a horde of little animals ready to swarm into the house.

The Egyptian rushed out after her and clasped her elbow. "Hang on a second; where ya going?"

"Home to get some sleep," she said, and tried to free her arm. He wouldn't let go of it.

"This is senseless," he panted. "You're at least a mile from the road, you don't know the way . . ."

"Let go of me. *Now*," she threatened quietly.

"And what about that creature on the loose?" He breathed in her face, intoxicating her with the reek of bourbon. "Laura, let's look for a room upstairs, and I'll hypnotize you to sleep."

"I bet you'd like to," she said icily, and tugged with her whole body, but he held on.

"Laura! Laura, wait!" Charlotte was storming out the door after them, guilt trembling in her voice.

"Let go of me, you astral asshole!" But he still wouldn't take his filthy paws off her. Only when she raised her other hand as if to slap him did he free her elbow and pull back, protectively closing his eyes. At that moment, Charlotte was dashing toward them . . .

Les, crouched behind a bush, saw it all happen—or thought he did. A pale wave of mist rolled forward, and the woman fighting the Egyptian lost her footing and tumbled into it just as the quadroon flashed onto the scene, so fast she looked like she'd taken the other's place. When the Egyptian opened his eyes and saw Charlotte running after Laura, he thought she *was* Laura and took off after her. Laura, meanwhile, had gotten up, kicked off her shoes, and grabbed them in one hand. She was able to sprint off into the thickening mist. Charlotte couldn't see the Egyptian, but she heard the clumsy clodhopper shaking the earth behind her. Leaving both of them behind, Laura saw wan tree.

"Laura! Laura!" She could hear Charlotte behind her, pursuing now just mist.

Behind Charlotte panted the Egyptian, groping after her uncertain form. Les had started after both of them, and the three entered a thickness of trees.

Far ahead of them, Laura ran another ten steps, then stopped and looked back. No house. No pursuers. Just the pallid bandage of mist rolling away, into the trees.

But she heard footsteps, behind and to her left, moving away from her. Good. The last thing she wanted was to be captured and carried away by a rescue party of local boys in jocks. She looked up. The sudsy clouds seemed lit from inside. Above their confusion, there was the useless moon.

Under her bare feet, she felt the hardened coolness of a dirt-track. They had arrived this way, in a cab. She could make it to the road, she was sure. She took her high-heeled shoes, untied their straps of snakeskin, ran one through her waistband and retied them, freeing her hands. She pulled down the sleeves of her wraparound dress. It was cool, but pleasantly so—calming the nerves, stopping the rush of the blood. She started to walk, looking right and left. Treetops. Trunks with hollows. Stumps. As she passed them, they seemed to turn and look after her—night's family, carved full of meaning.

This is gonna be tougher'n the toughest scag bust, thought Les, pursuing Laura and the Egyptian, aware of his urban shoes grinding rotten beds of leaves and broken branches. Aware of the night, cool on his neck like a witch's breath. Aware of his Model 20 Magnum. It felt very frail and ineffective against his hip, though it weighed three pounds.

Charlotte, lost in the midst, realized soon that she wasn't going to find Laura. She stopped to look back for the house, saw the Egyptian emerging from the mist behind her, breaking weeds like a groundhog. "Laura, stop! The blockage, the astral blockage—it's over!" *Fucking pig in heat,* swore Charlotte, and ran, thinking it useless to turn and explain who she was. He was going to throw himself on her anyway, that was plain, to clear *her* blockage.

Just then, the Egyptian stumbled and slammed into the ground so hard that he saw supernovas. He sat up, beastly drunk, and saw that Laura's silhouette had doubled before him—who else was there?

That was all he saw of Les, who was racing past him pursuing Charlotte, his steps so synchronized with hers that she could hear only her own body breaking through the screens of twigs. Still thinking he was chasing Laura, Les saw the girl unclearly, but well enough to stay on her trail. He heard torn branches behind him, and turned to see if it was the swami, catching up with them again.

He saw a dark branch come alive and slip off a tree. As if a creature of the forest had been lying there, waiting for their passage, so it could leap down and pursue them. An agile, though not tall, body started passing through the comb of the forest, nimble and light as a shadow.

Pausing by a tree trunk, Les looked back, eyes widening, skin chilling off, fingers beginning to creep toward his Magnum. The form stalking him was dark and definitely human-shaped. It seemed to wear dark clothing, but the clothing fit the body tightly, like a skin; he could tell by the way the feline form was advancing, without flap or flutter. He saw a patch of milkier complexion, the face. Barely breathing, Les controlled his fear, and let him come even closer. A pair of eyes kindled up in the face, yellow-greenish, like big fireflies.

At that moment, all three heard the river ahead. Charlotte mistook the lowering of the ground toward it for what she remembered of the dirt track leading to the house, and kicked into high gear. The beast in pursuit uttered a sort of bray of joy, short and low and perfectly audible, as if the river, his home ground, reassured him of the imminent contentment of his lusts. He stalked with more confidence, and Les, seeing him so close, his movements so instinctively perfect, was instantly convinced of who and what he had here. And the bray, animalistic and hungry, reinforced his conviction. "I've got 'im, Dale!" he whispered to the absent Cabot. "This is him, the big one!"

Big rivers make little noise, except at the edges, where their weeping gets snarled in the unkempt hairiness of half-unburied roots. Charlotte heard that rustle/murmur, too, and realized that she wasn't near the house after all. She turned. "Okay, mister, you win—I don't know where I am," she told the approaching figure behind her, and saw how much thinner he was than the Egyptian, how sprightly in his run across the shrub, and how clear green his eyes had become.

"Help!" she cried too late, feeling around for a weapon, a branch, or something. She tripped backward, balanced herself, and bumped hard into a body. She turned and saw right next to her face the twins of those green eyes. She felt a body clad in rough woolen cloth, and as her hand drew away from it, repulsed by its coarseness, she felt a cold hand, moist, flaccid. Her fingers dug into the flesh, flabby and clammy like a cadaver's. And underneath another layer of tissue, she felt the merciless toughness of bone.

The eyes behind her came closer. Held by the second creature, Charlotte suddenly knew that she was doomed. "Oh, Mother," she said softly, her big body shaking from head to toe. The creature advancing on her whipped out a sort of cane.

Les pulled the Magnum just as the second creature gave Charlotte a jab in the chest. It was enough to send Charlotte wading backward into the water. "Freeze!" faltered Les, but the two were so inebriated by the smell of the prey that they simply didn't hear him. Teeth chattering, Les marched on the girl's aggressors, beginning a Hail Mary in Latin: *Ave Maria, gratia plena, Dominus tecum* . . . He interrupted it to holler "Freeze!" again, much louder, and point the gun just as the creature with the cane leaped in the water after the girl, pulled a blade out of it, flashed it in the dim luminescence of the moon-impregnated clouds.

The blade made the noise a machete makes slashing a taut gunnysack. Charlotte felt her neck explode open. The other creature sprang to the spot, and its hungry mouth sealed its lips on the gash, airtight like tentacles. Les, rushing through the shrub, let a shot roar above the killers' head, stopped, took aim. The second shot banged across the dark, hitting fully one of the bodies, the feeding one, but the creature barely moved. The other turned, baring its teeth. It flashed the saber, and started for Les.

In the next few instants, Les felt this was the end. And if he survived, then it was the loony bin for him, making baskets and doormats that said God Bless Our Home.

Charlotte fell in the river. Looking up, her dying eyes saw the moon, bluish through the quivering film of water, and then pinkish from a wisp of blood, her own, mixed into the river. That was all the blood she saw, a wisp, though her throat had been opened more than halfway.

The creature sucking at her throat plunged into the water with her. The other had climbed onto the shore, and Les let him have it again: ka-*boom*, from all 8.75 inches of the barrel. The bullet ripped the air, whipped into the creature with 972 Joules of energy, or 717 foot-pounds. The creature gaped at the hole in his chest, then kept advancing. The saber was almost upon Les.

The little cop realized that he just couldn't, wasn't allowed to, had no room to panic. Slowly, he lowered the gun again. *Benedicta tu in Mulieribus.* Ka-BOOM. *Et benedictus fructus ventris tuis, Iesus.* The saber flashed down and nicked his ear. Les stuck the gun into the hole made by the two other bullets, right where humans have their hearts: *Ka-BOOM!* The creature neighed like the devil's own steed asking for hell's gates to open, and collapsed at Detective Vitrolly's feet.

Only now did he remember that he had a flashlight. He flicked it on, and pointed it toward the water. The girl's body was floating on its back, and Les saw that the victim wasn't Laura.

The mist was muffling the sounds. The Egyptian heard distant yells, and shots that sounded as if fired from a B-B gun. He was too drunk to care.

For a while he lay where he had fallen, then got himself up, staggered on, came finally to a hardened roadway. He thought it must lead to the River Road. Without knowing it, he was following almost in Laura's footsteps.

Laura was far ahead by now, deep into the night. She'd heard neither shots nor yells for help.

Her feet had gotten used to the soberingly damp ground. She wondered remorsefully what had happened to the Egyptian. She had been so bitchy to him. She had taken out on him her bitter disappointment at seeing Alain with another woman. She'd call him tomorrow and apologize.

There was no way to tell if she was moving in the right direction. There was no moon, and no stars—she wouldn't have known how to read their position anyway. But there was a road under her, and it had to lead somewhere, to another road; hopefully, a well-traveled hardtop to a house with a phone.

Where was Alain now? She flashed on the blond woman in his embrace. Perhaps opening his shirt, the way she had planned to do it, button by button. She saw red picturing the scene, and chastised herself. He'd been a jerk, but she didn't own him, or anything.

The darkness was deepening. The trees were richer, weaving branches into branches over the road, which had shrunk to a path. Go back? But she had already passed a fork in the road: how would she know now which diverging course to take? *Walk on, Laura, you might be in Florida by tomorrow.*

The hum of the trees was addictive. She felt like opening her lips and murmuring with the trees. The night was deepening inside her and she found herself in a state of electrified palpitation, loving the darkness for its cleansing effect, and yet dreading what it might shape itself into. Demented fantasy: meet Alain, now, on this benighted pathway. Let him stand abruptly in the brush, between two trees, with a smile of demonic lechery on his lips. He'd horrify the wits out of her, and how wonderful that would be. Silence her jealousy, let her fall into his arms, sedated by terror as by wine, that incredible wine they'd had at the Paris Cafe.

Be sane, Laura. She heard a noise, like that of an engine. *Groll, groll, groll, groll,* a boat of some kind. She wasn't far from the river, or one of its canals. It gave her heart; her shoulders threw off a weight. *I'm not scared.* She started to walk faster, and heard dogs howl. The pathway took a turn, and the trees ended; an opulent garden lay before her, and towering behind the geometry of flowers, two Greek temple structures seemed to grin with the bared teeth of their columns. She stopped, noticing there was no light whatsoever in them. *I hope this isn't the ruin that cabdriver was mentioning.*

She encouraged herself: The effect came from the columns, looking like mouths with torn-off lips. There were no lights because everyone was asleep. But she didn't have the energy to go on. The garden and the mansion had somehow spellbound her into not moving.

She looked back, to the canyon of the winding path between the masses of trees. Something moved on it. An animal.

Something like a minor devil trotted toward her. She saw eyes in a long black face, like a muzzle, a pair of rigid projections above the low forehead, like little horns. The devil's face on a four-legged body. It trotted unhurriedly toward her, making no other noise, as if it wanted to sniff her, and the eyes beamed up at her. Fascinated, she looked at the immobile horns: They seemed related in their fixedness to the fixedness of the eyes.

She spun around, headed at an unbridled gallop toward the temples, and the howls and barks immediately revealed their source: a dog kennel with tall wire walls, just by the first temple, with seething masses growling and snarling ferociously inside. But somehow they were less spooky than the little quadruped with horns, or the dark, lifeless mausoleums that loomed over her. Laura raced past untrimmed bushes of boxwood looking like shaggy beasts themselves, hopped onto a cracked set of steps, identified the faint reflection of a beveled door, leaned on it. It gave in. A cavelike vestibule was what she saw ahead. *I'm in one of those tourist plantations,* she thought. *But where are the guards and what about that dog kennel?*

"Good evening," tolled a voice like a bronze imitation of a human's. "Welcome to Belle Hellène."

It nearly whisked her off her feet. She looked, and to her left, in the opening of a corridor, there stood a shockingly thin old man, raising a brass candleholder. In the candle flames, his eyes shone like balls of painted crystal. The bags under his eyes were grotesquely wrinkled, and his chalk-white hair was a mass seemingly not of strands but of stone: like a chiseled marble wig over an ovoid skull.

"Oh, God, you gave me a start." She pressed her hand on her heart, and swallowed repeatedly. Emory advanced with the same voracious glint in his eyes Laura remembered from the airport and had also noticed the day he passed her in the brougham. Like a carnivore spotting his catch. Her hand moved from her heart to make sure her dress was covering her. "Good evening, sorry to bust in like this. Something . . . something out there scared me," she explained her presence. "Something with horns."

"Malcolm," called Emory.

A colossal black valet in a livery approached from the other end of the vestibule, also with a candle.

"I think Zoltan has slipped out of the kennel again. One of my younger dobermans. He just had his ears trimmed. They're in little casts; that's what looked like horns out there."

"I see. Can I use your phone?" she asked. Malcolm had disappeared as if by sleight of hand; he'd been there a second before.

"Of course. What's the emergency?"

Come on, she told herself, *the old mummer's harmless*. "I left a party next door," she said, "and I need a ride back to town."

"You're welcome to call, but I'm afraid no one will come out here at so late an hour. Laura, is it?"

"Emory, is it?" she mimicked him.

His glance changed, softened, enriched by a tinge of vanity—pleased to be recognized. "My age drives me to oversleep, but sometimes I find myself awake at an hour like this, at the height of my often slumberous senses," he said with beautiful poetic cadence, as if he was remembering the baroque, complicated lines. "Wouldn't you prefer my society for an hour, and then Malcolm could put you up in Alain's room until morning? We can get you a taxicab then."

"Well, I don't know," she answered uncertainly. "What were you doing up at this hour?"

"Having a glass of wine. Rereading books I've read a thousand times. Doing and undoing my future in a game of cards."

His eyes had changed completely. From imperious and cold, they had turned velvety and soft, even humble. He held a hand out.

"Okay, I guess," she murmured, not admitting to herself that it was Alain's room, even without Alain in it, that had prompted her decision.

She hadn't guessed what reaction her acquiescence would bring out in the old man. He suddenly straightened like a red-coated guard outside Buckingham Palace, took her arm, and escorted her up a stairway wide enough for his horse-and-brougham. "Malcolm, bring another glass to the Carpathian room," he called to the dark behind him. Emboldened by his style, Laura pulled back her shoulders, boosted her breasts forward, and tried to be regal even barefoot, her snakeskin shoes still dangling at her waist.

For a few moments, the world was a nebulous orbit around the glow of the candle moving up the stairs, to which the man and woman seemed attached. To Laura's right, family portraits in oil paraded, brought to a yellowish semblance of life by the passing of the candle. And Alain's own face, not oil, a photograph in an oval frame, passed too, staring at her. "Where's Alain?" she asked.

"I think up on the river. You know, he wasn't destined to take the reins, but this family lost an older heir, and the mantle fell on his shoulders. I'm afraid we're like the Augean stable, you remember? Three thousand oxen fouled it for thirty years, then Hercules was called in to sweep it. Well, Alain's sweeping ours. Gallantly."

"You speak like a poet," she said.

"I was one. Not one of the best . . . I believe Alain and you are acquainted . . . *closely*?" He accented the word, and for some reason she wasn't offended. "Not closely," she said, seeing a vast hall open before them.

Malcolm must have taken a short cut. He was adding candles to a table with an astrolabe, a piece of bone in a bauble of glass mounted in gilt fringes, a set of cards, several books, all open. She felt the cool wind of steeply high vaults above her, and saw a grandiflora of red stained glass, over a coat of arms with the Lecouveur name in Gothic fonts.

The old man guided her into a chair with a steely grip of his hand, explaining that the emergency team still hadn't arrived to restore power to the estate. Malcolm was marching back and forth, each time bringing more candles, till two dozen of them crowned the long table like living gems. The room, though a little decrepit, was fully and grandiosely visible now; Emory's grace of speech and gesture were also sufficiently well lit. Laura noticed how amazingly timed and unprecipitous his movements were, as if no inelegant reflex was ever permitted inside that body, along those aged limbs. Or as if he'd done it before, over and over, and the movements had grown into their own rhythm like a second heartbeat.

"Cards! Cards!" he surprised her, rubbing his hands vivaciously, boyishly. "You play?" She said she played gin rummy. "I hope you lose," he said, shuffling the cards. "Because, *qui gagne au jeu perde en amour:* Who wins at cards loses in love. I hope I'm not putting you off with my ostentatious deportment?" he said, worried suddenly. She shook her head, and tasted the wine that Malcolm had poured for her.

She recognized the deep lack-of-taste kind of taste. And then an inebriation of the strangest sort spread in her head. A sort of connection with the high vaults above, and with the unseen cellars, basements, whatever they were underneath, as if her mind was on a vertical axis between them, free to move up and down with the agility of quicksilver. "Of course I'm not put off," she said hurriedly. "I think you give sparkle to everything you touch: You shouldn't be so selfish with it, though; it seems to be for the family and for no one else."

He was pensive for just an instant. "You Americans," he said. "The *world* is your family, and the present is your tradition. You are right," he continued, as if conceding defeat. "Alain is more like you than like me. Choosing the family was a sacrifice for him. But he made the sacrifice. Like any Lecouveur before him." He rolled his voice at the room, with pride. "Alain paid homage to these walls with furs from beasts slaughtered in the Carpathians. With weapons whose steel remembers how it was tempered by our enemies' blood. With portraits of men who share one trait: loyalty to oneself, and that means loyalty to the clan. How can Alain escape such a heritage, and such a wealth of meaning?''

"Or such a curse," she said, feeling quite safe for some reason. His pouchy eyelids fluttered.

"Or such a curse," he admitted. "But better a curse than anonymity. You see, mediocrity was never befriended by us Lecouveurs. We can be vile and raw, yet remain stately and exemplary. We can shine or succumb to darkness. But we can't just *be*. Being is a state of mediocrity. And we're anything but mediocre." His hand groped on the table for a tattered old edition, and it nearly crumbled under his touch: "Do you like Lord Byron?"

Laura smiled. "Yes. What I remember of him."

"He had a word for the others—the mediocres: the flower of Adam's bastards. We, of course, are not bastards. We are the legitimate few." He stopped to appraise her reaction, continued: "Let me be conceited. I find he wrote his lines for me."

She shrugged, lenient. All this smoke, noise, and fire, for her. Nice stroke on the ego. "For instance?" she inquired.

Lecouveur was quiet for a moment, remembering. Then:

> I have not loved the World, nor the World me;
> I have not flattered its rank breath, nor bowed
> To its idolatries a patient knee.

She liked it so much that she clapped. He looked so harmlessly overweening that she felt like kissing him on the cheek—but the pouched eyes repulsed her a little. "Bravo, Emory. One more!"

> Let there be light! said God, and there was light!
> Let there be blood! says man, and there's a sea!

"And how is this one about you?" laughed Laura.

"It may not be about me, but I like the callousness of its truth."

"Did he write anything on how you feel about life?"

He paused, drank a little wine. "You are, though untrained, so naturally astute," he complimented her. "He wrote about how I feel now, in my sorry old hour, turning over the reins. It runs:

> What is the worst of woes that wait on Age?
> What stamps the wrinkle deeper on the brow?

He gave suspenseful resonance to the question. His hand rustled across the tableful of cards, and grasped hers. Laura started: It was colder than anything alive she'd ever touched, and intimidatingly strong. She didn't feel like breaking his flow, though. *I'll pull it back as soon as he's done with his classics.*

Holding her hand, his expression became unexpectedly close and sincere. Younger, too. "What is the worst of woes?" He answered:

> To view each loved one blotted from Life's page,
> And be alone on earth, as I am now.

There was a silence.

"Did you love many women who died?" asked Laura.

She was stunned by her own question. She hadn't been aware of any thought process leading to it.

But Lecouveur was impressed. "Amazing perception!" he whispered. "Yes. That has been my life. And being of good birth and seductive in my prime, I piled up conquest upon conquest. To find myself lonelier now than the words of the poet can express. Not like Alain, " he added brusquely.

"Alain?" she frowned, taken by surprise.

"Alain is clever. He wants one love. He'll get it. I scattered myself into many flames, poured my youth into many chalices. Alain," he said with firmness, "knows the worth of love, and does not use the word lightly. The trouble is . . ."

She was sipping his words, savoring them, a smile unconsciously starting to widen her mouth. Lecouveur's look changed from mellow and nostalgic to direct, regaining the amused malice she'd seen in it before. "You like him, don't you?" he asked, and grinned.

He waited for her reaction, with a hungry, almost prurient interest.

"I do," she answered uncomfortably.

"This may just not be his time to seek a mate, to build something stable. The fortunes of the clan are taking precedence."

"But that," she retorted, "is up to him, isn't it?"

She heard her voice in the big room, colder, more aggressive than she wanted it to sound. *I love him. Look how I rise to his defense . . . And he loves me.* She sipped more wine, to relax.

"Of course it's up to him." Emory looked down into the cards. "You lost," he said.

She felt the wine, and reclined in her chair. "I'm glad. I'll win at love."

"You already have," he said with a smile. "I mean, love is in you. It's written in your fate, and in your body."

The prurience had vanished from his eyes. Sweet strange granddad, he enveloped her in a look of moist warmth. It would have been manly vigor fifty years before. "Malcolm will conduct you to Alain's room," he said. "And forgive my prolixity."

"You can be so charming," she said, rising, "and so can Alain."

"Alain more than I," said Emory. A tickled little chuckle animated the heavy cheeks, the flab under the eyes. "Alain is entirely addictive."

Alain knows the worth of love. Emory said it. And he doesn't use the word lightly.

She followed Malcolm's candle down the colossal stairway, across the lower vestibule and along a glass-enclosed gallery, humid with potted plants. Outside the gallery, the moon had finally emerged. The trees, the bushes, everything was silver. She saw the brougham Emory had ridden in two weeks before. Silver, too. In the enchantment of moonlight, it seemed impossible to imagine that Alain would leave the sion, no matter how otherwise tempting the outside world was.

She couldn't wait to see his room.

The stairway to it had no family portraits. It was a bare flight of polished wood between whitewashed walls, surprising in their starkness. At the top, it gave onto a kind of lobby flanked with doors, and the door to his bedroom was the last, after a bathroom that Malcolm showed her by shining the candle toward a deco interior, with ceramic-decorated tub and frosted glass enclosing a shower. Alain's room was deco, too, black deco bed with white sheets and pillows and black comforter, deco chest of drawers, and photos and etchings of ships and barges, looking as if they had been taken or printed in the thirties. The furniture was reasonably well kept, but the style didn't seem his. She asked Malcolm if it had been someone else's before. He was arranging candles on the deco dresser.

"I wouldn't know, Miss," he said, dull, lifeless. "Don't you start a fire," he warned her, then brought a stack of towels and put them on the bed and wished her good-night.

She wished him good night, too; he closed the door, and she lit more candles. Inspecting the walk-in closet, she found jackets and slacks and shirts, all pretty straight stuff. A magazine rack by the bed contained issues of *Fortune, Business News, Newsweek*. There were sections of the *Wall Street Journal* and the *Times-Picayune* between the rack and the bed. The window was shaded by curtains. The bed was made, but when she brought her face close to it, she found that the bedding wasn't fresh. A slight musky odor, the smell she had smelled on him after he'd been a whole day on the river. She felt a delicious fear of taking off her dress and lying in his scent. Where was he now? Still with that woman?

She showered, and even the touch of the water seemed to bring some intimacy with Alain. She was sure he came back sometimes so exhausted that he collapsed in bed full of that musky smell, without bothering to scrub it off first. Young males, alone, unobserved.

The soles of her feet were bruised and scratched from the long barefoot walk. She felt like touching her own body: She hadn't done it in so long, she needed to learn it again. Then she thought of the old man in the other wing of the house, and resisted the urge. Her watch read four in the morning.

She could leave no candles on. She blew them out, and the dark was so sudden and total that she had to grope for the bed. She lay down and pulled the covers over her. Softer than she had expected. She had felt so intensely that tonight she'd be making love to Alain—well, this wasn't such a bad second.

Out in the kennel, a dog howled unexpectedly.

Then, before Laura could open her eyes, her door opened. She had been dreaming something about Alain. Back from the river, he had pierced the night with strong headlights that had reflected into the bedroom. Emory was on the porch in her dream, insisting to Alain that she had come here of her own free will. The suddenly opening door had shattered the dream. Her head bobbed up from the pillow: The door was open wide, a dark-clad man silhouetted against it, the square opening of the lobby dark and cold behind it, like a trapdoor into a catacomb.

Feverishly she grabbed her left wrist and dug the nails of her right fingers in it, staring all the while, as if aghast alertness could cancel out the intruder. Her fingernails stung hard at her skin, but she was wide awake, and the silhouette had a sort of familiarity, although it was so dark that she could make out no details of the face or clothes.

"Alain?" she whispered.

The whisper crystallized in her throat. He made a leap she thought only a master dancer could manage, the reflection of his eyes streaking the room like lightning. He fell on her like a devil, and in a growl that sounded like Alain, asked "Why did you come?" He suffocated her with heavy lips, and she fell back under his weight. He pulled back his mouth and his teeth chattered feverishly. She threw her arms around the pleasantly muscular mass of his back. His mouth touched her ear, slipped below it, his teeth played with a spot on her neck.

"Alain . . . wait", she managed to whisper, feeling him so frenzied, so feverish in her arms, that she wanted to help him, to relieve him, to soothe him. He moved as if he was ripping his own clothes off, while keeping her locked in the hold of his other arm. She wanted to take off herself the little she was wearing, but her fingers dug into his back as his teeth ripped her skin. "No!" Laura cried out, stunned, and it sounded like a helpless squeal. Her arms flailed, pulled at him in a supreme but vain effort to throw him off.

"*Nooooooo!*" She screamed fully this time, from the pain and from the horror, and tried to knock him off her again, and couldn't. Well saddled on her body, he cut deeper. She twitched. Her arms fell.

Something flowed out of her. Something was being drawn out of her, a slow, painful draining that was a torture, and yet at the same time a relief. He shook in her arms more, but remained attached tightly to her neck. Then he rose between her parted knees, clutched the side of her underwear, and pulled. It snapped noiselessly, and Laura didn't, couldn't try to resist it. She lived a second of girlish fear: She wasn't ready. He found the crib of her body open, couched himself in it, and throbbed and vibrated with a passion that came from the dawn of time.

As the dread subsided, she started to breathe, possessed in this monstrous manner, but conscious, surviving. A curious sad langour, a sort of shamed lasciviousness filled her, and almost a sort of pity for this beast whose uncontrollable thirst for one liquid of her body motivated the uncontrollable urge to give her one of his. But she was too frightened and re-pulsed to touch any part of him: she let her arms lay defeated by her sides, and a defense mechanism made her start bab-bling mangled words: "Alain . . . please . . . easy, sweet-heart." At the word *sweetheart*, he throbbed mightily and although not letting go of her neck, he neighed a muffled neigh of pleased confirmation, or of abject scorn.

Laura passed out.

When she came to, the darkness was as full, as tangible, as before. So little light came through the shutters that she barely made out his face, on the pillow next to her.

It was, the little she could see of it, beautiful.

Alain at his loveliest, satisfied, replete. Lips dark, they would've probably looked a resplendent crimson by candle-light, or any other light. Forehead smooth, dark hair flowing wavily on the pillow. Cheekbones gorgeous, the dark mass of his chest heaving peacefully.

One love, she thought. *One love.*

His hand was next to her face. She touched it, felt the porous flabbiness of the skin . . . and *stared*.

She felt fear hammering, pounding inside her. The hand looked like time's hand itself—a monster of antiquity—and the arm springing from it looked ancient like a forgotten piece of sculpture.

This isn't Alain.

Carefully, stealthily, she could slip out of the bed, perhaps light a candle. *This isn't Alain.* She didn't care who he was with right now. With another woman, somewhere in the big indifferent town, under the vulgar lighting of a bar, in a bed smelling of another woman's body. Thank God *this* wasn't Alain.

She was shaking. She was trembling from head to toe.

The floor creaked. The thing on the bed opened its eyes.

It looked at her, and the memory of the ordeal rushed into her brain. The fear of that giant leap was, above all, unbearable. The thing stirred upward. Laura threw herself away from his reach, landed with a brutal thud on the rug by the bed. She heard the bedsprings protest under his violent movement, felt him almost on her. She screamed frenziedly, flipped over on her belly. To crawl away, away from the bed.

He leaped again, landed on her, and his nakedness slapped against the whole length of her back. She opened her mouth to scream and a hand clamped over her lips. Through the repellent fingers, she uttered a grotesque bray of fear, and shook him off. His other hand raked her shoulders with overgrown nails.

She flew toward the open door. One step ahead, he was on her again. She brought up one foot, kicked back hard into yielding flesh. She fled into the lobby, toward the obscure light at its other end. A roar of pain and anger rose behind her and an arm coiled itself around her stomach. In the struggle, she fell on her face and he collapsed on top of her. His mouth went for her old wounds. The teeth didn't nibble this time. They sank in. The draining feeling, monstrously scary and pleasant, sent her body suddenly all atingle. But her mind resisted it. *I'll survive this. I won't die. Or go crazy. I'll think of Alain.*

She felt a knee behind her, knocking her knees apart. An unexpected defense mechanism kicked in, with thoughts and visions of Alain. Alain needed this from her, she told herself. He loved her so. After quenching his first frenzy, he would be such a generously patient lover. "Alain," she moaned distortedly, "wait." Her insides were contracted by fear, but he was becoming by the second turgid again. Like a beast mounted by another, Laura groaned sweetly, "Alain . . . not so hard, honey . . . let me move . . . with you. . . ."

He seemed to take pity on her, and slowed enough for her to unclench the tautness of her muscles. Forgetting about her neck, she uttered little gasps of feverish concentration, making herself accept the man. His hands freed the submitting woman, and began to stroke her shoulders, her back, her thighs. . . .

Her mind had saved her. This wasn't so terrible. This didn't seem impossible to overcome, scarring beyond repair. She felt tears growing behind her hot eyelids, soothing tears, and called them to flow faster and richer, like a cure. . . .

She fainted again. He let her sprawl forward, and her body, whitened by the polish of the night, kept stirring, pricked by little spasms. He moved on her, leisurely now, unhungry, just feasting.

Predawn light started to gray up the narrow spaces between the shutter slats. He finally detached his body from the woman's and stood. He contemplated her satedly, eyes following her curvatures, as if remembering them for a later, lonelier time.

Then his grotesque-looking hands scooped her off the floor, and carried her back to bed. He took a towel and wiped the drops of blood off her neck. Her body was young and strong; her blood coagulated superbly. He stepped into the bathroom, wetted another towel, moved back to her, and, with an artist's gentleness, washed the face, neck, and shoulders of his most recent masterpiece.

9

Indistinct shapes, unclear colors. The amorphous movement of fireflies, wheeling, whirling, as in a kinetic painting.

Her vision adjusted and she saw what they were: specks of dust, multicolored, suspended in a bright beam of sunlight.

She saw her wristwatch on the floor: 9:42.

She was lying on her stomach. Her face was hanging off Alain's bed above the floor. Her watch lay before her eyes, close to her abandoned wraparound dress.

Hungry. She was ravenously hungry.

Suddenly she froze and whipped her hands up to her neck, clearly aware of what had happened. Her hair stood on end so hard and so quickly that she heard its ends crackle electrically.

Am I still alive?

Try walking first. One step. Then another. Don't push yourself. Everything starts with just one step.

Birds chirped and twitted outside.

Somehow what had happened was both incredibly simple, and impossible to comprehend.

The voices! she thought. *The voices!*

They had been right, those voices, mercilessly right. She should have stayed away from New Orleans. The Egyptian had warned her, too. Alain . . .

Oh, Alain. Oh God, Alain. Everything had happened for him and because of him.

She tried to get her wits together. Pull energy from every cell and fiber, make fistfuls of courage out of it, build a frame for the battered body and scarred mind.

Let's get out of here first. But to what? What sort of world, what sort of future?

She slipped into her dress, put on her shoes, then took her shoes off again. She needed every advantage she could gain. With luck she would make it to the freeway and hitchhike into town. Hitchhiking seemed such an undangerous sport now.

She didn't have the guts to look in a mirror. She stepped into the stark lobby, walked along to the stairway, and downstairs. On the ground floor she found a living room with scattered boxes: new sets of glasses for a bar had just been brought in, and the bar was there, too, a nice one, with stools and a phone.

Not a sound, not a stir from another person. The ground floor had wide French doors opening into a French garden. No human shadow crossed it in any direction.

She walked to the bar and picked up the phone. With no difficulty she got the operator, who offered to ring a cab company for her. She did. All very simple. A cab would be there in half an hour. Yes, Belle Hellène, drivers knew the place.

Where was he, the degenerate? Lying in state in his Carpathian room, waiting for the sun to set again? She thought about it, and decided that nothing in the world would get her to climb the stairway to the other wing, to find Emory, to throw more cruel light over this horror.

What about Alain? What was the truth about Alain?

Tears stole up on her. Looking behind the bar for something to wipe her eyes, she saw herself in the bar's mirror: a pale but reasonably normal looking female. Dress crumpled like she had slept in it. As she stared at herself, she remembered that she had promised Cabot to let him know about every move she made. She hadn't told him about the dinner she was supposed to have with Alain.

But the dinner hadn't taken place. And she, alone, of her own free will, had chosen to leave that party last night. She should've stayed at the party. Bored perhaps, grossed out maybe, but protected.

I'll call Cabot as soon as I get home. Wait a second, what am I going to tell him?

The first time she had been attacked, everyone had behaved as if it was exciting. Marion and Charlotte drooling for more details. The cops, interested in the real, the truly important cases. The murders.

She had been examined by a doctor. Her blood tests had been fine. Maybe they'd be fine this time, too, except that the last thing she wanted was to tell anybody, to ask anyone to look at her body. Or to retell the story. To reenact it for the police, who'd repress lecherous grins while a homicide stenographer would tap hieroglyphs on long bands of paper about how it had happened, how long it had lasted, had she struggled, had she *seen him*?

She felt that a shameful secret was filling all of her, from her scalp to her toes. Inside this little body, five feet four, a giant tunnel was opening into an unknown world. Twin to the world she knew, yet unseen like the reverse side of the moon. She felt ready to fall through a dark and thunderous space, and land on a nightmarishly subplanetary surface. What nameless revelation was awaiting her there?

The cab!

Holding purse and shoes, she darted outside, and the glare of the sun hit her like a rain of liquid brass, cascading its fiery revenge on her face, her shoulders, her arms, her whole body.

There was no one anywhere as far as her eyes could search the grounds.

Orienting herself, she started toward the gates, then turned back for one last look. Staring at the mansion, she did something she had never done before, but occasionally seen done by Catholics. She raised her palm, and plowed the air with it in a sign of the cross that covered half of her. Then, behind that unseen protection, she hurried toward the gates and the salvation lying beyond them.

The cab deposited her on Ursulines Street.

She paid the driver, then climbed the outer stairwell, marveling at her own resources of vitality.

A manila envelope lay on her doorstep. She picked it up.

Quite heavy, feeling like a book—who was sending her a book?

Then she saw the note pinned to it: *Call me when you get in. The Egyptian.* And his phone number.

Must be some catalog of astral encounters. She unlocked her door, expecting subconsciously to step in and be sucked into a pit cracking open right under her feet. Or the rosewood walls might suddenly draw together, boxing her into an untimely coffin. She heard the phone, and its realistic ring calmed her down a little.

"Hi there," said Cabot. "I thought you and I had a deal."

She puffed air through her open mouth, feeling an intense thirst. "What about it?" she asked defensively.

"You were supposed to let me know when you went out and with who," he said, and she heard irritation in the way he crumpled his words. "Why'n't you do it last night?"

"You were supposed to have your men one step behind me at all times," she retorted. "What happened to that part of the deal?"

"Les was right behind you. He saved your life last night."

"He what?" Little Les with his big nose had tailed her to Belle Hellène? Pulled the beast off her body? Kindly carried her back to the bed and let her sleep it off?

"We've got the killer," announced Cabot, and she realized that it wasn't irritation that deformed his speech—it was elation.

"You got him?"

She was breathless. Mind blanked out.

But Alain rose above her blank mind. He was clean. Uninvolved. Nothing to do with the whole bloody mess.

"Who is he?" she managed to ask.

"We haven't established the identity yet. Can you come over here?" asked Cabot. "I think it'll help my inquiry if you see him."

The white shroud was pulled back brutally. Mayberry unraveled it off toes stiffened by rigor mortis.

"I found some anatomical modifications inside him that are absolutely astounding, but it's still beyond question that he's a human. The digestive tract has the most amazing peculiarities. You know, the gut breaks down food into amino acids, fatty acids, glycerol, sugars. Now the absorption of these products is done almost exclusively in the small intestine, which has an enormous surface of activity, due to the *plicae circulares*, or folds of the intestine's inner mucosa. To this area is added more area from the *villi*, those little fingers 'bout one millimeter tall that grow over the whole mucous membrane. Now, this guy's got more little creases or fingers than any human I've ever dissected—as if his diet was the hardest to break down of all known diets."

The dead creature seemed to measure about five one or two. His forehead was low like an angled roof, and the pro-tuberances over his sunken eyes appeared conic. Good-sized ears stuck out of his rich hair, but there was little hair grow-ing on his face, or on the rest of his body.

Abundant lighting had been set up around the tray he lay on. The light entered the fist-sized hole on the left side of his chest, which showed no shininess of coagulated blood, be-cause the burned gunpowder from Les's gun had coated it in chimneylike soot.

He was bestially muscular. Under his rib cage, his stomach was collapsed inside, as if from endless hunger. His waist was amazingly thin, and he had almost no buttocks. But the thighs, calves, and feet bulged with sinew. "When he leaps, he flies," had been Mayberry's earlier assessment, as he had touched the blocks of muscles on his legs.

The nose was sunken at the bridge; the mouth had round lips, vitriolically purple. The eyelashes looked like they'd been snatched off his lids; underneath, the eyes had a staid glaucousness.

Somehow, the people looking at him couldn't shake the feeling that his mouth was suppressing a leer. That the eyes, though fixed, were watching. That the ears, which appeared cocked to catch the unheard sounds of the living, perhaps received the amorphous rumble of life from beyond the trans-parent veil of death.

"So what if he's got that many creases and thingamabobs in his gut?" asked Cabot nervously.

"Well, he's a marvel of nature," said Mayberry, "because when I cut him, I found the *villi* lying flat on the mucous membrane, which means that he'd been fasting for quite a while.''

"That makes sense," intervened Les. "He only cut her up. The other fellow done the suckin'.''

"After such fasting he should've had zero energy," protested Mayberry. "Anyway, he's got no large intestine to speak of. When I got into what should be the distal colon, I found no longitudinal muscle. Now, how this gut could empty its crap without such a muscle is a mystery to me. Moreover, his rectal sphincter is tightly grown together, as if really never required to function. I think it's almost atrophied.''

"So what are you saying?" asked Jackie Webster. She was aware of the young woman beside her turning green.

Les slapped his forehead. "Either he makes no shit, or he gets rid of it some other way, right?''

"Where is the bathroom?" asked Laura. Mayberry gave her a look, but couldn't help concluding, "That was my original assumption: this creature's physiologically adapted to an exclusively liquid diet.''

Cabot's eyes were glowing like cigars. "Blood, huh?''

"Blood," confirmed Mayberry. "Which renders him, uh . . . nonexcremental.''

"Please," said Laura, wiping clammy face with clammy fingers. "I'm going to be sick.''

"Thataway, ma'am," said Les, and she staggered away.

The genitals, clearly exposed, built up a rich pyramid between his muscular thighs. The penis was thicker than a grown cucumber, and the testes stuffed up the sac like plump purple tennis balls.

Cabot paced, his enthusiasm mitigated by worry. Caught him, they had, and caught him in the act. The other one's body would turn up somewhere along the river in a day or two. But was this a human? A valid candidate for the department's idea of a culprit?

"When's Knowles coming over to see the body?" he asked.

"He called from Will's Point, said he'd drop in this evening," informed Jackie.

Cabot prowled again, struggling to save a sliver of remembrance from a bog of time. "Hey, Cahill," he called at the technician, "Don't this guy remind you of them mooncalves used to live down by the river? Used to be known as muck-skins?''

"Yeah," said Cahill. "Fished by night and slept by day. Mixed English with some pay-tois of their own.''

"I'm going there," announced Cabot, "and I'm taking her with me. Either she reacts somehow when she sees them, or they react when they see her." And under his breath. "Must be some reason why these fucksome wenches happened to be hanging out just where those two were fielding for fresh blood. I'll be back later.''

A soft padding of female feet heralded Laura's entrance back into the netherworld.

"We're going someplace where you might help identify some suspects," said Cabot. She nodded, drained of all will-power. She had been like that ever since she had seen Charlotte on the other tray, a macabre caricature of the girl she had been.

She stopped by the dead man. Mayberry had opened the body's mouth, demonstrating how it almost didn't close over the double row of teeth, crowded and sharp like needles.

"This ain't a man's mouth. It's a piranha's.''

Laura looked down into the crater of teeth. Their pointed-ness was evil—no respite, no mercy for whatever pulsing vein came within their reach. And beyond the teeth, the throat was a chasm of hunger.

"Let's go." Cabot started leading her toward the exit.

"I honestly don't know how blood could feed a mammal this big," Mayberry shook his head after the departing couple. "Unless his organism developed a way of breaking down each protein cell in the victim's blood more efficiently than we ever would.''

In the car, she kept thinking, *I've caused Charlotte's death.*

Then she said it aloud, to Cabot, and he asked how did she figure. Charlotte had taken her to that party, not vice versa. Charlotte had run outside after her. Laura had been in mortal peril, and only the mist-provoked confusion that had fooled detective, medium, *and* killer had saved her hide from a similar end.

The car driven by a younger detective followed a two-lane road right by the river. Laura's window was open. Agglomerations of trees zoomed past, their rustling foliage opening instantaneously as they passed, like a green and herbal music box. God, there was still a world of innocence and normality out there. Was she already and forever cut off from it?

What about last night? The evidence of fresh molestation, two pinpricks on the other side of her neck, completed symmetrically the almost-healed wounds Dr. Gattery had examined.

Cabot was recalcitrant, almost hostile, about having Emory Lecouveur incriminated.

"Lady," he said, "Mr. Lecouveur's been a founding father to this city. Always a little quaint, I'm sure he's made women feel peculiar in his company at times, with those fiery eyes and all. But a killer, he *ain't*."

Laura took a deep breath. "What about his nephew?"

"He ain't one either. Look, you're talkin' about people with pull, with reputations, pillars of the community. Mister Alain's gonna renew his term as councilman; their business is gonna flourish again. That's the way it is with that family. Born winners," he said with the tone of a definitive grasp on reality. "You want to press charges? Fine, we'll do it, but I don't know for what—for those li'l hickeys? And can you swear it's the old man who gave 'em to you?"

She thought. No, she couldn't swear.

"Can you swear it's th' other?"

No. Not even that.

"Some women would beg for such treatment," was his conclusion. She lost her temper and said maybe in *these* boondocks, and that he sounded crassly male chauvinistic, and look, she was coming with him now, but that was all, no more cooperation, it didn't lead anywhere, anyway. She didn't even know how much longer she would stay in this town.

"That's your business," he said evenly. "And mine is that I see you don't get attacked again as long as you're in my jurisdiction. Attacked by a killer, not by a lover."

"You're being extremely rude in your insinuations, and you're invading my privacy," she replied sharply.

He apologized, and they rode in silence for another half hour. Sickly, she kept replaying last night's events in her

mind: one moment in particular from the whole ordeal, an
almost touching one. When he had taken her, so eager, so
desperate in his feverish addiction, that she had been strangely
moved by so much need. And by so much loneliness. Like a
jailed man seeing sun, like a child sensing its mother. His
brute and selfish force had been almost forgivable, his tremor
above her and inside her intimate, almost binding. Something
beyond normal emotion, something superhuman, had passed
into her.

He had subjected her to a vile initiation, but at this instant
she had almost accepted it. From the depth of her unconscious, through layers of time, from the roots of the earth
moving under the police car, into her limbs, into her womanhood, a call for warm and dripping sacrifice seemed to find
audience within her.

How would it all have felt with Alain?

She started, afraid that her face had betrayed her thoughts.
She looked at Cabot. He was staring ahead, inert, indifferent.

Oh, that second of panic, when teeth and manhood deflow-
ered her simultaneously, that would've been hot with Alain!
And the frenzy of his uncontrollable appetite, to which she
could only respond with disarmed pain. And later, the monstrous movement, back-forth, back-forth, thirst quenched, primal lust appeased. A quiver of tiredness and building fantasy
stretched her legs. Alain's pleasure. Alain's pleasure.

"There they come!" said the driving cop, with near alarm.

The car penetrated between weeping willows. She saw a
horde of small men drop a vast fishing net on the shore, turn,
and start running toward the car.

"Look 'bout as unsightly as the dead 'un," confirmed
Cabot. Laura saw a mixture of jeans and T-shirts and dark
brown trousers of a sort of peasant cloth, and faded shirts
with ornaments of red embroidery into which was sewn an
occasional silver dollar, or earring, or some other cheap gar-
nish. The same low foreheads, purple lips, and glaucous eyes.
Some limped, but even those who did approached the car with
amazing agility while their throats quacked and tittled:

"Come 'ere, *ba. Or vinit din oras sa ne vada.*"

"*Ce zici, ba?* Where?"

"Right by the *tarm—nu'i vezi, ba, in caru politiei?*"

"Cine's, ba?"

"Ba, lume, ba: care'a furat sa vie la judecata."

"Ba," barked explosively, was the staple word. Half-wit smiles, hands wiping snot, quick-batting eyelids, all rolled toward them in a tide and engulfed the police car. They started pounding hands on hoods, on the trunk, on the windows. Hands with overgrown nails, greened by the river.

"What are they yammering about?" asked Cabot. She listened, heard nothing remotely like French in their jive. But their mouths looked full of bladelike teeth, and moved fast, like mowing machines. The green hands started pulling sticks from their belts—nice polished canes. A thin, stiletto-like blade suddenly shone out of a cane, and came down hard on the windshield.

"Back to the road!" ordered Cabot. The driver reversed, and Laura felt the back of the car thudding into something soft, a body. Wheels blowing dirt, the car screeched into the roadway, and the swarming invasion was left behind, shaking fists and sticks. Cabot's nose was almost glued to the window. "Jesus, what's happened to them?" he whispered, appalled.

"Gotta come back with a team," opined the driver, and turned the patrol car around. But it was clear to Laura that the two cops were shaken. "I always knew they were a little funny," gasped Cabot.

"Could be the water pollution," the driver muttered, glancing back. The whole settlement of dysfunctionals showed now as a bracelet of thatch-roofed houses around an arm of the river. "That's what makes killers," muttered Cabot. "Backwaters like this one."

The sun was setting when the police car drove back into town. Cabot dropped Laura at her place, warning her that from now on she'd be watched *personally* around the clock, not just the house. She could make everyone's life easier by checking with him daily.

Out of a desire to transport herself into another reality, she turned on the TV. *"Bam—pee—ros! Bam—pee—ros!"* a crowd of Latinos were shouting on the news, somewhere on the dockside, while stretchers with blanketed bodies were carried past them to open ambulance doors, and the newsman explained that a grisly incident had happened on the river. The bodies of several union men had been discovered murdered and eviscerated on a barge returning from an unloading site upriver, and the word was that the site adjoined a Lecouveur property, or that the barge belonged to them. Apparently out of control by now, the rumors that the slashings were the work of vampires had permeated into union circles, too, and an organizer was interviewed. He called the barge owners "bloodsuckers," and the newsman asked him if he meant that *literally*, and the organizer's English was too basic to understand such words. "A bloodsucker's a bloodsucker, what the f—" He was bleeped off the air and replaced by another organizer, a Tarzan with a golden bead and an Irish brogue, who said smartly that management had screwed up worse than ever before, and the bomb just needed a fuse to be ignited. What about these apocalyptic rumors that the river traffic was being controlled by vampires? "I don't know about that, but me and my local have been to survival courses and training grounds, and we're armed and prepared for any sort of emergency," the man said. Laura wanted to switch the damn thing off, but the phone rang before she could do it.

"My dear girl, I'm so glad to find you," cooed Marion Voguey. "What are you doing there all alone? I thought to myself, I can't let you be alone tonight, not after what happened to poor—"

Laura ground her teeth. "How'd you know?"

"It was in the afternoon paper." Slow police, fast reporters. "Listen," pursued Marion in the same dulcet tone, "come spend the night at my place. I have a lovely guest room, and good locks on the doors. I'll make us a nice country steak and rice and butter beans, and if you can't sleep, we'll talk into the small hours."

She hesitated a second. "All right." Why fight fate? "Thanks," she added. "I'll be there in half an hour."

She packed a few things, added her unopened mail and the envelope from the Egyptian. Whatever it was, it might distract her.

Let Cabot watch her empty apartment. But wait: He had promised to have *her* watched.

Before walking out, she switched off the TV set, just as it

started to replay the news. For a second, the Latinos rushed back onto the screen, chorusing, righteous in their wrath: "Bam—pee-ros!"

Cabot was listening to the news on the radio, driving from home back to the office, shaven and in a fresh shirt—no need to give that skunk Knowles anything else to gripe about. On top of the situation, he had found the time to offer to the world a face of the law that could be esteemed and trusted.

But he was nervous, and for good reason.

The sight of those Cajuns had baffled him. True, he hadn't trespassed into their parts for a while, yet how much inbreeding could change a community so fast and so completely?

There were also these rumors . . . If he listened to them, New Orleans was being taken over. But wait—*he* had started those rumors. He and Jackie and Les.

They had made up a vampire, certain that there couldn't be one. Yet now real vampires seemed to be coming out of the woodwork, like bedbugs smelling the odor of a heavy sleeper.

Where was all this going to end?

And what was this *new* mess? Those union men, mysteriously massacred on the Lecouveurs' barge?

And who was Laura Walker, really? An innocent bystander? If she was so innocent, why was she such a catalyst for strange passions?

The sun had set for maybe half an hour, but its lingering blaze had drawn a burning path across the clouds. The air felt strange, as if the day was dead, yet night was afraid to fall and the earth was preserved in the crystal ball of dusk, for the attention of a distracted wizard.

He checked his gun at the morgue, took the down elevator, so lost in thought that he only heard the snarling voice at the last second.

"He left, huh?" roared Knowles from inside the crime lab. "Answer me, boy! He just and up left, with three magnum slugs in him?"

Les whined something unintelligible. Cabot moved his adipose legs under his pursy body, sensing a catastrophe.

"Why didn't you lock 'im in a crypt? And where were *you*, Jackie?"

Cabot stormed in. His glance tumbled and slipped on the empty shininess of the tray, still lit copiously by bulbs hot in their grooved sockets.

The toothy little vampire had disappeared. From the tray, Cabot's eyes scanned to the left, totally by instinct. One of the windows was broken, and the feet of passersby flashed on the sidewalk past its irregularly jagged opening.

"I bust my ass to be here tonight, to see what you got and hopefully close this case that's sinking the whole department into ridicule," Knowles blustered on. He took a breath and directed the rest of it at Les, shaking the little Italian on his feet with the pure vibration of his vocal cords. "And when I get here you tell me that he got away? He just got up from the tray, nice and dead, and walked to that window, broke it, climbed out, and vanished in the traffic, thank you very much?"

He spotted Cabot, who wasn't even looking at him. He was looking at the window. Past a mortified Jackie, whose fat was quivering on her like gelatin.

"Aha, who have we here? Our veteran homicide wonder-worker? You're off the case, Cabot." He screamed and seemed ready to fall into a fit of epilepsy.

Then he promenaded his gaze over the others. "I'll make a report to the commissioner tomorrow, and God willing, I'll fire the lot of you." Swinging his fists spasmodically, he rolled out of the lab, and his hysterics filled the lobby, all the way to the elevators.

The silence was broken by Cabot, who asked quietly, "Were the doors locked?"

Jackie nodded. Cabot peered back at the broken window. The street was dark with dusk.

Marion lived on St. Charles Avenue, in the Garden District.

Caught in traffic congestion between 1st and Louisiana, Laura opened the manila envelope and pulled out of it a tome. The covers felt like parched leather, darkened by the passage of time.

It was a black book, almost square. Since the traffic still

wasn't moving, she thumbed through the first few pages. The paper was yellow, lined horizontally with streaks that had almost faded. Uniform, orderly handwriting filled the pages. She saw it was in French, noticed the date of an entry: April 3, 1869. An old diary.

Well-tailored, the covers held evenly between them a thick wad of pages. Three hundred or better, she thought. The paper was thin and, though yellowed, seemed to have taken well the mutations of time. The traffic started moving again, and she had to put the diary aside.

Marion's house was a masterwork of gingerbread, exactly the way she had pictured it. Turrets, cowls, double roofs, Victorian steeples, it had them all, enough for three houses. She rang the doorbell and Marion opened it with a martini shaker in her hand.

"You won't believe who's here to see you," she prattled, eyes glowing. Over a mat, Laura walked through a smell of rug detergent, and saw so many cute little pieces of bric-a-brac that she realized Marion's house had to be *just so*. A doll's house, every surface covered with collector's items, every square inch of finish well protected. She was taking all this in when a rocking chair creaked, and Alain rose and came straight toward her.

10

"ALAIN'S been looking for you all over town," announced Marion, agitating the cocktail shaker.

He was wearing the tweed jacket and jeans he'd had on when he bumped into her at the airport.

"Not quite all over town," said Alain. "Just at your place and at the store."

. The faint haze of a beard was back on his face. But he didn't look harried or drawn this time—on the contrary. A resplendent glow came from his skin, vital and fresh, as if he'd slept like a baby until minutes before. His eyes, emerald clear, took in her face, her body, all of her, and seemed satisfied that she was all in one piece. She struggled to keep her head turned at such an angle that the fresh scars wouldn't show, and then she remembered that she didn't have to. She had changed at home, into a green turtleneck.

"He finally came here," Marion went on, "and I told him you were on your way. I thought you'd enjoy any extra company. Try this. I'm afraid I haven't kept my hand in, but I used to mix great martinis about fifteen years ago."

Laura took the cocktail, and gulped it. But she felt no bite from the alcohol, as if it were gin-flavored water.

"Alain was telling me how the unpleasantness with the unions was almost over, and then those maniacs boarded a barge the other night and killed the crew, simply to keep up this senseless rift . . ."

"Well, we don't really know who started the fight, but it's not helping," said Alain. "Laura, I'm sorry about Charlotte."

She just looked at him, a thousand thoughts churning in her mind. *He's not a pervert, not like Emory. But even if he is . . . No, look at those eyes. I'm thirsty. I want to be with him, to be kissed by him, to fall back on a bed, on a lawn, on any sort of surface, and bury myself under his lovely weight. Hold him. Talk to him. Untie all those knots of mystery. I'm thirsty. I'm thirsty.*

"Thank you," she managed to say. "I had grown to like her a lot. The police caught one of the killers."

"Laura, care for another martini?" asked Marion.

"A lieutenant called and told me," said Alain. "Cabot. He said the killer lived in a Cajun settlement. Not far from our property, in fact."

He took her hand. She blinked, afraid of the touch, surprised to feel a sensation of peace, of security. It entered her wrist and spread through her body. She remembered Marion's question. "No, thank you. Could I have a little water, though?"

Marion just stood there, like a spectator watching two performers. "Of course," she said. Finally she rested the shaker on the table and vanished into a hallway.

"She's not going to let us talk to each other," said Alain as soon as she was gone.

"What shall we do?" Laura asked, despondent, captured by his eyes and having no other wish.

"Can we take a little walk? I mean, unless you're totally exhausted."

"I'll walk with you," she said. Marion was just stepping back in with a tall glass of water. "We're going out for a few minutes," announced Laura. She took the glass from Marion's liver-spotted hand, drank it till she was staring through the glass bottom at the ceiling and the overhead light. "Thanks," she said.

She laid it down by the shaker. "Come on," she said, and started toward the exit, hearing his footfalls behind, in sync with hers, the nicest sound she could think of.

Wide like a freeway, St. Charles Avenue welcomed them

with the bell of a streetcar just stopping at a station, twin
tracks shining away down the center of the avenue on their
long bed of cracked stone, the trees rustling lazily with a
breeze, the streetlights nesting in the trees. *He's going to take
me in his arms and kiss me as soon as we round the corner.*

"I want to explain about last night," said Alain, the green
of his eyes dark now and crisscrossed by shiny reflections
from the lights, from the traffic. "I was trying to keep myself
away from you."

She breathed.

A wrinkle of pain crawled along his forehead. "Please understand me," he said almost vehemently. "There's nothing
wrong with *you*!" Luckily, they were alone on the tree-shaded
sidewalk. "You are a strong young woman. You can decide
on the course of your own life. You owe nothing to anyone.
I suppose that's one reason I care for you so desperately."
He averted his eyes at the word *desperately*, as if it was
embarrassing. "I care for you very much," he continued. "I
more than care for you, I'm in *love* with you," he said with
a tortured tone of sadness that she enjoyed. At least his feelings were *strong*. "Laura, I liked you the instant I saw you
at the airport. Saturday night, after my dinner plans collapsed, I drove around in the Quarter, daydreaming about
glimpsing you walk across the street. I wanted to see you so
badly that when I heard you quarreling with that drunk at
Preservation Hall, I felt I had *planted* you there by my fantasy
alone. Later, at your place, after we kissed, I was glad you
made that mistake, glad that you called me by another name.
I had an excuse to storm out thinking that I was still
safe. . . ."

He was striding next to her, and she saw for the first time
that his gait could be uneven, that the strong and well-
coordinated body was now agitated by emotion, and the contained passion she had watched on his face before . . . that
passion was burning its way out of him, in the glow of his
eyes, in the feverish flutter of his nostrils, in his quickened,
almost faltering speech.

"Wait a second," she said. "I, I, I, that's all you're saying—*I*, Alain. What about *me*?"

He looked at her, the mist of misunderstanding in his eyes. "You?" he asked. "I thought we *were* talking about you."

"We were talking about Alain. Alain's in love," she said, delighting in the line. "Alain's in love, and it's quite scary for him, quite tormenting. But what about Laura? Why should she wait in anguish, wondering if he's all right, in this city where killers prey on whomever crosses their path? Why should she keep herself ready for someone who says he's in love with her, and count the seconds, and then see him with another woman? Yes, you drove right past me last night, with some cheap blonde," she said, as his eyebrows flexed into question marks. "What makes you think that only *your* agony is important? The famous blueblood of your family, of which I've been hearing ever since I landed in New Orleans?"

He stopped under the full shade of an oak whose swollen roots had cracked the sidewalk. She was surprised to see a sort of angry envy in his eyes.

"Freedom," he murmured. "It must be sweet to be free."

"You can *make* yourself free if you want," she said. "It only takes the will to do it."

He contemplated her somberly, looking instantly ten years older than the lovesick little boy whose pathos she had interrupted. She shouldn't have done it. She should have let him go on, trilling and warbling his infatuation—she had been reveling in it. "I spent some time last night with a woman I didn't know," he said flatly. "It only taught me how unique I found every second I've spent with you. Nothing happened, no closeness, no romance. I took her home, then went back upriver and spent the night thinking about what my life was supposed to be before I met you, and what I'd like it to be now. I imagined my life with you," he said almost with hostility.

"And was it so awful?" she asked.

He stared and stared at her, then said, "It was wonderful," in a crumbled tone. She looked, but there were no tears in his eyes, just a sort of stoic pain that deepened them even more than usual.

She put her hand on his arm. "Alain. slow down. Nothing's taking me away from you."

He stepped out of the oak's shadow. He even moved as if

he was in pain, and she panicked a little. *This is serious. This isn't just bachelor immaturity.*

"You're free," he said.

"And you're not?"

"No," he replied, the passion back in his voice. "What's this?" he asked suddenly, pointing down at the cracked sidewalk. She started and looked down, and saw just the sidewalk, polished by the melancholy light of the street. "To you it's just a slab of concrete you're walking on. To me, it's a lid entombing me. My destiny plunges beneath this sidewalk, into time, into the roots of my family, into events I didn't cause and decisions I didn't make. That, all of that, lies down there." He tapped the sidewalk with his shoe. "Blood flows down there—our blood. And I can't leave it."

They walked in silence for a few seconds. They had walked almost the length of a streetcar stop; the next one loomed a few hundred yards ahead.

She pondered, while cars rolled past them, and to their left houses swept slowly by, monumental, with porticoes and loggias and circular driveways and glittering entrance doors of beveled glass.

"If you can't leave this place," she said, "why can't I stay and share it with you?"

"Because you don't know my family," he answered promptly. "You don't know who they are, and how they live. Because you don't share our blood." She started to open her mouth, and he took her shoulders and turned her toward him. "Laura, listen to me. These are things I'd never tell anyone else"—his voice was cracking, his hands were squeezing hers—"There's more to the Lecouveurs than their money, their sacrosanct old manners, their morbid pomp. *Evil* lies at our foundation. Take my uncle Emory—people think he's a harmless old eccentric. They don't know, you don't know, how devilish he is, how clever and selfish, how determined he is to hold and control everything he touches. But he only holds and controls so that he can destroy, and nothing stops him from having his way. Nothing."

She had listened to him, aware of the sidewalk beneath her feet, aware that somehow they were standing atop a subterranean vault of wickedness—the past of the Lecouveurs.

"Nothing?" she asked.

"Nothing," he echoed.

She thought of last night. Of the apparition in Alain's bedroom.

It wasn't Alain. I can swear it.

It was the old man with his seductive manners and his favorite poets. And those horrible hands, that body, damp and full, like a leech's. Made young again through its revolting vice.

Emory.

I don't want Alain ever to know about last night.

"Alain," she said. Her heart pounded. *This might be the last time I see him.* "Why are you such a prisoner? How did they gain such power over you?" She said *they* because she didn't want to mention Emory. Afraid of the words she was pronouncing, as if Emory could hear her from miles away at Belle Hellène, and materialize next to them, blowing fire from eyes and nostrils, and whirl them both into the raging hell beneath the sidewalk. She clutched him by the lapels of his tweed jacket. "Alain, I can help you. We can go away. Let's run away together."

The sadness in his eyes was inconsolable. It seemed as if a clock was moving inside his irises, recording for the thousandth time a chance at freedom; he had encountered it before, yet he had never been able to seize it.

"I can't abandon my destiny," he said.

"Can I join it?" she asked, hoping against hope.

His eyes widened in revulsed shock; his hands clasped her shoulders. "Laura, please, don't even think of it," he whispered, shaken as though he'd seen a ghost; she noticed little pearls of sweat on his forehead. "You could never become a Lecouveur, and thank God for that."

"Alain," she asked gently, "is your family somehow involved in those slashings?"

"No," he said, slowly, solemnly. "We didn't kill any of those miserable people." He paused, added in a doleful tone, "Cabot told me the killer was caught. Out here, they always turn out to be some backwoods imbeciles. They're sentenced to life and thrown behind bars and forgotten—a punishment as useless as the crime."

"Alain, can I help you in any way?" she begged.

He looked at her, reactionless for a moment, as if inebriated with some mysterious thought. "Yes," he said finally. "Leave New Orleans. Too many gruesome things have happened so close to you. I'm telling you to leave because I love you. Go clean, as you came."

She turned and walked ahead, because she didn't want to cry in front of him. He caught up, walked abreast of her. Through her tears, she saw the streetlights liquefy, the contours of the trees ripple. To hell with it. She had no handkerchief. She mopped her eyes with her hand.

"What is love to you?" she asked.

"I read this once," he said after a pause. "Love is a crystal of fear. People see themselves in it with such clarity, no wonder they get scared and run away." She was crying in earnest. He put an arm around her waist to support her, and cradled her head against his chest.

"Alain, Alain," she whispered, "you're so strong. And so weak." He was silent, acquiescing.

"What do you get out of sacrificing yourself to such a family?" she asked when her tears finally dried.

"Power. And mastery over time."

"Mastery over time—what are you talking about?" she asked incredulously.

"We do have mastery over time, we Lecouveurs. Would you like to see it?"

She shrugged, not caring whether he could walk on water. They had reached the next train stop. A streetcar was rumbling to a halt: an old set of two greenish, dusty cars, poorly lit, with narrow windows, its trolley blowing electric sparks as it occasionally missed the feeding cable.

"Come on, I'll show you," said Alain, taking her elbow and pushing her toward the streetcar. Confused, she tried to resist him, but he lifted her and put her in the car before it came to a complete stop. He jumped in next to her, took her face in his hands, and covered her mouth with his.

Depressed and exhausted, she drank in the kiss, and felt that a shot of oxygen was bringing her back to life. Eyes closed, she heard other people's voices next to her: the conductor giving a passenger directions, a woman urging a child to get on the streetcar. A breath of cool air touched her, as if the roof of the car had opened, and a joyous song sprang from many chests, drunkenly off-key. She opened her eyes to look at the inside of the car.

There was no inside. She and Alain were standing at the prow of a float: It was pulled by two horses, down a street with wooden sidewalks, thronged with people holding torches. She saw more floats ahead, turned to examine the one they were standing on: a hot waft of air, sickeningly mixing camphor, eau-de-roses and human dirt, hit her in the face like a limp pelt. A hospital scene was what their float was carrying. On half a dozen couches, men and women in stained robes foamed at the mouth or raised skeletal arms toward a priest with a scarf wrapped around his nose and mouth, assisted by two Ursuline Sisters.

Laura began to shake uncontrollably.

The floats ahead carried other moribunds, other moving hospital wards. Abruptly, the meaning became clear: These were no carnival floats, but simply carts hauling away the flotsam of filled hospitals toward the common grave. And she and Alain were standing on one of them, listening to a drunken, joyful song pouring from French throats, raspy with rotgut wine.

> *Quand on est mort on est foutu-uu-uu,*
> *On est foutu dans une bier-ree . . .*
> *When one is dead, then one is screwed,*
> *One is screwed inside a co-o-offin . . ."*

She could think of one word to say: "Jesus, Jesus, Jesus," she repeated, seeing that all the windows and doorways they were passing revealed sights of doom. In candlelit rooms, half-naked bodies lay in rumpled beds. On a floor, a woman was crawling miserably toward an overturned bucket. Laura looked at the crowd, in maskers' garb, dancing, passing bottles, collapsing to the ground—here fell a man, there went another. Entering a crossroads, the float jolted over something—a body? Her own body twitched, feeling the agony of mashed flesh and broken bones beneath her, and she saw a band of Choctaw Indians on horseback, each smoking a big pipe as an amulet of protection, seemingly entertained by the Mardi Gras of death.

She threw herself on Alain's body, buried her face in the breast of his jacket. "Enough, please!" she cried.

The song faded. She felt that she was lifted, then lowered. Her feet touched something solid. She opened her eyes. She was back on St. Charles Avenue.

With a clang, the streetcar took off. The vision hadn't lasted as long as the streetcar's stop at the station.

"There was an epidemic of yellow fever around 1853," said Alain.

She kept saying, "Jesus, Jesus," with chattering teeth.

The streetcar was diminishing in the distance, like a toy. She saw it stop a quarter of a mile down, heard the faint bell clang.

"I didn't mean to scare you. It just happened that we passed close to that moment in time," said Alain.

He helped her across the traffic lanes back to the sidewalk. She felt like crying again, but she had no tears. "Don't you hate having this kind of gift?" she asked.

"Yes," he said simply. "Time, anywhere you open it, teaches you some hideous lesson."

"You're not like them!" she cried, so hard that her temples throbbed, ready to explode. She threw her arms around his neck: "Alain, you *can't* be like them! I love you! I love you!"

He put his arms around her. "I'm not like them," he said soothingly.

"Then why do you have to live here? Why do you have to give them your life?" She thought her tears had dried up— she was wrong, she had plenty left, and they started rolling warmly down her cheeks again. "Alain, we can leave right now. Go to the airport, get on a plane to San Francisco. Alain, please . . ."

She stammered on, while he turned her around and started walking her gently back toward Marion's house, telling her it was too late for him, he wasn't like his kinfolk but the bonds were too strong. Gently, like an adult pacifying a disconsolate child about a lost dog, he told the story of his childhood of fairy tales and midnight scares at Belle Hellène. How his father had disappeared one day, leaving behind a twenty-year-old wife and a two-year-old son. And how his mother had married another man and moved away from Louisiana, leaving Alain with the maids and cooks and the outlandish uncle. And of all the people in his life, it was Emory—crazy, quirky, awful Emory—who had never abandoned him, and now he'd asked Alain to take over. Because the family needed him to get themselves back on their feet . . .

She listened like a child, pain sweetened by his voice.

On Marion's doorstep, they said good-bye. He would see her soon.

She didn't believe him.

They didn't kiss.

Long after midnight, after Marion had gone to bed, Laura sat down on a couch in the living room, and called the Egyptian. At the third ring he answered, hoarse from sleep. "What's the story with this book in French?" she asked him abruptly.

Her bare foot was weaving the telephone cord between two toes. Instead of tickling her, the curly plastic line produced almost no sensation.

"I'm sorry about last night. I don't usually drink and I got kinda loaded," the medium apologized.

"Spare me," she said. "What's with this book?"

"Aaah . . ." he sighed, reorganizing his memory. "Yes . . . I followed Charlotte in the dark, thinking it was you. Poor Charlotte, she was—"

"For God's sake, come to the point," she implored. "I barely have the energy to listen to you."

"All right. I lost both her and you in that mist. Then I found a path I thought would take me to the road. Usually, encompassable space is a cinch for my faculties, but this time I was too fuzzy to use my astral beams, so I just followed the path to a sort of . . . big garden." He stopped.

"Mm-hm. A big garden. Go on," she urged him.

"The place looked deserted, but I guess it wasn't, because I could hear yelps and barks. But darkness and alcohol combining . . ." he laughed oafishly, and paused again. She wished she had him right there so she could grab him and shake the story out of his pudgy mass. ". . . I collapsed under a tree till about noon the next day."

"I'm so glad," she said.

"Then there was a real astral storm."

"Really."

"Yep," he confirmed seriously. "Almost like a meteor shower of beams and glitches and fragments of aura, and I deducted that it was being generated by that house. The house, you see, was protecting itself against my presence. Then . . . wait a minute, I've got coffee here someplace, let me pour a cup."

She tried to imagine him, on his bed, between ramparts of books, hairy feet groping into musty slippers, to get up and grab that cold cup of coffee.

"But my aura resisted the shower, and soon it was over. Now the house had temporarily exhausted its defenses, and lay before me unprotected." She heard a slurp of coffee. "At the same time, *your* voices began speaking again. They told me that a partial key to your confusions lay in the house. I started for the house, noticing no human activity, in fact no life at all—oh yes, there were those dogs, barking away in their kennel."

She breathed deeply, passed her hands through her hair, and found it unkempt and coarse. But she felt a feeble renewal of hope. Maybe this deranged babble meant that all was not over, that all was not lost between her and Alain.

"I met no one as I was directed inside, to a library, where that book was indicated to me. I took it, carried it out of the property unmolested, hitched a ride to Metairie, and got a cab back from there. I rushed to your place, but naturally I didn't find you, so I left the book on your doorstep. Isn't it peculiar that I always reach you, but never right away?" he finished.

"Everything's peculiar," she murmured. "Did you read the book?"

"I couldn't. It's in French," he replied.

"What?" She started to laugh and clamped a hand over her mouth, for fear of waking Marion. "You can't read French?"

"I'm sorry," he growled, offended. "I'm a channeler, not

a language major.'' But Laura laughed on. The clairvoyant who summoned spirits from all corners of space and time, beset by such a ridiculous obstacle?

''Why didn't you go into a trance and call someone to help you with the translation?''

''No one was available. And if you don't stop jeering like a moron, I'll interrupt this communication,'' he threatened, terribly irritated.

''Oh, come on, have some humor,'' she chided him. ''I read French. I'll read it and tell you all about it.''

''Oh, great.'' He sounded satisfied. ''We have to meet that family,'' he said resolutely.

''We?''

''I need you as an introduction. They are great travelers, it's obvious, even though they have passport problems.''

He explained that the Lecouveurs had an incredible time/space ability. Did Laura realize what that gift would mean, combined with *his* passport? Streamlined in his aura like a super-spaceship, not even the remotest reaches of the universe, of the past or future, would remain uncharted to him. Or to Laura, he hastened to add.

''You don't have to be polite,'' she said. ''I don't want a ticket for your astral trips.''

''Okay.'' He was only too glad to gallivant on the outer plane all by himself. ''You'll let me know, then?''

She reassured him one more time, hung up, and felt faint. She leaned her forehead against the couch, blanked out for a few seconds.

Then she sat up again. She had cried. Stains of tears and a thin streak of saliva had defaced Marion's perfect couch.

She listened. The apartment seemed to be floating in a sleepy stupor. Two table lamps burned on in the living room. Laura sat next to one of them, wondering what was wrong with the Big Plan that God was supposed to have for every living being, and for her. She couldn't hear the streetcars. It was too late. They were sleeping their sleep of oiled wheels, their power poles folded on the rooftops like huge fishing rods in the vast municipal garage where streetcars rest before another day.

She stumbled toward the guest room, carrying the book.

By the bed, a lit bedside lamp promised a long, peaceful read. Laura got in bed, thanking fastidious Marion for the crispness of the sheets.

Love is a crystal of fear.

No, Alain. Love is a struggle for one's self. Too bad you've lost yours.

She opened the book again. The paper was time-yellowed, but the hand was calligraphically legible.

Je commence ce journal en ce jour du Seigneur . . .

"I start this diary in the day of our Lord . . ." She paused, noticing that Lord was misspelled—*Seingeur*, instead of *Seigneur*. *Singe*, she knew, was monkey in French. As if calling God a dog.

She felt a quickening of her heart, for just a second, then she dismissed the implication, and read on.

PART THREE

VARCOLAC

11

Varcolac, varcolac
din padure si din lac,
care musti obrazul lunii
sange sugi din ceafa lumii,
si scoli noaptea din sicrie
ucigasii si nebunii . . .

Vampire, vampire, rise and flutter
over magic woods and lakes,
at the moon's cheek gnaw and nibble,
bite the world's ripe neck, and stir
out of rotted, moss-grown coffins
the self-murdered, the demented . . .

Romanian ballad

I start this diary in the day of our Lord, April 3, 1869. I, Amar Calovaru, *boyar* and *ban* of the Lower Danube, shall record the shapings of time that are setting us forth now toward an inscrutable destination. And I shall reminisce and mix the present with the portentous, irreversible hours that made us what we are.

Hours lost in the forest of time past. Five hundred and thirty-nine years since, at Posada, we reddened the snow-capped Carpathians with the blood of the Hungarians, winning our status and our title.

That night, after the battle! What glorious apocalypse!

My forehead was gashed. My left arm, elbow crushed by a cudgel, followed me like a vulture's broken wing as I dragged myself across the snow. Other parts of me bristled with arrow points and spear ends, but the pain had captured my entire body. I crawled up a pile of corpses, hearing a call that came from deeper within than my flesh, deeper even than my memories of ancestors and settled lands—it seemed to seep up from the bowels of the earth itself and find its way into my battered, destroyed body.

I felt that I needed to be up, higher than the heaps of the fallen, higher than the environing peaks. The pine trees, martially dark, pinned the stars against the sky with their sharp tops, and the moon rose over the battlefield like a dizzy survivor.

The pile I climbed on was still warm. Blood trickled from a face I recognized. I had crossed paths with him three times, but he had finally escaped me in the pandemonium of battle. The moon put glitter in the blood, and the half-open eyes seemed to look upon me with friendship. After death, the issue we had chopped and hacked and slashed each other over, so ardently, was finally meaningless.

Mystically, the moon was showing me my medication.

I murmured a word of apology and foregiveness to the dead man. Then drank him, like the blessed manna of rebirth. When I had acquired enough strength to see, to hear again, I became aware of other crawlings and squirmings all across the silent battlefield. Others, barely surviving, had heard, with the heightened senses of near death, the same pagan oracle. I prayed that my own kin, the Calovarus, would heed it.

Then I dozed off, finding soft couch in the tender flesh of the bodies. I woke up in time to chase off my face hawks that had been busy plucking the others' eyes. They had thought me dead, too.

The moon had fled, shy like a dishonored virgin. Instead, the sun broke through the clouds with triumphant vulgarity. For the first time, its life-giving glow, its cheering warmth, seemed strange to me. Not unwanted, not inimical, and yet it provoked an itchy agitation in my blood, and though my broken limbs moved freely, I was nauseated and angry. I looked at my arms. The paleness of fatigue had sculpted the veins out and upwards. Mixed in my life-stream, untellable, inseparable from me now, was their other flow, whose roots I couldn't unearth, nor its age fathom. A strange twin. A wild mate, to whom I had entrusted my life.

But I looked up at the sun with a sense of rival achievement that bested the war we had won, the loyalty to Ralph the Black, our prince of the land, and even life itself as I had known it. From now on, I felt that time was mine. Like a dark sun, I would be suspended over all creation, privy to its daily life, yet sovereign in my orbit. Time, space, would tick and stretch around me.

I was forty-two then. Unwed, childless, embittered by life's blows. Oh, what a rebirth. What a sweet secret to nurse in my convalescing heart, to let out only in enigmatic glimmers as my eyes would rest on the world from which I was separated by my superior power.

How could today's king, brought to the throne three years ago into a Romania finally sewn back together by a coalition of political upstarts, understand *me*, my longevity of thought and power, the dark sacredness of my needs? How could he understand a Calovaru?

The king is a man of his fast-perishing day. He was fashioned by the "three elements of modern civilization: gunpowder, printing and the Protestant religion," as Mr. Carlyle summed it up. Nothing tribal in him. No primal fever. No wedding to the moon.

We are to meet and speak in three days. I shall listen to his arguments from my perspective: eternity.

APRIL 4.
My anniversary was last night. I traveled to the mountains, and arrived after sunset. Like a fresco dedicated to the birth of a nation, long columns of kinfolk and tenants walked across the passes to gather at Posada, where we had followed the native prince, crushed the invader, and found ourselves.

The sloping plateau where I had begun my covenant was verdant, sprinkled with mountain flowers.

I shall leave it, leave the country. The rest of the world, I know, swarms with brethren clans, born of different races, initiated into our subterranean brotherhood through different mythic rituals. But varcolacs they all are. Like us.

APRIL 6.

The king and I talked this morning. My liaison with his niece is his only official charge. Of my power and my following, no mention.

Where is Dorothea? I asked. At Tusnad Spa, taking the waters. His lisping Royal Majesty sent her there to cure her nubile inflammation for me. O Cherub of Darkness! O Osiris, guardian of the mysteries of the moon! This man thinks I'm a skin rash! I shall go away with a German prescription ointment!

No, upstart kingling. No, Bavarian dachshund. The fever of my blood is in her, in her opulent and somewhat sottish Germanic parts—neck, breasts, rump, et cetera. Odors of blood, redolence of grave have bitten deep into her liberalminded chastity. She talks of peasant reforms but speaks not the idiom of those peasants.

We are to sell our farms and vineyards, liquidate our other interests and sail away with nothing but our money. I plead for soil from Romania. Dirt from my ancestors' graves. My blood, my earth, I want to take it with me in boxes, to plant it upon my next shore.

Asking, I whine. He witnesses a Calovaru sobbing. Abject, I feign readiness to kiss his hand. But he's a hypochondriac. Details of my savant sexual practices have reached and disturbed his sanitary Majesty. He won't let me kiss the hand I feel like spitting on, for fear of infection.

He grants the favor, eyes rounded at my depth of superstition.

A week and we depart. By steamship.

Oh, Dorothea. I never loved you when I had you. How I regret your whiteness, your somnolent resignation to the number of my appetites. Soon, soon, Dorothea, my blood will wake up in you. You will be the scourge of Danubian manhood. Wives and sweethearts will cry their eyes out while you cruise among the Danube's male flowers, snatching hearts.

After my royal audience is over, I take a walk along Bucharest's main boulevard. I want to be seen and remembered.

Mansions, gates, windows. Carriages. Men in black top hats. Walking sticks sparking up as their steel ends hit the sidewalks. Pomaded mustaches. Gypsy florist girls. A cafe, another.

A huge pain, even for my fortified heart. This string-puppet pantomime, dressed à la mode. Is this my home-land? Is this all that I'm leaving forever?

Was it always just this? Will the next shore be nothing but its slightly broader, slightly louder repetition?

APRIL 13.
I write as the ship's siren shrieks.

Twenty of my family are leaving with me. Almost the whole clan.

My drunk nephew stays ashore till the last minute. He's taught a gypsy band a song. They strike it up as he rushes to the gangplank.

"We're rich and damned, we are the Calovaru-uuus . . ."

Laura looked up from the diary. She closed her eyes to see the ancient name in her mind.

Calovaru. Amar Calovaru.
Ca-lo-var. La-co-var. Le-cou-veur.
Ca-lo-var. Var-ca-lo. Var-co-lac.
Le-cou-veur. Var-co-lac.
Amar Calovaru. Emory Lecouveur.
The same man?

But even born on the year of the diary's inception, he'd have to be . . . she counted quickly. One hundred seventeen years old.

And what about the other five hundred years? Were they just a poetic metaphor?

APRIL 26.
Aboard the steamship.

I look at the sea; blue-gray, unyielding, terrible reposi-tory of meanings lost. In fantasy I change its color to red.

I want to be a sea that engulfs and batters shores. A tide that rises inexorably, kept back illusorily by dams, until one day the dams collapse, the break-through explodes into the unprotected land and the blood tide is here, dawn of a new geological epoch.

There is a woman on board, a Spanish soprano, who sings arias in the first-class salon after dinner, delighting

the passengers with her trills, and me with the swannish-
ness of her neck. Her neck and arms are admirable, white
tubes of live Carrara marble. She excites my poetic sen-
sibilities.

How to catch her? She is exasperatingly shadowed by
a gross duenna, a fiftyish matron who never leaves her
alone, except at night when she goes out for a moment to
empty the cabin's chamber pots.

Crusades, legislations, utensils, tomes of philosophy,
works of art, how inconsequential and purposeless they all
seem when The Woman passes. All the episodes of history, occurring and ending and being remembered just so
they form the deadweight of our life, until a living body
swings along, so ill-protected by its thin armor of flesh.
Legs, breasts. Curves, openings. They sweep history into
oblivion with one lowering of the buttocks onto a sofa, with
one turn of the neck, the veins flexed, the projection of the
thyroid cartilage, so delicate, almost unseen in some
woman, like a maddening invitation. Oh, when they swallow . . . That dear swelling, slipping up, down . . . I think
there's a coordination between its movement and the
movement of women's eyes. Women's eyes flutter up,
down, perfectly in tune with their precious throats. (Note:
must look it up in *Punziger's Anatomy*.)

The only way to meet her seems to be to get the old one
first. Surprise her on her nightly round, immobilize her,
leave her dazed in some lobby.

What a terrible taste, the old one's, before that freshness . . .

APRIL 28.
We're approaching Marseilles. It's tonight, or never.

She knows of my interest in her. She sang straight at
me the last few times.

No. Don't try. This voyage is so important. For the family. And all those boxes of earth in the holds. A scandal?
A crisis imperiling our settlement in France? The *police
maritime* waiting at the dockside? Think of the future. This
exile is our chance to build a world-ramified empire. All
that put at hazard, compromised perhaps, for one neck?

Cloak yourself in renunciation, Calovaru. Lie down in
darkness. Close the lid. Let the future take shape while

the sea rolls under you, the sea-mews shriek, and the winds formed by air pressure in other continents roam tirelessly, untaxed, unarrestible, as one day you will.

I'm a poet at heart. Canine-toothed Ovid, one day I'll write my own *Ars Amandi*.

Laura lowered the book. She closed her eyes, massaged them with her thumbs. They ached from the long day, from the long night, from the calligraphic little letters.

He had told her he was a poet. She smiled, like an author's friend, recognizing in a line a shared conversation.

She leafed through the rest of the book. Page after page of the same disciplined handwriting, even and small, loading the paper to capacity with Calovaru/Lecouveur's life. They couldn't have been written over the years, much less over the giant span of centuries. The hand had inked out the letters with assurance, passing from one page to another with such unbroken regularity that it looked like the book had been written in one long session. But the paper *was* old. Was it fiction, then, all released in one long spurt of inspiration? Was it a chronicle of many years, put down in a single strenuous effort?

She skipped at random, started another entry.

JANUARY 2, 1898.
Incredible! Someone dared!
I write this as I sit at a desk of the cotton exchange in New Orleans. The shipping business has been satisfactory to brisk most of the time, and apart from other merchandise we are beginning to make a dent in the market with our imported wines. Calling them French, of course, as we call ourselves. In America—vast land that loves no nationality, not even its own—one is lucky to be despised as French. One is reviled, second-guessed, envied, gossiped about, then received with open arms, and asked with sincere ignorance for the clue to a thousand mysteries. How to serve white wine. With what dishes. In what shape of glasses. How to kiss a lady's hand signifying erotic interest that wouldn't shock her prudish Calvinistic background, nor alarm her husband. How to kiss her mouth. What to say in bed—before and after. We are America's fantasy of decadent elegance and unflagging male erection; we are

the ones the Americans love to hate, because . . . I think because we helped their Revolution (not that we did it for the love of them, but quite clearly rather to hurt the English), and our help is still the perverse pill their culture cannot digest. *Ergo*: Be French in America—you'll be rewarded with hatred, and prosperity.

But then, for quite a while, New Orleans has been French on its own.

What irony. Twenty-nine years ago I moved my clan to France. We bought land in the south—vineyards, vaster and better-tended than the ones we owned in Wallachia. But for the French there, we were Wallachians. That branch that stayed in France—rich by now, well-known, influential, forgetting its mother tongue—is still considered Wallachian.

Instead, we're French, unquestioably French,—in America. As a result, I'm deprived of a companionable circle of Wallachian literati friends who could chuckle with me at the publication of the nightmares of some whiskey-imbibing Irish hack named Stoker who's selling cartfuls of a composition called *Dracula*.

I had a copy ordered in London. The next mail boat will bring it.

Imagine: my past in print.

According to the reviews, it contains plenty of folklore. Where did he glean his documentation? No mealy-mouthed British subject could invent all that by himself.

MAY 8.

The book arrived, but I couldn't have it right away. The ship's second officer was reading it as the ship put in; then he lent it to the harbormaster's daughter. From there it went a circuitous route of swooning uptown literary circles, filled with pimply local prosefiers.

I finally got it back, covers parched by hardened candlewax.

I'm reading it.

MAY 11.

I'll sue!

Hold yourselves. We, the clan, *the purest*, WE—

We are, according to Mr. Stoker, an assemblage of

bloodlines from which Icelandic berserkers are not ex-
cluded! Huns, Lombards, Avars, Bulgars, Turks complete
the salad! *We Romanians* are more mongrelized than the
gypsies! Alas, those centuries of careful intermarriage and
obsessive selection of our prey! How often we shrank back
from a natural beauty in order not to break a line, and
settled for a cross-eyed purebreed instead! How often *I* did
it!

Even King Vlad's name is deformed! Of Ralph the Black,
no reference at all! And some other patent fallacies, like
never suffering one ray of sun!

I can't repress a flattered feeling, though, seeing how
well this deacon's inflations are catching on with the pop-
ulace! It's doing a raging business in Europe.

Is it the tip of a vast public change? Are we, the subterranean zeitgeist, finally coming into our own?

You've come a long way, baby, thought Laura. *Nowadays
people watch* Dracula *movies on cassette.*

Later that evening:
Nostalgia, as painful as unrequited love. Nostalgia for
Romania, lost forever. Those dusty little roads in the country. Those craggy mountaintops, jagged and scorching all
summer long, smoothed into the winter by the first snow-
falls.

Horrible thought: Did that confounded *Stoker*, in his
zealous neo-phytical clumsiness, stumble upon the true
mystery? Has he heard from some authentic Romanian
shepherd of the *minuna*?

Minuna: the ritual that would free a varcolac, if ever he
was sufficiently healthy of body to resist its racking pains
and come out of it not feet first but still alive, still breathing,
still thinking.

Minuna. The magic remedy.

Would I ever have the courage to try it? No. But I know
myself. Endless pleasure is what I'm here for. Why would
I reverse my condition? To live the rest of my days in colorless mortality?

But what if Stoker is preparing some sequel, containing
the actual information? Some pioneers in science, some
holy bigots, would quickly jump on it, and armed with the

antidote, they could hunt us down and put us in camps, administer it to us by force, TRANSFORM US, KILL US!

I shudder as I write.

He couldn't have learned the secret. It's known only to a single pocket of villages, locked in the impregnability of the Carpathians. It's locked away, in Romania. Like a ring slipped off a finger during a shipwreck, it tumbled to the bottom of that sea. It lies there now, intact but useless.

It will never kill *me*. I'm safe, I'm alive, alive, ALIVE. I feel like roaring it to the swamps of blessed Louisiana. Swamps, pleasures, here I come!

She let the book fall and leaned back. Tired images formed behind her eyelids, but none had the power to scare her anymore. Emory on that medieval battlefield, keeping himself alive by preying on his dying enemies. Emory, the haughty Balkan aristocrat, humbled by a romantic scandal. Emory, the poet, who entertained under a moth-eaten coat of arms, and rode across the Quarter in a brougham, and telescoped five centuries of mystery in a book with black covers.

She was exhausted.

But not frightened. The sensation hit her suddenly, like a familiar ache abruptly stopping, leaving instead a sense of numb normality.

She wasn't scared.

She sat up, then stood, then paced. She sat down again, wondered why she felt so accepting about all this. Reading, she had expected to stiffen with revulsion. Instead she had felt a mildly shocked sense of . . . familiarity.

She called fear back. It responded only when she remembered standing next to Alain on the streetcar's front platform, her face buried in his jacket. And then, turning, finding herself in that grim pageant of the past, a doomed Mardi Gras more than a century before. *That* had been horrifying, and at least by the judgment of her senses, utterly real.

That she feared. That eternity, that infinity, available, ready to open to a power that Alain had called mastery of time.

Without that demonstration, she could have comfortably believed that Emory was nothing but an old reprobate who took his epic fantasies for truth, occasionally getting to act them out, getting to reward his tired old lust by assaulting a guest. A guest lured to Belle Hellène by the young Lecouveur.

No, it couldn't be that way. If Alain could travel back and forth into eternity, so could Emory. Yet if they could, what kept them here? Battling taxes and unions? Fighting for seats on the city council? Falling in love, or at least pretending to? Why were they so faithful to the parts they played? Emory, the cynic, the scintillating rogue. Alain, the torn soul, the loyal successor.

In any case, they weren't involved in the murders—Alain had sounded totally sincere. And the killer had been caught. She needed no more protection. Besides, Cabot had said it: He'd protect her from a killer, not from a lover.

No, I don't believe it. It's too pat, too simple, too logical, too impossible to be possible. I'm going mad trying to accept it. Yet I'd be mad not to accept it. What do I want? What did I ever want?

Love. That was all she'd ever wanted.

And if it was meant to happen? Now, here? This strange bloom on her path, the richest, most inebriating flower? Love. Love for Alain. And from Alain.

I'm one of them! boomed a voice inside her. Fear—palpable, tangible—clenched suddenly at her vitals.

That's why I still love him, after all the revelations! That's why I didn't tell him, didn't tell on that disgusting old letch! That's why I'm not afraid!

It whipped her out of the bed.

No, no, this isn't possible, this isn't happening. Not from two silly little punctures. Four silly little punctures. She needed to see her body, her neck. There was a bathroom across a little hallway. She flung the doors open, stormed into the bathroom, clawed the wall to find the light switch. The corner of a mirror was the first thing she noticed. She popped her head into it, so terrified at the prospect of not seeing herself at all that she stabbed her upper teeth into her lower lip. Jesus, no, *nooo!*

The mirror threw back her reflection perfectly. It was simply her. She pressed her face against the glass, seeing a monstrefied likeness of herself, one-eyed, nose tip squashed into a grotesque umbrella-shaped proboscis. *I am Laura, Laura, LAURA. Laura is a good girl. I believe in God, the Father Almighty, maker of heaven and earth . . .*

She pulled back, drained. Her breath had misted the mirror. Her forehead, nose, hands, had left greasy blotches on it. She saw the glow of her bleeding lower lip.

She licked her own blood and felt a bizarre certainty that she could recognize it. Hers. Not anyone else's. And sweet. Soothing.

Then she examined her neck. The tiny pricks were still there. Looking so benign, so innocent.

I need sleep, she thought. No one could take so many shocks. So much exhaustion.

She went back to the bed, but didn't sleep. She talked to herself feverishly. She was all right, she was absolutely certain of it. She didn't want to be one of *them*, she was positive, and that was additional proof that she hadn't been contaminated. And how *could* she be, from losing just a few drops of blood? She felt the rest of her life fluid pulsing in her, strong, abundant, untainted. No, she was fine, healthy, able to feel, to love, to bear children.

But Alain . . . Alain's heart was in the right place, she was sure. He couldn't free himself, though. Apparently. He needed help. But he hadn't asked for it. Why should he? What proof had she given him of strength, of uncommon determination, of resources beyond the average? And he wanted to spare her, to protect her—he *loved* her. He was ashamed, too, of who they were. Of their infamy, real or imagined, it didn't matter anymore. Picture a clear-eyed little boy, growing up under such a weight of degrading myth. Feeling so much ignominy and disgrace, no wonder he had exiled himself up the river, grateful to spend his energies, his frustrations, his revolt, in exhausting work for the family. That disgusting, execrable family.

Poor man, caught between love and shame.

She could help him. If Alain couldn't free himself, *they* could free him together.

She looked at her wristwatch and found that it was six in the morning. Soon she'd hear the first streetcar.

Tomorrow . . . But it was already tomorrow.

Her lingerie show was now in three days. Marion had helped with the organizing, with the invitations, but there was still a lot to do.

I've got to take care of that. I can't quit before the show.

Muscles, nerves, emotions, sensations, all crowded together inside her, crying for rest, for sleep.

She laid her head down, and it came at last.

12

THE FOUR union men were buried with honors.

Arata had no family, nor did one friend of Candy's, but the other friend did, and so did Candy himself. Their families, locals with continuity in the area, owned family plots in two separate graveyards, but it was decided that the four had gone down together and should be buried together. So a four-casket granite mausoleum was acquired in the Metairie cemetery, close to its northern edge, to the roar of Highway 10. Arata, in a dark jacket, his neck concealed by a stiffly starched collar, looked almost like a bridegroom, while Candy, who had been pulled out of the water green and bloated, showed an obese face—the morticians had layered makeup over makeup on him, and now he had the cheerfulness of a country-fair dummy waiting to be shot with BB-guns. The other two had been similarly repaired.

Mass was at a neighboring church. The interment was scheduled at six in the evening, so that people could make it after work—and everyone came, in battered cars and pickup trucks, in Sunday bests and white shirts, some men in clip-on ties, some in hats or caps so that they could pay their respects to the dead by taking them off.

An after-funeral dinner had been catered back at the church, in a basement hall and in the churchyard outside, for the attendance was massive. Dixie Rebel flags, tricolor Mexican flags, union slogans, and cardboard shamrocks for Candy, who was Irish, swayed in the steamy air, along the main pathway of the cemetery, into the fourfold plot built on top of the Louisiana clay.

Braulio staggered between his widowed mother and his married sister and her family, following the coffins, which were carried into the cemetery on union shoulders. He had been prostrate for two days after the horror ride in the little dinghy, which had ended at the docks in the harbor. He hadn't been pursued or attacked, but sailing back alone after watching Candy drown had been the worst hell he'd ever wish on a man.

He was to give an address at the memorial dinner. He had written down nothing. All he could think of was that he felt like throwing himself into one of the gaping caskets.

The morning papers had reported in the business sections a massive loan the Lecouveurs had just received, engineered by the young Lecouveur, to modernize their fleet of barges and buy a number of new ones.

Uniformed police were visible around the cemetery, but there were plainclothes detectives around, too, because an investigation was in progress. Braulio had been questioned, and expected to be questioned again.

In an old leather jacket, with a tie, Cabot sat behind the wheel of an unmarked Nova Special across the road from the cemetery gates. Les was inside with the mourners. Cabot had switched on the radio for news, and dialed past a disc jockey announcing the formation of a new local band: the Vampires.

He had taken two days off. It wasn't known as yet who would succeed him on the case. Doubtlessly, someone more to Knowles's liking.

Everything seemed to be disintegrating—not only around him but inside him. He felt a depression that someone so jaded had deemed himself protected from. Something new was moving into the city he thought he knew so well. Into the streets, into the people, even into the air. Something difficult to identify, a mysterious flux, responding to alien laws. A wave of change, a menacing tide he didn't understand, and wasn't part of.

Yet as he sat in the unmarked police car, at no point did his suspicious mind stop to examine more closely the Lecouveur family. Though the men being buried behind the gates had been killed on their barge, and the quadroon girl had died at the edge of the estate, and the Walker woman had been babbling Alain's name, Cabot simply refused to consider the possibility that they might be involved.

Like Alain's father—mayor of New Orleans during Cabot's rookie years—the Lecouveurs weren't above or beyond the law—they *were* the law in these parts, a law more absolute than any book, for it was unwritten. They were history, draped in its imperial arbitrariness. In Cabot's mind, they would never stoop to murder, or to conspiracy. They didn't have to.

Cabot felt like praying. Not for the dead behind the gates, but for himself. Begging any power, even the darkest, to descend from its lofty seat and bring him absolution—or oblivion.

After the burial, the union men returned to the church. A security service of young members screened out the strangers and the cops, and only the faithful were allowed to enter the churchyard and the linoleum-floored basement hall. Drinking had started as soon as people started arriving; little tumblers had been filled with tequila and whiskey, placed on the tables, and set afire. The hundred-proof grog burned for their fallen comrades; but even with three drinks in him, Braulio couldn't find any words to say. The general mood was frightfully silent anyway, but he really lost his nerve when he saw that he'd been steered into the basement with about fifty people, all men. The reassuring smile of his mother and sister weren't floating nearby anymore.

Sudden panic bathed his shirt and suit in sweat. What would happen to him after the service? Would he be taken in for an interrogation? A truly merciless one, bringing to the surface how, like a coward, he'd left Candy prey to the waters and the others prey to the monsters? In the grim faces of the men staring at him, he thought he might be able to read his sentence—but with a good speech he might move a few hearts, and win a lesser penance. Even without a hand, or an arm, life was for the living. "Brothers," he began, his mouth dry with fear, and faces turned to listen to him, odiously tight and grim.

"Brothers, he was . . ." Braulio searched for a word of praise for Arata, then remembered that he wasn't the only victim. "They were, *all* of 'em . . ."

"Wait a second," a brutal voice cut him off. "Did anyone check the room?"

"We did; it's clean," answered someone.

Braulio looked around, trying to understand what was happening. He noticed how laboriously everyone seemed to be breathing. Holding in a tension that could spill out at any second—venting itself on him.

"And the priest?" pursued the voice.

"He's okay," someone else responded.

"Good. So we're just brothers here."

"No *culebras*!" someone shouted. *Culebras* meant lizards, which meant snitches, and he pronounced it Anglo style.

Braulio saw the man who said it. Smaller than him, pasty white in the face, dirty blond hair, shoulders vibrating with muscles, cowboy boots worn under the unironed trousers of a faded suit. His suit looked cheap, but the boots, of 'gator skin, were flashy, snazzy. The man stepped forward, shot an inquiring glance at Braulio, *Okay if I say a word?* He stood against the table with the burning liquor glasses, head lowered, like a bull appraising a herd before joining it.

"I guess y'all know me, but for those who don't, I'm Royce, from Local 91. . . ." Suddenly, his mouth popped open, his eyes widened, and he let out a sneeze that echoed in the packed hall. "This is from the stench," he yelled. "It's so thick and smelly, brothers, it makes me sneeze an' choke an' don't let me sleep. And I know it don't let you sleep neither. It's the stench of brimstone from them goddamn Lecouveurs!"

He stopped. The silence was explosive, as if the whole crowd was holding its breath.

"We've all been thinking the same thing, so it's about time somebody came out and said it aloud," he shouted. "And I says the Lecouveurs are a bunch of demons and they ought to be sent back to Hell, where they came from. I says forget the negotiation table, and forget the law. Let's go get 'em, brothers!'' he bellowed at the crowd, with long-stored-up feeling. "Let's get 'em *now*, before they get more of us!"

Silence. One second. Two. Three. And then the crowd began to shuffle their feet with excitement.

"Let's get 'em!" repeated Royce for the third time. "Let's go out and set their unholy lair ablaze, and then drive stakes through their black hearts!"

The crowd's heavy breathing could be heard, almost in unison. And then the voice answered solitarily, but Braulio heard it like an approval from all: "Righteous!"

Laura's fashion show started at six P.M. on Thursday, at the New Orleans Hilton, whose Lavender Room had been rented through one of Marion's connections.

The half-hour scheduled for cocktails and hors d'oeuvres mushroomed into an hour, as women Laura had never met walked in and kissed almost all the women already there, and then, after an introduction from Marion, everyone kissed her and wished her welcome. They were all dressed up, even though the only men present were the hotel's assistant manager, the pianist (a solo piano was to be the show's accompaniment), and a couple of designers. These women had cloakrooms full of clothes, and needed such events to show them off. Conversations of saccharine Southern genteelness filled the room while the models were getting ready to parade down the makeshift runway in lacy-silky outfits from ornate Victorian to sexy contemporary—peignoir sets, teddies, camisoles with matching tap shorts, negligees that could double for evening wear. For the first time since she came to New Orleans, Laura felt in her own element at last, presiding over this sea of elegant and excited females. Then a gong beat behind a curtain, Marion grabbed the mike to emcee the affair, and a parade of beautiful women with great bodies and no money flowed down the runway—to the *ooohhs* and *aaahhs* of women who had plenty of money and spent a lot of it to maintain their bodies. And the few who had both, the fifteen percent or so really pretty young ones who had married well— those would be her best customers.

Laura was standing by one of the exits, next to a fashion photographer who was flashing away, when the assistant manager was called out by a busboy. He came back and, holding the door open, asked her to please come outside for just a second.

The next room was a small foyer decorated enticingly in lavender. The light came from candle-shaped lamps, pronged to the walls in sets of threes. In the pale purple of the room, Emory's dark suit looked like black agate, and his eyes leaped on her like spiders.

All the flirty lightness of the show drained out of her. As the assistant manager stepped back inside and closed the door, the room closed in around them, still and airless, like a padded coffin. She couldn't look Emory in the eyes and focused on his brightly polished shoes. Though he hadn't moved, she could swear he was a foot closer to her. She stepped back, crumpling in her hands an invitation to the show.

"Please don't run away," he said, staring at her hypnotically. "I won't harm you. No one of my blood ever wished to harm you."

She let out a whimper. The black suit he was wearing tonight was pressed so perfectly that the crease of the trousers seemed to stab the air. The weighted tails of the coat moved as he pushed a lapel away and rested a fist against his hip, in a young man's attitude. The waistcoat under his jacket looked coffered like a carved figurehead's on a ship's prow. She couldn't help marveling at the disquieting complexity of his appearance. The face and the hand on the hip were alive, but the posture and the drape of the clothing were sculptural, as if he'd just walked off a pedestal, only momentarily human.

That hand.

She could almost feel the craggy fingers back on her body, the sharp undulations of the fingertips tracking marks on her back, the porous heaps of old tissues slapping against her naked shoulders and thighs, with the dull sound of air cushions. But the ugly hand stopped at the curt edge of a perfect white cuff, and the black sleeve above, so well tailored, restored the loathsomeness to a sort of macabre esthetic.

That unequaled effect was his elegance, and he knew it. With indulgent cruelty, he smiled. "A bit shaky, aren't we, after our little party?"

She was wretchedly aware of being alone with him, with

no weapon at hand. The roomful of people behind the door seemed beyond reach or hearing.

"Leave," she said, to the shoes and suit, to the porous hands. To the crawling memory of their "little party."

His eyes narrowed with curiosity. "Why should I?"

"If you don't leave, I'll get the security guards and have you removed."

"That would be interesting," Emory said. "Perhaps you don't know that we own part of this hotel."

"Good night," she said, and found the strength to turn around and step toward the door. Like a giant jack-in-the-box, he sprang from where he was and stretched his arms. She wanted to scream, but her vocal cords just wouldn't do it. He raised his hideous hands in a conciliatory gesture. "Laura, please, there's no need to make a scene out of this."

She could throw herself at him, she thought. They'd crash into the other room together, and everyone would leap to her assistance. What stopped her was the thought of her body touching his. Also, curiously, the thought of Emory let loose among a hundred females, some down to the scantiest attire.

"Laura," Emory pleaded chidingly. "You can't be as impressionable as this."

She could turn and try to run. But she dreaded his shadow, spreading rapacious wings behind her.

His eyes glowed like green embers. Held under their gaze, she made a huge effort to think without fear. *He has no power, except his lechery. That's his only power, that's the only power he ever had over me.*

She talked softly, but loud enough for him to hear. "You vile, despicable degenerate."

She felt better, less frightened.

A smile of gratified vanity split the red lips over the white teeth. "Call me what you will, Laura."

She felt enraged by the familiar, proprietary way in which he said her name, and ordered herself not to feel the rage, not to react, to be cool.

"The night we spent together," he whispered, "will be

our precious little memory. Our cherished secret. It will never happen again.''

"Damn right it won't!" she said through her teeth.

He frowned, astonished by her firmness. But his voice came out sweeter, with no trace of threat. "We'll just smile at each other now and then, struck by some innocent detail of reality that will bring the memory back for a fleeting moment." Her face told him clearly that he'd be smiling alone. He drew nearer.

"Laura, is it so monstrous of me, old as I am, to have breathed for a second your life-giving fragrance?"

"What do you *want*?"

"Tomorrow," he said, "is my birthday."

"Oh." She laughed coldly. "You want me to wish you many happy returns? To send you a card with compliments on your methods of seduction? Well, I can tell you my feelings right now," she snapped. "I don't care if you drop dead on the way back to your peeling castle. As for your prowess, it made me want to puke. And the only reason I didn't do it," she said, groping for the weak spot in his armor, and thrusting at it wickedly, "is because all the time I was thinking that you could've been Alain!"

He narrowed his eyes, and a slim line sealed up his lips. Closing all openings and cracks, his face looked like a death mask, except for his eyes, which reddened at the insult. His hands twitched, grabbing at the air.

"You love him, then?"

She didn't deign to answer.

"He loves you," he said cavernously.

She nodded, but again graced him with no reply.

"After seeing you three times, he loves you. It's no youthful fancy, he really does," repeated Emory. He stepped aside from the door, and his wizened claws hung to the sides of his tastefully dressed torso, like two tiny corpses.

She still said nothing, acknowledging her conquest. From inside the showroom, an ovation arose. One of the peignoirs had struck a nerve in the crowd.

"Laura," he said. His voice, sad, was almost melodious, cracked, not bronzed. Pleasant. "Laura, I've had my chances with you. Remember the little shaft inside the wall of your apartment?''

She stiffened, and her eyes riveted onto his flamboyant cravat.

''The roof grating can be moved. Those worthless policemen didn't even realize it. Laura, both Alain and I noticed you the very night you arrived. How could any man whose blood isn't water keep himself away from you?''

Another ovation from inside. Emory shot a glance at the door and talked faster. ''I'm not surprised Alain loves you so. But he doesn't *know* you, not the way I do,'' he whispered. ''Does he?''

She stood motionlessly, staring him back in the eyes. *You're not sure, are you, you scaly Caliban?* ''You'll *never* know me the way Alain does,'' she said.

A touch of steel parted the jealous redness of his eyes, and quickly vanished. ''Come to my party tomorrow, Laura. Come and meet the family. We are different, yes, but we aren't as terrible as you think. We have our own beauty, and Alain is part of it. Laura, the occult knowledge we brought over with us from the Carpathians,'' he whispered, ''our familiarity with the old rituals, has resulted in . . . in . . .''

He seemed reluctant to define it, so she helped: ''In the mastery of time?''

His eyes went round with surprise, then he smiled. ''That and other—little intuitive gifts. Nothing to harm anyone. We're not bad, Laura. The world is full of spoon-benders and table-shakers, and no one fears them.'' He moved really close to her, but she didn't fear him anymore. She felt his breath—stale, old.

''I want you to get to know us,'' he went on, ''because I feel that the little time we spent together''—he raised his bony hands to prevent a reaction from her—''made you, just a little, *like* us. Come, Alain will be there,'' he finished persuasively.

She hesitated. Indistinctly, she heard Marion's voice inside, amplified by the mike, and wished that the show would last another ten minutes, but it wasn't likely. ''How can I trust you?'' she heard herself saying.

''Come with someone. Bring whoever you want, even those

simpletons, the detectives who've been following you around. Watching for danger from outside, when the danger was within," he said, chuckling in a pleased aside to himself. When she bristled and glared, his voice instantly softened apologetically. "But you won't be alone with me, there'll be plenty of people there. And Alain, too, of course."

Alain. *Alain.*

He seemed to guess her suspicion. "I'm only here now as Alain's messenger, to invite you to our party," he said, simply, convincingly.

"What will you be serving?" she asked sarcastically. "That funny wine?"

"No, no," he said. "Good old Southern sour mash. Laura," he said with sudden solemnity, "I have to go now. It's up to you. But please come—let it be your decision to join us," he spoke the words carefully, "as Alain's bride."

She took a deep breath. She heard her voice—fattened by satisfaction. "That's for Alain to decide, too, isn't it?"

"He needs help—your help," he said hastily.

"Why?"

"He's tortured about who he is. About the roots he comes from. He needs to know that you accept him in order to accept himself." Long, rolling applause rang inside. The door to the Lavender Room swung open.

"Laura Walker?" asked an overdressed lady, stepping toward her. "Oh I'm so glad to meet you. I'm Hope—" She added a last name Laura didn't catch. "Your store is exactly what this city needs."

"Thank you," said Laura.

"Will you come?" Emory whispered in her other ear.

"I'll see," she whispered back. More women were walking out—one of them greeted Emory. Laura's hand, hanging at her side, was suddenly found by his hand and treated to a little squeeze of mute understanding. He excused himself, said he was being called away, bowed to the growing little group, and danced out of the foyer, as agile as a young man. Marion was coming out of the Lavender Room, surrounded by a colorful bouquet of socialites. The impressed wives of the high and mighty streamed out of the room to find the store owner and pull her back inside for congratulations, and questions, and orders for business.

With dreamlike steps, Emory strode away from the show's hub of excitement, his footfalls deadened completely by the thickness of the plush hotel carpets, to the sales director's office. He was recognized by a secretary who let him into the office, empty at this hour, to make a private call. Emory called Malcolm at Belle Hellène, was told that Alain's bags were all packed in his room, and Alain himself at the river camp. Emory had himself put through to the river camp, talked to the dispatcher. He waited patiently almost ten minutes, like a man whose sense of time could not be frustrated by delays, till Alain came on the line.

"Alain," said Emory with dignity, "tomorrow is the company's last board meeting in its present structure. I ask that you postpone your departure and attend it."

There was a pause, during which the line, extremely clear at that hour, conveyed the standard background noises from Alain's working post on the river: the clacking of an electronic printer, men talking, the muffled hoot of a passing boat. Then Alain said he saw no reason to attend, he had fulfilled his last obligation to the clan by securing the loan. That and his resignation from the board could be announced without him present.

"The family's throwing a little celebration for me after the board meeting. Are you going to miss that, too?" asked Emory, and then listened.

Alain said he was sorry, and hoped Emory wouldn't be too inconvenienced by his absence. He had business records to file, memos to pouch, last calls to make before leaving.

"Alain, I beg you to reconsider. There's no reason for you to throw away our whole family and a brilliant future. I know how aggrieved you are over your loss, but she is nothing but a female, *one* female. Dramatic departures of this sort are simply not *done* over just one person."

"One person can be important enough to me," replied Alain. "Not that I would expect you to understand it. Besides, I've reconsidered and re-reconsidered already. I've hesitated while people died. And the changes I've been fight-

ing for haven't been accomplished. I don't want to do it anymore, Emory, it's as simple as that."

"Alain," said Emory, "you're selfish."

Alain found that quite funny; he chuckled. "Where are you
calling me from?" he asked.

"From Belle Hellène," Emory replied quietly. "Alain,
you're fooling yourself. You'll never be free of us."

"I'll be as free as I can make myself be. And if I have to
carry a curse, it'll be only my own."

"Well, I suppose I have exhausted all my arguments,"
Emory said, smiling contentedly and looking around at the
office. The assistant manager was obviously an inveterate
fisherman; the walls were lined with pictures of him on boat
decks or wharves, arms bending under the weight of a catch.
"You know how much we shall all miss you . . ."

"Stuff it, Emory," said Alain calmly. "Good night."

The receiver clicked up on the river.

Emory put his own phone down and looked out the window. The moon, almost full, had risen over the waterfront.

He looked at a clock on the wall. He reviewed the scenario
in his mind, and decided to give all the players an hour, to
further their progress into their roles.

He leaned back in the fisherman's chair, and waited.

I'm here as Alain's messenger.

Laura accepted congratulations, exchanged cards, jotted
down phone numbers with a smile she had learned to repeat
each time she shook a hand or heard a word of praise. Warm
enough to engage the other person's good will, cool enough
to signal autonomy and competence.

*Come see what we're really like. Let it be your decision to
join us, as Alain's bride.*

Why hadn't he come himself? Embarrassed about the other
night's farewell? Why charge the old degenerate with such
an invitation? But, of course, he didn't know. About Emory
and her.

Thanking the models, posing with them for a last group
shot. Getting the wares packed, wrapping the show. All the
while playing back the scene with Emory.

If only she'd had the presence of mind to say, "Wait a

minute, I want to talk to Alain first. Is there a way to reach him up in that wilderness?'' But the chance had been lost. Alain had remained out of reach, though only a phone call away. All of a sudden she felt trapped in the belief that Alain was real, of flesh and blood, part of the present, *only* when he was standing right next to her.

She felt she had peered into a hole in the face of reality. Beyond it, a vertiginous tunnel blinded her with its unlit opaqueness, and the hum of its empty air whizzed by her face and gave her a chill. No, no. She called in for support all the physical sensations she'd experienced with him. His eyes, his mouth. His smell and touch. The tantalizing fever in her belly, in her thighs, as she had mounted his thigh that afternoon at the store, when he was leaning back on the wall, kissing her. The urge she had felt in her breasts, in her nipples. All that was real enough.

He was real. But as elusive as quicksilver.

What kind of a husband would such a man make? What kind of a father?

She couldn't escape Marion, so she joined her in the hotel's bar, for drinks with two of the models and two young socialites and a fashion reporter. She warned them that in half an hour she'd be driving back to Marion's to take a hot bath and crash. Marion pouted; she wanted to stay and whoop it up a little. She was gloating and gushing as if the success had been all her own. Laura said that's all right, she could go back alone, she didn't mind.

Half an hour later, she got up, kissed Marion. Kissed everybody. And left.

In the jeep, she thought about calling Cabot, trying to reach Alain through him, then dismissed it. Why bother to check? It was now or never. If Alain had ever intended to be taken seriously, it had to be this time.

If he was real.

The thought of what he had shown her in that streetcar scared her the most. Maybe she didn't live here at all. Maybe he lived back *there*, in time, and simply came to visit, and Emory was his grotesque agent in the current world. No, no, his arms, his lips, they were anything but ghostly. His body was male, and swelled with male desire. She prayed, driving past a set of streetlights, that Alain was real. Enough fantasy. Enough living with the dead. Enough voices.

She had created those voices—now she was quite sure. She had invented them, with the same detail and believability with which she constructed those fantasies, so complete and sophisticated that her body responded to them with actual sensations, and wriggled alone in bed, and had orgasms, and then slept, sated and damp, as if after true lovemaking. She had given them such strength and allowed them to call and cry out so loud in her subconscious, small wonder that that psychic, the Egyptian, had heard them, too.

She had foreseen, in leaving San Francisco, that the bonds to the past would break. That a man, the extraordinary Alain, would appear and fight Michael's lingering memory, and expel it from her body. And she had created the voices.

Of course, seen from this angle, everything figured. There were a couple of loose ends, but in the main things made sense. The killings, the tragic end of someone close, Charlotte, had wrapped an ominous cloud around something much simpler: that she had met and fallen in love with a man of uncommon powers acquired by his family and passed down as an incredible mental gift.

Seen from this point of view—she was lucky.

Poor Charlotte.

Given a different set of circumstances, Charlotte could've been Alain's choice. While Laura could have been the victim, the blood-desiccated corpse in the forest. How little separated one woman's good fortune from another's disaster.

She parked the jeep close to the corner of St. Charles. She and Alain had walked around that corner three nights before.

She glanced at the street corner. Fondly. Alain's message had erased the pain and disappointment of that walk.

If he was real. Fear of finding out that he *wasn't* devoured her fear of going back to Belle Hellène. She had to find out, and going to that party was the way. *I'll go, and I'll take Cabot with me.*

With a righteous sense of resolve, she stabbed the key into the lock.

She turned the lights on in the living room.

Now everything felt, if not normal, at least consistent. Absurdly consistent. A couple of coincidences here and there, like crumbs fallen off a loaf of bread after the passing of a straight blade. Alain was always appearing and disappearing at the right moment. But maybe she was responsible for that, too. Michael, unimaginative Michael, used to make fun of her. "Serendipitous Laura," he called her, when she looked down just in time to locate dimes lying before her on the sidewalks of San Francisco. When she complained about needing money, and the postman took care of it with a check in the mail an hour later. Hadn't she had, as a little girl, an uncanny sense of who might talk first when she played on the living room rug while several adults were having coffee? Of knowing whether the lights were on or off in a room before entering it? But that was long ago. Puberty had blunted those abilities, and confronted her with an unpredictable world full of unsuspected issues: What she should do with herself after high school, boys were so different from girls, Mom and Dad won't live forever, money was important.

The child she had been, the girl she had been, still seemed alive in her, a piece of the woman she had become. All in preparation for meeting this man, who had rejected her three nights before, only to reverse himself through the message brought by his grotesque uncle: "Let it be your decision to join us, as Alain's bride." What a dizzying satisfaction, what a conquest, to return to Belle Hellène tomorrow, to pass judgment on whether he and they were worthy of her.

She hesitated, then called the Egyptian, and found his line busy. She undressed, called him again, got a busy signal. She ran the hot water in the bathtub, called again, same busy signal, called Cabot. She found him right away and told him about the invitation to Emory's party tomorrow night, and that she wanted him to be there.

"Cain't come uninvited," said Cabot, "it's against etiquette. What makes you want me there, anyway? You got any reason t'feel uneasy about anybody?"

She said no, but she sort of had a feeling, a hunch that something would, could turn up to help his inquiry.

"Ain't my inquiry no more," said Cabot. She was shocked and asked why. He laughed rather bitterly and said the law business wasn't like the lace business. He said he could tag along by himself, though; he was free, he was taking it easy these days. "If it's the old boy's birthday, every walk o' life will be there, from church to gin mill. So they'll have some cops for security. Wouldn't be no big deal to slip in." He reflected for an instant. "Okay, you got it, 'ol Cabot'll be there."

"Thanks." She pictured his big red face, felt like stroking his gray hair, like a mutt's.

"Later," he said monotonously, and hung up.

She called the Egyptian again, but again it was busy. Finally she got through to him after she took her bath, and asked him if his phone had been out of order.

"No, I've been answering calls," he replied. "This vampire scare is turning into an epidemic. People are calling me to ask how they could insulate their auras for anti-vampire protection. I'm actually thinking of giving a talk about it. Would you like to co-chair it with me?"

She was speechless, then started to laugh. "Are you serious?"

He replied that he was dead serious, and offered her thirty percent of the take. She said she thought that would be a rip-off of the audience. Was she an authority on vampires, or even the Egyptian, for that matter? And quite stunned, she realized that she felt a need to defend . . . well, not quite to defend . . . but certainly not to join in this sudden hysteria. No, she said, thanks, no—she was going to a party at the Lecouveurs'.

The Egyptian couldn't wait to learn what the black diary had revealed to Laura. Feeling the same unexpected protectiveness, she sanitized the contents as much as possible, then asked him about the time-machine experience she'd had with Alain. The Egyptian thought it was possible, but simply as a projection of her mind. Laura interrupted impatiently: She had *seen* those streets, that Mardi Gras pageant. Could a mind projection be so elaborate?

"One can do amazing things by mind projection," said the Egyptian. He quoted the example of seventeenth-century slaves captured in Dahomey, Africa, and brought across the Atlantic in the fetid holds of blackbirders. Chained, possessing no weapons or freedom of movement, they found a way to commit suicide . . . by holding their breath. Now, anyone just trying to hold their breath would get light-headed, and the brain would give the breathing system an instant command to start functioning again. Killing oneself by not breathing was clinically impossible. But those tribesmen from Africa projected themselves as dead, and accordingly, they died, the Egyptian explained. Changing the subject abruptly, he asked Laura to take him with her to Emory's party.

"You weren't invited. It's against etiquette," she echoed Cabot.

He insisted stubbornly; he was dying to be with the Lecouveurs, to observe them, so that he could understand them. "They're the new thing—the *in* crowd," he said quite unastrally.

"I can't. I'm sorry."

He warned her that he might just crash it anyway. She shrugged and wished him good luck, and they both said good night.

At about the same time, Emory emerged from the office, crossed the hotel's lounge, and walked into the bar. He was rewarded as usual with heads turning and whispers running around the room. He stopped suddenly, eyes concentrating, senses sharpening. He'd sighted a table of girls, gorgeous girls, five or six of them. They looked like models.

He was looking for females. The talk with Laura had gotten his blood up, and it was boiling even higher now as moonlight whitened the street outside and streamed in through windows, rivaling the bar's dim illumination.

He directed his steps toward the girls, thinking of an amusing excuse to seat himself at their table. One of them turned to look at the approaching man. He felt the call in her movement, and his muscles hardened under the heavy flap of his clothing. The shine of a smile cut into the darkness of her face, and she jumped up, running among the little tables toward him.

"E-m-m-ory!" she called. He blinked disbelievingly, pulling the corners of his mouth into a polite smile, and offering his hand to be taken by a smaller hand in a white glove.

"Alone, you, at this hour?" cooed Marion Voguey, and over her shoulder he saw the others, the young ones, interrupted from some conversation, looking to see who Marion was talking to.

"I see," he said, "you're taking out your cheerleaders."

"Oh, aren't they adorable?" she laughed. "They made our show such a smash, they deserve a little fun!" She threw back toward them a maternal smile, but Emory noticed that she wasn't moving out of his way: She was carefully blocking his path to all that young flesh.

"I would be delighted to buy them a couple of bottles of Cordon Rouge," he said.

They had overheard their dialogue, and were turning in their seats now to face Emory. He tried to imagine the bodies under the dresses, under the butterfly-gauze of Laura's lingerie. But Marion skillfully slipped her arm under his.

"I'm glad I have an escort—they just chased me from their table," she said, and pushed him one step further away from the girls.

He frowned, smelling a trick. "Why would they do such a thing?" he asked. One of the girls turned back toward the table, away from him and Marion. "They just made me understand," chuckled Marion, "that one hour with mama is enough. Now they want to be on their own, so they can flirt with guys their own age."

"You look like a very desirable mama," he said with a congealed smile.

"Really? Emory, you just made my night," bloomed Marion. "You look quite desirable, too. What's your secret? Are the rumors true about those embarrassing predilections of yours?" She breathed gin and tonic in his face, her body swaying slightly as she clung to his arm.

All the girls' faces were back huddled over the table now, no longer paying any attention to him. He felt a surge of anger, and was sure she had noticed it. But she kept undulating before him, with an innocent smile.

She didn't look bad, he decided. The low cut of her dress revealed capacious breasts, but otherwise she seemed slim. And she smiled like an eighteen-year-old.

"Maybe you should buy *me* some champagne, Emory,"

she whispered cutely, pressing herself against him. The touch didn't put him off this time.

"All right," he surrendered. And then, like a mask falling, replaced by another, he grinned, his eyes lit up by a new plan.

"Let's get out of here. I can't hear myself think." He steered her out of the bar and toward the double set of elevators. "You know, we own the hotel's penthouse. What about some champagne up there? The view over the river is breathtaking."

His eyes stared straight into hers. A direct question was asked silently. It was rewarded by a clear, wordless answer. "Why, Emory," she said aloud. "I'd be delighted. Are you going to order me the champagne by telephone? I adore things ordered by telephone."

He looked around. The lounge was empty, and a clerk behind the reception desk was bending over a computerized list of guests. He wished the lounge had been crowded. He wished that the world could have watched him now taking up to the penthouse a twenty-year-old. One of those stunning fillies with a prematurely cynical smile should have been walking beside him right now, swaying in high heels, inviting a push to topple her onto the penthouse's bed. A proud pair of legs that wouldn't mind his age, as they would open with honest lust not for him, but for a brooch, a bracelet, a set of earrings brought in the next morning on the breakfast tray.

But there was no such prize for him tonight. There was just Marion. Eager and predictable Marion. However . . .

However, she was this night's gift. And he'd never passed up a gift in his life.

"Why, Marion," he imitated her coo, "I'd be happy to order by telephone anything that strikes your fancy."

13

Laura lay down on her bed. Sleep stole her body and carried it over some wide dark river, which she knew well, though she had never seen it.

She experienced a sensation of utter peace, deep and satisfying, a peace with herself that she couldn't remember feeling before. All the while, her body moved above the dark water, flying without wings, walking without steps. She was alone but felt presences around her, from friendly beings, related to her. They were traveling in the night, unhurried and content, just like her. The night was lit not just by the moon, but by four or five other planets that orbited around the earth, moving about as fast as a blimp would over a big city.

She looked down at the water. Though dark, it had a sort of inner luminosity. She knew suddenly that this was the river of life—vast, broad, unending—and it felt quite natural that she would hover over it like this.

Still asleep, she heard the mistress of the house returning. A key rattled in the front-door lock, and uneven footsteps announced a rather tipsy Marion—quite drunk, actually, because she bumped into a chair in the dark, something Laura didn't expect from a woman with such punctilious knowledge of where every little thing should be. She woke up completely as Marion began noisily pulling out drawers, and moving things around with the energy of a young girl spirited by some great night out. Then she heard the shower.

Laura had left the bedside lamp on; she reached her hand out and turned it off. The river of sleep had been waiting. It rolled over her again.

In her sleep, she heard Marion talking on the phone in the next room. Loud with excitement. She thought she heard her tell someone, "You were terrific," or something like that. Then she heard Marion open the windows of the living room and start pacing. Then she heard nothing.

She was floating over that river again, and the friendly planets were spinning closer—in fact she could feel on her skin a slight rise in temperature as they appeared from behind the crest of the horizon and circled, before disappearing again. Then, from space, a dark dot sped toward her, and it became Alain. Alain—his gorgeous naked body made of a sort of dark marble—was hurtling through space in search of her. He had eyes like the cowrie-shell eyes of African gods, but they were beautiful, and she wasn't afraid. He slowed down when he saw her. She lay on her back in the air. His astral body floated above hers, and his face, carved like a statue's, slowly pressed down on hers.

She closed her eyes, ecstatic. That coupling of their faces felt like a mystical orgasm. The features of his face dissolved into hers, the shape of his mouth informed the curvature of her mouth, his brow and eye sockets reshaped hers, and their profiles meshed completely. Now she was him, and the flight through the universe began again, and it seemed that the word "wedding" had never had a clearer meaning to her. *This* was a wedding—this passage of his features into hers, of his body into hers. And then, as one, this planetary honeymoon.

She got up after nine. A note from Marion told her of beignets in the microwave; they just had to be warmed up. The coffeepot was brimming with aromatic Creole brew. The day was warm and overcast, and yes, all the windows to the living room were open.

The day stayed warm and overcast. The day of reckoning, and revelation.

Was she excited? Anxious? Fearful?

For Christ's sake, Laura. Just for once, stop splitting every loose end into 36,000 smaller ends, only to braid them back together into one.

The party would be in full swing by six. She had no intention to go and face that bunch too early. Her entrance would be timed for maximum effect.

Little by little, she had taken outfits and nighties and make-up over to Marion's, had populated the guest-room closet and the bathroom with them. Now she packed them and took them back to her apartment. It seemed symbolic, as if her period of adolescent night-frights was finally over. She put her clothes back in her dresser, found the forgotten airline headset in the bottom drawer, and threw it in the trash.

Then she spent a short day at the store. She called Marion twice to thank her for helping with yesterday's show and for everything else, and didn't find her. And at four she was at home, washing her hair, moving around with calm control, as if the last few weeks had never happened.

She had a peculiar sensation looking at things and people—she had noticed it driving back from the store. Everything seemed new somehow, even though it was utterly familiar. People's faces had acquired a sort of indefinable meaningfulness. The minutiae of their features were so clear to her, as if her eyes had just learned to take things in, to observe them in depth and detail, with a speed and clarity she had never experienced before. Colors were more vivid. The outlines of shapes against other shapes were sharper. Even the magnolia tree before her balcony, its jagged black leaves stabbing into the sun's red laceration between two clouds, had a sort of music to it. The seen was fresh and vibrant—while the unseen behind it called out at her with a melodic, enticing voice.

Even her face had changed, though she couldn't say how. It had a lascivious candor that made her want to lean into the mirror, to reach across the cool barrier of glass, and touch herself. The pores of her skin had a life all their own, and seemed ready for adventure. "We'll have fun," they promised from myriads of little smiles spread all over her face.

At five, her hair dry, she called Cabot.

"I'm just leaving," he grunted. "I'll be there before you."

She felt guilty. "I'm sorry," she said. "I hope you didn't cancel something important just to watch over me."

"Don't be silly. There'll be free food and drinks. What better bargain can a guy like me hope for?"

"You're not serious," she said. *He was such an old tiger two weeks ago. What's happened to him?* "I'm sure it's depressing to have to give up an investigation after putting so much into it . . ."

"Either I'm serious," he said mockingly, "or you're very young—it's one o' the two. I'll see you there."

He hung up. She shrugged, looked at the three dresses she had pulled out and laid on the bed, and chose the silver-blue satin. It was strapless—she'd need a jacket to cover her shoulders later. But the dress was flowy, sexy, terrific. The smallest movement made it ripple, and then it resettled on her body with long shimmers of disturbed light.

A diamond necklace, she decided, worked perfectly with it. And two diamond studs in her ears. Against the never-still reflections of her dress, the jewels had a heavy, static glow. Together, they made her look vulnerably young. Then she put on silver pumps, not her tallest, but all right for walking or dancing.

She pulled the Jeep out of the carport and cut through a back alley, toward Esplanade.

The sensation of ineffable novelty persisted as Laura drove off Highway 10, with the declining sun in her eyes, the green and white scrim of houses and trees stretching shinily on both sides of the busy traffic lanes. Veering south, she took River Road. Passing a gas station, she glimpsed an old 1959 Cadillac with its hood up. Turning to see its outrageous shark fins, she thought that the rounded shoulders bending over the steaming engine and the mass of hair crowning them looked familiar. It was the Egyptian! A bend in the road swept gas station and car and Egyptian out of sight, with the same symphonic grace, and the trees rustled at the Jeep's passage just like her dress rustled when she moved in her seat. The trees, the road, the buildings seemed drawn up by a giant hand directly onto the liquid film of her irises.

Belle Hellène announced itself a mile in advance, with cars parked on each side of the roadway. Car parkers, posted at intervals of a few hundred yards, waved at her to slow down, and when she stopped, the massive iron gates were in sight.

"Miss Walker?" asked someone into her rolled-down window.

She turned. She saw a reddish mustache and glasses.

"I thought this would be you. I'm Clark Chadwick," said the man, opening her door. He clicked his fingers with a show of authority that didn't go with the servile, almost cringing smile he beamed at her. The snap of fingers brought a valet running.

"Park it right here," he ordered the valet, "so Miss Walker won't be standing forever to get it back," he switched back to smiling at her.

"Thank you," she said. There was nothing else to do but surrender the keys and step out of the car, into the bright light of his relentless smile. "Thank you, mister . . . ?"

"Chadwick, Clark Chadwick. I thought Alain might've mentioned me?"

"I'm afraid he hasn't," said Laura, trying to match half of his smile.

"I'm the family attorney. I bend the laws so that they don't have to break 'em. Miss Walker, it's so wonderful to meet you at last. And you look just *per*-fect," he rhapsodized, admiring her dress so overtly that she felt uneasy. "Might I have the pleasure to walk you in?"

"Why not?" Was the family attorney acting so obsequious because the word had spread already that she might become, *just might become*, Alain's bride?

The heavy carriage gates were open just a crack. Chadwick pushed them open further, then offered his arm. They stepped through. With a quick palpitation, she looked for the decomposing garden and unkempt trees she had run through that doomed morning.

She saw instead that the driveway's gravel had been raked carefully. Trimmed, the line of trees was bordered by regular little heaps of grayed moss. The bushes that had looked like shriveled witches' faces were now shaped back into geometrical silhouettes. Symphonic music was coming from somewhere, sounding in character with the recovered dignity of the garden.

Belle Hellène had primped herself. For Laura.

What poetic justice, to be accompanied regally into the

place she had left humbled and terror-stricken. The feeling sent a buzz through her body.

"This place sure has changed," she said.

"Hasn't it?" Chadwick agreed enthusiastically. He was holding his arm right under hers, palm cupped up to fit her wrist. "This loan is the first breath of fresh air into the family business, and look at the difference already."

"I'm glad they got it," said Laura with goodwill.

"Alain is the one who got it for them. He's got such a head for business." He fawned his smile away from her, at the unseen Alain.

"Oh yes, he's great with business," she said, feeling like a fraud. How much did she really know about him and his abilities? *But I know I love him—shouldn't that be enough?* "Where is he?" she asked.

The ramparts of boxwood opened, showing resuscitated flower beds. Behind them, like taller flowers, she saw women in cocktail dresses with glasses in their hands, and some men in suits, about fifty guests in all.

"Alain should be here any minute. He had to take care of something upriver. Excuse me, I'm sort of a factotum here tonight." He detached his arm and ran toward a dour-faced liveried maitre d'. Laura let him go, still feeling that dizzy sense of contentment, that everything here, even Clark Chadwick, belonged to her.

She watched him whisper something into the maitre d's ear. Both had to take a step aside as a striped tent started rising beside them, and the maitre d' turned and vanished behind it.

Laura tried to recognize the loud music—was it Mahler? One of his later symphonies? Flowing into the driveway, to make room for the tent, the crowd engulfed Laura. A tray of champagne stopped right by her. She took a glass, heard a woman shrilling above the music: "So who's out there for you if you're over thirty-five? Married men? How much time can they give you? Guys twice divorced? They're the worst tightwads."

I know I'm being selfish, but I don't have those problems. I've got Alain, and he's got me.

"If I find a guy I like, I want him for good, I'm tired of flings," answered another woman.

Controlling a second palpitation, Laura turned toward the house. Yes, there it was, the Greek temple to the left, where she and Emory had talked under the stained-glass window. She was holding her purse against her hip. From under her purse, from an unknown niche in her body, fear suddenly reached out with a pair of pincers and tweezed at her heart. Very fast, and then it shrank back into hiding.

"And if *he* wants someone for good, it's gonna be some twenty-year-old, not you. Come on, dawlin' "—the first voice started laughing—"settle for a foreigner with an accent, and pray it's not a speech impediment."

"Sorry." Chadwick rushed back to her with every indication that even while away his main concern had been Belle Hellène's new mistress. "Let me get you a drink—oh, you got one."

"Yes, thanks," she said. She felt that her natural modesty was returning, that she wouldn't be able to enjoy this smug vanity much longer, and was almost angry, like a child who rarely gets to play with a much-desired toy. "It's nice and cool out here," she said, sipping the champagne, "much cooler than in town." Talking, she glanced over Chadwick's shoulder. There was the glass-enclosed gallery—she remembered how silvery the night had looked as she had walked through it. And beyond the gallery, the other temple. A ray of setting sun streaked its ground floor, carmine red, making the Greek pillars look like bared, bloodied teeth. Because of the sun, she couldn't tell whether the lights inside were on or not. She looked at the mansion, and it looked back with hypnotic muteness, as yet untouched by the fresh signs of affluence.

"Oh, yes," he agreed quickly. "You'll see—the summers at Belle Hellène, they're a blessing here in the Delta. You thinking of any changes you'd like to bring to the property?"

That's it. This place is mine, because Alain's mine.

She couldn't help it. In her brain, in her lips, in her arms, in her breasts and crotch and everywhere, she felt it. The pride. A thick, milky giddy shot of pride.

"I don't know," she said. "Make it less . . . ancient. Less Gothic. It's a little spooky. I'd like to cheer it up a little."

He took that in, his expression suddenly pensive, his look serious. "Maybe," he agreed softly, after a beat. "Maybe."

"But then again," she said, "I'd have to talk to Alain about it." She looked around; the well-dressed crowd, its poses urbane and complacent, didn't seem to find anything odd about the house. She saw the woman named Hope who had congratulated her after her show. And at the other end of the crowd . . . yes, there he was: Cabot. In a J.C. Penney suit, split open by his belly. Cabot. Safety.

"Miss Walker," a deep bass voice asked quietly next to her, but with such resonance that she jumped, as if the earth had opened and emitted an echo from its core. Malcolm, in a tuxedo that seemed to expand his chest, grinned at her. "You're expected inside. Would you please follow me?"

"I'll take it." Chadwick hurried to grab her glass.

"Nice talking to you," she said, and he answered that they'd be seeing a lot more of each other, he was certain. Laura said oh yes, for sure, rewarded him with a smile, and followed the broad beam of Malcolm's back past the tent.

Let's see you, Alain, sweet Alain, she sang in her mind. *Let's see you in the midst of your dear crazy old family.*

As she and Malcolm stepped off the grass and onto the geometrized gravel before the front steps, the sun wrapped them in its glorious last ray.

"So how are you, Malcolm?" she inquired benevolently, behind the man's formidable back. He slowed down, letting her walk abreast of him, "Ev'thing's fine and dandy, Miss Walker," he said darkly, as if speaking inwardly to another Malcolm, whom he had to reassure and pacify.

"Why is that music so loud?" They had passed some unseen amplifier, blaring Mahler: his Eighth Symphony, she had finally identified it, written for a double-size orchestra.

"Fellow what did the riggin' this mornin' done somethin' funny to the switches." The entrance door, of massive oak, was open. Malcolm pushed the beveled-glass inner door behind it. The musty chill of the house rippled the satin around Laura's body. Her eyes, acclimating from the sunlight outside, saw for a second just circles of darkness, and Malcolm seemed to rise in the air and disappear. When she looked, he wasn't on her left. She remembered how he had vanished from her side the first time she'd walked into the house, and rematerialized at the top of the stairs.

To her right, it seemed that a woman's portrait on the wall liquefied and flowed down from its frame. Suddenly, a tall gaunt female with long arms and dark hair was standing next to her, saying, "It's all right, Malcolm, I'll take her upstairs."

From somewhere, the mysterious Malcolm grumbled acquiescence, but Laura couldn't see him.

"Hi," said the female apparition. "I'm Rose Janice, Alain's cousin."

"Oh, hi!" countered Laura enthusiastically, and stretched her hand into the dark. Five cold bones squeezed it, and a redolence of mouthwash blew out of Rose Janice's overwide smile. Laura concentrated her gaze, made out a black dress and a dog collar of black velvet around the scrawny neck.

"This way," breathed Rose Janice. Behind the mouthwash, a raw stench came from her throat.

She pointed at a long, ill-lit lobby. The darkness at the other end was carved with the steps of the giant balustrade she remembered from last time.

"You're a skinny one," commented Rose Janice. She was walking with long strides, and Laura had to adjust hers and strain her ankles to take firm steps on her high heels. "I am?" she replied. "You're not exactly overweight yourself."

"I mean, for an outsider. All the girls we've taken from the outside have been fuller than you," explained Rose Janice. Before Laura's mind could fasten on "the outside" and what that might mean in terms of the cohesion of such a family, the five cold bones grasped her arm. "You're strong, though. You can take it," said the tall woman, and her foul breath engulfed Laura's face again. *Poor girl, she's got a very nervous stomach. What is it I can take—making babies, perhaps?*

"I was like you when I came back from boarding school— I could take it. I couldn't take it now, see how narrow I am? Touch," Rose Janice invited, just as the two of them mounted the first step. Feeling her hand confiscated again, Laura swallowed nervously. The skeletal other hand pulled her fingers toward Rose Janice's body, below her waist. They touched a hip that felt like hard wire under the black dress, and right next to it, a loosely stretched drum of skin.

It was like a grotesque joke, like a partially deflated balloon gaudily painted to resemble a human body. Laura's fingers sank into the flesh; a mortified piece of Play-Doh seemed to stretch next to the hip bone. "Ow," Rose Janice moaned softly under Laura's touch, eyes staring straight into Laura's, with a sort of morbid pleasure. Laura snatched her fingers free. *Jesus, what sort of dystrophy is she suffering from?*

"You know, I was Alain's intended," said Rose Janice.

"What?" Laura bristled so fiercely that the apparition shrunk back toward the railless edge of the stairs. *"I was,"* stressed the mad woman. "Now that he's gone . . . ."

"Wait a second—where is he gone?" *Is she delirious?* "Where is Alain?"

"I don't know where he moved, maybe Houston. . . ." Laura felt like grabbing her by the neck, but the thought of touching that monstrous flesh again checked her impulse.

"What are you raving about? Isn't Alain here?" The top of the stairs flattened itself beneath her steps, and a rectangle of better lighting opened before them. Peering in, Laura saw the grandiflora of stained glass, considerably better lit now by the setting sun, with the coat of arms underneath it. Its bottom half was concealed by what looked like a huge family portrait. Standing, leaning against each other, even seated on the floor, a dozen or more people aimed flat canvas glances at the two entering women.

"I've got her," said Rose Janice.

Not "I brought her"—*I've got her.*

It seemed that she had talked to the portrait. Seeing that the people in the painting were dressed in turn-of-the-century garb, Laura scanned them quickly to see if Alain and Emory were among them. She saw long dresses on three or four women whose bodies had once been sumptuous, but had now lost firmness. Two men, looking like twins in their sixties, examined her from eyes set low under the slanted arcades of their foreheads. Several pale youngsters looked like they had never played with a ball. On the floor, two young girls had the mangy expressions of cast-out orphans.

It was then, in the middle of the bizarre diorama, that one of the twins took off a hat to Laura, and the portrait, breaking its arrangement, advanced toward her.

Flabbergasted, she stared. A phosphoric yellow luminescence played in their eyes. They were all farinaceously pale.

"Alain!" she called, not convinced that he was away in Houston.

Just then, something hit her on the back of the head. She spun around, and Rose Janice's long hand caught her across the face—it felt like a coat hanger. A stinging pain flashed from Laura's forehead to her lips. "Stop!" she screamed, but the hand slapped her again, at random, with the impotent clumsiness of deep anger, nails cutting against her cheek.

"He was mine! He was mine!" Rose Janice screeched like a rabid cat. Laura caught the skeletal arm, and the third blow went nowhere, but Rose Janice seemed to want to be stopped. She let herself fall back against Laura's body, face close, lips curved backward, revealing uneven teeth, the revolting smell of her breath nauseating Laura. Laura felt that the only way she could wrestle with Rose Janice was not to have that face so close to hers. She jumped back, feeling the other bodies all around her. She'd never be able to fight them off once cornered, or down. She made fists, lashed out as fast and hard as she could, broke open a space of darkness between two bodies, and a white ghostly mask rushed at her, from outside the circle, and as if from outer space.

"Mmmm!" hummed Emory, lips sealed together by a ravaging lust that he was fighting to keep inside. He grabbed Laura's arm in a viselike grip, so hard she feared he'd break her bones. *"Leave her alone!"* he yelled, and the mass of other ghostly faces rolled off her. *"She's mine and mine alone!"* he crowed in the cackliest and most ridiculous Gallic rooster's call, but Laura felt no comic relief whatsoever. The huge white hands, luminescent in the dark, held her with irresistible strength, turned and twisted her body like putty in their grasp. *"She's my youth!"* he exulted. *"She's my sap, my blood!"* he clucked. The moist hands went over her breasts, and one slipped libidinously under her dress.

"No!" she screamed, and hit him in the face, and felt that

she had fractured her hand on the stony relief of a statue. He grabbed her again, held her still, incapable of fighting him.

"Isn't she pretty? Pretty, pretty, ecksssciting," he hissed.

"I was prettier than her!" squawked Rose Janice, throwing herself on the old man, hitting him with her coat-hanger hands, "and you drained me, drained me, drained me!" she chanted insanely, and Laura saw her teeth: they were worse than uneven, they were climbing all over each other. "And then you promised me Alain, the way you promised him to *her*!" Laura tugged at Emory's hand, managed to free herself, but for a second didn't know where to escape: The Carpathian room stretched away in all directions.

"Flora!" shouted Emory, whipped by bony hands, "control this animal!" One of the women in long dresses sprang forward and seized Rose Janice by both arms, pinning them to her sides. Emory rid himself of Rose Janice with a dry whack on her cheek, leaped and caught Laura again in that undefeatable clasp.

"Let go, I'll scream!" she warned, screaming already, and knowing that whatever sounds she uttered wouldn't make it outside, and if they did, they wouldn't overpower Mahler at his loudest.

"Scream. Who will help you?" he taunted wickedly.

"There are people outside—" she started, and he cut in: "Who? Those men without manhood? Those women without men? They need *us*!" he bellowed, and the Carpathian room's vaults vibrated so loudly that they shook Laura's body, and she clapped her hands over her ears, fearing that the roof might disintegrate in an avalanche of masonry.

The echo subsided. Near silence followed. Everyone kept their positions. Emory holding Laura by the arm. Rose Janice collapsed against Flora. The others poised to jump in and join the action as much as their old, frantically quivering limbs would let them.

Toot-toot! Toot-toot! a crude trumpet bugled outside the Carpathian room's far window. Out front, Mahler's arabesques continued to rain on the crowd. From the back of the house, *toot-toot!* came another trumpet, and another, and a chugging sound, round and mechanical, and a ruckus of voices. "Come on!" Emory grabbed her hand. "You've got to see this. It's for you!" He propelled her toward the window and she almost crashed face first into its greenish filminess of cobwebs and dirt stains. But Emory restored her balance. With strength unthinkable for his age, he grabbed the heavy window frame and pushed up. It jolted noisily and opened. He grabbed Laura by the neck, forced her head out into the evening air and into a vision of . . .

Barges.

She saw behind the house a landing site. Narrow wharves, fanning out into the water as far as she could see amidst the foliage of oaks and cypresses. A barge was just pulling in, decks darkened by two dozen rivermen, some in workshirts and jeans, but most of them in some sort of wool jacket with embroidered patterns of black-and-red needlework, heavy wool trousers and socks, and round black hats appearing to be of fur. Several had trumpets, some had rifles and handguns. They started jumping off the barge—and another barge pulled in immediately behind it, round sides bumping mightily against the half-collapsed wharf.

Emory twisted her face toward his. "You like?" he crowed.

The little breath she had left, she put all in one question: "Where's Alain?"

"He loves you too much," he brayed. "He didn't want to *taint* you!" Taint was a word that amused him greatly; he guffawed and started coughing. "He threw the family business in my face with a moralistic tirade"—his voice creaked, rusty from the cough—"and dropped everything, including you—all because he loves you! Well, I love you, too, my precious, but not enough to spare you. He wasn't strong enough for you, anyway."

"At least he had a heart!" She felt like plucking his eyes out, but he was clutching her wrists. "You lied! You lied when you said he was waiting for me here!" she screamed. "You lied, you filthy bastard, bastard, bastard!" she cried tirelessly, and threw at him the only blow she could throw, held powerless as she was: From the depth of her chest, she spat in his face.

Wiping off the spit, he drew back, affected. "Please," he asked. "Don't call me a bastard."

"Bastard! Bastard!" she hissed.

"I am a Calovaru!" he said, stung by the insult. "My purity of blood is my virtue! Don't call me a bastard! Those—" he pointed down toward the faces of the boatmen streaming across the backyard, "those are the bastards. They're crossbreeds. They were sired by peasant women too weak to carry our seed, to foster and enrich the blood of the Calovarus."

She remembered: the halfwits she had seen with Cabot in that Cajun settlement. Oh, God. Those degenerates. Oh, Christ. Where was Cabot?

"Cabot!" she cried uselessly out the back window.

Emory watched her with a smile playing on his crimson lips. "He won't hear you, and even if he does, he won't help you."

She felt she hated him so much, she could simply poison him with her eyes.

"Chadwick is talking to him right now. He'll persuade him to work for us."

"I don't believe you!" she cried.

"He's an inferior man, but not totally unintelligent. His chief's trying to boot him off the force. He needs powerful friends, and we're on the rise again. We have the money now."

"Yes, the money." She felt like crying. Alain had brought them that money, Alain had endowed them with it, the duty-bound fool.

"We'll win back the power as soon as we beat the unions, and that should be accomplished in a few days. Then nothing can stop us. We'll roll over the city like a tide," Emory prophesied.

Trying to imagine that, she felt that her very brain started to ache.

"You'll be stopped," she whispered hatefully.

"By people like you and Cabot?"

"By me, by all sorts of other people."

The light that flared up in his eyes seemed to consume his irises from inside: From green, they turned purple. He squeezed her wrists so that her hands felt cut off, and hissed venomously: "Don't you ever think that anyone, anyone can stop *me*. Aren't you wondering about all the people who started dying around you as soon as you arrived? I *devoured* them"—his voice rose to a yell—"to allay my lust for you. Each time I tasted you, I had to stop myself, or you'd have awakened the next day looking like a desiccated mummy. So I mastered my thirst, and slaked it on others, and saved you. Only *I* can stop me!" he boomed. He let go of her wrists. She almost lost her balance. Two numb masses hung where her hands had been.

"There's a cure for vampires," she whispered. "You mentioned it in your diary."

The mask of demonic wrath fell from his face. Underneath, another Emory smiled courteously—the flattered author. "I thought that would be instructive reading for you. You're made of the same stuff." He grinned, interested. "Were you naked when you read it?"

"There's a cure . . ." she moaned. He cut her off.

"In the old country. No one knows where it's hidden," he snarled.

"Someone will go back there and get it, and rid the world of you forever." It felt like the last line she would ever utter.

"Come here," he roared. "Come with me, you naive lover of mankind, you ingenuous little prude. Come see what the future has in store."

He yanked her after him like a puppet. She didn't feel her feet touch the floor—they were suddenly in the lobby outside the Carpathian room. He grabbed a doorknob, twisted it and hurled her in, and a male shriek rose from the couple on the bed. Legs in lowered pants were hanging over the edge of the bed. An organdy dress straddled them. The woman rubbernecked to see the intruders, and Laura gasped in horror: face artfully made up, eyes blinking in shock, a trickle of blood seeping from the corner of her mouth—Marion! *Marion!* "Get out!" Merritt Bonheur shrieked from underneath her, and Marion spun her head back, hoping perhaps she hadn't been recognized. But Emory's reaction was just as fast. He pulled Laura out, slammed the door shut, opened another, propelled her into a second room.

He let go of her. Her temples were hammering, tolling, crashing with bells and cymbals and drums from Mahler's Eighth Symphony, and the stark interior of the room sobered her a little. A floor-to-ceiling window opened straight ahead. She didn't remember seeing it from the outside.

"There," said Emory. "Look at the river."

She looked at the river.

But it wasn't the river anymore.

She wobbled to the window, over a dark high-tech flooring whose color she couldn't determine: it wasn't black, or gray, or green, it was a dark color of its own. Pointillistic little thorns grew out of it, embracing the sole of her shoes in a firm suction, making little *flak-flak* noises as she advanced. Above the floor, the walls were light-colored—again a shade she'd never seen, a curdled hue that wasn't white, wasn't cream, wasn't anything but itself.

But the strangeness of the floor and walls was eclipsed by what she saw outside: a walled drainage canal, looking miles wide, filled from wall to wall, and flowing viscously with a dark, thick, crimson tide.

"That river," she breathed, aghast. "It looks like . . . ."

"It *is*."

There was light out there, but she couldn't tell where it came from. The sky looked like an unbroken sheet of brownish-gray clouds. "Where is the sun?" she asked.

"Behind the clouds," replied Emory. "Conventional sunlight is a thing of the past. That, of course," he chuckled, "gives us a more generous share of the time we can spend exposed."

Looking down, she saw the ground. Rusty like the canal's walls, without vegetation, hardened in irregular patterns, like cooled lava. There was no particularly striking terrain formation, except for the walled river, and a bulging roundness of cement interrupting one of the walls, miles away. Pipelines curled up from the river, and curled down again into the top of the bulging structure, making it look like a giant still. The still had a grille at the front facing the rusty desert. A dark line of people was crawling up to it.

"That," said Emory, "is a blood station. That's where people buy their blood."

She was staring, mouth open. A fuzzy question came to the surface of her mind, and she struggled to remember the words necessary to express it: "Who's selling the blood?"

"We are," he answered simply. "We own the franchise."

She looked at him. He wasn't wearing any futuristic clothing. He was dressed in his habitual black suit, chin hugged by another one of his flowing ascots.

Unexpectedly, something moved out in the desert. A horde of quick-bodied, black-clad creatures appeared at a gallop, running with skill over the craggy boulders and other protuberances of rusty lava, heading for the line of blood buyers. The spearhead of the horde hit the line right in its middle, and it squirmed and shook, like a bitten worm. Bodies started to fall out of it, under the blows of the black creatures, and were dragged away to be finished among the rusty boulders, but the people spared by the attack made no movement to leave the line, to run away, or hide or repulse the attack in any way. On the contrary, they quickly filled the vacancies, finding themselves a step closer to the precious dark fluid.

She couldn't believe her eyes. She was watching humans watch other humans being dragged away. Then some of the creatures returned to drag still more bodies from the line. Again the survivors showed no instinct for solidarity or self-preservation, no sympathy for the victims. Again they stepped closer to the dark grille dispatching rations of the red tide that rolled indifferently past the tragedy.

"Why aren't they doing something? Why aren't they helping each other?" she cried, looking at Emory, expecting that even he would have the same reaction to such desperate passivity.

"They don't want to help each other. All they want is their blood. A great illustration of how human nature functions, don't you think?" His fingernail tapped the window pane, in the direction of the slaughter. "People in concentration camps were no different."

"And you want to live for such a future?" she cried. He shrugged.

"What I want isn't the point. The cycle must continue. The succession of power has to be insured. In any case, it's better to be one of us than . . ." He didn't continue but she knew his meaning. Better to be one of them, than human.

"Come closer," he said suddenly, and she obeyed, leaning forward without thinking. His tongue suddenly lapped with gusto at her cheek. She screamed, jumped back, and touched the spot. She felt the pain where the other woman had scratched her.

"That fool, Rose Janice," he muttered. With the tip of his tongue, he stretched a rosy film over his lips. "I love you, Laura," he whispered, sweetly, poetically. She wanted to look away, but even the sight of him was less frightening than the bleak panorama from this high-tech tower.

"Shut up," she said.

"You're my youth restored to me," he murmured. "You're my life."

She knew he was right. What an obscene joke. But the death outside was obscene, too—indecent, humiliating beyond belief, the defeat of everything human.

"Take me out of here," she begged.

"I shall," he responded gravely. "We're expected."

She felt numbness seeping into her body. From her ankles. From the floor rich with suction dots. Numbness. Despair. The end of her will, the end of Laura.

"Who's expecting us?" she asked, surrendering.

"Everyone. The dance can't start without us."

He turned and walked toward the door. For a second she was tempted not to follow him. And do what? Remain behind in this doomsday?

After all, back in the present, the game hadn't been played out quite yet. She caught up with him, almost grateful that someone—even someone like Emory—could pass her safely through the Customs of time and space. And she loathed herself for the feeling. *I'm despicable. I'm not better than them.*

She had never felt as diminished, as devoid of pride and hope, as she followed him through the door: So sure of himself, so damnably authoritative, so utterly depraved.

He was going to have her—*her, her life.* He would suck years of strength and power from her youth and her body. She noticed how the door sill transformed halfway across from that eerie no-color material back to the solid oak of Belle Hellène. There was no boundary, though, no visible demarcation line—all of a sudden, one substance became another, just like the future became the present. And Emory offered his arm to help her down the shadowy stairs.

I'm going to kill him.

The thought entered her body and stayed; she felt it like an alien presence. But no repulsion followed. It was a clear, cold decision.

They were beginning to pass the family portraits. She looked in vain for Alain's photograph. Of course, it had been taken down—a minimal penalty for his treason.

I must hold myself together. Keep my eyes peeled, think carefully about what I could use as a weapon. Gather my courage and my strength—and not fail.

I'm going to kill him.

A sort of elation raised her head, straightened her posture. It felt like a gesture she hadn't performed in eons. It felt good.

They were reaching the bottom of the stairs.

The onrush of the half-breeds had surprised the party at the point when tipsiness had untied all tongues, feet had started shifting and shuffling unsurely on the grass, and eyes were turning, searching for the delayed food. The half-breeds flooded the place, seemingly from all sides. Those of the guests who tried to escape toward the gates were met head-on by a second wave of rivermen, running in along the drive-way and trampling over the flower beds. The screams of the crowd caught in the middle began like one voice from hundreds of throats, streaked with shots from the rifles and pistols that the rivermen discharged liberally into the air. All that pandemonium rose and crashed into the clouds of Mahler that solemnly draped the air above the front yard, drowning out all but the loudest yelps of terror.

Higher still, above all the pillage, the evening air was somnolently quiet, absorbing some of the commotion, and letting it fall back to earth, inert. Like in a huge mural by an anonymous Italian master, its bottom section full of the sound and fury of a fierce battlescape, above the carnage rustled the peaceful and sun-loving trees, which would survive the slaughter unaffected. Still higher in the fresco, above the rich masses of foliage, were depicted those classical crowds of onlookers: the gods of war and peace, floating in the air, with their retinues of fat cherubims. The gods, with smiles from swollen cheeks, watched the elite of the city being assaulted by the rivermen. And each and every one—chaser, chased, and divine observer—was listening to Mahler.

Laura and Emory reached the ground-floor hallway, and she shrunk at the growls, calls for help, howls of agony, and mad laughter, remembering she had heard the same nasal, ugly chortling from the Cajun crowd she'd seen in that village with Cabot. Where was Cabot, where in hell was Cabot?

In hell was appropriate. Had he been converted, killed, thrown off the property?

"This way," said Emory, pushing her to the left. "We'll take the gallery." He had loosened his grip a little, but she felt his fingers on her arm, ready to squeeze again at the slightest provocation.

They stepped into the gallery. Like a hideous replay of her glimpse into the future, she suddenly gaped at what was happening behind the wall of glass, and all the shrieks and yells made sense. She saw Cabot, standing like a bizarre fixed point in the midst of human turmoil, his cheeks florid among the pallid faces, looking crazy with shock. Clark Chadwick stood right behind him, apparently murmuring something in his ear, to which the cop responded with catatonic little nods, like an automaton. Around them, she saw the guests being chased, caught, dragged onto the grass by the rivermen. Above knots of thrashing bodies, an arm shot upward occasionally, or a torso, or a horrified face. She saw the woman who had complained about tightwad divorcés being chased by several black-capped rivermen, one limping, then overthrown on the grass and gang-sucked. From amidst the fury the Egyptian suddenly appeared, trying to rescue a neurotic-looking hippie-girl from the tumbling couples, threesomes, and foursomes. Laura saw them both clearly, advancing toward the gallery, he talking with his usual astrally concentrated expression, while she eyed his neck. A *hora* of leaping and shouting rivermen swept between them and the gallery, hiding them from sight, shaking arms and legs and convulsing with unbelievable frenzy.

"That's the way they are"—Emory had raised his voice,

but his tone was sweet, affectionate—"till they quench their thirst a little. Enjoy them, Laura, they're here in your honor."

She watched submissively, staring blankly at the leaps and contortions.

"They aren't really Cajun, are they?" she asked, as one short demon collided into the iron-framed glass of the gallery.

"Oh, not at all," replied Emory, laughing. "There's not a drop of Cajun blood in them. They're from the old country. Serfs who came as bargemen, watching over the shipments of soil. And we settled them along the river."

"They're disgusting," she said.

"Forgive them, they're celebrating your initiation," he replied. "Remember our first night together, in Alain's bedroom?" he crooned romantically. His paw slipped down her arm, to take her hand in his.

"I thought you were Alain," she said, shutting out her awareness of his touch. He jumped furiously, dropping her hand, stamping his foot on the tiled gallery floor, coattails flurrying comically around him. "That sissy? What do all the women see in him?"

"He's more of a man than you'll ever be," she retorted, watching him, her lips curling up despite herself. She loved to watch the way he reacted to Alain's name—like a devil sprinkled with holy water. Angrier still, he shouted, "Alain has always been too squeamish to kill! He was christened into the tribe too late!" Her eyelashes beat fast, in confusion.

"He wasn't meant to be one of us, ever!" screamed Emory. "But his father deserted his duties and we had to take Alain!"

She thought she hadn't heard him right. He saw her features, strained, trying to make out his words over the tumult of the garden.

"He doesn't kill." Emory slowed his voice to a patient, careful delivery. "That's why he can stand the sun. He's been surviving on that blood wine. Now he's left an empire, and me, and you, to save his precious conscience. How contemptibly *human*!" Emory spat out the words in tones of glacial scorn.

As terrified and exhausted as she was, a regenerating warmth spread inside her. *Oh, God, thank you. Oh, Alain, I knew you couldn't be like Emory.*

She straightened herself, directed at Emory a glance of near triumph. Suddenly a drop of hot acid fell onto the bottom of her stomach, fear sizzled inside her, and she felt ready to be sick. What about *her* blood?

He read the question in her eyes. He smiled.

"That's right, you're one of us already."

Nooo! was the sound she wanted to utter—a scream not just out of her mouth, but from all the pores of her body. But no voice came from her lips, and her pores seemed to open into a dark chasm. Sucked through, she fell, hearing Emory's voice diminish. "Too much of you has passed into me already. And the other night here"—his arm stretched over her head, toward the bedroom on the upper floor of the opposite wing—"I fed you some of *me*."

She was still falling. The nausea she felt was plummeting with her into the abyss.

"No," she said almost soundlessly.

She didn't remember. She had blanked it out completely.

"That's how the best of us are born again." He smiled. "Not depleted in one night, so that they crawl out of their graves as disgusting undeads. But fed subtly with the dark sacrament, with the everlasting infernal eucharist."

"Stop," she begged.

She had never thought of herself as truly religious. This time the blasphemy burned inside her.

I'll kill him. I'll kill Emory.

"You'll soon believe as we do—and behave as we do," he assured her. He gazed at her, trying to guess her emotions. "Tell me something. Do you *really* love Alain?" he asked incredulously.

"Yes," she breathed, feeling that no other word had ever contained more truth.

"You'll get over it." He took her arm, pushed her toward the other wing. "You need a man, not a boy," he said consolingly. "A traveler through time." He stroked her back through the delicate transparency of her satin dress. "Together, we'll conquer the future."

"I don't want any part of that future," she said, trying to slow his steps, to resist being taken into the other wing. Eyes darting around for a weapon, she noticed that the tumult behind the glass walls was subsiding.

Amazing. Chased and chasers were reappearing, in mixed groups, apparently talking to each other. Very few signs of fighting continued to agitate the shrubbery at the far end of the garden. Straightening their dresses, women were surfacing from behind the tent and away from the bushes, pursued less fiercely now by liver-faced Carpathians.

"I don't want that future," she repeated.

"Why not?" he stopped rhetorically before the door to the other wing. "We'll be the absolute ruling class, we'll control the fluid of life itself, we'll make sorties out of our towers to hunt that scum for sport."

"How awful," she said. She had noticed a pair of big gardening scissors. "And what if you fail? What if the future doesn't work out the way you're planning it?"

"It will," he said definitively. "We'll give everyone what they need, and then we'll cast them aside like empty husks."

His eyes swept over her, noticed the scissors. Quickly she shifted her gaze. Cabot and Chadwick were approaching. Cabot seemed less comatose. Chadwick was offering him a cigarette from a gold case.

Suddenly, three beats of music resounded from the other wing, and this time it wasn't Mahler. Violins. Old-fashioned violins. "Come," Emory said. "They're all waiting to see you." She dug her heels in the floor, tightening her body as if the cold chill of a guillotine had touched her neck.

"What are you doing this for, Emory?" she asked. "What's your reward?"

"The sweetest drink is my reward," he said. "The divine elixir—blood. You shall see how sweet it is when we drink it together. This is your new life—one that can last not merely the pathetic span of a human lifetime, but *forever*. Laura, don't you see how fortunate you are? Come," he added urgently, "the bargemen will lose their patience."

He grabbed her arm. The scissors remained behind, unused. She took a deep breath.

Through the door at the other end of the gallery, she walked into her new life.

As she blinked at the bright lights, a round of clamorous applause deafened her.

She had expected the dimness of the Carpathian room, slightly brightened by candles. There were candles here, too—so many, burning animatedly on stands loaded with at least two dozen each, that the blaze of all of them together, multiplied in vibrating flickers, lit the room more spectacularly than a row of klieg lights. Splashed from all angles with such reverberating illumination, the faces she saw were glimmering, beyond pale or tanned. In two long rows, they waited, about a hundred to a row, and as she and Emory passed between them, a cloud of excited whispering followed in their wake.

Instead of looking ahead, or at her escort, she peered leftward. Spellbound, she saw a pharaoh headdress like the one in the Egyptian's painting, but this one, lined with three tiers of encrusted jewels, was sitting on the erect head of a man with olive skin and almond eyes, his bare chest smeared with some aromatic unguent. Next to him, fanatically skinny, stood a crusader in mailed armor: overlapping chains and scales seemingly corroded by blood. A leap forward in time, then a leap back: a Viking in wolfhide. Phoenician sailors and Cistercian monk-scholars lined up after them. She glanced to her right. Past Emory, she saw prioresses and witches and slave girls and Byzantine dancers—the facing row was exclusively women. Turning back to the other side, her captivation so complete that she could barely walk, she beheld the caved-in cheeks of hermits, the beastly arms of cavemen, the glassy stares of zombies. Punk rockers appeared, teddy boys, jazzmen. Were they all in costume, or had they traveled across time to attend her coronation? Were they all vampires who had survived their own time to feast on this one? Quickening the pace, Emory threw the centuries at her until they reached the end of the room, and faced an all-white band, troubadouresquely pale and long-haired.

The bandleader bowed toward her. Emory asked for her hand. She realized that they would be dancing in a moment. Dancing this grotesque ritual, as if vowing her soul forever to the millennia.

A sudden shiver of fear cooled the blood in her veins as

the music began—a stately eighteenth-century gavotte. She looked in all directions, certain that after the dance, somehow, she'd never be able to free herself again, even if the gates opened and Emory let her go untouched.

"I don't know this dance," she objected.

"Oh, but you do. Try to remember," he answered imperiously.

He took her hand. The touch of his fingers had such weight that she felt they could crush her like an egg. Yet if she let go of them, some infinite tomb could open under her and swallow her up. It seemed that only Emory made sense in this scene, that he was her odious salvation.

Easy, Laura. You're still alive.

He bowed to her and she bowed to him before she could think about it. Then he stepped back, and she stepped back symmetrically. The music was surprisingly simple, almost primitive, but the number of the instruments improved its poor harmony. With a rattle and a sway, all the centuries began to move, and scabbards and high boots, laced sandals and armors, added their fracas to the harmony of the massed violins.

In time with the music, Emory retreated backward to the opposite wall, his lips open in an abstract half smile. Mincing his steps, he approached her again, and she minced hers to meet him, following not the music, or him, but some obscure instinct. They passed each other, and she crossed his path at an angle, changed places with another woman, came back, met Emory again. He gave her his arms, and twirled her in the middle of the floor, their pair the first in a row long like a reflection of mirrors in mirrors.

How well Emory danced. How gracefully he rounded his arms, and the statuesque block of his body displaced the air with such commanding confidence. She crossed away again, met one of the ladies she had seen overpowered on the lawn outside the gallery. Her dress was a little ruffled. Laura looked for the marks on her neck; she saw two pinpricks almost covered by fresh makeup. The woman was transfixed. She had crossed over already. She had passed through the strange doorway of her new fate.

Laura danced back. The man opposite her was now a warrior. A Greek hoplite, heavily armed, who instead of trampling with the coarseness of the foot soldier was gliding balletically across the dance floor. His short square sword glided with him, unsheathed, hanging in a simple rope strap at his waist. She fastened her eyes on the sword, and danced toward him.

Perm: Lucevic
c. A Greek hoplite, heavily armed, who instead of brass
'ng with the coarseness of the foot soldier was gliding

14

I *COULD DO it. If I held that thing with both hands.*

Swallowed behind the lip of the horizon, the sun reached back with a dust storm of red that powdered the tops of the trees, leaving the house and French garden untouched. Violet shades began to weave themselves between the tree-lined driveway and the pillared entrance.

A few bodies had been left, twisted, emptied, in the garden. A team of housemen were walking the complicated filigree of the pathways to find them and pick them up. Finished, they regrouped among the trees, sat on the grass, and lit cigarettes. Far at the driveway's other end, the iron gates, not locked, appeared like a sealed bandage on the cheek of the evening.

Through six dance movements, Laura had roughly reckoned that most of the guests were inside, dancing or massed along the walls. Now was her chance to stab Emory—and cause such a scene that she could sprint across the room and make it outside uncaptured.

Her car was parked beyond the closed gates. But there was that other road, the one she had followed into the property on the night of Charlotte's death. If she could find it.

Her jaws were tight, her teeth clenched against each other. She had long since lost her purse. She'd have to kick off her shoes as soon as the sword hit the starched shirtfront under

Emory's ascot. To give herself strength, she thought of Charlotte. And of Alain.

Where are you? Houston?

I'll find you in Houston. It's not big enough to hide you.

The Greek warrior followed the music toward her. The pommel of the sword ended in a polished ball of metal, which she had to grab first, and then pull the whole thing out of its strap. It had to be done just as her body and his crossed each other and he started his next movement, away from her. Fast, plunge it into Emory as he filled the warrior's spot, using his own weight and movement to drive the sword in deeper.

The multitude of candles pierced her eyes. She closed them for a moment, to rest them.

When she opened them again, she saw that the polished handle of the sword had glided right under the palm of her outstretched hand one instant earlier. She closed her fingers over it, but the man took an extra step, and her fingers slipped. She grabbed it again, lower, and pulled it from the strap in one swift motion, right under his stunned gaze. The handle was shorter than her palm, and the bare blade cut the side of her hand; she felt it, yet didn't feel it. While the music played on, she turned and lunged. Emory, parting the air like a vessel's monumental prow, saw the square, heavy shaft of iron rushing up toward his breastbone. With a starved glint, it hit him, punctured his shirt, ripped into his chest.

So amazed that his fingers curled up around empty air, he gazed with fascination at the face of the woman who had attacked him. The scratch from Rose Janice's fingers gave her features a sort of unfeminine ferocity, but she was so attractive that lust moved inside him just as a twinging cough spread from the wound to his throat. He felt no pain. Raising his hands to call for attention, he managed to gargle a yell, but she was out of reach already.

Turning and seeing the dancers' patterns still undisturbed, Laura dashed through them as if among the figures on a huge chessboard. Only when she reached the open doorway did she hear someone calling for help. Not Emory. *God, I hope you croaked.*

The purple phantoms of the evening waited right outside. On the stone ledge outside the door, before the first step down,

Laura stopped for just a second to rip off her shoes, and only then she felt the depth of the cut in her palm. The air was warm and humid, but being outside felt like such deliverance, if she could only swell her lungs with enough air she'd surely be able to fly away. An explosion of yells behind her covered the violins, but for a second nothing moved to catch her, and she saw that the phantoms were trees and bushes and the forgotten tent. She ran into the driveway, blessing the roundness of its gravel on her stockinged feet. A noisy rush behind her told her that they were bursting out of the hose, too many at once for the size of the door—she heard a glass pane shatter, and ordered her knees and thighs to pump harder, and in a flash that happy morning came back to her when she and Charlotte were running through the greenness of Audubon Park . . . *Charlotte, may you rest in peace, wherever you are.* Shouts and barked commands burst out behind her like a garland of Roman candles. "There she is! There she is!"— the shout rose to meet her this time, and she saw the housemen get up from the grass, some armed with their shiny canes, some spreading bare hands to block her path. *Oh, no. Oh, God.*

She made eye contact with one of them as he lunged forward. She zigzagged back, bending almost to the ground, heard the fierce thudding of feet after her, widened her eyes at an unexpected shape in her path—an old carriage, a well-polished brougham, triple steps hanging under the door embossed with the family L. She saw her chance, grabbed the door handle—blood was dripping out of her palm, and some of it would stain the handle, but in the dark . . . She opened the door, threw herself in . . .

. . . and fell at Emory's feet! She just couldn't hold her scream. Hollering at the top of her lungs, she stared at his drooping cheeks and fixedly shiny eyes and eyebrows so rich and stylish that they looked plucked and replanted over his eye sockets, and could do nothing but hit him hard in the face with her bleeding hand. The face popped open like a wax effigy, and split in two uneven halves, and she screamed louder.

He *was* made of wax.

She thought she'd gone mad; that was his voice, outside in

the garden. But he was made of wax in here; a stuffed dummy, an eerily realistic replica. The Emory who promenaded himself around in the proud brougham in the French Quarter, in the daytime, under the annihilating sun.

The voices were approaching, the footfalls pounded nearer; her screams had betrayed her hiding place. She tried to crawl over the effigy, revolted at the thought of touching even a likeness of Emory, and in the corner of her mind she marveled at how she had kept her nerve back on the dance floor. How she hadn't fainted each time he'd come closer, touched her, pirouetted her around the dance floor. Behind her, the brougham's door was thrown open. *"Aici! Aici! Uite-o aici!"* rattled someone in the patois she hadn't understood out there at the river settlement. Hands caught her ankles and she was pulled out, her face brushing against the dummy's unfeeling body, her dress rolling up under her in a crinkled wad of satin. Hot breaths blew over the bared backs of her legs as she clawed uselessly at the brougham's cushions. Arms slipped under her to save her face from bashing on the floor of the brougham. Hauled out, she saw by the glimmer of flashlights on gravel that the night was fully here, the night that restored demons to their full powers. She was mauled so brutally that she actually started to cry out for Emory, and her captors let her down on her feet. He was approaching, supported by Malcolm, in the middle of a group of pale-faced men and women in incongruous costumes. He was holding his hand over his heart. Dark gobbets of clotted blood soaked the shirt under his hand. His face was so crumpled with rage that she knew she'd find no mercy, that he was coming closer only to enjoy feeding her to that filthy pack.

Something like a gong resounded, distantly but clearly, at the end of the driveway. The sound was repeated, and all eyes, even Laura's, turned toward the gates. The gates' iron wings suddenly crashed inward and the headlights of a truck glared in, with more headlights behind them; the light from the following vehicles seeped around the sides of the first like a golden fuzz. Fireflies seemed to spark up and die instantly, and the irregular tapping of shots reached everyone's ears; gunpowder flames were igniting at the round end of pointed barrels. A hole opened in a column behind Emory. Someone screamed in pain; another volley of shots whizzed above the clustered faces before the entrance. The roar of another vehicle covered the gunfire: Alain's Dodge truck careened into view.

He saw Emory's group, and Emory. Emory saw him. Another salvo came from the advancing trucks. Alain saw Laura, arms and legs in the grip of the woolen-stockinged Carpathians. He looked right, at the advancing column; they were inside, no one could throw them out without a battle. He seemed to hesitate just one second, then locked the truck into four-wheel drive. Fanning gravel with his mud tires, he drove the Power Ram right into the midst of the Carpathians.

They left the woman, sprang aside to safety, and Alain leaned out. Laura thrust her hand at him, felt lifted, heard a pop in her shoulder joint, was dragged into the Ram all in one movement. Emory was yelling at Malcolm. "Get the guns! Stop Alain!" but Malcolm wouldn't budge, just looked over his shoulder to find someone else to yell the orders at, because he felt Emory's body weighing inertly on him, and feared that if he let go the old man would sprawl on the steps in front of his guests and his servants.

Cabot somehow found his way through to Emory. "You gotta get out of here," he yelled, and ducked his head to avoid another deadly hail of bullets. "Them union men got Macs an' AR-15s—where's the nearest phone?" The guns rattled viciously, chipping at the masonry, at the Greek pillars, trimming branches that had escaped the morning's pruning. Cabot turned to see what the younger Lecouveur was doing, saw his truck reverse mightily into a carved flower urn that it shattered completely. The young woman's head bobbed at the vehicle's movement, but her eyes were glittering, full of life. For a second, Cabot, wondered why the younger Lecouveur was here—had he thrown in with the unions?—then turned and trotted on fat legs, inside, to find that phone.

In the Ram, Laura's nerves gave way and her teeth chattered uncontrollably. *What have I done? My God, what's going to happen to me? I've killed him.* She wanted to turn and look—maybe he wasn't dying, maybe she'd only scratched him. She couldn't find the energy to do it. The cruel joy she had felt hearing Emory's rattly voice had vanished, leaving a stunned sensation of being someone she didn't know. Who was she now? A killer? Someone separated from the rest of mankind? Cabot was there, too—so the police had witnessed her attacking Emory.

Her eyes devoured Alain, every atom of him. Dressed in his river outfit, shaven but pale, his eyes ringed with shadows. She felt she was seeing him across an invisible wall. "Get down!" he shouted over the thunder of the engine, grabbing her shoulders brusquely, forcing her below the windshield. Bullets hummed over their heads.

She clung to Alain's arm, twisted it, and he looked at her with a grimace of pain. "I stabbed Emory! I killed him!" she yelled over long, repeated salvos from automatic guns.

He inched up, glanced out of the Ram: Malcolm and several other men were hustling Emory back into the house. He swung the wheel, gunned the Ram away from the path of the bullets, looked down at Laura: cringing, as white as a sheet, teeth clacking. "No, you didn't!" he yelled back. "You couldn't, he can't be killed!" He looked ahead again, saw the tent in front of the Ram's broad nose, mowed it down. Laura grabbed the door handle, threw the door open, tried to jump out. His arm harpooned after her, pulled her back in.

"I killed him! I gotta get out of here!" she moaned. Desperately fearing that the gunfire might find the Ram, seeing nothing but the darkness of the garden ahead and trying to helm the giant mud tires over bushes and flower beds, he opened his palm, cracked it over Laura's cheek. "You didn't kill him! No one can kill him! Shut up!"

The slap stunned and silenced her. The Ram rumbled around a tree, stopped, momentarily out of the attacker's sight, and she raised her head, feeling whiplashed from the ride over bushes, or from his blow—she wasn't sure. He knocked the gearshift into park, put his arm around her, and forced her close to him. "I'm sorry. Are you all right?" She felt like laughing and crying. This time *his* teeth were chattering. Maybe from fear. Maybe from the fever of the moment.

Tttrrrraaaaa-CKCK! went a gun behind them, an AR-15.

"I'm okay," she breathed. *I'm okay, I'm not a killer.*

He inched his head left, peering from behind the tree trunk. "How did you know I was here?" she asked.

"I called you to tell you I was leaving town, and when I couldn't reach you I called Marion. She told me you were coming to the party. I knew what would happen if you did."

Alain came for me! He came to save me!

"Why, why on earth did you come here?" he shouted, shifting the Ram back into drive. "What sort of lies did he tell you this time?"

"He said you'd be here."

"I wouldn't have left without talking to you." He was zigzagging the truck among overgrown bushes and trees.

"Where are we going?" she asked.

"We might find a boat there," he said, pointing to a dimly lit boat landing. "We can't get away by car, they've blocked all the roads in." Her heart beat at the thought of the dangers he'd confronted. "Why didn't you call Emory?"

"They cut the lines," he yelled. "They're terrifically well organized." He shot the Ram into the landing site, cut the engine, and didn't even bother to pull the keys out of the ignition. He ran to her side, lifted her by the waist, and landed her on the ground. "Let's go!" he ordered, grabbing her hand. He felt the cut in her palm, stopped, and raised her hand to examine it, worried, squinting in the light from a flare that was arching into the sky in front of the house. "It's not deep," he said. "It'll stop bleeding in a minute."

She let him hold her hand, deliciously pleased with his concern for her. Another flare. Half-hidden by the side of the house, she saw the brougham. Burning.

"They'll set the house on fire!" she whispered, awestruck. He looked back. Fusillades of gunfire were coming from behind the stopped trucks and the natural ramparts of bushes, and the guns inside the mansion were firing back. Laura saw Alain swallow, fighting to keep his control. "Come on," he told her. There was a vague expanse of terrain between them and the landing. He pulled her under the low branch of an oak.

She stepped on dirt that felt fresh, as if overturned moments before. She saw a collapsed tombstone next to an open grave. A mute cry of fear opened her mouth, and he shushed her with a fierce gesture. There were more open graves to her left and her right, and ahead. Crawling, staggering silhouettes were wandering among them, all over the family plot. She saw a pair, white-haired, in rags: the dried-up husk of a woman clung vulnerably to a man's skeletal arm as he led her toward the house with small, unsteady steps. They looked sweet and small, ideal lovers still, after an eternity spent lying in twin graves. Someone else came up from behind Alain and Laura: a greenish man with flaming hair and eerie eyes. He locked his eyes suspiciously on Laura, then seemed to recognize Alain, and walked on by them.

"Wait," said Alain, stopping her. He squeezed her hand, drawing her face to his chest to muffle her cry of pain. She looked up and saw his fingers. Bloodstained. He smeared some of the blood right by the corner of her mouth. "There," he said, satisfied with the diguise. Then he pulled her face up, reached her lips, kissed them long and deeply.

Now they were ready.

Crust of blood on her mouth, trying to stare glazedly at whoever they met, she walked with Alain past solitary figures in tattered shrouds and once through a group of ten or twelve silent children, until they reached the wharves. Below an eroded pier of wooden boards, a rowboat bobbed on the black water.

He jumped in, turned something on, an engine awakened and sputtered, and he killed it instantly. "Come!" he called, offering his arms.

She let his hands catch her under her armpits. Her shoulders were bare in the strapless dress, and she remembered that she'd brought a jacket along when she drove to the party. It was still out there, in her Jeep, which she had parked by the road outside the iron gates, a million years ago.

As he undid a rope, the boat tipped, reflecting her face and his in the water: they looked creole-dark, with the white of their eyes embedded in them like two underwater creatures peering upward.

Inside the house, Cabot ran from one phone to another. He never managed to make a call.

They brought Emory inside, seconds before the gunfire became so intense and well directed that everyone had to seek refuge in the house; a hundred voices yelled behind him. Some guests rushed to try the phones, as uselessly as Cabot; others started pulling tablecloths off the tables to wave them as white flags.

Chadwick ran to catch up with the group carrying Emory upstairs. "Aren't you gonna try to talk to them?" He had lost his glasses, and his red mustache twitched frantically from the quiver of his lips. "There must be a bullhorn someplace . . . we'll open the upstairs windows . . . they gotta stop . . ."

"They won't stop," said Emory.

"Bullshit!" yelled Chadwick with uncharacteristic vigor. "Make a deal, Emory! You can always make a deal."

"Rome didn't make a deal," sputtered Emory bloodily. "Remember? Rome shall perish. In the blood that she has spilt?"

"Oh, for Chrissakes, this isn't the time for your poets." He looked away from Emory to someone who might make better sense. "Where are you taking him?" he asked Malcolm.

"He wants to lie under the family coat o' a'ms," said Malcolm. Chadwick made a hopeless gesture, turned and stumbled back down to the ground floor, and was met by a councilman he knew well, face bloodied. "What happened?" Chadwick screamed. The man couldn't speak, he just pointed, explaining through gestures that this was from the rivermen's fists. Chadwick saw the massive front door, barricaded with tables and chairs, pocked with chips from the gunfire. He ran toward it, met the wicked fists of the rivermen, and was thrown back.

He fell into a chair and lay in a stupor, trying to make sense of what he was feeling. His wife was in Florida with the children. A woman he saw now and then in her apartment in Gentilly wouldn't miss him. He popped his collar open and stared vacantly at the multiplying chips and splinters on the inside of the door. There were several bullet holes, and one of them was smoking. Bewitched, he contemplated the

smoke as it grew thicker, turning slowly into a blond core of
fire.

When the fire started to spread through the ground floor,
the guests began to run upstairs. This pleased Emory, who
had recovered a sort of coughy second wind. The frantic yells
of panic made him rise shakily to his full grandeur, lit crimson by the light through the grandiflora from the flames lick-
ing the outside of the mansion. "We can't be killed, don't
you know that?" he almost yelled. "From the contagion of
the world's low stain," he declaimed, "we are secure!" He
felt like the captain of a sinking ship, skipper and chaplain
all at once to this cowed rabble.

Yet what if . . . what if there *was* death, even for him?
Dear, beauteous death. The Jewel of the Just. *Pallida Mors,
aequo pulsat pede* . . . But they *couldn't* be killed. And those
who hadn't joined their ranks yet could still save themselves
by accomplishing a quick conversion. He wanted to laugh,
but the stab of pain in his chest wouldn't let him.

The fire had gained hold. It was spreading up to the roofs,
to the entablatures, to the gables and the spooky jutting hooks.
The heat grew pearls of sweat on every forehead. Someone
not far from him was babbling through panicked sobs about
a life-insurance policy.

Emory looked up: The beams above him were the oldest
in the house. Even Louisiana's swampy moisture had been
chased out of them. They were as dry as a field of bones up
on the moon.

Alain had thrown the boat into motion by pushing at the wharf
with a pole. The boat floated away into the side canal, and
he started the engine. Sputtering, it took them almost to the
river, then died. He grabbed the oars and rowed until the
main stream opened before them. By that time, Laura's feet
were splashing in water. He dropped the oars, grabbed a plastic bucket, and started bailing the water out, while the reflection of the blaze on the shore lit his face more and more
clearly.

"I can't row and get the water out," he said defeatedly.
He looked at the house. Even the thickness of the trees

couldn't blot out the light. The blaze was raging five stories high. His dark eyes grew darker still, with tears. A man's tears. Shamed, scant, lasting but one instant. He took a deep breath, put away the bucket. "We'll let her drift, and she'll take us ashore."

She crawled clumsily to him, joined her body to his, not knowing how else to show her compassion. Feverish, his hands stroked her arms, went up toward her face. One palm touched her neck. He narrowed his eyes, grabbed her, and twisted her toward the dancing flames.

"Laura," he whispered, with the bitterest amazement.

She put her palm where his hand had been and felt the pinpoints of her last scars. He pushed her palm away, touched her again, then for a second stood gaping, his eyebrows painfully joined, his eyes empty.

"Alain," she moaned. She felt like a leper. Worse than after striking Emory.

He could barely speak. "When?" he asked hoarsely.

"The night . . ." She couldn't speak either. "The night you were supposed to take me to dinner . . . and you didn't . . . Charlotte took me to a party, next to your property . . ."

He collapsed on the gunwale. She went on, her voice thin and helpless, telling how she took the path that led through the darkness to Belle Hellène.

Even the strongest of men wasn't made for such blows. He turned away from her toward the burning mansion, and his black shadow against it looked void of purpose and willpower; like a tattered scarecrow silhouetted against a field of flames.

"Do I disgust you?" she whispered.

He didn't seem to hear.

I'm not going to cry. But she was crying already, staggering clumsily toward Alain, with an uneven movement that tipped the boat. "Alain, my love," she whispered, "I didn't mean to hurt you, I didn't mean for any of this to happen."

He was silent. She knew the meaning of his silence.

She stood next to him, but he made no attempt to touch her. She looked at the fire, but instead of hating it and everything that was being devoured by it, she felt a sort of distant sympathy. Those poor, blood-obsessed creatures. Some of them were being awarded, finally, the release of death.

In the dark, his hand moved. It found and accepted hers.

She sat next to him on the gunwale. "Do you think we might be picked up by one of your barges?" she asked.

He laughed. "I doubt there will be any barges coming this way tonight."

They sat silently, and he rose twice to throw the water out. Waterlogged but somehow still riverworthy, the boat followed an unseen path in the current, changing the perspective of the dancing flames, gradually shrinking them in the distance.

Perhaps an hour passed. Suddenly, Alain got up, stared at the fire. Far behind them now, it looked like one purple dot in the night sky. "He's dead," he said, with grim certainty.

She couldn't tell what he was feeling. She put her arms around him.

Sure to be rejected, she advanced her lips. He let himself be kissed. His mouth was sweetly bitter.

She tied her arms around his neck, pulling him closer. He shivered and squeezed himself into her, as if trying to hide whole within the refuge of her embrace.

Miles downriver, a sandbar shone in the shallow water, like a long brown finger. The bottom of the boat hit the sandbar with a harsh sound, and the pole and oars and plastic bucket rattled inside it.

Alain looked out over the gunwale. Dawn was beginning to scorch the horizon. Laura's wristwatch showed almost five in the morning. He helped her up, they stepped out of the boat into hip-deep water, and started wading across.

She took a look at him when they stepped ashore. He looked like he had survived a nuclear blast. "That way," he said, "is River Road." He helped her advance step by step, because she could barely walk. They sat to rest twice, and walked more, and then the gray flat ribbon of the road showed through the trees, and a red fire truck ripped across the landscape, looking brand-new, followed by an ambulance, and another ambulance. Alain ran through the trees to the roadside and flailed his arms. Leaning against tree trunks, she inched closer and saw that he had stopped a police car. *Great*, she thought. *Now, they'll arrest him, or me, or both of us. That kiss-ass attorney, or that morbid giraffe, Rose Janice, or whoever else is left, they'll find a way of accusing us of the attack . . . I'm being so paranoid . . . I just don't want anything to keep us apart anymore. . . .* They had gotten so far, they had survived so many perils, it seemed only fitting that divine retribution would be lying in wait close-by, ready to grab one of them, to separate them again forever.

But when she limped to the door of the police car, she found the cop answering Alain's questions deferentially—yes, Belle Hellène had been attacked and overrun, it wasn't clear by whom or why, and a fire had started, and consumed the house, in fact it was still burning, unresponsive to water cannons. Alain asked him to take Laura back to town, and the cop said just a minute and grabbed his radio. "He'll drive you to your place, to get your things," Alain instructed. "Then tell him to take you to the Moisant Hotel, by the airport. Take a room in my name and wait for me there."

She was looking at him, pressing in her mind his face, the torn shirt under his unbuttoned fatigue jacket, his soiled khaki cotton pants. "My purse is back there. How can I get a room at the hotel without any identification?"

"Just register in my name. They'll give it to you."

"I don't want you to go anywhere without me," she said, and grabbed his arm. He detached her fingers, gently but inflexibly. "I have to go back there. I have to see what's left . . ."

If that old bastard's still alive, I won't let you go. What difference does it make whether ten feet of the house are standing. Or even whether Emory's dead or not. He won't be bothering you or me anymore. The cop walked over from the car and said it was all right, he had been given permission to drive her wherever necessary.

"Go and rest, and I'll see you tonight," he promised, from his lips and from his eyes.

Don't let him. They'll kill him, or he'll disappear again.

"Alain," she said in a breaking voice. "Be careful."

"Don't worry. I'll be at the hotel by eight."

"How are you going to get back to Belle Hellène? You're not going to walk ten miles?"

"We've got another car coming to give Mr. Lecouveur a ride," said the cop. He had curly hair and a little nameplate over his breast pocket that read: LOVE. That was his name. He opened the car's passenger door, and Alain helped her in.

She turned for one last look at him as they pulled away. Standing in the roadway, framed by the untamed trees of Louisiana, his face dirty, his body thinned from the incredible night and morning, he looked like a spirit of the swamp.

Oh, God. I don't care who I am. I don't care who he is. Just give him to me. I'll do anything to have him.

15

WHEN SHE couldn't see Alain anymore, she turned and asked Officer Love his opinion about the attack on the Lecouveur property. Wasn't it strange that it had occurred after those mysterious killings, and so many other unusual happenings? Driving like a traffic-school manual, the policeman said yes, it *looked* strange, but it wasn't that strange really, because since olden times humanity had been split into two groups forever at war with each other, and though it seemed that there were a lot of warring factions in history—black and white, Americans and Japanese, Jews and Arabs, Christians and Muslims—those were the temporal appearances of only two forces, fighting incessantly, and the Lecouveurs and the longshoremen happened to be the latest link in that chain of dubious battles. And there were no victors, since the war never ended. The Lecouveurs had given it to the unions, and the unions were giving it back to them with interest. He wouldn't be surprised if the killings and rumors of vampires had been the work of the Lecouveurs's enemies, to justify last night's raid of the estate. Astonished at the unlikely erudition of this Louisiana police officer, Laura listened while he went on about Alain's family and their place in town and how the future would carry them again to prominence after a passing eclipse . . . until her head fell on her chest; moments before arriving at her apartment.

She woke up, told Officer Love she'd only be a minute, and climbed the stairs.

There was a second key to her door in a pot of flowers on the top landing. She had kept it in her purse with the other key while the house was being watched by Cabot's men, and had put it back in the pot yesterday morning after coming back from Marion's, reckoning that it was safe to leave it there again.

She had no energy to do any serious packing. She simply changed into a fresh outfit, brushed her hair, folded some underwear and a dress into her suitcase, and packed her make-up. The rest would be retrieved later, somehow.

Back in the car, while Love took the highway to the air-port, she meditated on his philosophy about irreconcilable groups locked together like twins in their need to fight each other. And who were she and Alain? Did they belong to any group? Or were they just a pair of innocents, idealistic lovers trying to flee from the path of war?

The Moisant Airport hotel was a horseshoe of stacked-up floors, its entrance deep inside the horseshoe's hollow, flanked by two elevators running up and down in glass encasements. The view from all the rooms was Lake Pontchartrain, boiling with hard sunlight. She took a room overlooking the lake, two stories below the constant thunder of outgoing planes.

She washed, then slept, too tired to mind the planes, though they seemed to roar right inside her pillow.

Belle Hellène's roof had collapsed, bringing down with it half the walls of the upper floor. The bullet-chipped pillars of the two porticoes were gray-black. The fire had been defeated in the mansion proper, but the adjoining buildings and some of the trees were still aflame. Alain covered his eyes when he saw the dog kennel, its wire hellishly black, the dogs charred to ashen masses in various poses of agony, one with a car-bonized paw still caught between two strands of blackened mesh. The stench of roasted meat was insufferable.

Bodies under blankets striped the lawn. The firemen had just opened the stairway leading to the Carpathian room, and Alain followed them up, a wet handkerchief pressed against his nostrils.

The paramedics already inside had found a black face blinking under a piece of masonry. Les Vitrolly screamed, seeing the burnt gray hair: It was Cabot, and he was conscious.

A stack of family portraits, stored in a now-destroyed attic, had crashed through the torn-up ceiling and fallen on and protected another survivor. "What's your name?" a paramedic was asking. Very hairy, with knit eyebrows and dark tufts coming out of ears and nostrils, he seemed shocked but not badly injured, and Alain thought he looked familiar. "What's your name?" repeated the paramedic.

"Maynard," the man whispered. "Maynard Cooks." He looked at Alain, and Alain recognized the Egyptian. A darkened hand waved toward Alain, and he stepped closer, and bent down. "The voices . . ." whispered the Egyptian, "the voices . . ."

"Ssshhhh, take it easy," urged the paramedic.

"They sent me to the diary . . . I gave her the diary," stammered the Egyptian, and the paramedic shot Alain a glance of complicity: How could the survivors of such a calamity not rave insanely?

A wall panel suddenly fell, exploding into dust. "I'm sorry, Mr. Lecouveur," grumbled Knowles, appearing from the cloud of dust, "Your uncle didn't make it."

A shiver, deeper than anything he'd experienced before, got hold of Alain and electrocuted him. He felt like a huge chain was falling off his body, and trembled, frightened by so much freedom. Then the thought sprang up in his mind: *Come on, he can't die. He'll never die.* And it wrapped the chain around him again.

"He's over here. Wanna see him?"

He acquiesced wordlessly, and moved to where the grandiflora used to be. The flames had melted the glass. Its upper half was now air, a piece of sky, the trees doused with water by the firemen.

The coat of arms, gray but shockingly intact, still hung under the destroyed grandiflora and Alain stared at it, realizing only after a moment that it had burned, like everything else, but its texture of ashes had kept the exact contour of the motto, *Mors Elude*, and the *quartiers de noblesse*, the moon and the shovel. If he were to blow on it, the ashes would fly away, eluding death no longer. And under his coat of arms, impaled by a burnished beam of solid oak, lay Emory, eyes open, lips open, as if seeing and smiling still.

"When the ceiling fell in, that beam caught him right in the heart," said Knowles. "Let's hope the smoke had asphyxiated him already."

A cluster of Lecouveurs had died around Emory, bunched around him like a guard of chess soldiers surrounding their king, all knocked down by a bored hand. Alain identified masks of ashes: Ernest Lecouveur, Jack Lecouveur, one of the Lignacs . . .

"What a way to go," said Knowles, and bent down to close the open eyes.

Alain reached out and pulled back Knowles's hand. "Don't close them," he said.

Knowles frowned, surprised, but held back whatever he was about to say. When he spoke again, he offered condolences for Rose Janice, who had been found crushed beneath a fallen wall, and for several other relatives. And he informed Alain that Marion Voguey had been taken to the hospital with severe burns. "You'll be relieved to hear that Mr. Chadwick survived, too," he said. "Unbelievable, but he made it outside." Knowles shook his head. "He was sitting right behind the front door, and the bullets spared him. Somehow, he didn't choke from the smoke, and when the door fell down, he just walked out. Musta been just about when the Mexes pulled out, figurin' we were comin'."

"Jesus," murmured Alain.

"He's made an inventory of what's been destroyed, just in case you're fixing to sue, Mr. Lecouveur," said Knowles in a deep-felt tone. "I know this is no happy way to inherit, but I guess now you'll have to take over, so congratulations."

Alain nodded numbly, a gesture that could be taken as an approval, and reeled away from Emory's crushed chest and staring eyes.

Outside, Clark Chadwick was finishing a padful of notes. His shirt was ashen gray, one sleeve of his jacket was missing, and he was staring cockeyed through a pair of borrowed glasses. Seeing Alain, his eyes lit up myopically. He rushed to the new heir, enthusiastially grabbed his arm, and started to unfold a vision of how the business should be conducted now that the stifling old way was gone forever; how the breath of the new and bold could be fanned into every corner of the Lecouveur empire, and how even the latest events, sad though they were, could be capitalized on.

Alain was thinking of Laura. And of Belle Hellène.

Now, keeping one meant keeping the other.

He looked around, at the garden. At this property he knew so well, this realm of jealous tragedy, which he had tried to conquer by serving it from outside, exiling himself in the wilderness of the river. The barbaric celibacy of those years. He'd run the place, out of duty, yet he had kept himself clean of it. Each time he came to visit, he felt triumphant and virginal. He managed to leave it, unspoiled, aiming each time a smile of relief at the undomesticated river.

Somehow, Emory's death, the property's destruction, had dragged him back and tamed him in one night. And Laura belonged to the place already. Meeting her tonight, falling into her embrace, he knew he wouldn't hold himself back anymore. He'd sink into her arms as into a bath of blood—the stored, liquid record of five centuries of Emory's unholy exploits.

He had a fleeting fantasy of her naked body. Of her lips. They floated forward, close to his face, and opened hungrily.

The fantasy somehow showed in his features. Chadwick stopped talking and looked at Alain. His cockeyed stare shone lecherously.

"The young lady . . . escaped?" he asked.

Alain frowned, and didn't answer.

"Are you all right?" inquired Chadwick. And then, solicitously, "We can continue this another time."

'I'm all right," whispered Alain. "Go on."

"Once you rebuild, she'll love it here," Chadwick prophesied.

Alain nodded, without a word.

Like a knife cutting a slice from a lean surface, a layer of his mind opened and shut again. Laura was in it. Naked. Smiling.

He remembered one of Emory's favorite quotes from Aeschylus:

> "Things are where things are,
> and as fate has willed,
> So shall they be fulfilled.

The corpse upstairs had wanted him to continue the empire. His wish had been fulfilled.

At six, when the lake looked like a twilight-polished tray, Laura was up and dressed in her white dress, waiting behind a tourist family at the cashier's counter in the hotel's curio shop. Her turn came, and she asked if they carried candles.

Candles. Peaceful spots of tremoring light, on her face, on his. Glasses of wine, half full. Hands touching. All that, to help them forget about death, and smoldering rubble, and the past.

And if he came, what would it mean? That he loved her. Even though her previous innocence was gone. He had tried to protect that innocence, to keep it intact, even from himself. This time, no longer pure, she would have no other way to explain his reappearance.

The shop had only voodoo candles, it turned out. Imitation conjure çandles. The saleslady explained that they were manufactured by some young artists in town, after the originals used by the Creoles in their conjuring. They were of black wax, shaped like animals: owls, roosters, cats. She bought two cats.

It was 6:15. She went and sat in a chair in the lounge, knowing that time wouldn't pass here any faster than up in her room.

At 7:00, the lake turned turquoise. At 7:30 she felt she couldn't even begin to guess whether he'd be showing up or not. She sat with the wrapped voodoo cats in her lap, wondering if she'd light them up by herself, in a wake over a solitary room-service dinner, or whether her breath and his, united, would make their flames quiver by a bed filled with their bodies.

She looked at her watch again at 7:40, looked up from it. Her breath stopped.

Across the lounge, Alain was walking toward her, in the same torn clothes, shoulders sagging with exhaustion, but smiling.

She got up and flung herself in his arms, candles and all.

In the elevator that crawled up the outside of the building, they kissed, and she couldn't take her eyes off him.

"Emory is dead," he said with finality. She didn't even bother to say I'm sorry.

"I'm going to draw you a bath," she planned out loud, "and put some bubbly salts in it. It'll be the best thing for your body."

"Whatever you want," he said.

"Whatever *you* want," she said.

"I want to feel," he said, "that we know nothing about each other, yet we trust each other completely."

That sounded romantic, but what did it really mean? *Well, why not? Why the hell not?*

"All right. I read a great diary once," she said, "about vampires. I think it was written by one."

The door of the elevator opened and he reached out to take her hand. Poor guy had helped her in and out of so many cars, boats, streetcars, dumbwaiters, and other risky vehicles, it had become a reflex action for him.

"He wrote that there's a cure for being a vampire." They started down the lobby toward her room.

"You mean against being one?" he asked.

"Whatever," she said. "A cure, a remedy, an antidote." She took out her key, opened the door, let him in. "Wait just a second, I'll get your bath ready."

She couldn't remember what the remedy was called, but the diary was at her apartment, and she could get it and look it up. She ran the taps in the bathroom. She started sprinkling bath salts in the hot water.

"It looks too hot. I'll melt in that water." She started. He was right behind her, looking enormous in the narrowness of the bathroom.

"You scared me," she said, pressing her hand on her heart.

"I'm sorry." He started pulling off his jacket. "Am I bathing by myself or under your supervision?"

He dropped his jacket on the floor, started unbuttoning his shirt. She suddenly chickened out at the thought of him stripping off everything—shirt, pants, underpants—before her. "Get in the water," she said. "I'll be right back."

She walked out of the bathroom, back to the safety of the bedroom, and paced between the window and bed, her fists closed up, her fingernails dipped into her palms.

She stopped by the window and peered out. The lake, darker than ink. The hotel building—an endless repetition of boxlike balconies and windows like her own. The two lit elevators crawling up and down in their glass encasements. She decided to close the curtains.

She fumbled behind the stiff cretonne of the outer curtains, looking for the strings. She almost couldn't do it—it seemed that once they were pulled shut, there was no return from being alone, really alone, with Alain.

She stood there for a beat, trying to control the movement of her chest—it was almost heaving.

Then she felt better. Calmer.

Over the top of the building, the sky looked now like dark blue enamel. Right then, the shape of a plane appeared, thrusting upward into the sky. The glass pane vibrated in front of Laura's face.

Another plane had brought her here only a few weeks ago. A lifetime ago.

She found the strings of the curtains, pulled on them, and shut out the night sky. The thunder of the plane faded and she heard Alain in the bathroom, moving in the bubbly water.

She unpacked the voodoo candles from the curio shop— they were shaped like unnaturally elongated bodies of sitting cats. She lit the wicks sprouting out of their black heads, then dripped wax in two ashtrays and stood the cats up in them. She rubbed the waxy feeling off her palms, then touched her cheeks—they were flushed.

She looked around the room—a temporary set arranged for strangers to act in, a furniture-store display, with no place to hide, and no true memories. The people who had been here before, standing on this carpet, using this bed, seemed unreal to her.

God, am I dreaming this? For a second she doubted that

Alain was real. Yet the first thing she saw, stepping back into the bathroom, were his clothes: the khaki pants, the fatigue jacket, the torn shirt, like a dead heap on the floor.

Alain was sitting in the tub, smiling at the sensation of the warm water, eyes closed. The size of the tub made his chest look even more formidably muscular. Little garlands of foam clung shinily to the dark hair striating his pectorals. On his left breast, the water had parted his hair, showing a nipple. It was tiny and pink; it looked so innocent, such a sweet little bud lost in that display of manhood, that she started to titter nervously—and Alain opened his eyes.

"I must look ridiculous in this bath," he said.

Even his voice betrayed his exhaustion. It was rocky and cracked; in a flash she remembered the old man's voice, those dragonlike bronze tones that had made her jump the night she wandered into the Lecouveur mansion.

"No, you don't." She had never had fantasies of being dressed in front of a naked man, and the fact that he was immersed in water made him seem somehow in her power. She moved behind him, lowered her face, and inhaled. His hair smelled sourly of burnt wood. From the soiled clothes on the floor rose an even more acrid stench—carbonized fabric, roasted flesh? At the same instant, he tilted his head back and caught her lips with his. Laura had to put her hands on the rim of the tub. She wanted to close her eyes, but the sight of his body kept them open. Every piece of him was built like a rock, and tanned everywhere except from groin to navel. She wrested her lips free. He *couldn't* be one of them— the light of the sun had seen his body too many times.

"I missed you," Alain whispered. "Today more than ever."

"I'm glad you're back in one piece." His voice was starting to flow again, and hers sounded almost normal. She looked at his eyes, then managed to look back at his body without embarrassment. Seeing the evenness of color that coated his shoulders, his sinewy forearms, the thighs and knees that appeared even browner under the foamy water, she realized that Alain's tan couldn't be recent—this was a deep change in pigmentation, from all the months and years of sunshine he had spent on the river, starting in childhood. A tan that won't ever go away, no matter how much or how little sun will caress this body from now on.

The brief sense of relief she felt at seeing the tan vanished. The pit of her stomach dropped lower again. She felt the low, sadistic burn of acid dripping into her stomach. And then a sort of indifference, washing over her. The anguish, though not gone, grew quiet and remote, as if happening to someone else.

"Come on. I'll wash your hair," she said maternally.

He sank lower in the water. She poured shampoo in one palm, then used both hands to work it into a rich cream, at times pushing on his head, and feeling how the strength of her hands could barely move this huge body. Alain's head bent obediently under her palms, but the solid trunk of his neck, the battlements of the shoulders and chest, just wouldn't give in to the pressure—like when, as a child in California, squatting down on a wharf, she had pushed at a big moored boat. The boat was brown, silent and masculine, a heavy, unknown body, for which her hands were no match. She felt that her hands, like all the rest of her, were so intensely female now.

She got up, brought a towel, and laid it on the toilet seat. "Shall I rinse your hair?"

"No, I'll do it."

"Do you want me to leave?"

"It's all right." His knees flexed upward, the rich little island of his groin streamed out of the water, and all of him rose. Laura stepped back, trying not to stare. He turned on the shower and chased the foam from his hair, chest and belly, smiling at her. As if hearing a silent permission, she spread the towel and began to dry him off. With the towel draped around his shoulders, he suddenly put his arms around her, and lifted her.

"Don't do that, you're too—" Laura started to say. He covered her mouth with his, and she heard his feet splash out of the tub and pad on the bathroom tiles. Her dress billowed as he carried her under the doorway, and their entrance into the room made the candle flames flutter. He stood between the dresser with its square mirror and the impersonal bed, kissing her, and she saw their reflection in the mirror.

His body looked like bronze; columns of polished muscles ran from the neck down, along his sides, thighs, calves. Surviving beads of water glittered here and there and she noticed fresh scratches on his legs: a deep one above the knee, lighter ones on his calves. From trampling around the smoldering ruins of Belle Hellène.

Gathered at his chest, Laura seemed small. Under her back and her knees she felt the throb of his arms. He was beat, wiped out after breaking out of the party with her, bringing the boat ashore, and returning to Belle Hellène to face the aftermath of the disaster. Lust alone kept him standing in this barbarian pose of conquest.

She watched herself in his arms. Her hair had lost its shape and was bristling, giving her a panicked schoolgirl air. Her bared knees were shining vulnerably. The nail polish on her toes caught the light of the closest candle—and suddenly Alain wrinkled his forehead. "Where did you get these?" he asked.

She followed his eyes: Half of the black wax head of one of the cats was gone. Like an Egyptian ritual statuette with a flame growing out of its top, it looked frightening.

"At the curio shop downstairs—they're supposed to be used in spells. It said so on the package." She tried to laugh, and Alain smiled—he *was* exhausted. Even the smile seemed to take something out of him.

"I bought these because they didn't have any others," she continued. "This room is so unmysterious." He nodded and stepped toward the bed. He freed one hand, grabbed the bedspread where it was tucked under the pillows by the headboard, and pulled. Held in his other arm, Laura saw the bedspread peel away until Alain let if fall to the floor. The laundered whiteness of the naked sheets hurt her eyes.

Breathing long exhausted breaths, he laid her on the bed, and sprawled down next to her.

"Don't be afraid," he whispered, "there's nothing to be afraid of."

Like a teenager, to his virgin lover. She felt a tremor under her chin and swallowed hurriedly.

I'm not afraid. Whatever has to happen, will happen.

"Are you all right?" he asked.

She wet her lips, but couldn't utter a sound.

"Laura?"

"Yes, yes," she whispered.

His eyes, so close to hers, seemed of a different color now. A different green. The rings of his irises: thousands of green lacelike patterns, intertwined with other patterns of brown and gold. In Alain's eyes, in the light of the candles, Laura saw the reflection of her own face: two tiny Lauras, waiting to be made love to by this man, so unlike other men.

Unexpectedly, he slipped his palm under her, freed her dress from her body, and pulled it up toward her waist. Laura barely had time to think of what she was wearing underneath: a transparent white teddy, top tied with a ribbon, bottom sealed under the crotch with three snap buttons. Alain took her shoulders and pulled her to a sitting position. With the same silent efficiency, he clutched the top of the dress and peeled it off over her head. Laura blushed. *He's undressed a lot of women.*

When she could see him again, his eyes stared straight into hers, dominating her will completely. He put his cheek against her heart, and his weight pushed her back onto the white sheets. As if hearing with his ear, she listened to a growing pumping inside her, until her heart beat loudly inside her eyes. She touched his knee with hers—a burning stab inside her, like a shot of alcohol, made her squirm. To keep her in place, he pressed his head on her breast. Her face bobbed nervously to the right, and she flinched: The cat-candle's head, or what was left of it, was just beginning to fall off the wax neck. Unsupported, the melting blob, still carrying the cat's features—pinched mustachioed lips, nostrils, high cheekbones—tilted, broke off, and fell by the stylized wax paws.

"Don't move," he whispered.

He caressed the outside of her thigh. A very light touch, just the tips of his fingers, past her knee, calf, ankle. His palm rounded her heel, then touched the inside of her calf. When it reached the inside of her thigh, her senses were so vibrant she thought she could feel even the movement of the air in the room: invading it silently from the gratings of the air-conditioning vents, lighting on the bed, and on her flushed face.

"I was such a fool," he chuckled, sounding young and boyish, "trying to keep myself away from you . . ." The end got muffled by a kiss. The tension in her body, rising toward a peak, fought the kiss, then started to break. Unconsciously, she moved her legs, wanting to remain like this, lost under him. Alain opened the top of her teddy and moved his mouth onto her left breast. *Sweep me away*, she thought, and closed her eyes.

He moved to the other breast.

She couldn't keep her legs still—her heels rubbed against the fabric of the bedsheets. Alain tortured her nipple with such delicate strokes and tickles and more strokes and more tickles and little not-quite-bites, that a knot inside her started to come untied.

Almost afraid of how ecstatic this might turn out to be, she wanted to slow down her reactions. To do that, she tried to visualize that knot inside her, and what was happening to it. It was tied fast, with one loop undone just a little. She felt a touch lighter than fingers, picking at that loop, trying to pull it out, so that the knot would slip apart and let go of what it had sealed up. One more pull, and one more. She felt she couldn't stand Alain's mouth on her nipple anymore. She put her hands on his head, pulled it off her breast, and tried to kiss his mouth. But he resisted, easily slipping out of her hands, and wouldn't let go of the nipple. She felt the muscles in her back tighten and arch themselves up—almost lifting his much bigger body. Inside her, the minute, teasing, tireless, excruciating pulls were slowly opening the loop. With brief halts followed by little spurts of progress, and more stubborn but impotent halts, the tie was sliding out of the knot—the knot was snapping open!

His mouth ravaged her nipples. She locked both arms around his shoulder blades and squeezed as hard as she could. Unable to reach his mouth, she fastened her lips on his shoulder, and bit him. She moaned . . . and climaxed.

She felt she couldn't catch her breath. There was no knot inside her anymore.

She heard a plane and wondered how many others had landed and taken off in the last half hour, the thunder of their turbine engines ignored by both of them. Alain rose on one elbow, and smiled. "That was a pretty savage bite," he said.

She looked. A round little flower was blooming on his shoulder. Dark droplets were filling the imprints left by her teeth.

"I'm sorry. Oh, Jesus, Alain."

She wanted to kiss the bite, and as she moved in his arms, she realized that the bottom of her teddy was open.

Skillful bastard, when, how did he snap the buttons open? Probably with the same hand that untied the knot inside her.

"You can kiss it if you like." He grinned.

She matched the contour of the bite with her lips. It tasted sweet, for want of another word. She had never tasted anything like it. She kissed it again. Sweet? No, not sweet. Deep. Like the wine she had tasted out of his glass at Cafe Paris.

"Do you like the taste of blood?" Alain asked, shifting the weight of his body and grabbing the top of her teddy. Its silk flapped off over her head even faster than the dress.

"I remember . . ." she heard herself stuttering a little, ". . . I remember when I was a kid." The teddy floated in the air next to her face, then vanished below the side of the bed. The thick hair on his chest instantly assailed her breasts. "I cut my finger and sucked on it—it felt nice."

"What do you mean—nice?"

She felt the inside of her thighs copiously wet. *It's going to be wonderful.*

"Sort of . . . soothing." His body found its way between her thighs, his waist feeling so muscular and big—*I'm too small for him*, panicked Laura. His face was close, his lips smiling, and the lacelike pattern of light in his eyes seemed to be growing even more complex.

"Soothing," Alain murmured like an echo. And then he filled her.

It happened so fast, it was so smooth and painless, that Laura gasped. She felt him not only inside her crotch, but literally in her whole body, reaching up to her throat and stopping her breath.

She fought to breathe, forgetting what else was happening. She rolled her head to the other side and saw in the mirror the dark mass of Alain's back, and her own legs, escaping past it, pointing upward: two frail stems, pleading mutely toward the indifferent ceiling. Alain's back moved, and almost immediately her legs took their cue from it and began to flutter in his rhythm. It was amazing that he could move at all; she felt he was filling every atom of space inside her. *I'm not going to like this.* But the flesh and muscles inside her tightened around him. For a second the squeeze was so unbearable that sweat erupted on Laura's temples.

And then, as if Alain and the inside of her had found a way to occupy the same space, the choking sensation subsided. A delicious *frisson* of pleasure crisped up the skin of her inner thighs, belly, and breasts, responding to the man's feel and weight. She tried to pull herself back, to not be possessed so completely, but he had found another knot inside her, and wasn't trying to untie it anymore: He was simply crushing it. Flattening it with long, luxurious, pounding strokes. A milky stream started rolling inside her. She looked for his mouth, found only his shoulder, and bit into it again, with renewed pleasure and total selfishness and no concern whatever of his pain.

She only let go of it when she started to call his name: "Alain. Alain." He was saying hers: "Laura. Laura." They were babbling like two idiots. His mouth came back to hers, and they kissed brutally, building and building, until finally a shudder seized his entire body, and she felt a primitive spurt bursting deep inside her. Trying to match it with one of her own and not quite managing this time, she glanced again in the mirror and she saw her legs lashed together behind his towering back. A female mounted by a minotaur.

He rolled over on his back, still holding her. She found herself atop his body, pinned on it.

"Laura."

"Yes."

Alain's face was awash in sweat. So was hers.

"I love you."

She found no strength to respond. She nodded, content, and stared at what she saw of him—his shoulders, his chest, his face—proudly, proprietarily.

"I fell in love with you at . . ."

She could guess this one. "At Cafe Paris."

"Yes."

"You're such a wonderful lover," she whispered, curling the hair on his chest with her finger. "The best I ever had."

His eyes smiled.

Suddenly something darkened their limpid light. Laura's arms tightened, and she felt the coolness of the room on her body. Alerted by the shadow in Alain's eyes, she wanted to turn, to find the reason for it. But his hands closed over her shoulders and he held her on him like a prey.

As if a cloud had passed over, as if a chill wind had flapped above them, they felt that they weren't alone. It lasted only a second, but the presence was so powerful and clear that Laura fell on Alain's chest, prostrate. His arms tightened around her. All senses awake, he looked ready to rise, to meet the invisible rival and wage battle.

Then, slowly, the vile presence seemed to dissolve and vanish. The weight of his hands on her shoulders eased.

"I love you," he said, to her and to the air around them.

She breathed, wishing she could arouse him instantly, that the strange spell would be forgotten.

She lowered her face and kissed his mouth. Doing it, she found one of his nipples with her breast.

She teased it with *her* breast. Under her, his heart began to beat faster, until it was hammering furiously. She started to kiss his neck. His hands kneaded her back; his body was preparing to do it again. Good. She was ready, too. Exhausted, but ready.

This time she lay on his chest, feeling his breath on her throat like a soft breeze, letting him move slowly, almost dreaming.

Bizarre scenes from some unknown mythology started to parade under her closed eyelids.

In the scorched steppes of Assyria, after a battle that claimed thousands of lives, survivors were opening corpses' veins to drink blood, the only liquid under the deadening, mummifying sun . . .

A high priest atop an Aztec pyramid was drinking the ritual red balm from a skull-chalice. Two knives poised for sacrifice pressed on a prisoner's chest. A wave of the high priest's hand and the knives penetrated the chest with such precision that the heart popped out, shrinking and distending still, like a bird flapping in flight though its head has been already shattered by the shot . . .

A woman was squatting in childbirth by a fire, in the wet thickness of Africa. Birthplace of the Nile, a pierced rock sputtered with clear water nearby. Other women surrounded the birth-sacrifice. Eyes shining, mouths panting, they uttered guttural growls, like hungry pregnant cats . . .

Herself, naked, stepping toward a throne of bones under a mystic moon. The beast on the throne has a furry body, and of his inhuman face all she can make out are the eyes. They steam, those eyes, like little hellish vats. He's waiting for her. She can see his lust, rising straight and turgid from his crotch, standing for her to straddle it . . . black, menacing, bloody from the virgin before her. Her white body opening carefully, fitting onto that stem of darkness.

She wasn't afraid.

It's all fantasy, her mind murmured reassuringly.

The sleepy mating went on for awhile, then she woke up, feeling that Alain was awake, too.

He was making love to her with concentrated skill, tired and yet too greedy to overlook any move, any effort that could bring them further pleasure.

Her brow furrowing in the effort to match his prowess, she felt his heart beating slower, more distant, as if in another body.

She pulled her face back, and looked at him. His cheeks were sunken, his skin pale under its tan. "Stop. Alain, please stop."

He seemed not to understand.

"Stop. Let's stop. You're too tired."

"I'm not."

She felt his body quiver under her. In a supreme effort, he rose to his feet, still holding her locked around his waist.

"I told you I wasn't tired," he said, smiling.

He carried her toward the mirror. She caught a glimpse of the candles: Both cats had melted down to their paws. Like the stone lions guarding the entrances of temples at Karnak and Luxor.

"Look at us," he said. She shrank away, shyly. "Look," he urged.

Laura turned. She saw herself clinging from his neck, her open legs hugging his middle, her bottom spread from the attempt to keep him inside her, to not lose any of him. She thought fleetingly of pictures she had seen. Erotic positions immortalized in stone on Hindu temples—the man/god always standing, the divine mate always carried, legs arched around his erect stature, giving and receiving pleasure.

"Put me down," she pleaded, embarrassed.

"No." Holding her waist, he began to rotate her. It was a little uncomfortable, but exciting. "I love you," she whispered. He moved her more, then turned and laid her down on the bed. Hastily, afraid of breaking the rhythm, he made room for himself between her legs, and she received him. She squirmed sorely under him, astounded that after so much lovemaking she could still respond—and realized that she was moving alone.

"What happened?" He looked haggard, staring at a fixed point somewhere over her head. "Please, don't stop."

But he wasn't moving, and she felt a desperate fire inside her, to keep making love, to feel that joy again, overcoming the soreness. She took his face in her hands. "Alain. My love, what's the matter?"

He stared at her. "I did try to protect you. From me—from all of us."

In the silence that followed, one of the candle wicks sizzled hard and loud, dying in a pool of liquid wax.

Suddenly, in his arms, she felt that her eyes were playing a trick on her; though his face was a few inches away, the perspective stretched and deepened, and the loved face, the loved eyes, seemed to loom a mile above her. Minuscule, like an offering beneath the giant profile of a Buddha carved from a whole mountainside, she lay under her man.

"What did you feel, what did you think the first time?" he asked.

"What first time?" He was miles away, he wasn't Alain.

"When he first came to you. The first night, right after you arrived in New Orleans."

"Em-Emory?" She stammered, and felt the cool presence back inside the room.

"He was so experienced and clever," continued Alain, "he could make himself feel like a dream, a hallucination, a fantasy to his victims."

"I thought he *was* a fantasy, Alain." She touched him, struggling to bring him back close, out of his coldly oracular posture. "I thought he was a fantasy the first time. The second time, I thought he was that killer. Until that night at Belle Hellène, I never knew what was really happening to me. Alain," she said, trying to give her voice the ring of honesty. "Even though I was terrified, I wished it was you. I was dreaming about you, fantasizing about you. I would've done everything with you . . . Alain, where are you?" she cried, frightened. "Come back!"

He shook, as if surfacing from a dream. He looked at her, and now he was normal again. His body salty from love's sweat, his eyes guilty. And deeply angry about something irreversible.

"Alain," she said sadly, "I wish it had been you all the time. Why didn't you come to me? Why weren't you there to protect me?"

"I *was* around," he answered with contained anger, "the first few nights."

"I don't understand."

She looked at his face. His eyes had grown in luminosity, as if to compensate for the dying candle. A stony kind of look made his cheeks rigid, like those of a statue. But he was still devilishly handsome. Inside the stony mask, his eyes lived, human.

"The first night," he said, disgusted, as if confessing a shameful secret, "I couldn't keep myself away anymore than he did. So I came to your place—and found him there already. You were lying on your bed, half-asleep, half-possessed. I chased him out of your bedroom, but didn't stay one minute more, not one more minute, for fear of doing myself what I suspected he had started."

He paused. When he began to talk again, his voice trembled with rancor.

"We found ourselves outside your house. Both shaking with unsatisfied lust, both mad and manic, both hungry. He killed not one hour later, close to the house where you slept. With such ranvenousness that I was convinced he hadn't had a chance to really feast on you. And he wouldn't tell me that he *had*. He had simply decided that you were his. Such was Emory."

She felt the coolness of the room. And she felt revulsion, but no fear. "Where were you after that night?"

"He came to you again. I had been shadowing him, but I couldn't follow him all the time, and if I stood guard by your bed night after night, I couldn't possibly hope to resist the temptation myself."

"There's nothing we can do about that now," she said quietly.

The second candle started to die, sizzling. Her body, not touched by his, was cool now.

The second candle quivered once more, then vanished.

Without candles, the room was almost pitch black. A dagger of light stabbed the dark where the curtains met, and Alain's eyes were pierced by it.

"What *are* we going to do now?" he asked bitterly. She smiled in the dark. "We're going to love each other, you fool," she said. "And we're going to find that remedy."

She didn't want to think about it anymore. She just wanted to be a woman, naked, with a naked man.

"Can you see my eyes?" she asked, like a child learning a new game.

He nodded. He could see them. Her eyes glittered in the dark now, lit by a gleam of their own, more than human.

"We'll try to find the cure," he agreed belatedly. "But I doubt that it exists."

"Emory said it does exist," she replied.

"Emory was a poet," said Alain. "It could have been no more than one of his poems."

"Poor Emory," she said, feeling a strange melancholy. "By trying to make me his, he gave me to you."

He was silent. Laura expected to hear a plane, but heard only silence. Then an elevator door *whoosh*ed open not too far away; human laughter spilled into a lobby and died again.

Outside, the world lay at rest, gathered within itself, whiling away the precious hours of the night, and the bayou, bubbling with nitrogen acids and fumes from the souls of dead plants, was silent, too, deadly silent. A witch's cauldron before the witch's hand lights the match, setting the chopped wood on fire.

"Come here," she said. Gratefully, he moved closer to her in the dark and took her in his arms. "Cover me with your body—I'm cold."

But his body felt cold, too, although his manhood was rigid. She lay open, he filled her again, moved in a zombielike, somnambulistic way for a few seconds . . .

. . . And then, as if floodgates had opened, his body began to warm up again. He started to warm up her insides, and soon her body, though tired and spent, was ready to respond again. The roots of her hair crackled, stiffening on her forehead, and her body started to ooze more sweat over dried-up sweat. "Come on," she urged him with authority. "Come on, faster."

Impatiently, she pushed him off her, detached herself, rolled him over, straddled him, and began to ride him wildly, her body so greased in sweat that her flesh slipped on his. "Faster! Faster!" she cried, feeling ready to hit him, and she did, banging her fists on his chest. She wanted to scratch him, to bite him, to beat him into moving as fast as she did, but she just couldn't be bested, galloping ahead of him like a loose mare. His hand groped for her face, and she bit it. When he pulled his hand free, she whinnied like a wild horse, and went for his neck. It felt so big, such a muscular stack, that her small mouth would never get a good chance.

But she tried. *This will be demonic!* her mind cheered, like a girl fulfilling suddenly and completely a long-cherished fantasy. Drawing blood, she savored his manhood more deliciously then ever.

Everything was happening down there. Knots were being crushed every second, buds of delight were opening and wilting, others sprouting and blooming. At fever pitch, attuned to the smallest sounds of pleasure, Laura heard a deeper, slower rumble. *Boom*, something went under her, *Boom*, like the greatest drum from the darkest tropics.

It was Alain's heart. Alain's beloved, more-than-human heart.

Throbbing under her, he seized her shoulders and began to pull her downward, forcing the white neck closer and closer to his open mouth. Then, just before his glittering teeth could fasten onto her flesh, he growled, "No, I can't!" and tried to thrust her roughly away from him. She held on.

"Don't stop, love," she crooned, as a colossal orgasm was about to blow her womb apart. *Impossible*, she thought, *it's too big, too grandiose. I'll lose it. I'll never survive it. I'll die before it happens.*

And it started to happen.

And then and only then, when she was so sure of it, when every muscle and tendon in her body was vibrating from it, when her heart began to race through space, then . . . she brought her neck over his face and fed it to him . . . she gave him her pulsing throat.

About the Author

PETRU POPESCU was one of Romania's most provocative young novelists before he came to the United States as a guest of the University of Iowa's International Writing Program and chose to stay in this country, writing in English. With IN HOT BLOOD, he brings an erotic shiver to a genre that inspired masters like Poe and Stoker. His earlier novels include BURIAL OF THE VINE and BEFORE AND AFTER EDITH. As a filmmaker, Popescu wrote and directed the feature DEATH OF AN ANGEL, and wrote THE LAST WAVE, which has become a classic.